Anne Melville is the author of the highly acclaimed *Lorimer* series and *The House of Hardie*, *Grace Hardie* and *The Dangerfield Diaries*. The daughter of the author and lecturer Bernard Newman, she was a scholar of St Hugh's College, Oxford, where she read Modern History. She and her husband now live in Oxford.

By the same author

The Lorimer Line
The Lorimer Legacy
Lorimers at War
Lorimers in Love
The Last of the Lorimers
Lorimer Loyalties
The House of Hardie
Grace Hardie
The Hardie Inheritance
The Dangerfield Diaries

ANNE MELVILLE

The Tantivy Trust

Grafton

An Imprint of HarperCollins*Publishers*

Grafton
An Imprint of HarperCollins*Publishers*
77–85 Fulham Palace Road,
Hammersmith, London W6 8JB

Published by Grafton 1993
9 8 7 6 5 4 3 2 1

First published in Great Britain by
HarperCollins*Publishers* 1992

ISBN 0 586 21382 1

Set in Times

Printed in Great Britain by
HarperCollinsManufacturing Glasgow

Contents

She is one of the richest women in the world.
But where is she?
Who is she?

Prologue

1946

Magnificent as a golden oriole in the silk brocade gown of a Doctor of Music, the Maestro paused for a second in the dimness of the cloister. On the lawn of the Fellows' Garden clustered the red-robed dignitaries of the University of Oxford, talking earnestly to each other. Each held in his hand a glass of champagne. As usual, Ludo had brought his employer to the right place at the right time, and wearing the right clothes.

Earlier, there had been a moment of anxiety. Ludo, Scottish by birth, had enjoyed a peripatetic upbringing as the son of a military attaché, and from it had developed an unerring ability to discover in any country, any language, precisely what arrangements needed to be made, and to make them. But as the taxi drove away, it had left the Maestro standing in front of a college whose black, crumbling stone walls seemed to offer no warmth of welcome. The front quadrangle was silent; not with the emptiness of a space through which no one happened at that moment to be passing but with the echoing loneliness of a building abandoned. The porch was littered with trunks waiting to be collected and carried to the station, but their owners had already left Oxford, perhaps for ever. It was a relief to be reminded by the porter who hurried out to show him the way that only the undergraduates' term had ended. The life of the University continued.

So here they all were: the Chancellor himself, with Heads of Houses and Doctors of Divinity, Civil Law, and Medicine. The academic gowns which lent them

9

dignity also removed them from this current year of austerity, 1946, into the timelessness of tradition, for the bright and peaceful scene now being enacted would have looked little different in any year during the past two or three centuries. Even the topics of conversation had probably not changed. The professors might look as though they were discussing grave points of scholarship, but were almost certainly exchanging gossip and spreading rumour about new appointments.

Catching sight of the honorand, the Chancellor came striding towards him. The Maestro, his golden robe shimmering with the movement, stepped politely out into the sunshine so that the formal greeting could be a public one.

'Your Highness! Welcome to Oxford. The University is greatly honoured by your presence amongst us.' The plummy voice spoke with the careful enunciation suited to fools or foreigners.

'The honour's all mine.' On this occasion the Maestro did not attempt to shrug off his rank. He preferred to be known by the appellation conferred on him by the orchestra which he had conducted for the past twenty years, taking more pride in this than in the ancient title which was merely inherited from the bastard son of a pope. As a rule he allowed himself to be called Prince Fiori only when in the company of his wife, who valued such things. This Encaenia, though, with all its ceremonies, was not the day on which to insist on informality.

But another misapprehension must be more quickly corrected. Doubtless his recent and much-publicised decision to live and work in Rome had misled the Chancellor into thinking of him as a wholly Italian Italian. To avoid later embarrassment, it was important to make clear at once that he spoke English fluently, albeit with a North American accent.

As a young man he had recognised the inevitability of

Fascist rule in Italy sufficiently early to make his departure an unobtrusive one. His widowed mother, remaining behind on the estates which were less easily moved than other assets, had spread a tactful story: her talented son feared that his noble birth would make it impossible for him to be taken seriously as a professional musician in his home country and so had found irresistible the offer of a position and the prospect of a career in Canada.

In truth no such employment had been offered. The great wealth of the Fioris made it possible for the young prince not only to support himself but to raise and rehearse an orchestra at his own expense and to build a concert hall in which it could play. Only then was his adopted city invited to put its name to the package and bask in civic pride as the fame of its conductor grew.

That fame alone, he had assumed, was responsible for the invitation which had brought him to Oxford today in order that the honorary degree of Doctor of Music might be conferred upon him. It was only ten minutes later, as his champagne glass was refilled, that he began to suspect another motive.

'This delightful hour before the ceremony begins is known as Lord Crewe's Benefaction,' the Chancellor told him. 'Lord Crewe was Rector of Lincoln College and Bishop of Oxford in the seventeenth century. He left money to the university when he died specifically to provide champagne and strawberries on Encaenia days for the holders of certain positions and higher degrees. I always think that it must have given him great pleasure, when he drew up the terms of the donation, to think that he would be remembered for ever in such a pleasant way.'

So that was it. What did they want of him, the Maestro wondered? A scholarship for a student? An endowment for a fellowship? Or something more substantial: a practice room or concert hall?

11

He had never wasted time on deploring the misdeeds of his ancestors and the sources of his own wealth. Music was his only passion, and although he had married money as well as inheriting it, he had not done so for the sake of the fortune involved but because Stella was a decorative and sensible woman who could be trusted to honour a business arrangement. He had made her a princess and she had provided him with an heir. They were good friends, and it was understood between them that she would behave discreetly with her lovers while he would never allow it to be guessed that Ludo was more to him than merely an efficient young personal assistant.

Antonio was the apple of both their eyes. One day he would be one of the richest men in the world, for through his mother he was descended from a miner lucky in the Yukon gold rush and from a family long established in the Canadian fur trade. The Maestro had wanted an heir to inherit his fortune, and now that he had the heir he was obsessed by the need to preserve the fortune which would one day be inherited. As a young man he had been generous, even spendthrift; but these days he preferred to husband his resources so that it could be for Antonio, if he wished, to show immense generosity one day.

Besides, if the presentation of an honorary degree were to be followed too swiftly by any kind of gift, it might come to seem only a bribe. And there was no need to respond to the Chancellor's comment with anything more than a smile of agreement.

Soon it was time for the procession to form and make its slow way into the Sheldonian Theatre as an organ played and the audience respectfully rose. The proceedings were conducted in Latin, which the Maestro spoke and understood as a living language. He was able to bow his head at the right moments in appreciation of the Public

12

Orator's elegant compliments, and was the first to smile at his jokes. Ludo had coached him in the elaborate donning and doffing of hats which would be expected and there was, thank goodness, no need to make any speech of thanks. Within an hour, newly endoctored, he was making his farewells to the Chancellor.

Ludo was waiting for him. As a rule they were careful not to touch in public, but the younger man was able to give a quick squeeze of congratulation as he helped to take off the voluminous gown.

'We have to return it to the shop,' he said.

'Why? I told you to buy it.'

'They wouldn't let me. They haven't been able to get hold of any more brocade since the war started, so they have to hang on to their last gown for anyone who needs it to rent. I've taken the details. I'll get one made up in Rome.'

Not altogether mollified by this explanation, the Maestro allowed himself to be led into the establishment of a university tailor. While Ludo dealt with the tedious details of returning the gown, the Maestro inspected the stock of academic wear, college scarves and sweaters and blazer badges and, in a separate room, school uniforms. His eyes flickered with interest. It was his custom to buy a tie for Antonio on every trip abroad. Since he had time to spare here he studied the rack of school ties.

They were all striped, differentiated only by combinations of colour, but one caught his eye at once by its oddity. Woven in green, it was crossed only by two narrow bands of gold, close together. And between the gold lines was a tiny steam engine. As a piece of design it was a mess, but the boy would love it.

Antonio was mad about trains. He had refused to leave Canada unless he was allowed to travel the whole length of the Canadian Pacific Railway as a farewell treat. This tie would be the perfect gift for him. Smiling at the thought of his young son's pleasure, the Maestro carried the trophy back to the room in which Ludo was settling the bill.

'I'll take this,' he said.

The tailor looked up in surprise. 'Oh, you have a son at Tantivy, do you, sir?'

'Uh-uh. I just like the tie.'

'I'm sorry, sir, but we aren't empowered . . . The tie is restricted to pupils of the school.'

'Who's going to know?'

'I'm afraid the Colonel is very strict on the subject. Especially on that particular version of the tie, with the train. We can only sell it when we receive an authorisation like this.'

He pulled a piece of paper from a drawer. Frowning with incredulity, the Maestro read aloud the words written in neat copperplate.

'"This is to certify that Hodgkins, P. has qualified to be Train Marshal of the Remove and may wear the TM Tantivy tie. Signed: Edward Twist." What sort of gobbledy-gook is that?' But without waiting for an answer to his own question he took a fountain pen from Ludo's breast pocket. Crossing out Hodgkins, P. he wrote in its place Fiori, A. 'Now let me buy the tie.'

'Really, sir, I can't . . . This is most improper. My instructions . . . Besides, it's on coupons.' The tailor produced this last objection triumphantly, recognising that his awkward customer was a foreigner and unlikely to be carrying the necessary entitlement.

'Here you are.' Ludo, as always, was prepared for any emergency and produced a tiny scrap of paper from his wallet. 'And the tie will never be worn in England. Your Colonel friend need never know.' He spoke in the soft voice with which he was accustomed to smooth away difficulties all over the world. More to the point, he had managed to get the tie into his own hands and clearly did

14

not intend to return it. In grudging acceptance the tailor added the item to the bill.

The Maestro smiled in approval. Now there was a train to be caught. He dismissed from his mind the insignificant purchase of an eccentric prep school tie.

PART ONE

1962–1971

1

The flat – unfurnished, uncarpeted, undecorated – was, like its new owners, in that exciting stage when anything was possible and no mistakes had yet been made. Andrew Craig and Hilary Mortimer had spent a morning stripping off wallpaper and now, on a spring day in 1962, sat side by side on the floor.

'Is that the most you can manage?' Hilary asked her fiancé. They were comparing their wedding invitation lists.

'You have to remember that I'm an orphan.'

She giggled. 'Your explanation for absolutely all your deficiencies! But exactly how is it meant to excuse the fact that my half of the church is going to be crammed while you'll be lucky if you fill two pews?'

'Well, just look at your list. Seventeen relations to start with, while I've only got Grandma.' Andrew's father had been killed in the war and his mother died only a few years later. 'And then all these friends of your parents. Do we really want them?'

'They're part of the wedding present revenge tradition. My mother and father have had to cough up for their offspring, so now they're expected to do the same for me. I confidently expect to receive ten identical pyrex dishes.' This was not quite true. She had a bride's list at Peter Jones, but suspected that he might prefer not to know about this. Andrew, who hated to feel under any obligation to anybody, was not good at accepting gifts even on an occasion like this.

'Well, there you are, you see. My mother wasn't around to be asked to contribute to other people's weddings, so nobody owes us.'

'Doesn't matter. There must be people you called "Auntie" when you were a little boy.'

'But if I haven't seen them for twenty years . . .'

'They'll be tickled pink that you remember them. And you'll be offering them a good party. Just sit and think. And while you're doing it, hand over your address book.'

'In my briefcase.'

She found the book, sat down again and began to turn the pages. 'This is going to be *very* educational. Who is Sheila Bowden?'

'Oh, she was just . . . I haven't seen her for ages. We don't want . . .'

'Yes, we do. That's one of the purposes of a wedding. To let the bridegroom's old flames see that he's managed to hitch up with someone far more beautiful and generally marvellous than any of them, and is now to be considered out of circulation.'

'And the bride's old flames?'

'Those too.' They were both teasing. Hilary had fallen in love with Andrew when she was in her first year at Oxford and he was in his third, and had never been seriously interested in anyone else. She continued to look through the address book. 'Tony Fiori. Who's he?'

'A school-friend.'

'Winchester?'

'No. Tantivy.'

'Close friend? Blood brother?'

Andrew flushed. His complexion was naturally pale and made to seem even paler by the blackness of his hair and the severity of his horn-rimmed spectacles, but now the blood rushed up from his neck. He left it too late to turn his head away and Hilary's brown eyes widened in delighted amusement.

'Have I hit the nail on the head? Pricking of fingers? Writing of names in blood? The real thing?'

'Not exactly, but you're not far off. There was something

20

special to the school; a ritual for becoming best friends. The Tantivy Twist it was called, because the Colonel, Colonel Twist, claimed to have invented it.'

'What was it?'

'A kind of knot. I can't remember how to do it now. But we'd tie our fingers together and each of us would hold one end of the string, and the thing was that neither could get free until the other one let go of *his* end. We probably said some kind of mumbo-jumbo while we were hitched together, but I don't remember that either.'

'I bet you do really. Faithful unto death, that sort of thing? Well, let's have a look.'

'A look at what?'

'At Tony Fiori. Somewhere in those cardboard boxes, don't attempt to deny it, will be the sort of photograph which has all the school in rows in front of the cricket pavilion; and you being you, you'll know exactly which box.'

She was correct in her guess. Andrew hauled himself to his feet and hesitated for only a moment before pulling out a rolled photograph.

'Let me find you first. Oh here, right in the middle. You haven't changed a bit!'

She was only half joking. Of course there was a difference between the earnest twelve-year-old head boy, neat in his school uniform, and the lanky twenty-five-year-old who was lounging beside her in tee shirt and jeans. But even at school he had been very tall for his age and notable for his extreme thinness. Already there he was wearing spectacles, and his earnest face held the familiar expression of a man whose concentration would at any moment show itself in a frown. 'So which is Tony?' she asked.

Andrew's long finger pointed at a boy in the second row, smaller than himself and plumper.

'I thought schoolboys were never allowed to be best friends with boys younger than themselves.'

'It's not considered such a serious crime in a prep school.

21

I was his shepherd when he first arrived at Tantivy, so you could say we were thrown together.'

'What did that mean?'

'Oh, every new boy had one of the older boys to look after him for the first couple of weeks. Show him where to go and what to do. And take his punishments for him. So if Tony talked in Prayers, I was the one who had to do extra prep. But the real thing was, he didn't have any family in England, and nobody had told his parents about Sundays. As well as half term, there were three Sundays in the term when we were allowed to go home, or be taken out to lunch and tea if our homes were too far away, and Tony was going to be the only boy left in school.'

'So you took him home with you.'

'My mother got quite fond of him, I think. She went on inviting him even after his mother had realised what the system was and could have made other arrangements. And then, as a sort of thank-you, his family invited me to Rome for each Easter holiday, so we finished up by seeing more of each other than most school-friends did.'

'Well, there you are then.' Hilary looked meaningfully at the wedding list.

'I'm not there at all. We haven't seen each other for years. He went off to school in Switzerland and university in America; Harvard. An international man, is Tony.'

'Doesn't matter. Once a best friend, always a best friend. I can tell from the way you talk that you *are* still friends, even if it's only by correspondence.'

'Yes. But I don't want to send him an invitation.'

'Why not?'

'Because we couldn't expect him actually to come. He'll probably be in Rome or New York or California. If we invited him, it would seem too much as though we were simply asking for a present.'

'Would that be such a crime?'

'Yes. He's rich, you see.'

'Better and better. *Two* pyrex dishes, perhaps.'

'No, I mean *really* rich. Rolling in the stuff. He wouldn't be able to give a small present without seeming mean, and I don't want . . . I mean, when a family's as wealthy as that, people are always cadging, asking for charity.'

'How rich?' Hilary was interested in this prep school friend whose name had never been mentioned to her before. 'Gulbenkian-rich?'

'Perhaps not quite. But pretty near.'

'Fiori.' She rolled the name round her mind. 'Any relation to the conductor? The Maestro?'

'Only son.'

'Well, I know he's the tops and he must earn a packet, but that can hardly put them in the big league, can it?'

'There's big family money on both sides and Tony will get the lot one day. Land and property and businesses all over the world, and palaces full of art treasures. On top of that, he's got golden fingers himself. His parents just spend the cash, but Tony wants to build his own fortune. And I suppose money attracts money. He was only a month out of Harvard when he set up what you might call his personal merchant bank. To take risks, finance projects and rake in the profits.'

'How on earth did a boy from a family like that come to go to prep school in England? And a crazy prep school like Tantivy, of all places?'

'It wasn't crazy.' Andrew put on an expression of mock-indignation. 'It may have been forty years out of date and run by a nut-case, but it got me a scholarship to Winchester.'

'It was your own natural brilliance which won you that scholarship.'

Andrew shook his head. 'No. Old-fashioned cramming. Discipline and hard work, to Colonel Twist's personal recipe.'

23

'But how would an internationally-famous conductor ever know about that?'

'It's a long story.'

'We have world enough and time.' Hilary rearranged herself so that her head rested on Andrew's shoulder. His arm, around her waist, pulled her even closer. 'Andrew, I do love you.'

'Me too.' There was a pause while they kissed. Hilary would have liked to do more than kiss. All their friends – and perhaps even her mother – probably took it for granted that she and Andrew were already making good use of the privacy offered by the empty flat. But Andrew was oddly old-fashioned. Hilary, on her wedding day, would be that rarest of creatures in the 1960s: the bride who was still a virgin. She was tempted to force her way through his restraint, but knew that if she did so they might both later regret it. Conversation was a safety barrier.

'Right,' she demanded. 'The story of Tony Fiori.'

'Well, in the spring of 1947, when I was ten, my mother took me to Italy. She wanted to see the place where my father was killed, and his grave. But after we'd done that we had an ordinary sight-seeing holiday in Rome. And one afternoon we got on to a tram and found ourselves sitting opposite a boy – he was only just eight at the time – wearing the Tantivy tie. And not just the ordinary one: the Train Marshal's tie.'

'Do I know about train marshals?'

'Well, this is a digression. Colonel Twist was bats about model engines. There was a huge attic at the top of School House entirely filled with a train lay-out. He had a lot of scenery – mountains and lakes and villages. It was one of the things we all had to do in Art, make tiny models of trees and cars and people and animals. And then there were these elaborate railway tracks which ran side by side or over and under each other, with points and junctions and everything you can think of. You could run eight trains at the same time if you knew what you were doing.'

'Sounds like a small boy's heaven.'

'Yes. The perfect bribe. Or incentive, I suppose it would be called these days. What happened was that on the last day of term each form was allowed an hour in the train room. And the boy who'd got top marks was appointed Train Marshal and could tell all the others what to do. As long as there weren't any accidents, he was allowed to wear a special tie with an engine on it from then on.'

'Were you ever a train marshal?'

'Once or twice, yes. Anyway, to return to Tony. He was called Antonio in Rome, of course. When my mother recognised the tie, she naturally thought that he must be a schoolmate of mine, and started talking to him and the woman with him.'

'I suppose they didn't understand English.'

'*He* did. He'd been born and brought up in Canada. But he was being looked after by some sort of maid or governess, and she looked pretty alarmed. His mother was a princess, who couldn't be expected to travel on trams herself but allowed Tony a trip once a week as a treat. He invited us home for tea. I think he knew that he wasn't entitled to wear the tie. His father had joked about it being a terrible crime and he may have felt that he wanted his mother to get him out of trouble. She was Scottish-Canadian by birth, so there was no language problem there. Anyway, we went, and he showed me *his* trains. He thought they must be the best in the world, but I told him that the Colonel's were better. I never expected to see him again. But apparently after we'd gone he announced to his parents that he wished to go to school in England, to Tantivy, in order to become a Train Marshal.'

'At the age of eight!'

'I don't suppose he had the foggiest idea what was

involved. He just wanted to play with the Tantivy trains. But he was hopelessly spoiled. If he went on long enough he always got what he wanted. It's possible that when his parents talked it over they may have decided it was a good idea anyway. It was always their intention that he should grow up to feel at home in any part of the world. This must have seemed a good way of keeping his English going. And, mock though you may, a prep school like Tantivy delivered a good education in a happy atmosphere.'

'How could I mock something which must have formed the character I adore!' There was more kissing. 'If Tony was spoiled at home, it must have been a bit of a shock finding that he had to keep rules.'

'I'm surprised he lasted more than five minutes. His father's boyfriend had made all the arrangements and bought the school uniform and all that sort of thing, but the Maestro himself brought him over. I'd already been chosen to be his shepherd because we'd had that meeting five months earlier, so I was on parade when they arrived. "I've opened a bank account here for Antonio," says the Maestro. "I guess a hundred pounds will be enough to start with." So the Colonel draws himself up, all nine feet of him – as it always seemed to a small boy. "Each boy is allowed to bring one pound ten shillings to school each term. He will give it to Matron, and may apply to her for pocket money every Saturday. Parents may send their son a cake on his birthday, which he will share with the rest of his form." I think that was when Tony began to realise what he was in for. The first thing I had to do after his father had left was to show him a place where he could cry without anyone seeing.'

'Poor little Antonio!'

'The name had to go as well. There would have been too many jokes about ice cream carts.'

Hilary disentangled herself from Andrew's arms and stared again at the photograph of the plump little boy.

'It sounds to me as though you did him very well, one way and another. Did you keep in touch after you left Tantivy?'

'I spent some more Easter holidays in Rome. Hence my fluent Italian. Remind me to impress you some time. We haven't actually met since he went to Harvard. His mother died when he was eighteen and after that he spent all his vacations with his father. The Maestro had an orchestra in California by that time.'

'So did you lose touch?'

'Not exactly. He writes letters.'

'Don't sound so surprised.'

'Well, men don't as a rule. Not that sort of chatty, no-particular-reason sort of letter. But yes, we've kept in touch.'

'Then don't you see, Andrew, we *must* invite him. You don't know that he wouldn't be able to come. And just think how hurt he'd be if he discovered that you'd done something like this without even telling him.'

'Oh, I'd tell him. It's just that – '

'Worse and worse. You'd tell him without asking him. And all because you're afraid that he might give you too generous a present. Doesn't it occur to you that I might be interested in meeting someone who's going to be the richest man in the world one day?'

'*One* of the richest.'

'One of the richest, then.'

'I can't risk it. You might fall for him instead of me.'

'Idiot. Anyway. We're not going to discuss this any longer, because it isn't really anything to do with you. It's Sir Nicholas and Lady Mortimer who are sending out the invitations, and if they decide to ask your friend Tony, whose address I now know, there's nothing you can do about it. What I'll promise you, though, is that if he writes to ask what we'd like, I shall say nothing but his company.'

'You don't know Tony. He has the knack of asking or offering the one favour that you can't refuse.'

'There's nothing I can't refuse,' said Hilary confidently. They were, after all, discussing only the trivial matter of a wedding invitation list. 'And now, are we or are we not going to get this ceiling painted today?'

2

Andrew was ill. 'Too much sun, I suppose,' he said, angry with himself because he had tried to be careful. 'What a way to end a honeymoon!'

After twelve days of Italian sunshine Hilary's body was tanned all over, but Andrew's white skin had merely turned pink, refusing to bronze. That morning, though, he had awoken to find that his face was dark red, hot and swollen. Hilary, dabbing his skin with cotton wool soaked in calamine lotion, could tell that even her lightest touch was causing discomfort.

'A day in the dark and cool for you,' she ordered.

'We were going to Verona.'

'Verona can wait. Would you like me to read to you? Or play cards?' It was easy to interpret his hesitation. 'You just want to be left alone?'

'Do you mind?'

'Course not.' She collected her swimming things and a book, closed the blinds to darken the room and blew him a kiss.

'A couple of hours' sleep and I'll be right as rain,' he promised.

'I'll come in at lunch time and see how you feel.'

In the corridor outside a maid was waiting to clean the room. Hilary did her best to indicate that her husband should not be disturbed. Since their arrival in Italy she had discovered that Andrew's claim to speak the language fluently was well justified, and had left all communication with the servants to him. The fact that she could not understand what they were saying enabled her to pretend that they were not really there; that she and her new husband were alone on the island.

Andrew had been proved right in his guess that Tony Fiori would be unable to attend the wedding – and right also in suspecting that he would offer a gift impossible to refuse. The Fioris owned palaces, villas, apartments and ranches all over the world, using each for only a few weeks in the year. By spending their honeymoon at the Villa dell'Isola, on Lake Garda, and giving the servants someone to look after, the newly-weds were doing the family a favour. So at least they had been persuaded.

Only after their arrival did Hilary realise the perfection of the offer. The Villa dell'Isola occupied the whole of a small island. It even seemed likely that the island was man-made, so well designed was its shape to offer a vista from every window of the villa. From the bedroom balcony, on which as a rule she and Andrew took breakfast, the view was of an avenue of tall, slim cypresses leading down to the tiny harbour in which a yacht, a speedboat and a dinghy gently rocked. The terrace on which they dined faced across the water to a park which also belonged to the Fiori family, landscaped with temples and white marble statues, and with a miniature waterfall splashing down from the mountains behind.

This morning, though, Hilary made her way to the side of the island which faced out into the middle of the lake. Below a series of three terraces was a grotto lined with sea shells in the fashion of an earlier century but furnished with a modern collection of chairs and mattresses. A tiny artificial beach sloped down to the centre of a little bay whose two miniature headlands curved round almost to touch. Only in the split second of passing directly in front of the gap could any yachtsman glimpse the occupants of the bay. It was explained by the servants to Andrew without the slightest hint of prurience that he and his bride might consider themselves completely private there. If for any reason their presence was required in the villa, a bell would ring on the terrace above, tugged by a wire from the kitchen. In no other way need they ever fear disturbance.

During the previous twelve days Hilary and Andrew had made good use of this privacy and now, alone, she had no hesitation in taking off all her clothes and stretching out in the sun. Although she had brought a book to read, she did not open it immediately, but instead lay on her back, staring up.

There was not a cloud in the sky. The sun, not yet unbearably hot, bathed her body with its warmth. She had only to ask and she would be supplied with cool drinks, delicious food, more towels or cushions. It seemed to Hilary that she would enjoy being a millionaire.

Well, this was the nearest she was ever likely to come to experiencing such a life. Andrew had a first-class mind and a first-class Oxford degree in mathematics to prove it. But, ignoring his own considerable talents, he had turned his back on ambition and chosen the security of a career in the Inland Revenue Service. They were never likely to starve, but they would certainly never be rich.

Nothing wrong with that. Andrew's indifference to material success was one of the qualities for which Hilary loved him. She closed her eyes against the brightness of the sun and began to day-dream about the future until she was startled – had she been sleeping? – by the harsh clanging of the bell. Did Andrew need her? Was he feeling worse? She slipped quickly into her beach robe, tugged the sash tight and ran up the steps towards the villa.

There was more chatter than usual going on in the kitchen quarters. Unlike the English servants in her mother's house, who were expected to remain silent unless spoken to, there was always shouting and laughing to be heard on the island, but today she recognised a new note of excitement. As she approached the courtyard, a stranger who had been sitting in the shade of the vines stood up, blocking her way.

'Mrs Craig. Hilary. I'm Tony Fiori.'

She was taken aback by both his presence and his appearance. It was presumably because he looked so small in the Tantivy school photograph that her mental picture of their host had been of a short, plump Italian. But although he was not as tall as Andrew, nor as thin, the tight casual clothes that he wore showed him to be fit and muscular. His looks as well as his voice were North American. She reminded herself that his mother was a Canadian and that he had only recently left Harvard, and told herself not to be surprised.

His eyes laughed as he bent to kiss her hand.

'Flying from one culture to another I lose identity,' he said. 'Just came into Milan airport from Washington, with business to do in Milan but not till tomorrow. Italian propriety tells me that to intrude on a honeymoon couple is the height of bad form. But as an American college man I assume that anyone anywhere will be delighted to see an old buddy. So I thought I'd risk it.'

He was talking to give her time to collect her thoughts, but there was a look of admiration in his eyes as he straightened himself. Hilary, who had not paused to put on her bikini before answering the summons of the bell, was about to tug the edges of her beach robe closer together when something in her host's expression – the merest twitch of the corner of his mouth – made her suddenly sure that he had cheated on the island's rules. If he had already had time to scrutinise the whole of her body, there was no point in being prudish about an inch of cleavage. Her hand fell to her side again and she stared steadily into his eyes in the hope – unsuccessful – of making him look ashamed.

'Sorry to look so startled,' she said. 'When I heard the bell, I thought it must be Andrew.'

'What are you doing to poor old Andrew? I last see him as a normal young man and suddenly he's covered in white paint.'

'He's caught the sun,' she explained.

'Nonsense. He's got mumps.'

'What!'

'I sent Emilia in to have a look. She was my nurse once; knows all about children's diseases.'

'But how could he possibly – ?' She paused as a picture flashed into her mind: a picture of Andrew at the wedding reception with a young pageboy half asleep on his lap. She remembered smiling at the sight. Andrew loved children. One day he would nurse his own son in just such a way. But she recalled now how flushed young Peter was that afternoon, and how unusual his lack of energy had been. Over-excitement, they had all assumed, but perhaps he was already incubating the virus.

'We've sent for the doctor,' Tony assured her. 'Though I guess it's one of these things which has to take its course. I mustn't keep you away now. Lunch in about an hour, okay? And afterwards we might go for a sail.'

'I can't possibly – '

'Yes, you can,' he said easily. 'This is where I find out whether you're sensible or silly. Emilia will keep old Andrew supplied with cold drinks. All he'll want apart from that is sleep. You'll make him miserable if he thinks he's spoiling your holiday as well as his own. It's a mistake to think that marriage means that you both have to be unhappy at the same time. Ask Andrew if you don't believe me.'

Andrew in fact was already asleep again, with Emilia – delighted to be useful – beside him. Hilary, silently dressing in the dark, recognised that she would only be in the way if she were to stay. Tony was right: and two hours on the water would give her the chance to get acquainted with him. Once again he had made an offer which could not be refused.

3

Girls, in Tony Fiori's experience, could be divided into three categories. Tony's experience was not very wide, for his eyes passed unnoticingly over that large percentage of womankind which was poor or ugly or shy or stupid. There were glamorous girls and there were fiercely intellectual or ambitious girls; he had met many specimens of each at Harvard and during his vacations in California. In addition to these there were sophisticated girls, who were rarely to be found at university but whom his grandmother and other hostesses regularly produced for his approval at dinner parties in New York, Boston, Washington or Rome.

It was the glamorous girls who dangled their charms in front of him, but almost certainly it would prove to be one of the sophisticated girls whom he would marry one day. His existing fortune and his immense expectations made him a 'catch' in any language. Although he never put the thought into words, he saw it as sensible to choose a wife who would be accustomed to money – so that, having enough of her own, she would find Tony attractive for himself and not for the lifestyle he could offer.

Hilary Craig fell into none of these categories. He knew her to be an Oxford graduate, and so presumably clever, but in their conversation over lunch she had neither pressed him into philosophical discussion nor forced him to hear how she proposed to build a career. She was not sophisticated. From the wedding invitation he had already learned that her mother was a Lady, but this did not make Hilary herself an aristocrat. Her father, as far as could be gathered from the one letter which had been prised out of Andrew since the engagement was announced, spent his life hunting, shooting, fishing and grumbling about taxation. Hilary was a country girl.

Nor did she attempt to make herself glamorous. Her dark curly hair was cut so that it would spring back into place after she had swum, showered, and rubbed it dry with a towel. Her face was strong rather than classically perfect – wide cheekbones, wide mouth, thick eyebrows. She wore no make-up, and dressed to conceal her body, not to reveal it.

As she walked down the avenue of cypresses towards the landing stage, she was sensibly dressed for the water in shorts and sneakers, with a shirt to protect her shoulders from the sun. The very looseness of the shirt seemed to emphasise the trimness of the body it concealed. Not glamorous, that artificial, second-rate word: but beautiful. Oh yes; firm and slender and strong and beautiful.

As though she could read his thoughts, Hilary came to a halt before stepping on to the yacht.

'One thing I wanted to ask,' she said. 'Did you come down to the grotto before you rang the bell this morning?'

Her wide hazel eyes stared steadily at him. It was easy to guess that she knew the answer already. He was tempted nevertheless to lie, on the assumption that she would prefer not to know the truth; but those eyes forced it out of him.

'Right,' he confessed. 'Just didn't think. So crazy to see Andrew again after all this time.' He was about to add that she had a neat little ass when it occurred to him that she might not know the American word. Translating his thought into English he came up with 'bottom'; but bottom, in England, was something to be beaten with a cane. It seemed prudent to abandon the comment. 'I'm sorry,' he said.

Hilary's wide, generous mouth opened into a smile.

'That's all right,' she said, stepping lightly on to the little boat. 'Thank you for not fibbing. I wouldn't have come out with you if you had.'

'You mean you wouldn't have trusted me on the water?' He cast off and followed her on to the yacht. It was small enough to sail single-handed but, as he took his seat by the rudder, he noted that she had automatically moved into the appropriate crewing position. 'You don't think I'd flirt with the wife of my oldest friend – and a new bride at that!'

'You can only trust people after you know them,' said Hilary, leaning back as the yacht left shelter and picked up the wind. 'And really I know nothing about you – as an adult, I mean – except that you're rolling in money. Rich men are sometimes spoilt. They often look for challenges. No, I didn't think you'd do the dirt on Andrew. But you could have tried to humiliate me by making me wish you would.'

'Too complicated for me, sorry,' he drawled – and then, abruptly, 'Gybe!'

As he expected, Hilary ducked neatly under the boom as it swung across. 'You've sailed before,' he said: a statement, not a question.

'See what I mean? You're checking me out. Fair enough, I suppose. But you can understand why I feel the need to stay on alert. Yes, I can handle a boat. And swim.'

Nodding in approval, he came to sit beside her. Now they could really move.

'Sound as though you're just what old Andrew needs – someone with practical skills,' he said, turning the yacht close to the wind so that they were forced to throw their weight backwards. 'First-rate brain but fourth-rate fingers, I always used to tell him. In your new home, I bet you're the one who's putting up the shelves.'

'Too true.' But now the noise and exhilaration of their speed made conversation difficult. Not until almost an hour later did he turn into the wind so that the sails flapped idly, making them seem to be becalmed.

'Is this the moment when you tell me that we've run out of gas?' Hilary grinned as she asked the question.

Tony grinned back. They were friends already, he realised, just by deciding that it was what they both wanted. There would be no need to be cautious in making preliminary approaches; no need to feel at risk. 'Tell me something about yourself,' he said. 'Andrew's a hopeless letter-writer. I ask him questions and he never answers.'

'What do you want to know?'

'Well, I do know already that you met him at Oxford. What did you major in? And did it help you get a job, or don't you work?'

'I read geography. Yes, I do work – to the horror of my mother, who gives the impression that no female Mortimer has ever before earned an honest penny for herself. The part of the degree course that I most enjoyed was statistics, so I got a job in market research.'

'You mean you stand in the street with a clip-board asking people what brand of coffee they drink?'

'Nearly but not quite. I'm the one who stays in the office, making up the questions and analysing the answers.' She laughed as he made a face. 'I enjoy it. And it won't be for ever. We want to have at least four children.'

'Sounds like hard work.'

'They're not likely all to arrive at once. And not straightaway, either. I want to enjoy being just a wife for a year or two before I start being a mother. But we're both only children, you see. And with Andrew losing both parents while he was young, he feels a great need for a family. That's something I suppose you've always taken for granted, but – '

He interrupted her with a shake of the head and spoke more seriously than before. 'I've never had a family. Nor a home.'

'But Andrew said – '

'Oh sure, plenty of houses. Like a chain of hotels where I can always get a room without booking. But nowhere where I belong. Not even a home country. I was born in Canada, but I'm not a Canadian. I have an Italian pedigree, but I don't feel Italian either, except sometimes when I'm staying with my grandmother. I've been to school in England and Switzerland, but that doesn't give them any hold on me. I guess I'm more American than anything else, but I'm not an American citizen. As for family . . . Until I was about ten my parents always used to meet up for Christmas for little Antonio's sake. After that, until my mother died, they let me choose which one I wanted to stay with. Reckoned they were doing me a favour; but a kid wants to be chosen, not to choose. I don't mean that they were ever uncaring. They both loved me. But separately. The best way to describe my family life would be nix. Which could be why I set such store by friendship.'

He paused, surprised at what he had revealed. He was not accustomed to confess so much to a new acquaintance. As he turned his head to look into Hilary's eyes, which expressed sympathy without sloppiness, he was confirmed in his earlier feeling that they had managed to achieve friendship without needing to work through any preliminary stages. Smiling, he indicated that the moment of seriousness was over and that it was time to change the subject. He had been intending to talk about her, not himself, when he suggested the sail. 'Back to you. Sir Nicholas and Lady Mortimer, the invitation said. And a grand address in the country.'

'Grand? That's rich, coming from a man with so many palaces that he can afford to lend them out to impecunious honeymooners. Not grand at all. Just old and entailed and rather shabby.'

'But in the country. I have a kind of impression of you as an outdoor girl. Do you ride?'

'Yes.'

'And now you'll be living in a flat in the middle of London.'

'With Andrew.'

'Ah yes, that must make all the difference. With Andrew.'

'Well, of course it does!'

'Calm down, calm down.' Laughing, he put a hand on her warm brown thigh. It was firm, muscular – riding muscles, no doubt. 'Only kidding. I'm surprised, though, that your parents didn't set you up on a more spacious scale. So that you could go on with the country thing.'

'In the first place I didn't want them to. My job's in London, as well as Andrew's. And in the second place Andrew is prickly in that sort of way. He wants to stand on his own two feet, and to look after me by himself.'

'Yes, right, I remember Andrew's prickles.' Tony moved his hand away and dangled his fingers in the water, splashing idly. 'I remember when his mother died, while he was still at school. My father wanted to repay some of the kindnesses he'd shown to me. The scholarship helped with his fees at Winchester, but even so – you mustn't pass this on to Andrew, of course – '

'Stop!' Hilary put up a hand as though she was bringing traffic rather than a confession to a halt. 'If there's something you don't want Andrew to know, you mustn't tell me, because I shall tell him. We're not going to have any secrets from each other.'

'None at all? How very dull your lives will be.' He was silent for a moment, sure that curiosity would after all overcome her scruples. But instead she asked another question quickly.

'What kindnesses did Andrew show to you? What made you become particular friends? I mean, I know he was your shepherd at Tantivy, and took you home for half terms: is that what you mean?'

'There was one thing more than anything else that I shall

never cease to thank him for. Did he ever tell you about the Train Marshals?'

'Yes, he did. Were you one of them?'

'It was what I longed to be. It was the reason why I asked my parents to send me to Tantivy, so that I could have my hour of glory with Colonel Twist's trains. I was a spoilt brat: I expect Andrew told you that. My father was always away or busy and my mother didn't have much time to spare for me so naturally they both gave me everything I wanted.'

'So you thought that you only need wish to be a Train Marshal and it would fall into your lap.'

'Right. When I arrived at the school, though, I soon realised how clever all the other boys were. I wasn't exactly stupid, but my governess hadn't given me a good start. Reading, writing and speaking three languages, fine; but she wasn't any good with figures herself so she dodged that part of the curriculum.'

'The teachers must have realised that before you arrived.'

'Well no, because Uncle Ludo did my entrance paper for me.' He laughed at Hilary's startled expression. 'My father has a personal assistant, major domo, fancy boy, whatever you like to call him. Anything that has to be fixed, Ludo fixes. He was told to get me a place at Tantivy, and the Colonel wouldn't accept a boy he'd never seen except on the basis of an entrance exam, so Ludo made sure that I passed it. It was only the math answers that he had to give me. I could manage the rest myself. Heck, I was only eight. I thought it was the system. Don't look so shocked.'

'Sorry.'

'It didn't take long after I arrived at Tantivy for me to realise that I was never going to get top of the class because I couldn't do math.' He paused and corrected the Americanism. 'Maths. At Christmas and in July we had exams. Not much to be done about that. But at Easter the Colonel went on the marks we got for prep throughout the term. So after I'd been at the school a couple of years I asked Andrew for help.'

'You mean you got him to do your prep for you?'

'That was what I expected. It was his last year in the school; my last chance, I felt. And we were already best friends. He was supposed to do anything I asked, just as I'd have done anything he asked me. All I wanted was the answers. And he wouldn't give them me.'

Hilary's bubble of laughter suggested that she had guessed what was coming.

'He coached me instead. For a whole term. Taught me all the basic stuff I'd missed. Showed me whatever method I needed for the day's prep, went through an example with me and then made me do the sum myself. The only thing that seemed helpful at the time was that he told me if I'd got it wrong, so that I could have another shot.'

'So you got a hundred per cent on your maths homework, zoomed up to the top of the form, became a train marshal after all and lived happily ever after!'

'Right. Which enabled Andrew to deliver a short lecture on how true friendship meant giving someone what they needed and not what they asked for.'

'A fairly strong philosophical concept for a ten-year-old.'

'I learnt the lesson. More to the point, I became quite good with figures, for which I daily give thanks. Not a wizard like Andrew, of course. Poor old mumpy Andrew. What's he doing now, Hilary? Like I said, he hardly ever answers my letters.'

'Still working for the Inland Revenue. Tax, you know. He's passed all the examinations now and got his first promotion. He hopes to specialise in trusts and tax avoidance schemes. Making sure that they keep inside the law.'

'I suppose that is one way of making a fortune. Ten years of catching out tax evaders and the rest of his life making a fortune by showing people how to get round the rules.'

'I don't think that's quite what he has in mind,' said Hilary.

Tony found it difficult to judge from her voice what her own attitude was, and so asked her outright. 'Do you wish it were?'

'His career is his business. He must do whatever he's happiest with.'

'What a marvellously supportive wife old Andrew has captured for himself!' He was not mocking, but sincere; and after a single suspicious glance Hilary appeared to recognise this.

'Well,' she said. 'Do I pass?'

'Pass what?'

'You came here to vet me, didn't you? To find out whether I was a suitable wife for your friend.'

Taking a risk, he leant sideways and kissed her on the lips.

'Oh, you pass all right. With honours. Lucky Andrew, I say. But that's only half of it. What I really came to find out is whether you consider me a suitable friend for your husband. A wife can dispose of her husband's old buddies overnight if she feels like it. You might regard me as dangerous.'

'You mean that I might start to compare my hard-working but hard-up husband with a handsome, charming, wealthy young man who doesn't need to do a hand's turn if he doesn't choose to. And if he *does* choose to work, he can travel the world, setting up new enterprises and cushioned against all the discomforts and trivialities of life by servants and wealth?'

'Of course I don't mean any such thing.' He was not accustomed to reveal himself as serious so often in a single conversation, but there was more at stake than Hilary probably realised. 'I *need* Andrew,' he told her. 'Even if

I knew that I would never see him again for the rest of my life, it wouldn't make any difference. I need to know that somewhere in the world there is a man called Andrew Craig who thinks of me as a friend. I've found already, there are some wives who aren't willing to share.'

'We're hardly in competition, are we? I mean, Andrew presumably expects different things of you and me. Unless of course' – and now her eyes sparkled with mischief – 'unless you've inherited your father's proclivities.'

'Good God, no!' The vehemence of his reaction rocked the little boat, reminding them both where they were. 'We'd better be getting back, I suppose. Would you like to take over?'

'Love to.' Keeping low, they changed places and within a second began to tack back towards the island. Recognising that Hilary was showing off, he recognised at the same time that she was competent. Beneath her expression of sympathetic understanding, he suspected, was a strong character. How long would she be content to remain the adoring bride, ready to support her husband in whatever he might choose to do, whether or not she agreed with it? Well, that would be for Andrew to find out.

He waited until they were back at the Villa dell'Isola before asking one last question.

'May I write to you? Just from time to time; two or three times a year.'

'Of course. You already do, don't you? Andrew told me – '

'I mean you you, not half of Andrew and you. I take your point about no secrets. You can both *read* the letters; that's okay. But I can only write to one person at a time. Andrew's so hopeless at answering, I reckon I could do better with you.'

'So you're really asking whether *I*'ll write to *you*?'

'You have it.'

Jumping up on to the landing stage, he stretched out a

hand to pull her after him, but did not step back, so that she was held close to him for a moment. He stared into her eyes, reading her uncertainty. During the past two hours she had taken both his inquisition and his confessions at face value and had accepted them as stemming from his boyhood closeness to her husband. Only now was she realising that his greed for friendship was stretching to include her as well.

Tony had two special smiles. There was his Italian smile: charming, with a hint of secret admiration. And there was the all-American college boy grin. He gave her the grin, happy for her to recognise it as a caricature of his feelings. She began to laugh, shaking her head.

'I think I'm out of my depth.'

'You said you could swim.'

Her laughter sobered to a smile. 'Right you are, then. One of us will answer your letters. If Andrew doesn't do it, I will. And no, before you ask, we are not going to seal the bargain with a kiss.'

She disentangled her hand and ran lightly along the platform towards the villa, to see how Andrew was getting on. Poor old Andrew. Lucky old Andrew. Tony watched her until she disappeared. He was well pleased with his afternoon.

4

Rome. July 3, 1962

Dear Hilary,

It's important for anyone who's granted a privilege to take advantage of it at once, in case it lapses through disuse. So I'm writing to you just because you told me I might, without having anything to say. Except of course that it was a great pleasure to meet you, and that old Andrew's a lucky dog. (One extra advantage of seizing you as a correspondent is that I can practise my English, which has grown rusty during all these years in America.)

I hope that by now all the germs have departed and his face has returned to its normal shape. It's a lesson to us all to catch all possible illnesses while we're still in the nursery. Remember that when your four children start to arrive.

Ciao,

Tony

Santa Monica. November 8, 1962

Dear Hilary,

Many thanks to you both for your letter. Yes, his death was a great shock. I'd tried all my life to persuade my father that trains, not planes, are the civilised way to travel, but if you're conducting one orchestra in California and another in Germany I suppose that sort of leisurely progress simply isn't possible. Plane crashes have become almost an occupational hazard of a musician's life. He knew that.

At least it was sudden and final. Ludo was one of

the survivors. I've just come away from the hospital. He's been terribly burned, but he'll live. At the moment, though, he doesn't want to. As a boy I used to resent him; and when I grew older I was disgusted by his closeness to my father – as though it were a one-sided relationship for which only one of the two could be held responsible. But now I find myself feeling warm and glad that the Maestro should have attracted such devotion. If my mother had been still alive she would have been sorry to lose a good friend, but not devastated. I wouldn't have needed to rush off and comfort her. It came as a shock to hear myself today doing my best to inspire Ludo with the will to live, telling him how much I'd need him to help me take over all the family responsibilities. All quite sincere, as it happens. He was never just a pretty face. Which is fortunate, since he's on his own now: a middle-aged man, badly scarred all over his face and body.

Yes, you're right that the Manhattan address is the one to write to, even if you feel sure that I'll be somewhere else. Anything marked Personal will reach me by courier.

Best wishes to you both,
Tony

Rome. September 21, 1963

My dear Hilary,

Many apologies for the long silence. These last months I've hardly known whether I was coming or going. You wouldn't believe the complications I've been trying to unravel. Well, perhaps Andrew would, since they're the sort of thing that presumably he's concerned with all the time, from the other side of the fence.

My father's will could hardly have been simpler.

The rest of my mother's fortune (which had been tied up in a marriage settlement) came to me automatically. From his own resources he left a generous lump sum to Ludo, together with the Santa Monica house and all its contents. (Not to be sneezed at, that last phrase, since that was where he kept his Impressionists and the Picassos.) All the rest to me without strings.

The complications arise from the way he'd been living for the past twenty-odd years. Neither he nor my mother ever needed to touch their capital and they didn't spend anything like the whole of their income. Ludo was left to look after the sordid details, and he did my father well, in a way, by re-investing income to provide more capital and yet more income. When you start off with millions, other millions roll in.

The problem is – perhaps you'd better not let Andrew read this paragraph, Hilary: no, no, only kidding! The problem is that Ludo didn't always bother with finicky little points like declaring the whole of the original income for tax. Most of it came through Rome, of course – he seems to have been properly scrupulous in the United States, where the rules are stricter – and Italy has an endearing system whereby tax liability is a matter for negotiation, with the odd sweetener not being entirely unknown. It may even be true, as Ludo claims, that the government did a sort of deal straight after the war in order to entice people like the Maestro, anti-Fascist exiles, back into the country. But to an Old Tantivian like myself, brought up on the Honour System, the whole thing stinks.

I was afraid at one point that Ludo would take his scarred face and his inheritance off to California and abandon me; now that he's a millionaire in his own right, he need never work again if he chooses not to. But a little moral blackmail has persuaded him that both he and the Fiori name could come out of this badly, so he's helping me to sort it out. Unwise, we've decided, to open up the whole can of worms, so we're merely doing some reorganisation, with everything to be strictly on the level from now on. This involves moving a lot of capital out of Italy, to avoid too great a contrast between the old and the new officially admitted income; so I'm having a great time investigating the relative delights of Liechtenstein, the Cayman Islands and some even more obscure islands in the middle of the Pacific.

I have it in mind to buy a selection of five-star hotels (judiciously scattered round the world so that I can flit from penthouse suite to penthouse suite on my travels). And I shall start in London, which is becoming – have you noticed this yourself? – the place where everyone wants to be. 'Where it's at.' So you may get a call before too long, to fix a meeting. I look forward to that.

All the best,
Tony

Costa Rica. Christmas

My dear Hilary,

It was great to see you both again and I hope that by now you have succeeded in smoothing down those ridiculous prickles of Andrew's. I can't tell you – or at least I *am* telling you – what an infinitesimal amount twenty thousand pounds is when compared with the fees I'm paying to surveyors and auditors and lawyers for the London hotels. It *has* to be an interest-free loan because I just can't be bothered with fiddly little bits of income. And I absolutely guarantee that in ten years' time you will be able to sell whatever house you buy, pay the money back and still be in pocket. I have studied these things: you have to believe me.

Besides, a cosy little flat like yours is fine for two people, but now that you've decided that it's family-starting time you need to get settled in something with space for all those four children. I'm sure that moving house when pregnant is not to be recommended. Do it now.

I've been thinking a lot about our conversation on the subject of wealth. Both my parents had very much the same attitude, I suspect. For my mother, being an heiress meant being able to buy absolutely anything she wanted or go anywhere she chose without having to think twice about it. For my father, it was the private money behind him which helped him to build a public reputation, so that you could almost say that he bought that as well. But his passion for music was genuine and his talent for conducting was genuine as well. He would have made the Hall of Fame in the end, however he'd started. Riches simply smoothed the way to begin with and made his life very comfortable. Neither of them was greedy, although I guess you could say that they were both selfish. They just took for granted what they'd been raised to expect.

I'm not a spender like my mother, and I have no overwhelming talent like my father. I *do* have a secret ambition, but that's going to stay secret for a bit – though if Andrew guesses that it's a hangover from my hour of glory as Train Marshal, he won't be far off the mark. What I positively enjoy is setting up successful deals, the bigger the better. Although that doesn't compare with any kind of creative vocation, as a career it's as respectable as anything else, so I'm not disposed to feel ashamed of it. Just think of all the employment I'm creating all over the world!

Anyway, get that house and invite me to stay in it.

With love,
Tony

Hey, hey, hey, Hilary,

It's all very well for you to say that I should give more of the Fiori fortune away, but disposing of money is a very time-consuming business. Once let it get round that you're a soft touch, and the begging letters never stop coming. Unless you're going to abandon any idea of only giving to the *deserving* poor, everything has to be investigated and supervised. Individual requests are hardly worth the effort, but if you start giving money away on a grand scale you have to give great thought to social consequences.

For example. This new contraceptive pill. I was approached two or three years ago by a laboratory in need of funding – not the one which has finally made the breakthrough, but it won't be far behind, and with what may be a safer formula. Personally I approve of this pill. I think it may prove to be the greatest invention of the century. Left to myself I would not only fund the lab but buy up the product by the million and distribute it free in all those countries where over-population is leading to famine. But this of course would be a slap in the face of the church to which I nominally belong. I could live with that, as a matter of fact; but my grandmother might never speak to me again. So I gave them what they asked for, but as an investment, not as a gift. And made it a condition that half of my contribution should go into research into infertility. That's the half I can tell Grandmother about. So now everyone's happy – but

50

only at the expense of more time than I really wanted to spend on it.

Later on, when I'm sixty, say, I'll stop trying to create wealth and change to disposing of it instead. But not yet. This is what comes of being descended from an 'old' family. You feel that having had so much handed down to you, you have a duty to hand even more down to your heir.

'What heir?' you may well ask. Yes indeed. Is it as a result of our conversation and correspondence that I conclude that what a rich man needs above all else is an heir, somebody to give point to working at the making of money? Or could it have anything to do with the fact that my grandmother, alarmed by my non-attendance at Mass and my little fling with the 'unsuitable' Hannah in New York, has recently been encouraging a friendship with the daughter of the newly-appointed American ambassador in Rome: a good Catholic girl.

Well, more of that later. I'm delighted to hear that the new house is a success.

Much love,
Tony

Manhattan. October 13, 1964

My dear Hilary,

Well, since you ask! Her name is Sara: Sara Morrell. She's a tiny little thing: I feel I could pick her up with one hand. But beautiful, beautiful. She has long black hair, and when she puts it up she looks stunningly sophisticated and when she lets it hang loose she looks stunningly young, which she is. She has very strong views about a great many things and tends to be a bit intense about them; but I agree with fifty per cent of her arguments and hope to laugh her out of the rest.

51

I first met her father at some diplomatic reception and we found we had a lot in common. He owns a world-wide chain of hotels – and, as you know, I've recently started to dabble my fingers in this pond – and he's also a Harvard man. So we chatted happily and he invited me to a private dinner and Sara was there on vacation. Grandmother, who claims not to be 'in society', picks up this sort of thing in about ten seconds flat and has her own network of elderly aristocratic buddies (what's the female of buddies?). Within two days Sara and I were discovering that whenever one of us was invited to a dance or opera or race meeting, the other by coincidence was in the same party. But I've never scoffed at matchmakers: they often get things right.

You'll gather from this that she's not the poor swineherd's daughter with whom princes in fairy tales always fall in love. But in practical terms it makes things simpler that she's already used to living the sort of life I lead. By which I mean not only luxury but a great deal of movement around the world. She has, however, given me notice that once the babies start to arrive, she'll want to establish one main settled home. (Strong View Number One: children need security of place as well as of parents.)

Nothing official will be announced until she finishes at college next May. But we both know where we're going.

Yours blissfully,
Tony

Rome. April 12, 1965

My dear Hilary,

By now you'll have received your official invitation. This is just to spell out the administrative arrangements. Even the Palazzo Fiori isn't capable of housing everyone I want to invite to the Wedding of the Century, but by great good fortune one of the Morrell hotels is in Rome. We've managed to empty it of all except two old ducks who have permanent suites and are not to be budged. They may be sorry when the Jet Set arrives!

I enclose your room card for a week – no point in making the journey just for a day or two. Also the air tickets. The return dates can easily be changed if, as I hope, you decide to explore a bit more of Italy while you're over. Give the old man a chance to show off his Italian.

Tell Andrew (yes, I know that you're already reading this over her shoulder) that there will be another Old Tantivian there. I don't suppose he remembers John Todhunter, who is exactly my own age and was in my form. I only became friends with him after Andrew had gone to Winchester. If he *does* have any recollection it will probably be of another little squirt who, like myself, could never get the point of cricket. In his case because he wore huge round glasses and still couldn't see the ball. He's a lawyer now, specialising in international law.

See you soon. Although there'll be a crowd, you're the ones I'll be looking out for.

With all (well, nearly all) my love,
Tony

Rome. In haste.

Dear Mrs Craig,

I am seriously displeased with you. After your success with the house, I thought you'd mastered the art of persuading Andrew to see sense. I'm not trying to *give* him anything: I'm asking *him* to give *me* a week of his time. And what right does he have to deprive me of the sight of you looking luscious in a frilly hat? Also, I've promised Tod the chance of a reunion with one of his boyhood heroes, the great Craig. And I want Sara to meet all my real friends.

There is no work, tell him, that can't be done a week later. If he'd got knocked down by a bus, Her Majesty would have found someone else to do her sums for a few days. So push him in front of the bus and bring him on a stretcher. I return the room cards. No will not be taken for an answer.

Yours sternly,
Tony

Villa dell'Isola. August 20, 1965

My dear Hilary,

It was really great to see you and you looked absolutely stunning. Don't get any thinner, though. You're perfect as you are.

Yes, you can tell old Andrew that I forgive him. I hadn't realised that he'd got to argue a case in court, and I guess it's not too easy to tell a judge to come back in seven days' time. Contempt of court, would that be it? If I thank him for letting you come by yourself, I shall have the Women's Libbers at my throat, so instead I'll just thank *you* for making the trip.

In any case, I couldn't have stayed cross for long. There's a lot to be said for married life, isn't there? I hope you remember our present address with affection, though I suppose Andrew's memories may be mumpier.

To my surprise, Sara has voted for making our main home in Rome. Except, of course, in August, when the city is insufferable. Her maternal family was Italian three generations back and she seems to have a kind of 'coming home' feeling. So I'm moving my headquarters there. Ludo is delighted.

He's already sold the California house, finding the West Coast boring; but he hated living in New York. I shall still have to spend a lot of time on the move, I fear, but for at least a few months Sara will be with me. By Christmas, though, she will have to settle down to the knitting of tiny clothes. This is really much too early for any official announcement, so don't refer to it in your next letter. But I'm so pleased that I have to tell someone!

With love to you both,
Tony

Rome. The Ides of March, 1966

My dear Hilary,

Many thanks for your card and gift. We're both over the moon about Giorgio, who is fat and happy and altogether perfect. We have talked through his future career as far as Harvard already, except that we still haven't decided how best to bring him up bi- or multi-lingual. The name – he will be called George or Georgie at home – is mainly for the sake of my grandmother, who is very old and very frail but has been hanging on to see me married and settled and a father. It's odd, as a matter of fact, how having a son makes one feel quite a different person. Older. More mature. More dignified. Even (don't laugh) for the first time princely. Tell Andrew he should try it some time. Although what you should produce is a daughter, so that Georgie can marry her. After Harvard.

Ciao,
Tony

Rome. November 3, 1966

My dear Hilary,

Congratulations to you both on your respective

promotions. How tactful of the Queen and Mr Shepherd to get together on the dates in order that neither of you should feel left behind.

I'm sorry that after all that flurry of telephone calls we didn't after all get to meet while I was in London. You were told, I hope, that it was my grandmother's illness which called me back. She slipped away peacefully about an hour after I arrived.

I noticed at the funeral how few relatives I have. Almost inevitable, I suppose. Heirs are heirs and (even more) heiresses are heiresses precisely because there are no brothers and sisters to share with. I have no aunts, uncles, parents. And now no grandparents either. Andrew will understand the feeling.

I've so many letters to write to my grandmother's friends that I can't do this one justice. I'll be in touch later.

Love,
Tony

Villa dell'Isola. August 2, 1967

My dear Hilary,

I write in sackcloth and ashes – horrified to realise that, because I'd been looking forward to a good chat in London, I never answered your last letter of long ago. I'm truly sorry to hear about your baby – or rather, no-baby – problem. Have you been to a doctor? I understand from my clinical friend that sometimes the problem is something quite small. If your local quack hasn't been able to help, please make contact with my friend Dr Sussman, whose card I enclose. I was at school with his son in Switzerland. Although his research lab is in Geneva, he runs clinics in London and Boston. I may have mentioned them to you in an earlier letter. Infertility is one of his specialities (the other being planning for the over-fertile). I've told him that he will hear from you, so you must write anyway, whether it's to ask for an appointment or to announce joyfully that you're already pregnant.

If you do go to see him, and if he manages to help, there will be no bills to pay. By which I mean exactly that, and not that he'll be sending them to me instead of you. I was able to help him out of a tight spot a while ago. Ever since then he has been desperately searching for some favour he can do me in return and I have been equally anxious to put one in his way to clear the slate. So Andrew is not to be allowed to interfere. This sort of thing is too important.

With love and sympathy,
Tony

Geneva. March 22, 1968

My dear Hilary,

Many thanks for your letter. I begin to wonder whether I did you a kindness, starting you off on what sounds a truly appalling series of tests. You must both hate it all. It can't do much for your love life, either, having to settle to the process of reproduction when the thermometer tells you to instead of when you feel like it. Until I got involved with Sussman, I'd never realised that the problem existed. So many babies turn up unwanted, at the worst possible moment, ruining reputations or sliding families into poverty; it's tempting to presume that one will come along whenever it's requested. At least, when your baby finally arrives, he'll certainly never need to doubt that he was wanted.

I was glad to hear that the clinic has found an explanation. I hadn't realised that mumps could have such consequences. Andrew must be kicking himself for his moment of folly in cuddling an infectious page on his wedding day. But even though the percentages may be against you, it's better than being told there's no chance; and if there's anything that can be done, Sussman will do it.

I confess that when your letter arrived I had no idea what you meant by the magic letters AIH. That's why I'm only answering now, having taken the opportunity of a business trip to Geneva to visit the lab and ask for a translation. At least that programme won't arouse any of the doubts which might come if they suggested using a Donor instead of a Husband. (You see, I'm showing off all my new knowledge.) But even so it must be an unpleasantly test-tubey process. Worth it in the end, though.

With love,
Tony

New York. February 3, 1969

My dear Hilary,

Your Christmas letter has only just caught up with me. It was forwarded to Canada, but missed me there and went back to Rome before finding me here.

My Canadian trip was for Sara's benefit. She gave away all her fur coats some years ago and campaigns vigorously against the trapping of wild animals. So it was tough on her – she hadn't known – when a gossip columnist broadcast the news that she was married to someone whose family connections went all the way back to the Hudson Bay Company. This is one of the businesses which was in my mother's marriage settlement and came to me after my father died. It's a general trading company, so I spent a little time in Canada trying to find a way of cutting out the fur trade and keeping the rest. In the end it proved simpler to sell the whole business.

You'd think that I might get a good press for an action which is high-minded in itself and a proof of a husband's devotion to his wife. Not a bit of it! All that the papers were interested in was the size of the sum raised by the sale. Begging letters are coming in by the sackful. I've had to take on two extra secretaries. Since Andrew knows such a lot about trusts, I'm seriously contemplating asking him to set up a charity for the benefit of orphaned ermine on my behalf.

Anyway, as a result, I'm now floating in unnecessary liquidity, and am just off to South America to investigate an interesting way of investing some of it. Sara, holding firmly to her principles (in this case, that young children should be brought up by mothers, and that nurses are only there to do the dull and dirty work) will be staying in Rome, where she is extremely happy and popular. Georgie continues to thrive and to do all the right things at the right times, or earlier.

I expect to be passing through London towards the end of the year. Dates not yet fixed, but I hope you'll be around. (Which being interpreted means, keep some of your holiday entitlement for me.)

See you then,
Tony

Rome. December, 1969

My dear Hilary,

It's always millionaires who save stamps by writing letters on their Christmas cards: have you noticed?

This is really just a note to say how super it was to see you again. (All my Italian friends look at me curiously. Super? What is this 'super'? You buy it at Biba, I tell them, leaving them even more bemused.) It was fun, being introduced to such an unexpectedly lively London. I'm glad you haven't dyed your own hair crimson, though.

And just as I'd written that, Hilary dear, your call came through with your news. It's always millionaires who are too mean to throw one Christmas card away and start another with a peon – no, I don't mean that. What's the word? Paean? Paean of congratulation. I'm so very pleased for you both and hope that everything will go smoothly from now on. As I'm sure it will, since you'll be getting more frequent checks than ordinary mothers-to-be. You didn't mention when the Happy Event was due. Keep us informed. Sara will be writing to you separately in the role of Experienced Mother, so you'd better stop smoking and drinking and eating green potatoes immediately, before she starts quizzing you.

No more of this gratitude business. It's Sussman you have to thank, not me. My part in it is not worth mentioning, but I'm delighted that there's going to be a happy ending.

Merry Christmas, and Hip-hip-hurrah!
Tony

Rome. January 30, 1969

Hilary, you marvellous girl,

I don't believe it! Quads! Are you sure? Can

they really tell so early in the pregnancy? Well, you're certainly making up for lost time. I thought Sara and I would be able to keep ahead of you indefinitely, and now in one fell swoop . . . Anyway, congratulations to you both. There could be nothing better calculated to wipe away the memory of all that cold-blooded clinical exploration than the moment when you hold all four babies in your arms.

Not that that's going to be particularly easy. Are you going to invite me to be a godfather to at least one of them, says he hinting madly – and preferably the whole lot. (I already have one English goddaughter, Tod's eldest, so I do know that the Church of England won't turn its nose up at me: it's only non-episcopal sects like Baptists that don't qualify.) I ask only because, if so, instead of sending them useless silver spoons, my christening present will be the services of a nanny for the first hectic year. Otherwise Andrew will have to spend his whole time changing nappies and filling bottles and the British economy will collapse through non-collection of taxes.

Anyway, I do hope everything goes smoothly. Make sure you have plenty of rest. I shall be thinking of you in July.

Sara joins me in sending all best wishes. She's in the family way again herself (only one, as far as we know: how ordinary!), but a couple of months behind you.

Look after yourself.

With all my love,

Tony

Rome. June 21, 1969

Dearest Hilary,

Andrew has just called me. By the time you read

61

this he will, I hope, have passed on our messages of love and sympathy. It must be a desperately anxious time for you. And quite apart from the worry of the babies being so tiny, you must have been upset by having to undergo the Caesarean instead of being able to hang on a few weeks for the experience of a normal birth. As far as I could gather from Andrew, two of the babies have been guzzling all the goodies and doing their best to starve and strangle their brother and sister: is that right? Who would have guessed that such dramas go on in the womb!

Although you must be mourning the little boy who died, I'm sure – knowing you – that by now you're thinking positively and giving thanks for the two who, according to Andrew, are reckoned by the doctors to have a good chance of survival. I gather that for the smallest of the three girls it's still touch and go, and will pray that she pulls through.

I hate to think of you unhappy or in pain, Hilary, and so I'm not going to. I shall concentrate all my thoughts on those two healthiest babies nuzzling up to their mother. You're to consider this letter as one of congratulations on your twins as well as best wishes for their triplet. Andrew says I can be godfather to *all* of them if I like, and I do like. And he has accepted the idea of the nanny. I think, frankly, that he's filled with terror at the thought of even touching babies who look so tiny and breakable. That won't last, though. In a few months' time he'll be tossing them up to the ceiling.

This is only a quick scribble. There should be flowers by now to remind you that my thoughts are with you. And I shall write again before long. For one thing, I must describe to you the beginning of Georgie's education. Sara, who is hot on child psychology, decided that it would be fatal to send him off to school for the first time just as a new baby arrives in the household. Rejection! Loss of status as only child! Superseded in parents' affection! So we started him at Easter instead, although at only just four he was a bit young for it. In my next letter – very soon, I promise – you will hear all about the extraordinary establishment run by a certain Mrs Bellamy in Rome for the sole purpose of producing English ladies and gentlemen.

Till then, allow yourself to be looked after. And give your three-quarters of quads a kiss from their godfather.

With all my love,
Tony

5

Mrs Bellamy's English School was situated at a good address just off the Via delle Quattro Fontane, in the heart of Rome. Its teaching methods were unashamedly old-fashioned but the quality of the staff, the smallness of the classes and the strictness of the discipline had built it a high reputation for turning spoilt four-year-olds into good-mannered and well-educated eleven-year-olds. It naturally attracted British expatriate children and the offspring of mixed marriages and had also long been popular with diplomatic families who believed that English and not French would be the language of future international relations. More recently it had enjoyed an influx of wealthy Roman children whose parents saw it as 'snob', a word of approval.

In the summer of 1970 the school was, as it always had been, exactly what its name implied. Not only was all teaching conducted in the English language but no other language might be spoken at any time on the school premises. Admittedly, a deaf ear was sometimes turned to lapses in the two beginners' classes, but any child who had passed his fifth birthday must expect to be reprimanded for even the briefest muttering in another tongue.

To this rule there was only one exception. Mrs Bellamy, the owner and headmistress of the school, was unwavering in her adherence to her native language but reluctantly recognised the necessity of communicating with workmen, officials and telephone callers in Italian. For this purpose she employed Miss Liggio as secretary and interpreter. It was not clear even to Miss Liggio whether the headmistress, after over twenty years' residence in Rome, had totally succeeded in resisting the infection of the language spoken all around her and in remaining as resolutely monoglot as she pretended; but no one had ever been able to trap her into admitting knowledge which she could only have acquired without benefit of translation.

Stout and dignified and unbending – for she had not been tempted by the freedoms of post-war fashion to abandon her corsetry – Mrs Bellamy sat at her desk, from which through one window she could see the assembly hall of the school and through the other could watch the street just outside and the steps up to the front door.

When she first opened her establishment the shortage of petrol after the war meant that most of her pupils walked to school. But as better times returned even the youngest seemed to become aware that it was a necessary mark of status to be delivered by car, preferably chauffeur-driven. Only more recently had Rome's permanent traffic jam become so horrific that parents were beginning to rebel against their children's demands. Those who lived near enough now once again arrived on foot.

Little George Fiori, trotting along the pavement at twenty past eight in his most un-Italian school cap and blazer, was one of these. For his first three weeks he had been brought each day by his mother, whom the headmistress knew to hold strong views on child development. The princess – Mrs Bellamy always used her correct title, especially when talking to other parents, although the Fioris seemed not to set much store by protocol – the princess had apparently thought it necessary to prove to her four-year-old son that he was not in any sense being pushed out of the way and that parent and school were, so to speak, on the same side.

Even at the beginning of the term, however, the princess's pregnant condition had been apparent and by now, with her gesture made, she preferred to rise at a later hour in the morning. It was the hand of a uniformed maid which George held as he skipped happily along, clutching his pencil box. Language was no problem in his case, for he spoke English with his parents at home; so his presence in the beginners' class was an encouragement to the other new pupils to keep the rules. George – she never used diminutives – was one of Mrs Bellamy's favoured pupils.

It was George, however, who caused an unexpected disruption to the timetable later on this particular day. At half-past twelve the bell rang as usual to end the morning's lessons. There would be half an hour for lunch, to be followed for the little ones by a compulsory rest before the afternoon session began.

The bell was still ringing when one of the Fiori cars, discreetly monogrammed, drew up in front of the English School. Leaving the driver to endure the immediate hooting of other drivers now obstructed, the maid who had brought George to school earlier that morning left the car and ran up the steps. She was still in uniform, but looked unusually flustered and dishevelled. She knocked rapidly on the door of Mrs Bellamy's office and was invited to enter.

The conversation which followed was, as usual, channelled through Miss Liggio, since the maid spoke no English. She had come to collect George, she explained, and to take him to the clinic where his mother had just – almost two months earlier than expected – had her baby. Mrs Bellamy pointed out that George was about to have luncheon and that pupils were not permitted to leave the premises during the school day. The maid gave an assurance that the little boy would be provided with a meal and would, if the headmistress insisted, be returned to the school by the time the afternoon lessons were due to start.

Why then, inquired Mrs Bellamy through her interpreter, was there such an urgency for George to visit his mother? Nothing, surely, would be lost if he were to wait until four o'clock.

While the hooting outside increased in volume, the answer emerged in a voluble rush of reasons. Mrs Bellamy waited patiently and was told, rather more briefly, that the Princess Fiori was anxious that her son should feel no jealousy of the new baby and for this reason had promised him that he should be the very first person to see it.

Mrs Bellamy did not for her own part believe in pandering to the feelings of young children in such a way, but everything she knew of the princess made this explanation unsurprising; and although the headmistress was happy to have the reputation of someone as strict with parents as with their children, she did not in practice wish to antagonise them. Reluctantly she nodded her head. Miss Liggio was despatched to find George and help him to put on his outdoor clothes.

He came smiling into the office. He enjoyed school, but this unexpected removal from lessons was clearly a treat. Bouncing up and down with high spirits, he greeted the maid and took her hand. After they had left together, allowing the traffic outside to move at last, Mrs Bellamy inquired of Miss Liggio what the maid had said to him, and was told that he was merely promised a surprise.

The incident was unusual, but not alarming. It did not even cause anxiety when he did not return, as promised, in time for his first afternoon lesson, since it had always seemed likely that there would be some delay. But at four o'clock the Fiori limousine returned. As the chauffeur walked round the car and opened the door, Mrs Bellamy rose to her feet in alarm and dismay. Stopping to exchange a smiling word with one of the other mothers was the Princess Fiori, seven months pregnant, come to collect her son from school.

6

'You let him go!'

Sara's knees turned to water. She staggered forward, needing to support herself by leaning both hands on the edge of Mrs Bellamy's desk. Miss Liggio, as white-faced as herself, hurried to bring up a chair and help her into it.

'How could you do that?' The half of Sara's mind which recognised what had happened had been anaesthetised by shock. She knew that she ought to be taking action, but for the moment could only protest, as though an exchange of words might reveal that Georgie was, after all, still on the school premises, held back perhaps by a tangled shoe lace, a detention for naughtiness. 'You have instructions from us . . . Your own rules . . .' She was trying not to believe what she had heard; but if proof of its truth was needed, it was to be seen in the headmistress's eyes, where self-justification was fighting with an appalled realisation of what she had done and what the consequences might be.

'Naturally I wouldn't have allowed him to leave with a stranger. It was your maid. The one who brought him to school this morning.'

'And the driver?'

'Wearing a grey uniform, as usual. I didn't notice his face below the cap. He was looking down at a book or map on his lap.'

Sara leant across the desk and pulled the telephone towards her. Tony was in South America. How long would it take him to return to Rome? The question – to which she did not know the answer – increased her panic as she was connected with his office and waited to be put through to Ludo.

She had never been at ease with Ludo. The scarring of one side of his face had distorted the shape of his mouth, giving a sinister appearance even to his smile. It was not his fault, of course, that he had been so badly hurt in the plane crash, and so she did her best to ignore his appearance. But while telling herself that his personal life was none of her business, she had always feared that he might one day lay himself open to blackmail. He had formed no new lasting relationship since the Maestro's death, and she often wondered how much he knew about the young men who were invited back to his apartment and sometimes offered employment as secretary or valet. But Tony trusted him absolutely, and in this emergency she must trust him too.

Her intention was to explain the situation calmly, but at the sound of his voice she found herself overwhelmed by distress. Tears poured down her cheeks and choked her throat and she panted for breath, unable to articulate more than one word at a time.

'Ludo. Ludo.'

'Is that Sara? Is something the matter? What's happened?'

'Georgie. Ludo, Georgie's been kidnapped. From school.'

There was a moment's pause. Ludo presumably was as startled and shocked as herself. When he spoke, his voice was deliberately calm and businesslike.

'Was it seen?'

'One of our maids came to collect him as though I'd sent her.'

'What time?'

'Half-past twelve.'

'Have you seen the maid since?'

'No. She came to me at about ten o'clock this morning and asked if she could take the day off. She has a small child who lives with her mother. He was sick, badly sick, she told me. I believed her. She was crying.' Sara had been sure at the time and was still sure now that the girl's distress was genuine, but it was all too easy to think of an alternative explanation: Lucia's own child held as hostage for her co-operation, perhaps; her tears those of regret for betrayal.

'What's her name and address?'

'Lucia Tarrmina. The address is at home. I don't remember . . . Oh, Ludo!'

'Steady. You've got to be brave now. Go straight back. I'll meet you there. First of all, though, I'll get in touch with Tony, to bring him home. And I'll plant a story in *Il Giorno* so that everyone knows that he's in Brazil. That'll make it easier to persuade any kidnappers that they'll have to wait until he's back in Italy.'

'But we can't wait. We must find Georgie at once.'

'We will. But they'll have to be the first to show their hand. Now listen, Sara. This is something to be kept secret. Who knows what happened at the school?'

'Mrs Bellamy. And her secretary, I suppose. I don't expect they exactly want the whole world to find out how careless they are with their pupils.' She looked the headmistress straight in the eye as she spoke, making clear the subject of the conversation.

'Make them promise. Don't make any comment to your driver. And when you get back, don't let anyone answer the telephone until I come. If you have to say anything at all to anybody, give the impression that Georgie's gone to stay with a friend for a few days, because the doctor's told you to rest more. Do your best to behave naturally, as though nothing's wrong.'

'Why – ?' But Ludo had already rung off.

'Why are you trying to give the impression that nothing's happened?' she asked him twenty minutes later. She found it unthinkable that she should be comfortable at such a time, and so had received him in the austere room which Tony used as a study.

'Two reasons. But give me the maid's address first. My confidential secretary will track her down.'

Sara waited impatiently while Giovanni was given the information and sent off. 'Two reasons, you said?'

'The first is that this situation, most unfortunately, attracts criminal hoaxers. Let it be known that a child is missing and you can find yourself receiving a dozen ransom demands without being able to tell immediately which is the genuine one.'

She gave a quick nod of the head. Even in her present distraught state she could recognise the sense of this.

'The second reason is that the police mustn't be allowed to find out.'

'Why not? Surely – I thought that would be the first thing you'd do, to tell them.'

'The last thing.' Ludo had been pacing the room, but now he sat down in Tony's chair on the other side of the desk and spoke to her forcefully. 'There have been three major kidnappings already this year that we know about, quite apart from those which the families have managed to keep quiet. The only single lesson to be learned from them is to keep the police out of it.'

'I don't understand.'

'The moment you report your belief that a crime has been committed, an investigating magistrate will be appointed to supervise the progress of the case. He is required to work on the principle that no ransom may be paid, so the first thing he'll do is to freeze all Tony's assets. Well, of course we might try to get round that by borrowing secretly from friends, but the magistrate can demand that all banks inform him of any large withdrawals of cash. If he has cause to believe that a ransom is being paid, he can appoint a surveillance team to find out where the drop is to take place and intercept it. Their orders would be not so much to save the victim as to recover the money and catch whoever has tried to collect it.'

'But surely, with a child's life at stake – '

'The payment of ransom has been illegal since 1945 and

the magistrate will have to uphold the law. And it's worse than that, Sara. This crazy business of having two separate police forces. The system is that whichever arrives first on the scene – the polizia or the carabinieri – takes charge of the case. But they hate each other so much that they won't share information. You can't even guarantee that they won't deliberately sabotage each other's plans. It may be that later we shall be forced to let it be known that a kidnapping has taken place. But before that happens we must set up a channel of communication that the police know nothing about, so that if they tap the telephones here and at the office – and of course they would – they won't learn anything about our final negotiations. As soon as Tony gets here, naturally he'll take charge. But until then, Sara, you must believe that I know what I'm talking about.'

Ludo had been speaking to her, as was his custom, with the scarred side of his face turned away. But to emphasise the seriousness of what he was saying, he turned directly towards her. The twisted mouth and livid skin which looked so sinister when he smiled made his present expression merely grim; for he was not smiling now. Sara knew that she must trust him to do whatever was best, but unhappiness burst out of her.

'Oh, Georgie!'

She and Ludo never touched. She could not remember even shaking hands when they were first introduced. A moment earlier it would have been the obvious thing for her to stretch a hand towards him as an indication of trust, and now it might have seemed equally appropriate for him to make some move to comfort her. Their inability to behave naturally created an awkwardness between them, which Ludo was the first to break.

'They won't harm him, Sara. He represents a fortune to them, don't you see? And we shall keep asking for proofs

72

that he is alive, to make it clear that if they hurt him, they get nothing.'

Sara made no comment on this. What Ludo said might prove to be true at the beginning of any negotiation, but surely there would come a moment when money had to be paid over before the kidnapped boy was returned. What would happen in that interval? She began to rock backwards and forwards in the chair, her arms crossed across her abdomen as if to keep her unborn baby safe.

'You should rest, Sara, for the sake of the child. I'll get the doctor to give you a sleeping draught.'

She shook her head. Even in this emergency she would not abandon her principles of motherhood. A drug for the mother would be a drug for the baby. Besides, how could she possibly allow herself to sleep until some message had been received? And so she sat all afternoon and all evening by the telephone.

Every few minutes, it seemed, she received some unwanted, frivolous call. In these last few weeks of her pregnancy she had reduced her social engagements; and her friends, from the kindest of motives, were using this medium to keep in touch. One day she would have to explain to them why she hustled each in turn so ungraciously off the line.

Finally, at ten o'clock in the evening, when Ludo had set his arrangements in hand and returned to sit beside her, the call they had been waiting for arrived.

'We have your child. The price is five miliardi.'

7

'We have to pay.'

It was not quite a command, not quite a question: a plea, rather, for reassurance. Calm again after the tears and embraces of their reunion, Sara faced her husband across a coffee table. Tony was grey with the exhaustion of his long flight home and the anxiety of the situation to which he had returned, but his eyes revealed a determination not to succumb yet to fatigue.

On the table between them lay Georgie's school cap: an English school cap of a kind hardly any longer worn in England, with a peak at the front and a button in the centre from which rows of stitching divided the crown into segments. The letter B was embroidered in gold in the centre of the front section and a tape bearing Georgie's name was sewn into the lining in accordance with Mrs Bellamy's regulations. The kidnapper had left the cap on the doorstep in a paper bag containing nothing else except the word ALDINI formed from letters cut out of a newspaper. This, according to Ludo, would be the kidnappers' identification in the negotiations to come – for they, quite as much as the parents, would wish to keep hoaxers at bay.

'Of course we have to pay,' Tony assured her. 'But not the whole sum. It's not expected. If we were to hand over five billion lire at the first time of asking, they'd tell themselves that they'd obviously pitched the demand too low, and would put in another one before releasing Georgie. It's taken for granted that we shall protest that it's impossible for us to afford so much. Then we suggest a much lower figure, and they retreat from their first demand, until we can reach a compromise.'

'You make it sound like some kind of bazaar haggle. But we're not buying a pair of sandals or a camel. We're buying Georgie.'

'That's why we must keep calm, darling. Yes, it is a haggle. But there are rules in bazaars and there are rules in kidnaps, and we must keep to them. It's best, I think, if we have a negotiator to speak on our behalf. I shall have my hands full trying to collect the money without anyone guessing what's up. And it's easier for someone who isn't quite so personally involved to keep cool. Gives more time, as well, because he has to keep saying that he must refer back and take new instructions.'

'We don't want more time. We want Georgie quickly. Now. Surely no one could talk to them better than you.'

'Ludo has volunteered to negotiate, and I think that's best. He's fixed up a room with a telephone and recording equipment. We'll give the Aldini that number. Then if the police – '

'Yes, yes.' She interrupted impatiently. 'Ludo explained all that.' She paused before asking her next question, because the answer was important. 'Tony, do you really trust Ludo?'

'Trust Ludo? With my life. With Georgie's life. Why do you ask that? My father – '

'Oh yes, I know Ludo was devoted to your father. But that doesn't mean that he's necessarily so faithful to you. He could be envious that you should be so much richer than he is. He might even – well, he seems so keen to get involved.'

'Most people would run a mile. Tangling with criminals is a dangerous thing to do. I'm grateful for his offer, not suspicious of it. Surely you're not suggesting that he could have anything to do with the kidnapping himself. If he'd wanted to be richer, he could have asked my father. Or he could easily have cheated me out of a small fortune at the time when I inherited, when I didn't know exactly what I was expecting to get.'

'Perhaps he did.'

Tony moved to stand behind her chair, his hands on her shoulders. He massaged them softly, as he had often done before during her pregnancy when her back began to ache.

'We've got a real enemy to do battle with now, darling. It's no time to turn our backs on a friend. Now, I want you to think of something precious to Georgie. Something for which he has a special name, which no one would guess.'

'His teddy bear? But he just calls that Teddy.'

'And they'd tear it apart, in case we'd bugged it. Anything else?'

'There's that blanket he sucks in bed. He calls it Pudding and Pie.'

'That'll do. Will you find it for me?'

'Yes, but why?'

Tony hesitated for a moment before answering. 'The cap could have been taken from a dead boy,' he reminded her at last. 'But if we demand that this blanket is given to Georgie and that its name is reported back to us – something that no one could possibly guess – then we can be sure he's still alive. We shall need to take a precaution of this sort at each stage, Ludo says.'

It seemed to Sara that Ludo knew much more about the mechanics of conducting a ransom operation than was normal. She still did not entirely trust him. But she had faith in Tony to do everything for the best and went without further protest to fetch the scrap of blanket.

In the days which followed her life was made intolerable by the fact that she had no role to play in the negotiations. It could do no harm, surely, for her to talk to Lucia, the maid who had played such a vital part in the abduction. She was prepared to appear sympathetic, to give the benefit of all possible doubts, in order to find out who it was who had issued threats and instructions, who had driven the car. But Tony forbade her to leave the palace. Her task was to look after their unborn child, he said, and at his request her gynaecologist called every day to examine and reassure her. Each visit was an ordeal, because she had promised not to reveal the true reason why she was unable to sleep at night and was nauseated by the sight of food.

'We're down to three miliardi,' Tony told her on the sixth day. Like Sara herself, his eyes were ringed with black circles of exhaustion. 'Ludo thinks we can get it to two, and that we ought to settle for that.'

Two miliardi was two billion lire: a million English pounds. But all that the words meant to Sara was that her son was still a prisoner. Even though he might be too young to understand what was happening, he would be confused and upset at being snatched from his parents. Would he ever forgive them for not rushing at once to his side when he called their names? Sara did her best to remember him only as the happy, chubby little boy who had come to her bedroom to kiss her goodbye before leaving for school on that last day. But the picture which dominated her mind was of a crying, terrified child, dirty and smelly, cowering in a cellar and bullied by his captors.

'How are we expected to pay?' she asked Tony wearily.

'We haven't got to that yet. The usual system is that they nominate a place where the money is to be dropped. After they've collected it and made sure that it really is money and not bits of old newspaper, they phone again and tell us where we can find Georgie.'

'But suppose – ' She was horrified by the answer, for she had assumed that there would be a formal handover, with the victim and the money being exchanged at the same moment. 'They could take the ransom and still hold on to Georgie.'

The nature of Tony's silence made it clear that this was not the imaginary fear of a worried mother.

'It does sometimes happen that a second ransom is demanded,' he admitted. 'A smaller one, usually, because it's easier for the family to argue that they've got nothing left. What's made this first haggle difficult is the publicity that I got when I sold the fur company. Anyone who reads the papers could have found out what I got for it. But as a general rule, kidnappers are as anxious to get rid of their hostage as we are to get him back. The whole business is a strain for them as well as us.'

'But they might cheat. You're dealing with a gang of criminals and you're relying on them to keep a set of rules!' Throughout this terrible week she had told herself that she must not become hysterical, but now a feeling of panic bubbled up from her stomach to her throat, ready to emerge in a scream. Tony, recognising the knife-edge on which her emotions were balanced, took her into his arms, kissing and stroking her.

'Sara, sweet, we can only try to do what is best,' he said. 'And everything is second-best to having Georgie here. Yes, of course there are risks, but they have to be taken.'

Sara pretended to be reassured, but her calmness was only an act. Why was Ludo pursuing this dangerous path when there was another way? It must surely be possible to find out who the kidnappers were and where they were holding Georgie. Why had she been forbidden to look for Lucia? Ludo had claimed that the maid had disappeared from home and could not be found, but that might be because he did not really wish to find her. Someone in her family would know where she was. Sara was still prepared to believe that she had played her part in the kidnapping only under some kind of duress. It would cost nothing to offer her forgiveness and freedom from prosecution on condition that she gave information leading to the discovery of Georgie's whereabouts.

Tomorrow, Sara promised herself, she would disobey

Tony and take the walk which the doctor had recommended every day for the past week. In a sense it hardly mattered whether or not her mission was successful. It was the waiting, the sitting at home and doing nothing, which was gradually driving her mad. She must *do* something. She must do *something*.

8

Ludo, who had the knack of acquiring expert advice on any subject, had hired an apartment for the sole purpose of communicating with Georgie's kidnappers. In its kitchen now Tony was examining a battered suitcase with great thoroughness, looking for the direction-finding bug concealed in it. He ran his fingers over every inch of the lining and stared intently at the locks and buckles before giving a nod of approval.

'Where is it?'

'In the hinge,' Ludo told him. 'If they take the case completely to pieces, they'll find it. But they're not likely to do that at the pick-up point. They'll be anxious to get away.'

'What sort of distance does it cover?'

'Only twenty kilometres. Anything more powerful than that would have been too big. But that's enough to let Giovanni keep his distance if they send me from one place to another. And then, if they have someone watching to make sure I go straight back, they'll have no reason to recognise the second car.' Giovanni, Ludo's confidential secretary, was already sitting in the hired car, black and unnoteworthy, which had been fitted with the receiving plate of the direction finder.

Together the two men filled the suitcase with bundles of used notes. 'Did you manage to get the numbers recorded?' asked Ludo.

'Not all of them. But I got a run of fifty new notes. I've made them as dirty and crumpled as I can and put one in each of fifty bundles. It's easier to get people to look out for a straight run of numbers.' They finished the packing and pressed down on the lid to close the suitcase. 'That's it, then.' Tony looked gravely across the table. 'I can't tell you how grateful I am to you, Ludo, for volunteering to deliver this. It's not something I could have asked of you, but you can imagine how much it means to us to have someone we can trust.'

Ludo's nod acknowledged the thanks while at the same time indicating that he saw it as his duty to undertake the ransom delivery now that the amount to be paid had, after sixteen days, been agreed. His expression remained grave.

'How's Sara taking it?' he asked.

Tony gave a helpless shrug of the shoulders. 'What can one expect? I thought she was going to go to pieces a week ago. But she seems to have pulled herself together. I mean, obviously she's frightened and upset, but she's got it under control. She just sits and rocks. Concentrating on the new baby, I suppose.'

'There was something about this morning's call that I didn't want to tell you in front of her,' Ludo said. 'It's all right as it happens, because what we offered today was what they were prepared to settle for. But – well, listen.'

He switched on the recording of the last telephone call. Although Tony was by now familiar with the thick Calabrese accent of the kidnapper who had been entrusted with the negotiations, he had to concentrate to understand the words.

The statement, irritably expressed, was simple. The talking has gone on too long. Until now the boy has been well cared for. But from this morning he has been left by himself. He has food for three days but will be given no more. If his parents don't wish him to starve, they should pay up without delay.

Listening to the ultimatum, Tony felt sick to his stomach. Thank God Sara had not heard it. The thought of Georgie locked up alone, not understanding what was happening,

81

not even realising that he must ration out whatever food had been left for him, would certainly have destroyed her precarious endurance. But at least now the arrangement had been made. There should not be too much longer to wait.

They were both startled by the sound of the telephone, although they had been waiting for the call. Ludo switched on the recorder and the loudspeaker and picked up the receiver.

The message this time was concise: the messenger carrying the ransom should take the Aquila road and stop at the last public telephone before the toll booths. Further directions would be found on a cigarette box hidden behind it.

Tony's mouth was dry with nervousness as he shook hands with Ludo. There were so many things which could still go wrong – including, of course, the unthinkable worst case: that Georgie might not be returned even after the ransom was paid. The two men were well aware how often it happened that a hostage was brutally murdered: they had spent fruitless hours discussing possible ways of insuring against this. But the kidnappers held all the cards. Tony could only hope that the four-year-old's helplessness would not only attract kindness but might persuade his captors that he could say nothing to identify the place where he had been held.

'I'll leave the message behind in the telephone box for Giovanni to read,' said Ludo. 'And I shall have the bugged suitcase beside me until the hand-over. So if there's any trouble there'll be two of us. Don't worry.'

How could he not worry? From the window of the apartment Tony watched Ludo get into the white car which had been chosen for its visibility. He felt strongly that he himself should have been the one to go, but Ludo had persuaded him of the real risk that in doing so he would present himself as a second kidnap possibility. His role –

too passive to calm his restlessness – was to be ready to collect his son.

So there was nothing to do but to wait. Ludo would make contact as soon as he could to say that the drop had been made. After that, please God, there would be a second call to say where the little boy could be found. For perhaps an hour Tony forced himself to sit still. But the pretence of studying the business papers he had brought with him could not be sustained, and he began to pace round and round the apartment. It was small and bleak, lacking any personal possessions at all, representing merely the space around a telephone line. Either Ludo or his secretary had sat there for the two hours each morning and evening specified by the Aldini but had done nothing to stamp the atmosphere with their presence.

The watched telephone never rings, he told himself, and kept his eyes away from it, but could not refrain from looking at his watch every few minutes. An hour, an hour and a half . . . He knew that it was foolish to be impatient. If the kidnappers were professionals, they would have laid a trail for Ludo to follow, like a macabre treasure hunt, so that they could make sure he was not under police observation.

Tony hoped to God that they *were* professionals. Sara had never been able to accept the theory that the demanding and paying of a ransom could be covered by any set of rules, but he knew it to be all too true that there were gangs or families who earned a steady living in this way. They usually came from the south, or from Sicily or Sardinia, but found the pickings richer in Rome or Milan. They knew how to behave if they were not to be caught; and they had just enough intelligence to recognise that each time they killed a captive, the next family to be threatened would be that much less likely to pay up.

Far more dangerous was the amateur kidnapper, the criminal who saw an opportunity and seized it. Such a man was just as likely as his victim to crack under the strain of the long-drawn-out haggle, sometimes with fatal results.

Three hours. Surely by now – and at that moment the telephone rang. This would be Ludo. But it was not. Apart from Ludo and Giovanni and himself – and, of course, the Aldini – only Sara knew this number: it was Sara's voice which shrieked into his ear before he had time to answer.

'Tony? Tony, you've got to come back at once. At once. The police are here. They've got a case full of money, which they say – Tony, what's going on? What's happened? They won't tell me anything till you come. Tony, I'm scared.'

'Keep calm, darling. I'll come at once.' But he stayed at the flat for long enough to record a message for the answering machine. If the police had recovered the money but not Georgie, then something had gone badly wrong and there could be no hope of any message giving the little boy's whereabouts. But it was desperately important that contact should be maintained. He set the machine and hurried back to the palace.

9

It was the carabinieri who had arrived and were standing, armed and grim-faced, around the suitcase which earlier that evening he had packed with currency notes. Why had Sara chosen to receive them in the salon, where the only table surfaces were the marble consoles beneath each huge gilt-framed mirror and the only chairs, straight-backed and uncomfortable, were arranged in lines against the walls? The little group was dwarfed by the size of the room, and the glittering Venetian chandeliers which hung from a ceiling painted with gods and cherubs illuminated a setting wholly inappropriate to the present crisis.

All the men were in uniform except for one, who now approached Tony and showed his identification.

'Fiscal police. I would like to suggest that your wife should now retire. She is distressed.'

'No.' Sara did not speak Italian as a native, but was sufficiently familiar with the language to understand what he was saying. 'I have to stay. I have to know what's happened.'

Shrugging his shoulders, he addressed himself formally to Tony.

'You will be aware that the promise or payment of ransom in cases of kidnap is illegal under the law of 1945 Section – '

Tony interrupted him with impatient anger. 'We can talk about that later. Where is my son? Where is Signor Leuchars, my negotiator?'

'Would that be the gentleman with the scarred face?'

'Yes.'

'I have to inform you that Sr Leuchars was unfortunately wounded in the course of the confrontation.'

'What confrontation?'

'You understand that we have a duty to prevent the unauthorised payment of any ransom. On receipt of the relevant information I was able to direct the carabinieri to the drop area. With great efficiency they were able to surround not only this spot but the place in which one of the two kidnappers was hiding, watching to see that the money was left. However, he became aware of their presence and held Sr Leuchars as a shield to cover his retreat. He was armed, and threatening to shoot. So naturally it was necessary for the carabinieri to fire first.'

'Wounded, you say. How badly wounded?'

'Well . . .' The civilian turned his head and beckoned to the uniformed officer to approach.

'Your representative, with the deformed face' – the officer put a hand up to his own cheek to indicate the site of Ludo's scarring – 'died on the way to hospital. This is greatly regretted, but of course he ought not – '

'Ludo dead!' Shock prevented Tony from listening to the rest of the excuse. 'And I let him go. I sent him. Oh God.'

'Where's Georgie?' Sara, not pretending to care anything for Ludo's fate, shook Tony violently by the arm. 'Have they found him? They wouldn't tell me anything.'

Although still stunned by the news of Ludo's death, Tony made an effort to press on with the interrogation. 'The kidnapper. You caught him, you said.'

'He was trapped, yes. After drawing his gun, of course, he could not expect mercy.'

'You're not telling me that you've killed him as well!'

'That is correct. Also his driver. He attempted to make his escape when he heard the gunfire, but we were able to shoot his tyres and the car skidded off the road.'

'But, you – you – ' Every insulting epithet that Tony had

ever learned flooded into his mind. He bit the words back, drawing blood from his lower lip. There was nothing to be gained from losing his temper. And so stupid were these men that probably they still did not understand what they had done.

If there was a gang involved, they would assume that it was the family, against all instructions, who had involved the police. Tony had no time at this moment to consider how the information had in fact been passed. Presumably the servants had gossiped amongst themselves about the suddenness of Georgie's departure on a visit and the equally sudden disappearance of Lucia. It had been impossible to act in a completely normal fashion on that first day, when it was so important for telephone calls to be taken only by Sara or Ludo. All of that could be investigated later. It was the present, not the past, which must concern him now.

Think about the gang. They would be angry at the deaths of two of their members: angry and alarmed. Whether their reaction proved to be one of ruthlessness or of panic, the effect was all too likely to be the same. They would kill their hostage. It was the easiest way out. There was a chance, just a chance, because he was so young, that they would drive him some distance away and leave him to be found wandering by the roadside; but it was not enough of a possibility to give any comfort.

Suppose, though, that it was not a gang at all. And suppose that the telephone threat had been the truth; that Georgie had already been abandoned in some isolated spot. It could be that only two men had ever known where he was; and now those men were dead. Tony's fury with the inept behaviour of the carabinieri was overwhelmed by the passionate love and anguish which he felt for his little son. Even his love for Sara, which he had thought to be the most important emotion in his life, was as nothing beside this. 'Oh Georgie, Georgie,' he muttered, swallowing the lump in his throat which threatened to choke him.

His weakness must be quickly conquered, for every second was important. He stepped towards the suitcase, but the officer moved in front of him.

'This money belongs to me,' said Tony.

'It will be returned to you in due course. It is required as evidence in the case of the dead man.'

They would keep it for months. And from now on they would be watching every source of cash to which he had access. Even if the kidnappers were prepared to wait, it might prove impossible to produce another sum of this size now that he was under official observation. But if Georgie was still alive, there was another way, for there was no further point in maintaining secrecy.

'We offer a reward,' he announced, raising his voice. 'One billion lire for information leading to the safe return of our son. If it is earned by your men identifying the villain they have killed and finding his hideout, good. I will arrange for publicity.' He could use newspapers and posters, radio and television. 'We shall ask that everyone in the country should search buildings on their own land or in deserted places. The matter is of the greatest urgency. You must know, if you have been tapping our calls, that the child has been abandoned. We have two days at the most to save his life. Two days. If he's not found by then, I shall complain directly to the Minister about the inefficiency of your men and their killing of my negotiator. But I'm sure you recognise the urgency, the distress caused to the mother – '

He turned to point to Sara and saw that she had collapsed on to one of the chairs and was hugging her abdomen and rocking her shoulders. It was a movement which had become familiar to him in the past two weeks; but now for the first time she was groaning as well. It might help if he could find something for her to do. As the carabinieri and the fiscal policeman left the salon, he did his best to speak calmly.

'We need photographs, darling. The clearest, the most recent photographs of Georgie that you can find. And that earlier one of him sitting on your lap. Even a kidnapper must have a woman in his life, a woman who may be touched by your distress. Bring them to my office as quickly as you can. I must make some phone calls.' Giovanni, who ought to have returned quickly to help and to tell what he knew of the day's tragic events, was no doubt still mourning his employer and lover in the hospital. 'As quickly as you can,' he repeated, for his wife showed no sign of moving.

She looked up and he saw that she was weeping.

'What did you mean,' she asked, 'when you told that officer that Georgie had been abandoned?'

Tony cursed himself for the indiscretion. In the heat of the argument he had forgotten that she was listening and could understand. To tell her the true sequence of events would be to terrify her. It seemed, in the circumstances, excusable to fudge the explanation.

'It was all arranged,' he said. 'You saw, we had the money. The drop was organised. Ludo was there. If those fools hadn't interfered, we should have received a call by now telling us where to go to find Georgie. But now we've lost the money and we don't know where to go.' He had wanted to put a cheerful gloss on the situation, but found himself unable after all to continue. 'I'm frightened, Sara. If those men they killed are the only ones who know . . . Well, that's why we must move fast. There's no one who can't be tempted by a billion lire. We shall hear something soon. The question of who tipped off the police can wait until afterwards.'

'Why was it such a bad thing to do?'

'You've seen the answer. Because what has happened is what was almost bound to happen.'

'But they might have been able to do something. To trace the telephone calls, to find out who it was who held Lucia's son at gunpoint.'

'How do you know about that?'

'I went to ask her mother, of course. I wanted to understand how Lucia could do such a thing. And I thought she, or her mother, might be able to describe the man. We didn't have any clues at all, and you didn't seem to be doing anything except collecting the money.'

'Not doing anything! You must be mad. We had private detectives – ' He stopped, aghast. 'You're not telling me that it was *you* – '

There was a flash of defiance in Sara's eyes as she turned her tear-stained face up towards him. 'I made Lucia go. To tell everything she knew.'

'She didn't know the telephone number.'

'I gave them that.'

'I don't believe it! I don't believe it! I told you. Ludo told you. All you had to do was to keep quiet, to pretend that nothing was wrong. Was that too much to ask?'

'Yes. Yes, it was.'

'Didn't you trust me? My own son. Could you really think that I wouldn't do everything, anything that was needed to get him back again?'

'Of course I trusted you. But not always Ludo.'

'So Ludo has died because I trusted my wife when I ought not to have done.'

'We ought not to be quarrelling. Not now. Tony, please – '

'The least you could have done was to tell me. If I'd known that the telephone was likely to be tapped, everything would have turned out differently.'

'You make it sound as though it's all my fault.'

'Well, that's just – ' With a great effort Tony closed his lips on what he was about to say. He was not a man accustomed to lose his temper. It was because all his

90

emotions – terror and love as well as anger – were so near the surface that he found it so difficult to control himself. And time was ticking away. 'The photographs. Get the photographs.'

'I can't – ' Sara checked herself in mid-sentence as though suddenly she had no breath. A moment passed before she was able to speak again. 'The baby's coming.'

It should have been a moment for tenderness, but instead he almost exclaimed aloud with impatience at being detained still further from the business of organising the reward offer. 'Stay there,' he told her and ran from the salon to telephone her obstetrician.

'You're to go into the clinic,' he told her when he returned, still running. The birth had been expected to take place in the palace, but Dr Visicchio had explained at unwanted length that an eight-month baby was in some ways even more vulnerable than one born at seven months. He would try to delay the birth if he could and, if not, would need to have the latest equipment to hand. 'A private ambulance will be here in five minutes. Stay here; they'll bring a stretcher trolley for you. I've told your maid. She's packing your things.'

'Won't you come with me?'

'I can't, Sara. The reward is our only hope. I must get it on to television straightaway. Get posters printed. There's so much to do.' Now that there was no longer any need for secrecy, he could make use of his office resources, but no one but himself could start the process of publicity.

She nodded her head in acceptance and, still unable to stand, held out her arms. Tony forced himself to bend down and kiss her, but was unable to provide the embrace she wanted. He was still too angry with her, and too worried.

Even when, four hours later, there was a telephone call from the clinic to say that his wife had been safely delivered of a baby daughter it was impossible to feel delight or even relief. Sara's behaviour had been unforgivable. It was not so much what she had done – because allowances must be made for a mother's natural distress – but the fact that she had kept her action secret, knowing how strongly he would disapprove. Hilary Craig, he thought – but why on earth should he think of Hilary at a moment of crisis like this? – Hilary would never have behaved in so crazy a fashion. But then, Hilary would never be likely to find herself involved in such a drama. Such things did not happen in England.

Perhaps he should have chosen to settle in England and to pay murderous taxes as the price of being safe from real murder and corruption and inefficiency. It was too late to think about that now. But he was surprised by the intensity of his wish to make contact with Hilary and Andrew, even in the middle of this crisis when there was no time to be lost; to hear their friendly, concerned voices; to be supported by their sympathy. He had lost Ludo. It was terrifyingly likely that he was losing Georgie. And so great was his anger at Sara's incomprehensible stupidity that he was unable to imagine how he could ever be close to her again. He was all alone in a fog of misery and fear.

10

Masked and gowned like a nurse, but with none of a nurse's dispassionate skills, Hilary was admitted to one of the intensive care cubicles in the hospital's neonatal unit. She herself had been discharged a fortnight after the birth of her quadruplets, but the three surviving babies had needed to stay in hospital care until they attained the birth weight of an average baby. Even the two strongest had weighed under four pounds each when they were born, and the third tipped the scales at only just over two pounds.

Now, ten weeks after their birth, two of the babies were ready to go home: she had come to collect them. It was the smallest one, who must stay behind, at whom she stared anxiously now.

'Baby Craig Three' said the plastic bracelet round the tiny wrist, and 'Baby Craig Three' said the notes outside the incubator. At almost every visit Sister made a gentle attempt to persuade Hilary and Andrew that it was time to choose a name for the baby. Andrew would have been willing to do so but Hilary would not let him.

She was sufficiently well-balanced as a rule to recognise that she was temporarily off-balance now. The process of becoming a mother had left her confused and over-emotional, torn in different directions by a conflict of feelings. Although she told herself that thousands of women had Caesarean deliveries, that this had been in the best interests of her babies – indeed, had been essential – she felt shame as well as deprivation at having been unconscious through what should have been an experience of excitement and joy.

And then, in an odd way, she did not know quite how

to feel about her children – as though it were a matter of choice instead of a natural maternal instinct. By the time she came round from the anaesthetic, they had all been taken away to be placed naked on beds of cotton wool in incubators, with tubes and wires attached to their tiny red bodies. She had been pushed along in a wheelchair to look at them, but of course was not allowed to touch. It was three weeks before one of them was placed in her arms for the first time.

During the whole of that three weeks she had been afraid, and she was still afraid now. The little boy had slipped into death so quickly and easily. It seemed all too possible that his sisters might follow him. She found that she did not mourn her son because she had never known him; and for a little while had held herself aloof from her daughters as well in case she should need to protect her emotions against further loss.

By now it seemed safe to love two of them, but Baby Three was another matter. Had she been born a generation earlier, she would probably not have survived for more than a few minutes. Medical expertise had kept her alive, but there might be a price to pay. When she was a month old, Andrew and Hilary had been warned by the doctor that she was not responding well to stimuli. It could be that she was still affected by the trauma of birth, but perhaps they should prepare themselves for the possibility that there was some degree of brain damage. It would not be possible to tell for certain for some time yet.

Hilary had cried all the way home on the day she heard the news, but by now her feelings were more complicated. She genuinely did not know whether she wanted the baby to live or die. Had it – she – been an only child there would have been no doubt in her mother's mind; no reservations about loving and caring for her. It was because there were two other babies to be looked after that the unwanted thought kept creeping in. If the damage were to prove severe, would it perhaps be for the best . . . ? Hilary was ashamed of the thought and angry with herself because she could not make it go away. She did not dare even to confess it to Andrew – although perhaps Andrew himself might be concealing the same guilty feeling.

He came to stand beside her now, having travelled straight from work to drive her home. For a few moments they stood in silence beside the cot. Only when Andrew offered her a handkerchief after they had left the sterile area did Hilary realise that tears were once again streaming down her cheeks. She dabbed herself dry and blew her nose vigorously.

'I don't know why I keep doing this. I never cry as a rule.'

'It's the most natural thing in the world. Your whole system's been shaken up. Hormones flying about all over the place. And – well, there's something to cry about. That pathetic little scrap. It makes me wonder, suddenly. I mean, I've always wanted a large family. But now I find myself asking what right I have to inflict life on a human being when so much of it may be struggle and unhappiness.'

'Selfishness, I suppose. On both our parts, I mean. The pleasure of having children.'

'But can we rely even on that? It's double-edged. There's pain as well as pleasure. Hostages to fortune, isn't that what they say?'

'This is no way for a new father to be talking.' Hilary shrugged off her distress and returned to her normal cheerfulness, turning her head to smile at him. Until that moment they had been standing side by side, looking at the baby rather than at each other. Now she drew her breath in sharply as she caught sight of his expression. His face was haggard and strained: he looked near to tears himself.

The sight of his distress strengthened Hilary's resolution.

'It'll be all right, Andrew. She'll pull through, I'm sure she will. A normal, lovely little girl.'

Andrew shook his head.

'It's not that,' he said. 'Something else. I'll tell you when we get home.'

'No. What? Tell me now, or I shall imagine all kinds of horrors.'

He hesitated, but only for a moment.

'They've found Georgie,' he said.

The question on Hilary's lips did not need to be asked, for only one answer could explain her husband's expression.

'Dead?'

He nodded, and she threw herself into his arms, embracing him as fiercely as if she were comforting Tony.

'Tell me,' she said at last. They had learned only three weeks earlier about the kidnapping of the little boy. Tony had kept the secret from them as from everyone else at first, but his offer of a huge reward made world news. When Andrew phoned up to express his sympathy and hopes for a happy ending, he was given an apology for the fact that they had been kept in the dark, but he and Hilary knew no more than the rest of the world what had happened.

'He was locked up in the cabin of a boat. A stolen boat moored to a buoy. The owner didn't discover it had gone from its usual mooring until he arrived for his August holiday, and it wasn't found until a week after that.'

'Does that mean that Georgie was dead all the time, even when Tony was trying to pay the ransom?'

'No. It sounds as though he starved to death over the past three weeks.'

'Oh! Oh, how horrible! What kind of beast could do something like that?'

'It may not have been intended that way. Tony said – '

'Have you been speaking to him today?'

96

'Yes. He phoned me at work. He asked – ' Andrew paused unhappily. 'He wanted to know if I could fly out to Rome for a day, at once.'

'I hope you said you would.'

'How could I say that when I'd promised to take the babies home.'

'But you must go,' said Hilary. 'If there's anything you can do . . .'

'What *can* I do?'

'That's for him to say. I mean, it's only for a day, you said. And I've got Nanny.' They had accepted Tony's choice of a christening present and the newly-appointed nanny had arrived in the house two days earlier to make sure that everything was prepared. She was trained and uniformed but had agreed at the interview to share the care of the little girls with their mother instead of demanding sole responsibility. 'Is that why you were looking so worried, because you wanted to go but thought you ought not to?' She kissed him warmly to show that she understood his divided loyalties.

'Are you sure?'

'Of course I'm sure. Since you're here now, you might as well drive us home first as we arranged, but then you must catch the first plane you can. Think how much he's doing for us. First of all the house and now Nanny. If this is a chance for you to do something in return . . .' She knew that this was certain to be a convincing argument and, as she had expected, he nodded his head in relief.

'Thanks, darling. If you're sure you can cope. I won't be away long.'

In a curious way, and one which she was reluctant to admit to herself, Hilary found herself calmed by what she had learned. Her distress on Tony and Sara's behalf was genuine and deep, but as she looked through the glass wall at the tiny, unstirring baby in the incubator, she felt for the first time a rush of protective love. At least the

97

little girl was still alive. No one had yet brought the news against which there was no appeal and which meant that there could be no future for her. Hilary felt her own fists involuntarily clenching with determination that Baby Craig Three should survive and improve and grow up to be a happy, normal girl. How lucky they were, Andrew and she, compared to Tony and Sara who would now be so unhappy. As soon as Andrew returned, they would together choose a name for the third of their babies.

'Yes, of course you must go,' she repeated.

11

On his very first visit to the Palazzo Fiori at the age of ten Andrew had found it hard to believe that anyone could regard such a huge and sumptuous building as a home. The central great hall, with its wide double staircase curving upwards towards a dome, reminded him then of a bank; whilst the great entertaining rooms on the *piano nobile* – the salon, ballroom and banqueting hall – were so elaborately decorated with frescos on the ceilings and pictures on the walls that they resembled an art gallery. He had assumed that the Throne Room must have something to do with his host's princely title, but the oddness of having such a room in a private house was made greater, not less, when he learned that it had been furnished and left untouched for three hundred years solely in case a pope should come to visit.

Even the drawing room and dining room used by the family could have been parts of a museum, so old and beautiful was the furniture they contained. The only room of a normal size which he saw was Tony's bedroom, on the floor above – and unlike Andrew's room at home in England it did not have to double as a study and hobby room, but was just for sleeping in.

Twenty-three years on from that first visit the palace was even less of a home than before. As the car which had met Andrew at the airport turned through the arched entrance just before midnight, it seemed at first that he was not expected, for everything was in darkness. The porter was quick to flick the welcoming switch which bathed in mellow floodlight the statues in the courtyard and the balconies above them, but there was still an atmosphere of emptiness as Andrew followed one of the servants up the stairs. He did not remember that his footsteps had echoed so loudly on previous visits, but quickly realised the explanation: the tapestries which once had lined the walls of the stairwell were no longer there.

He looked around curiously as he was shown into the drawing room. All the pictures which had hung on the walls had disappeared, although the six large paintings originally commissioned to fit into the panelling were still in place, perhaps because they could not be moved. Most of the furniture had gone as well, and a pile of chests and soft packing material at one end of the room suggested that valuable objects were still in the process of being taken away.

But there was no time to wonder what was happening, for through the open door he could hear Tony hurrying from his study.

'Andrew! Good of you to come! I'm sorry I couldn't meet you myself, but I hope Mario found you without any trouble. How are you? What will you drink?'

'Whisky and water, please.' Andrew wondered whether or not to make any further expression of regret about Georgie's death, and decided not to. In two telephone calls he had done his best to convey Hilary's sympathy and his own, and judged that while the tragedy was still so close, every mention of it might prove upsetting. 'What's going on here, Tony?' he asked instead, waving a hand towards the packing cases.

'We're pulling out. Sara refuses to live in Rome any longer, and I can't say I blame her.'

'Where are you moving to?'

'Not decided. New York is full of muggers. California is full of freaks and burglars. South America is even worse for kidnapping than Italy. The world's a dangerous place.'

'You should come to live in law-abiding England.'

'Might do. Nothing decided yet, except not Rome. I

haven't even settled what to do with the palace. Rent it out, I guess. If it was an ordinary house we could just sell up, but when something's been handed down through so many generations you don't feel you have the right to ditch it. Sara says what's the point in holding on when there's no Georgie to take over; but Isabella might like it one day.'

'Isabella? Hilary said she was sure that the baby should have arrived by now, but we didn't like to ask, in case . . .'

'Our fault. We should have let you know. Sorry. We haven't made any sort of announcement to anyone, in fact. Too much else on our minds. Say when.'

'Thanks.'

'Yes, the baby arrived early, in the middle of all the kidnap chaos. It was the strain. We tried to get Sara to rest, but she wouldn't. Naturally enough. It was a bit dicey for the first few days. You and Hilary had the same problem a couple of months earlier, didn't you? I shall want to hear all about that in a moment. Isabella's still in the clinic, but she's putting on weight and generally beginning to look human, so it seems that all's well.'

'And Sara?'

'Sara flew off to Tokyo yesterday, as soon as I'd confirmed that it was Georgie's body that they'd found. She wanted to be with her mother. Her father got the embassy there after he left Rome.'

Andrew made no comment. Surely, at a time like this, a woman's place was with her husband and new-born baby rather than with her parents. But how could someone who had never experienced it understand the stress and grief which she must have suffered? It was for Tony, not himself, to express disappointment if he felt it. He waited, sipping his drink.

'She ought to have stayed for the funeral,' Tony said after a few moments. 'For her own sake, I mean. I can understand, in a way, why she felt a need to escape after so many days of fear and uncertainty, but she went too soon. A ceremony, a kind of formal saying goodbye, it's a necessary part of . . .' His lips trembled and he could not finish the sentence. Andrew looked down at his glass, giving him time to compose himself.

'And you would have liked her there at your side,' he suggested.

'Right. I had it today, the funeral. No point in hanging around, once she'd gone. We used our own chapel. I was glad of newspaper interest while we were searching for him, but I wanted this to be private. Such a small coffin!' He walked across to the marble mantelpiece and picked up a photograph in a silver frame. Andrew joined him, looking over his shoulder at the picture of Sara, radiantly happy, holding her first baby in his long christening robe.

'We thought that only the good fairies had come to his christening.' Tony stared down at the picture. 'The child who would grow up to be one of the richest men in the world one day. But that was why he died. And took his mother away with him.'

'She'll be back soon, I'm sure. The baby – '

'I'm not sure which way the baby is going to work,' said Tony unhappily. 'One of the things which upset Sara most was the feeling that she was trapped in her pregnancy, so to speak, when she wanted to be out doing things. Not that there was anything she could have done, but I'm certain that she felt imprisoned. With Georgie, and before Isabella was born, she always used to talk a lot about the ways in which a mother should bond with her babies. I didn't go along with her theories particularly, but *she* believed them and so there's something very deliberate about the way she won't have anything to do with Isabella.'

'Nothing at all?'

'She wouldn't feed her – breast-feed, I mean – although that's another thing she always felt strongly about. I don't know that she's ever even touched her. Before she went, she was behaving like a woman who intends to give her baby away for adoption and so won't let herself love it.'

'It's a difficult time anyway for a woman. I remember, about three days after our babies were born, Hilary started to cry and went on for almost a whole day. Not because the boy had died. Not for any reason at all, as far as I could make out. She simply couldn't stop.'

'I'd have felt happier if Sara *had* cried. It would be easier to cope with ordinary distress than with this . . . this . . . Well, that's enough about that for the moment. Tell me about my favourite other man's wife. How's Hilary?'

'In fine form. Nervous, mind you. Babies are such fragile things, aren't they? You have – or at least *I* have – this feeling that you can ruin a whole life by squeezing something too hard. I can't tell you how grateful we are for your christening present, Tony. It's not just having an extra pair of hands, though that's certainly going to be needed. It's knowing that there's a professional on the spot in case of emergencies.'

Tony shrugged his thanks away. 'Have you dined?' he asked.

'I had a meal on the plane, thanks.'

'That's not a dinner.'

'Perhaps not, but it's food. I don't want anything more. And – '

'You're tired, of course. I'll show you up.'

'But there was something you wanted – '

'Tomorrow,' said Tony. 'We'll talk about it tomorrow. You can stay, I hope.'

'Of course I can.' He had already – before Tony's appeal arrived – arranged to take this week off work with the intention of helping at home.

'Tomorrow, then. I need you rested and clear-headed. I have a favour to ask.'

12

'We'll go to Tivoli,' said Tony at breakfast. 'Do you remember Tivoli?'

'I certainly do.' Andrew had been taken there for a picnic during the first holiday he ever spent with the Fioris, and on each subsequent visit had begged for a return. The generosity of a princely picnic hamper had something to do with his schoolboy enthusiasm for this particular expedition, but in addition he had been fascinated by the many fountains of the Villa d'Este: fountains which gushed from the heads of animals or showered over statues or played bird songs or organ music or trumpet calls by their force. He took it for granted that on a hot day in August both the palace and its grounds would be swarming with tourists, and was amused to realise from Tony's startled and slightly annoyed expression when they arrived that his host had not expected this.

They stood in silence for a moment, looking along the Avenue of the Hundred Fountains. Nothing else in the garden was silent, for water splashed all round them while children shrieked in delight as they ran from one carved figure to another or flicked water at each other.

'They don't know how lucky they are,' said Tony, a sombre expression on his face. 'Ordinary families. Ordinary kids, whom nobody wants to steal and kill.'

'Not all those boys will grow up,' said Andrew. 'It isn't only princes who can be bereaved. Some of those will fall ill, drown, get run over, crash their motor bikes. No one can go through life without loss.'

'Right. All the same, I don't think . . . Let's move on to the Gregoriana.'

Turning their backs on the Villa d'Este, they walked through the narrow streets of old Tivoli to the Villa Gregoriana which proved, as Tony had expected, to be off the tourist track. The gardens here were wilder, using the natural features of river and ravines to create waterfalls and caves. Within a few moments the two men were alone in a belvedere, their quiet voices cocooned by the thundering of the cascade below.

'This business about Sara,' said Tony abruptly. 'I guess it may be serious. When we got married, you know, she was like me – like you and Hilary – wanting to have a big family. Not the usual sort of beautiful rich girl, hanging on to her figure. But now it's not just that she's rejecting Isabella. The day before she left, she told me that she didn't want to have any more children. So much pain, she said, bringing babies into the world just to become the victims of murderers. Never again. Her doctor talks about post-natal depression, special circumstances, all be right again in the end, but . . .'

'Sounds reasonable.'

'I'm not sure. You see, while the Georgie business was going on, we had a quarrel. Just when we ought to have been at our closest. It was the strain of the thing, going on so long. Something she did, something I said – easy to forgive, but difficult to forget.'

'It won't last,' said Andrew uneasily.

'I hope not. But even if she comes back, it's never going to be quite the same again. She's a good Catholic, you know. Not like me. I don't know how she'd play it, the not having any more children thing. And I'd always hoped, you know . . . You and Hilary, you were a kind of model for me of what marriage should be. The people I move amongst, most of them, seem to flit in and out of it without any hearts being broken. There's no – what's the right word? – loyalty. But I always had the feeling that you and Hilary were best friends as well as being husband and wife, right?'

'Right.'

'That was what I wanted for myself, and I thought I'd got it. But now, well, we've let each other down and I'm not sure that the crack can be mended. This is why I asked you to come. I need support, Andrew. I need someone I can trust.'

'Trust to do what?'

'Just to be trustworthy, I guess. Someone whose advice and opinions are always honest, always in my best interests, so that I never have to doubt the motive behind them even for a moment. The Maestro had that with Ludo, and I trusted Ludo as well, although of course I didn't love him. But now Ludo's dead and Sara – I can't rely on Sara. Even if I forgive her, how can I ever be sure that she's forgiven me? I need *you*, Andrew.'

'You've always had my friendship. You know that. You can rely on that.' Andrew held out his hand in what he intended as a gesture of support; but Tony shook his head.

'I'm looking for something more formal, more informed than that. It isn't enough just to know that somewhere in the world there's someone who'll always be pleased to see me. Yesterday, for example. I asked you to come, and you came, and I'm more grateful than I can say for that. But I can't go tearing you away from your family and your job whenever I need a word of advice or a shoulder to blub on, just because we were at school together once.'

'There must be people in your organisation – '

'They all have their own axes to grind. I don't think the worse of them for that, but it leaves me sitting on top, making up my own mind. I'm not asking you to run a business for me, Andrew, or anything like that. But I *am* offering you a job.'

'A job as what?'

'As – ' Tony shrugged his shoulders in a hopeless attempt to find the right word for it. 'As my trusty. It might be a year before I had anything to discuss with you, but I'd want to feel that your time was at my disposal.'

'What's your proposition, then?'

Until now, as he discussed his marriage and his need for support, Tony's voice had been uncertain; but he answered his friend's question with a businesslike briskness.

'I'd like to offer you a retainer of three times the salary you're getting at the moment, in exchange for the right to call on your services at any time; with an extra fee whenever I do in fact call on them. The house loan would be written off, naturally, because you'd be using the place as a private office. You'd have to give up your job, and I'd like you to spend a few months familiarising yourself with all my business interests. But after that, you could do any free-lance work you wanted. As a private tax consultant, for example – any fees you earned like that would be your own. Or you might like to take some extra training – international law, different kinds of accounting, whatever you chose. As long as you were able to throw up whatever it was whenever I asked you to.'

There was a long silence before Andrew laughed. 'I've never known before what "dumbfounded" meant, but I know now. This certainly isn't what I expected when you phoned.'

'I can guess what might worry you. You had to watch your mother struggling to bring you up after she was widowed. You've never had any kind of financial security except for what your job offers, and now you're responsible for a wife and three children. At some point while you were at university you decided that you'd rather be safe than rich. And now I'm asking you to give up that safety. Well, I can give you a contract for life. Money is not my problem.'

Andrew turned to look at his friend. Since their last meeting – perhaps only in the past few weeks – Tony had aged. The light of enthusiasm which was his most attractive characteristic had left his eyes and his expression was anxious and strained. It reminded Andrew of the little boy who had been so anxious to marshal the headmaster's trains that he had tried to cheat on his maths prep. They had been Best Friends then in the strict schoolboy sense of the term, but even at that time Andrew had known and Tony had accepted that a Best Friend did not necessarily do exactly what was asked of him. In any case they were both now grown men. It would be sentimental to pretend that nothing had changed in the past twenty years, for there were other people to be considered.

'I'd like a little time,' he said. 'I came here under orders from Hilary to stay as long as you wanted and do whatever you asked; but neither of us had anything like this in mind. It's a big step. Why don't we walk a bit: and then when we get back to Rome you could drop me somewhere short of the palazzo for an hour or two.'

Tony nodded obediently and made no further effort at persuasion. They strolled in a roundabout and leisurely fashion back to the Villa d'Este, where they had left the car.

'Do you still play with trains?' asked Andrew, the question put into his mind by the flash of schoolboy memory.

'Real trains now. I buy as many as I can. And try to travel on the rest. I have this ambition, to ride over every mile of track in the world before I die. Well, no hope of achieving that, of course, but I go for all the oddities. Trains that are floated across rivers on rafts or which go up impossible mountains. Whenever I'm in a new country my local manager's expected to find me something interesting to add to the list.'

'You keep a list, then.'

'I have a map room. I draw in every journey after I make it. It's the best definition of a hobby that I know, that it should be completely useless.' He turned his head to grin at Andrew with the worry lines smoothed away.

'That's part of the fun of having money, Andrew. There's only so much that a man can actually use in sensible ways. As far as the rest is concerned, it doesn't matter a damn whether or not it's wasted as long as you enjoy the process of throwing it away.'

More than ever it seemed necessary to Andrew to give careful thought to his friend's proposition. If he was to be of any help to Tony he would need to empathise with an attitude of mind which at the moment was foreign to him. As they approached the Fiori palace he asked Tony to drop him in the Piazza di Spagna.

He had intended to walk down the Via Condotti to the Caffe Greco, but changed his mind at the last moment and instead turned into Babington's Tea Rooms. Although he did not go as far as to order tea, the old-fashioned atmosphere helped him to feel properly English as he considered the change which was proposed in his life.

There was no need for him to consult Hilary, because he was quite certain what her reaction would be. She had never tried to talk him out of his choice of career but he knew that she considered it fuddy-duddy and wished that he were more prepared to take risks. Not that she would consider this to be a risk in financial terms, any more than Andrew himself did. And she would certainly think it only fair to accept any proposition put forward by the friend who had so generously provided her with a nanny. What she might not understand was that Andrew Craig, trusted adviser to an international entrepreneur, would not be quite the same person as Andrew Craig, Inspector of Taxes.

'But don't you see' – Andrew could hear her saying this as clearly as if she were seated at the table beside him – 'this is your chance at last to give Tony something he needs. You've always been bothered about taking favours from him, but you'll be the one who is giving now. The money's not important to him; he won't notice it. So it mustn't count as important to us either. What matters is that he's making a request that you can't refuse.'

It was not as easy as all that. Andrew drank three orders of coffee before returning at last to the palace and finding Tony in his office.

'A couple of things to put on the table,' said Andrew. 'First, I'm not interested in a contract for life. If you're going to trust me, then I can trust you. All I'd need to ask is that if anything should happen to me within the next few years you'd remember that Hilary would no longer have a Civil Service pension.'

Tony nodded. A grin began to appear on his face as he asked, 'And the second?'

'The second thing is that I have to give three months' notice. But after that – ' For a second time that day he held out his hand. On this occasion Tony took it, but held it only for a second before clasping him with both arms in a hug of gratitude.

'Shall we write it again in blood, Tantivy-style?' he asked. The light of excitement had returned to his eyes and for the first time since Andrew's arrival he ceased to look unhappy.

'I think we should consider that the first time is still valid,' Andrew answered gravely. Then he too could not help grinning as he remembered the glee with which Hilary had once interrogated him about schoolboy rituals. 'After all, it was meant to last for life.'

13

It was in June 1971 that Tony Fiori gave up the struggle to work out for himself the best solution to the problem of Isabella. Already New York was too hot. By August it would be intolerable. By August, too, she might be walking. She could not be confined for ever in the Dakota, however palatial his apartment might be. 'Get me Andrew Craig,' he said to his secretary.

As he waited for the connection to be made, he spent a moment thinking about June in England. Andrew's garden in Weybridge would be sweetly scented by roses now. The lawn would be green and smooth. The first strawberries would be ready for picking. At this moment Hilary was probably weeding or hoeing while her babies kicked happily in the sunshine under the eye of the nanny. Tantivy had done its best to spoil Tony's English summers with examinations and that ridiculous game, cricket, but he nevertheless remembered them with pleasure for blue skies and fluffy white clouds and a temperature which was neither too hot nor too cold.

'How's the weather with you?' he demanded to know as soon as Andrew answered.

'Is that Tony? I thought it was only we Brits who insisted on talking about the weather all the time. Well, if you must know, it's raining. Good for the garden, Hilary says.'

'You won't mind leaving, then. Can you come over?'

'Of course.' At the other end of the telephone Andrew's voice sounded pleased. It was the great thing about Andrew, that he could not bear to be indebted to anyone. Tony had made a mental note when they first shook hands on their arrangement ten months earlier that he must think of something for his friend to do at least two or three times a year; but there was nothing contrived about this particular invitation.

'How's Hilary?' he asked twenty-four hours later as they made their way at crawling pace from the airport towards Manhattan.

'Cross with you. I bear a message from her. The fact that her husband has spent weeks as your guest in New York and is always chatting on the telephone is no reason for you to stop writing to her. It's not just that she likes getting your letters. She enjoys writing to you as well, but feels she ought to have something to answer.'

'Tell her that unsolicited letters are by far the most enjoyable. But no, I'll tell her myself. I was going to write anyway to say that I want her to keep the nanny on for another year as my first birthday present to my goddaughters.'

'You're too generous – particularly when we can afford to pick up the tab ourselves, thanks to what you're paying me. I must say, it makes all the difference in the world, being able to go out whenever we want to and having someone to take charge when we panic. It won't be the same nanny, though. The one we've got at the moment specialises in babies from birth. She's very firm about never staying for longer than a year unless there are signs that Mother is going to produce another little package in the foreseeable future. But we could certainly find someone else. Thanks a lot. Actually, of course, what Hilary sends is her love. Quite apart from everything else you've done for us, she's pleased as punch that you've got me out of the IRS.'

'The advantage is all mine. I want to thank you again, Andrew, for that report you wrote after you got back from New York. When I suggested this arrangement last year I suppose all I really had in mind was a shoulder to weep on from time to time. I'd almost forgotten that you were

112

such a wizard with figures. We'd been worrying for three years about those bad debts in South America, and you think of a solution after four weeks.'

'Beginner's luck. It really is true that an outsider can see a situation with fresh eyes. And you must give some of the credit to the Guggenheim. I spent a couple of hours at the top of the gallery looking down, letting my mind run with the spiral staircase and on and on. Perhaps I ought to make my fortune by writing a book on Geometric Solutions to Financial Problems. What have you got for me this time?'

'I'll show you when we get there.' It was not something to be discussed in front of his driver/bodyguard. In his love of driving fast, though in little else, Tony was a true Italian, and so on long journeys he liked to take the wheel himself. But in Manhattan, where anything over ten miles an hour was good going he was content to be a passenger.

'Gip and I went off to do a course of evasive driving together,' he said, nodding towards the driver's back as though bringing him into the conversation. 'So if, for example, someones pushes a baby buggy out in front of one of us in a narrow street where there's a car parked in the other lane, do we do an emergency stop? No, we do not. We just take it that there's only a doll in the buggy, run it over and keep on driving. What the course didn't teach us was what to say to the police and how to look the bereaved mother in the eye afterwards if we happened to have guessed wrong.'

By now they were skirting the southern edge of Central Park. 'Can we walk?' asked Andrew suddenly.

'Sure. Pull in, Gip.' Tony looked teasingly at his friend. 'You're never going to make a good American.'

'I have absolutely no ambitions in that direction. And after a flight – '

'Right. You need to stretch those long legs.' They left the car and turned into the park, strolling beside the pond before moving across towards West Drive. They had covered almost four blocks going north when Andrew came to a standstill and began to laugh.

'What's up?'

'I can't get over it. That such a building should exist here at all. Much less that someone I know should live in it! But I suppose what *you* find odd is that you only have a single apartment in it, and not the whole palace.'

He was staring at the Dakota, which was indeed a palace – a huge edifice, the width of a block: eight tall storeys crowned with an exuberance of gables and spires and chimneys and roof walks. Tony, who had taken over his apartment after his father's death and took its spaciousness and eccentricity for granted, looked at it through his friend's eyes and grinned in sympathy.

'What my American friends find odd is that I should go on living here when I could afford to move on to the East Side. Only a European would choose to rattle about in an unfashionable address when he could have something shiny-new and interior-designed just across the park.'

They walked on together, but paused at the main entrance of the building for the doorman to appear.

'Mr Craig is a house guest of mine,' Tony told him. The man was new since Andrew's last visit and was under instructions not to let anyone up without phoning for authority unless he had been given an introduction of this kind. Although the Dakota was a secure building in the sense of having walls like a fortress, it could all too easily be penetrated by someone claiming that he had flowers to deliver. 'Up we go, then,' he said to Andrew.

Tony's father had chosen the seventh-floor apartment for the high view it afforded over Central Park. As they approached the door, Tony glanced upwards to check that the security camera had them in its sights and was moving with them to prove that the security guard inside was alert. He stood for a moment with his arms stretched high and wide, pressing against the two hidden buttons in the door frame. These precautions were new since Andrew had last stayed in the apartment.

Some of the new measures would have to be explained to his guest. The balcony which ran right round the building had been one of the advantages of the seventh-floor apartments – and it was invaluable for providing baby Isabella with fresh air. But it also represented a hazard, requiring an elaborate alarm system. He followed Andrew into his bedroom and explained the procedure to be followed if he wanted to open a window.

'You'd like to freshen up with a shower, I expect.'

'Later. Spit it out, Tony. What's up?'

Tony sat down on the edge of the bed. Now that it came to the point, he found it hard to begin his explanation of why he had summoned Andrew to meet him here. In the early, happy, days of his marriage he would never have expected that he would want to discuss his relationship with Sara with an outsider. When he first sent for his friend and poured out his fears, it was because Georgie's death had left him in such an emotional state. But it was for just this kind of situation that he had asked Andrew to act as his adviser: there was no point in funking it.

'Sara's left again,' he said abruptly at last. 'This time I guess it's for good.' She had returned from Tokyo – at her mother's insistence, he suspected – during Andrew's familiarisation period in New York, and had stayed for three months. But Tony's new obsession with security precautions, which he had hoped she would find reassuring, had instead driven her away again. Every lock, every alarm made her feel a prisoner while reminding her that it had all come too late to save Georgie. Tony had tried to point out to her that it was Isabella who must be protected now, but Sara was not interested in her daughter, refusing to love her because she was so convinced that she would lose her one day. By going, she had made the loss real.

115

'I'm sorry. Really sorry. Same reason as before?'

'Yes. She rejects the child completely. And of course I don't, so all the time she was with me she was aware of me worrying about Isabella, wanting to spend time playing with her when I could, that kind of thing. Two incompatible attitudes springing from the same cause. I hardly dare let Isabella out of my sight. Sara can't dare to look at her. So we're out of sympathy on that. And then – '

He hesitated, feeling that even between close friends this was something which should not be discussed. But he had made the decision to trust Andrew with every detail of his private affairs. 'She's still adamant about not having any more children, but she won't go on the pill, or use anything or let me. She did suggest that I should have a vasectomy. God knows what the logic of that is. It's not something I'd do lightly, because really I'd like more kids. But I might have agreed if I'd felt safe with her. Seemed to me, though, that I might lose out anyway and then I'd be a double loser. So you can imagine, our reconciliation wasn't exactly passionate.'

'Are you going to divorce?'

'No doubt she'll have to ask the Pope,' Tony said bitterly. 'I shall let her make the running on that. I can always get a civil divorce after a bit if I want to. To be going on with, I've got a lawyer working on the terms of a legal separation. It's a bit outside Tod's field, so I'm using my local man. She's not likely to be greedy about money. Her father made a good settlement on her when we married, and she'll inherit a lot more when he dies. In any case, she's reacting against the life of a rich woman at the moment. Living in an adobe hut in the New Mexican desert. I shall settle a few million dollars on her on the understanding that she has no further claim on me either when we divorce or when I die and that she renounces any rights with respect to Isabella. That's what she wants now; but I need it to be watertight so that she can't change her mind in ten or twenty years' time.'

116

'You could let me have a look at the draft before you sign it,' Andrew suggested. 'In fact, a chat with the lawyer straightaway would be useful. There could be tax advantages in arranging the settlement one way rather than another – or even in one country rather than another. And if you want to make sure that she never tries to change the arrangement in the future, you mustn't make an outright gift of the money. Keep the capital in trust so that it can be forfeited if she breaks the agreement.'

Tony was pleased that Andrew should volunteer his help. Almost certainly the second suggestion would have been covered in the draft, but he had given no special instructions to his lawyer about minimising tax. His pleasure in manipulating money came from increasing it, not in deciding how best to dispose of it. Hilary, he remembered, had chided him once for not giving more of it away. In the new circumstances, it was a matter to which he could turn his attention before too long; but the Sara business must be disposed of first. 'Thanks,' he said. 'I'd be grateful.'

'But that wasn't the point you wanted me here to discuss?'

'No.' Tony stood up and began to pace round the room. 'Come and visit the nursery,' he said at last. 'This is really what I want to talk to you about. Isabella.'

14

There were fourteen rooms in the apartment, allowing baby Isabella to have her own suite of day and night nurseries, kitchen, bathroom and nurse's room. The nurse rose to her feet as the two men entered the day nursery.

'You remember Emilia?' said Tony. 'From your mumpy honeymoon.'

'Yes, of course.'

'She did such a good job of bringing me up that I've put her in charge of Isabella. How's my beauty then?' Yes, she was a beauty, with wide brown eyes and a plump rosy skin. She had lost the hair that she was born with, but it was beginning to grow again. He leaned over to pick her up and kissed the finger which she poked towards his mouth as he held her tightly. She was so warm, so soft, so loving. Georgie had been warm and cuddly in exactly the same way at this age. It was a thought which Tony tried to dismiss from his mind, for at such times he could understand a little of what Sara felt. To lose one child was a tragedy. To be robbed of a second could easily send anyone mad.

'Go and get yourself a coffee,' he suggested to Emilia. 'I'll ring through when we're ready to go.'

'I'm surprised that you persuaded her to come to a big city like New York,' commented Andrew as the door closed. 'She doesn't speak a word of the language, does she?'

'I doubt she's been outside the apartment since she arrived. And there were special circumstances.' He sat down in the chair which Emilia had just vacated and began to jig Isabella up and down on his knee. 'She has a granddaughter, Sophia, who came to work for us in Rome a couple of years ago. Too young, probably. Thought it dull being a maid and got a job as a waitress instead. Unsophisticated country girl: predictable consequence.'

'Pregnant?'

'Right. When I sent for Emilia to ask if she'd come here, she poured all this out. She wanted me to let her hide Sophia away in the Villa dell'Isola for a couple of years so that she could reappear as a young widow and avoid the disgrace to the family name. As though it would have fooled anyone. So I said, why not make it New York? In her sort of home village – in the south of Italy – anyone would believe that a wicked American might desert his wife. We were going to need a nurserymaid here as well as Emilia, and there was no need for us ever to notice that there was another baby on the premises. Sophia may even manage to find a real husband if she ever gets brave enough to cross the street.'

He put Isabella down on the floor and watched as she crawled towards a favourite soft ball.

'Yours are walking by now, I suppose,' he said.

'Not quite,' Andrew told him. 'They stand up and stagger and then fall over. We were warned from the start that they'd be a couple of months behind full-term babies in development, for the first year at least. And of course – '

Tony waited for the end of the sentence, but it did not come. 'It's odd,' he said at last, 'the difference it makes, not having a son. I mean, I didn't have one before Georgie was born, but I was sure that I would one day.'

'I expect you will again,' said Andrew. 'You'll want to marry again, start a new family, when all this is behind you.'

'Maybe. But for the moment . . . The Women's Libbers would say, wouldn't they, that I ought to think of a daughter in the same way as a son, but I can't do that. While Georgie was alive – and even before that, when I was sure he'd be along some time – I got a lot of pleasure in increasing his fortune. God knows, I don't need any more for myself, so I have to have an incentive. But when I look at Isabella . . . Christ, Andrew, what am I going to do?'

'Are you still thinking about kidnapping?'

'That's only part of it. A big part. I mean, she's only ten months old. I can keep her guarded while she's tiny. But she can't spend the whole of her life surrounded by bodyguards. What kind of a life is she going to have? How will she make friends if she never goes to school? I don't want her to grow up scared; but I'm scared myself, and she'll smell that when she's older. I even had a tattoo done, so that if she were ever snatched and kept for a long time nobody would be able to palm another child off on me.' For a moment he buried his head in his hands. 'I think it was that which was the last straw for Sara. As though I was so certain it would happen one day.'

'You said that kidnapping was only part of your worry. What's the other part?'

Tony took a deep breath to bring his emotions back under control.

'Just look at her, Andrew,' he said. 'One day, when I die, she's going to find herself one of the richest women in the world. What will it do to her, knowing that? When a man asks her to marry him, when people try to be friendly, how will she be able to tell whether they genuinely like her, love her? There are two ways she can get it wrong. She can trust people who shouldn't be trusted and she can push away people who might be loyal. And if she's intelligent enough to realise that, she'll never feel certain. That could make her insecure or it could turn her into a toughie. A rich bitch.'

'You've survived the same situation,' Andrew reminded him. 'Sara didn't marry you for money. And you have friends.'

'I chose them. Actively, not passively. This is one of the

things I feel about having a daughter rather than a son. It's more difficult for a girl.'

'You may be old-fashioned, thinking that. Girls these days don't take kindly to being thought softer than their brothers.' But Andrew's voice expressed sympathy, all the same. 'Is this why you asked me to come?'

'Right. I said when we first talked about this business of giving me advice that I wanted someone who was always on my side. But that's not it after all. I want you to speak for Isabella. Not in any sense of her against me, but of me only being happy if I know I've done the best for her. What should I do to give my daughter a happy life, Andrew?'

'Now that you've switched the ground rules, you might find me having to suggest that you should give all your money away to the poor.'

'If that's the answer, then that's the answer. Except that I don't want her to be poor herself.'

'I can see that we're going to have a very philosophical weekend,' said Andrew. 'How do we define a happy life? And I'm still allowed to take your personal interests into consideration, I hope. I mean, earlier on you were talking as though you'd lost your incentive to do anything with your money. But presumably you don't propose to spend the rest of your life doing nothing. So, for example – speaking just off the top of my head – it might be possible for you to set up a charitable trust and turn your money, or part of it, over to the trust but then make yourself responsible for continuing to work in the same way to increase its endowment. And then there could be another trust for Isabella which would prevent her having direct access to any capital. That would deter the greediest fortune-hunters.'

Trusts, of course, were Andrew's speciality, so it was not surprising that they should provide the first solution to spring to his mind; but it seemed to Tony that this might not be the perfect one. If the sort of trust proposed for Isabella was to keep her throughout life in the sort of comfort to which she was entitled as a wealthy man's daughter, the fortune-hunters would cluster round all the same.

But Andrew, speaking without time to reflect, would not expect an immediate reaction: and there was another point which Tony wanted to raise.

'Something else,' he said. 'Isabella's not the only one who might be kidnapped. It could happen to me. South America is a bandit continent, and I have to spend a lot of time there. Anything could happen, any time. It's an odd thing, but I haven't got any close family at all. Certainly no one of my own generation. Whether or not there's a trust, I need to appoint legal guardians for Isabella in the event of my death. Otherwise she might simply be handed back to Sara, whether she wants her or not, and I couldn't bear the thought of that. Too cold an arrangement. Could I name you as a guardian, Andrew? Or better still, you and Hilary jointly? Tod would act as well – I've asked him – and deal with all the legal side.'

He had expected immediate agreement, and was dismayed to see that for the first time his friend looked doubtful.

'Don't start telling me that I'm only thirty-two, that it's too early to worry about things like that. That's what wills and trusts are for, to cope with the unexpected. You know that better than anyone else.'

'That's not what's bothering me,' said Andrew slowly. 'Giving up my job, giving you advice, those are easy things. But taking responsibility for a child's life . . .' He looked down at Isabella, who had rolled over on her back, clutching the ball to her chest, and was kicking and gurgling with contentment. 'I mean, to look at it coldly, after your death Isabella wouldn't be an heiress any longer but an incredibly wealthy child, no matter how the money might be tied up. If we left her here, we'd have to take responsibility for all the precautions you've set up – but at a distance. And we couldn't do it, in fact, because it wouldn't be right for a child to be brought up entirely by servants, with no family life.'

'You might – '

'We could take her into our own family, yes, or Tod into his. But even that's not as easy as it sounds. One immensely rich child living cheek by jowl with other ordinary children who will have to earn their own livings one day. And the kidnap danger would still be there, but more difficult to guard against. We should have to impose on ourselves all the security business that you say has driven Sara away. I'm not saying that it would be out of the question; but . . .'

It had not occurred to Tony that his friend would even consider turning the request down, and he felt an urgent need to press it. But he managed to keep quiet, recognising that Andrew was still thinking aloud.

'Under the system you've set up here, how much time are you going to spend with Isabella, Tony?' he asked. 'Is she going to be brought up by servants even though she's got a father? All the things that are written about poor little rich girls, I'm not sure that it's always the money that turns them sour. It could be just the feeling of being neglected as children while their parents are either making money or spending it. What I'm getting at is this: is she going to have a family life with you?'

'Christ, I don't know. I just don't know. It doesn't matter while she's a baby. But when she gets older, yes, things will have to change. I'll have to stop travelling around, set up a permanent home base, bring her to live with me.'

'You'll marry again,' said Andrew confidently for a second time. 'It probably isn't something you're prepared to contemplate at the moment, but it's sure to happen. So what we're talking about will probably be only a temporary arrangement. I'd like to sleep on this, Tony. Can we talk about it again tomorrow?'

Tony nodded. Like Andrew, he stared down at the

contented baby on the floor before bending down to tickle her. For a moment she gurgled happily. Then the smile faded from her face, to be replaced by an expression of extreme concentration.

'What's the matter?' Tony was alarmed by the sudden change. Beside him, there was a sound which Andrew must have learned from Hilary: he was giggling.

'Your daughter is filling her nappy. Or diaper as the case may be. This is the moment when poor men summon their wives and rich men ring for the nurse to come back.'

Tony grinned as he rang for Emilia. Then, returning to stand near his daughter, he sighed.

'I can't see any way, not any way at all, that she can be happy,' he said. 'You're probably right. I ought to give all my money away and let her live as an ordinary girl.'

'Did I say that? If you took that course she might grow up to have some hobby like collecting Fabergé eggs or breeding racehorses that absolutely demanded that she should have a fortune of her own, and she'd never forgive you for depriving her of it. You can't change the fact that she's been born a Fiori. Besides, you don't really want her to be ordinary. You want her to be comfortably off in the most literal sense of the words – to have all the advantages of great wealth but none of the disadvantages. Am I right so far?'

'You make me feel ten years old again,' said Tony ruefully. He was recalling his consternation on that day at Tantivy when what he asked for was an easy way to become Train Marshal but what he got was a course of mathematical coaching. 'The bossy genius with his own definition of what's best for me.'

'What's best for *Isabella*,' Andrew reminded him. 'We're back to that philosophical argument again. First of all we have to define happiness. Only after that can we think of the best way to keep her happy.'

'We. You're going to help me then?'

'Of course I'm going to help you. Try, anyway. It's just a question of deciding what's best. Is there a telephone in my room? I didn't notice.'

'Yes.'

'Good. I'd like breakfast in bed at six o'clock, please. With an extra thermos flask of black coffee. And a typewriter. And no one to disturb me until I come out. I may go back to the Guggenheim later.'

'Right.' Tony was still in his Tantivy mood, remembering how that first annoyance had gradually changed to self-confidence and admiration. 'Have you got a plan already?'

'Not a plan. An idea, perhaps.'

'What is it?'

'Don't be in such a rush, young Fiori. Tomorrow. I'll tell you tomorrow.'

PART TWO

1973

1

In the course of his visit to Manhattan in 1971 Andrew had produced not one but four alternative proposals for Isabella's upbringing. Each of them had its own disadvantages – how could it not, when the problem was so intractable? But from the moment when Tony scribbled his approval and signature at the foot of one of the four sheets he had felt free to live his own life in the knowledge that his daughter was safe for the time being. He spent as much time as he could with her, but between these visits he continued to travel the world, keeping an eye on his far-flung enterprises.

November 1973 found him in Peru. The opening of a new hotel in Lima had gone well, and he had spent two weeks afterwards negotiating towards the realisation of a long-standing ambition – to be the man who linked the countries of the west coast by a railway system which would run from Caracas to at least Santiago on the same gauge of line and with services bearing some relationship to a timetable.

The obstacles were formidable – including mountains and rivers, national inflation rates and individual demands for sweeteners. There were vested land interests to be overcome, and absolutely no certainty that the first train to run would not be derailed by one of half a dozen guerrilla organisations, of which each country had its own example. Tony struggled to persuade each government of the increased prosperity which a new trade route would bring, but found it heavy going.

For the moment there was no more to be done, but before flying from Lima to Caracas to catch his plane to Europe he had allowed himself time for a treat. The manager of the new hotel, knowing that the president of the company 'collected' railway journeys, had suggested a trip from Cuzco to the Inca ruins at Machu Picchu; but Tony had made that journey in Sara's company during their extended honeymoon and had no wish to repeat it. Instead, he bought tickets for himself and his bodyguard for the journey from Lima to Huancayo and back.

This was the highest standard-gauge railway in the world: that much he knew already, but he had not realised quite how unnerving the trip would prove to be. Rocky, his bodyguard, was as strong as a bull and as brave as a matador where muggers, gangsters, kidnappers or terrorists were concerned; but as the train crawled up to its high point of 15,000 feet he was sitting frozen in a corner with his eyes tightly shut. Railway attendants were patrolling the corridors to offer oxygen to any passengers suffering from altitude sickness; but they had no remedy to offer for vertigo.

In order to climb from sea level to such a height within the narrow confines of the Rimac Valley, the train needed to cross and recross the ravine on the narrowest of bridges until it was as high above the floor of the valley as an aeroplane might have been. Between the bridges it made its way along equally narrow ledges hacked out from a sheer granite cliff. To wind its way up was impossible, so instead it proceeded in zig-zags. As the front engine came to a halt with its nose against the cliff, the guard at the back hurriedly switched the points to allow a second engine to carry the carriages forward and up in the opposite direction. There was one heart-stopping second each time before the brakes caught when there seemed nothing to prevent the whole train from slipping backwards, picking up speed, shooting off the end of the previous zig-zag. This journey came nearer than any other to shaking the firmness of

Tony's belief that it was always safer to travel by rail than by air.

On arrival at Huancayo there were two hours to wait before the return journey. None of the other passengers had been crazy enough to travel such a distance merely in order to go straight back again, and Rocky rapidly disappeared in search of somewhere where he could be sick. Tony, smiling sympathetically, made himself comfortable and began to write a letter to Hilary.

There was no longer any need for them to correspond, for he was a regular visitor to Kilcraigie Castle. Since one wing of the Craigs' new home housed the UK offices of the Fiori Foundation – and stored some of the treasures he had removed from the Palazzo Fiori in Rome – he could happily combine pleasure with business. But Hilary had made it clear how much she enjoyed receiving his letters and so he made a point of writing to her whenever he was anywhere interesting. He did not, however, post all the letters.

Did Andrew, he wondered, realise that his best friend was in love with his wife? The answer didn't really matter, for Hilary would never be disloyal – and at all sensible moments Tony himself understood that the delicate balance of the three-cornered relationship must not be disturbed. But it was hard to be sensible all the time. Under the appalling strain of Georgie's kidnapping he had realised how much he longed for the level-headed support of someone like Hilary; and from the moment of Sara's final desertion his longing had become desperate. This was one of the occasions when he allowed himself to express his true feelings, making no attempt to conceal his desire as the words which revealed his fantasies scribbled over the paper and he pictured Hilary reading them.

Instead of throwing the letter away immediately he had finished it, he tucked it into his passport pouch. As long as it remained there he could pretend to himself that on this occasion he might post it and allow Hilary to learn of his feelings – but knew that he would not. Common sense told him that he must not allow her to become too important a part of his life. As soon as his marriage to Sara ended in divorce, the fishing fleet of three continents had set sail in his direction. It would be the easiest thing in the world to find another wife and set up a home to which Isabella could be brought. That would be best for everybody – if only he could find another woman as cheerful and sensible and desirable as Hilary Craig.

Desultory stirrings suggested that the train might be preparing to start on its return journey. Pale-faced, Rocky reported back.

'Don't look out of the window,' said Tony sympathetically. His own nerves were good, but even he felt his head swimming when he tried from the highest of the flimsy bridges to count the number of those which crossed the ravine below.

During the zig-zags down the cliff face he felt more secure, and leaned as far out of the window as he could to take a photograph. His head swam in the high, thin air and he could feel a headache building up at the back of his eyes; but such small discomforts were forgotten as an unusual sound reached his ears, causing him to twist his body and look upwards. What was that sudden roar, that sinister rumble? An explosion? An earthquake? The sonic boom of a plane? Whatever the cause, the result was an avalanche. Rocks were sliding down the mountain: bouncing, crashing, picking up speed.

The noise came nearer, became louder. 'Watch it!' shouted Tony, recognising even as he yelled how ridiculous it was to think that anyone would hear or be able to take any evasive action even if he did. For a split second he managed to persuade himself that the zig-zagging railway line took up only a small part of the mountainside. There would be room for the avalanche to hurtle past without causing damage. He was still reassuring himself when the end of the train was hit.

Because he was already leaning so far out of the window he fell clear as the carriage was pushed off the track and out into the middle of the ravine. He was aware of being pushed out into space, and then falling in what seemed to be a slow, lazy manner. It was as though his eyes were floating in the air, watching the body which had once been attached to them tumble down the side of the mountain. He was flailing desperately with his arms, trying to swim his way back to land, and the effort must have been successful, for he crashed against the rocky cliff with a force which winded him: cracking his ribs, dislocating a shoulder.

For a little while longer he continued to slither downwards while his clothes and flesh were cut to shreds by knife-edge ridges. The train had disappeared, twisting outwards and looping over like the tail of a swooping kite before plunging down to the bottom of the ravine: he had heard the screams of the passengers merge and fade in a single high-pitched note, but could spare no attention for that. All his energies were directed to the need to find something to check his fall.

It came in the form of a lower section of the railway track. His bruised or broken arms were not strong enough to allow him a grip, but one foot caught in the rail. He heard the snap of yet another bone but miraculously, after it, was still. His eyes closed in relief and exhaustion.

Only slowly and fitfully did he regain consciousness some time later. There were moments when he felt on the brink of understanding what had happened, only to sense it slipping away again. There was no pain. Indeed, his body still seemed to be floating in the air, as though he were suffering from an extreme form of altitude sickness. If he kept very still, perhaps he would acclimatise and be able to place his feet steadily on the ground again.

133

Little by little he emerged from the solace of unconsciousness. Where was he? What had happened? He tried to move his legs, but there was no connection between the brain which issued the order and the muscles which should have obeyed it. His shoulders were resting on the low, narrow embankment beside the rail which had trapped his foot; his head hung out in space. There was nothing wrong with his eyes and he could see at once that if he tried to move he would be in danger of hurtling thousands of feet down.

How long would it be before anyone realised that there had been an accident? The train was not due to reach Lima for another two or three hours – and Peru was an unpunctual country. A delay of a further hour or so would hardly be noticed. Then more time would be lost while rescuers were found and transported to the scene. The train in its fall might well have crashed through some of the lower bridges. So how would they travel, if the railway line was broken? Would anyone have ropes long enough for helpers to be lowered from above? And soon it would be dark. They would have to wait until next day. For how many hours could he expect to survive, injured and without oxygen, losing blood from his many cuts, exposed to the air at an altitude of thirteen or fourteen thousand feet? Although at that moment the sun was shining brightly, Tony felt his blood chill at the realisation that he was going to die.

He shouted, over and over again; but if there was any response he could not hear it. He tried to raise and turn his head so that the narrow ledge would support it; but without success. It was hard to believe that this could be happening to Tony Fiori. He was only thirty-three years old. He was so rich that he could charter a fleet of helicopters or whatever else was needed for a rescue if only there were some means of communication. He had advisers and helpers to smooth his path all over the world – except here. He had always enjoyed the gift of finding solutions to problems: but this problem was too big for him.

Time passed, and his hour of clear vision ended. It became a struggle to remain conscious, and he found himself groaning although he still felt no pain. Over and over again as darkness fell he repeated his daughter's name. Isabella. Isabella. What would happen to Isabella? By the time the sun next rose she would have become the richest child in the world. Would her wealth make her happy? Would it compensate for the fact that neither her mother nor her father had proved able to make a home for her?

Andrew would become her guardian. Andrew would look after her. Although reluctant, he had promised, and Andrew never broke promises. By now Tony was becoming delirious. His mind was tying itself in knots and he remembered that other special knot with which two schoolboys had tied their fingers together once. The Tantivy Twist. Neither of the two could free himself from the promises they had made then until the other first let go.

Now Tony was being forced to let go. Andrew would be free. But Andrew could be trusted. If only Andrew were here now – anywhere in Peru – he wouldn't allow his friend to die. He would mobilise the Peruvian army and air force if necessary to search the mountainside inch by inch.

What was the point in thinking like that? Andrew was half a world away, with no reason to worry about someone who was not expected to arrive in Europe for another forty-eight hours. The days were long gone when ten-year-old Craig had been appointed as the shepherd of eight-year-old Fiori.

'It's my job to look after you for your first two weeks,' Andrew had said. 'So you can ask me any questions you like and I'll show you where you have to go and what

135

you're supposed to do. And if you break any of the school rules, then I have to do the punishment for you, so you'd jolly well better not. It's only for the first fortnight, though. After that you're on your own.'

Andrew's voice had been stern and he had frowned ferociously to show that there was to be no nonsense. Nevertheless, that first fortnight at Tantivy had in a sense extended itself for twenty-five years. But it was coming to an end now. Tony was indeed on his own.

2

Would the drive never end? In other circumstances Sara would have lingered to enjoy the panorama of the hills whose rocky heads and grassy shoulders rose above autumn skirts of bronze bracken – so different in scale from the snow-capped Colorado mountains which provided a distant backdrop to her New Mexico home. She might have stopped to listen to the musical flow of swift burns over smooth grey rocks or to the splash of waterfalls. She would certainly have stood quietly for a few moments to breathe in the peace of the loch, its calm surface broken only by a scattering of low islets. The sun was setting, and a mist rose gently to carpet the lower glen while more distant ranges of mountains softened into different shades of grey. It was a beautiful scene, but she had no eyes for it.

This had been a day of wrong decisions. Before ever leaving the United States she ought to have searched for a flight which would bring her to Prestwick rather than Heathrow, and found a domestic connection to it. When she did at last have the sense to study a map, at London Airport, her destination seemed almost equidistant from Glasgow and Edinburgh; but she realised now that she should have waited for a Glasgow shuttle instead of choosing the Edinburgh flight just because it could offer a seat immediately. On arrival, she should have insisted that the car hire company found her a vehicle with automatic gearbox. As it was, every traffic hold-up as she struggled out of the city and every approaching car along the present single-track lane sent her fumbling to change gear with an unaccustomed hand. She should – well, she shouldn't have made the journey in the first place, but instead should have stayed in New Mexico. What else were telephones for?

The trouble with a telephone was that you couldn't force anyone to give you a straight answer. It was too easy for a faceless voice to pass you on or cut you off. In a flurry of international calls before leaving the commune she had discovered that she was not going to be given any information. Her name was not on the need-to-know list. Whether from embassies or police headquarters, the answer was always the same: you must speak to Andrew Craig.

But where was Andrew Craig? Italy and England had pointed her to Peru; but Peru had passed her from office to office through what must surely be one of the world's worst telephone systems before announcing that he had left the country for the United Kingdom three hours earlier.

Only two of the voices had been helpful. The address she had for the Craigs proved to be out-of-date. They had moved two years earlier, said the present owner of the house in Weybridge; but if she would hang on for a moment the present address and telephone number could be dug out of an old diary. And when, armed with this, Sara had called the number of Kilcraigie Castle, a soft Scottish voice had regretted that none of the family was at home to take the call. But Mr Craig was expected late that night: would the lady care to ring again next morning?

That would have been the sensible thing to do. But by then Sara had lost track of time and time zones. Her nature had always been an impatient one, although she was doing her best to calm it down to the leisurely pace of the commune. She was simply not capable of sitting and doing nothing even at the best of times; and this was the worst of times. If nine or ten hours had to be killed before she could speak to Andrew, she might as well use them to get herself on to the same side of the Atlantic.

How much further could it be? She could not be lost, for the signs now pointed only to Kilcraigie and she had been told, when she stopped at the last village, that the road ended there, at the head of the loch. Why had Andrew chosen such an out-of-the-way place in which to live? And how had he been able to afford a castle? She supposed that Hilary's parents must have died; for, although she had never met them, she remembered that they had some kind of title. Neither the questions nor the answers were important. She was merely trying not to think about anything that mattered.

For the past five miles or so a hill which rose steeply from the water had obstructed her view of the end of the loch, which curved round behind it. Now, as she drew level with the hill, she was able to see past it – and braked with astonishment so sharply that the car stalled, blocking the narrow road. But there was no other traffic within miles. She allowed herself time to stare.

It was a real castle – a storybook castle with turrets and battlements. What else could she have expected from the name – a suburban condominium with ideas above its station? Of course not: but she had assumed that she was approaching a family house. What she saw now was a ruin.

It stood on what at first sight looked like an island, but which, as she drove slowly on, proved to be a rocky peninsula extending from the foot of the glen into the water. The ragged curtain walls enclosed a considerable area. Within them rose the remains of halls and towers, all in a state of collapse. No one could possibly be living here. Only as she rounded the end of the loch did another building appear, later in date than the fortifications on the peninsula. It stood a little higher up the hill, with its garden dropping in a series of terraces to the level of the water.

The house was large. One wing was sheltered by the hill and another stretched out into the glen. Behind them, in the centre, rose an incongruous round tower whose massive masonry walls linked it to the ruins rather than to the more modern castle which had incorporated it. The clash of styles was ugly and the lack of any sign of life gave the building, in the fading light, a forbidding appearance. It still didn't make sense that Andrew and Hilary should live in a place like this. But that was none of Sara's business. Leaving the car near the water's edge she climbed six curving flights of steps and tugged at the bell chain which hung beside a double wooden door.

There was a long wait before a smaller door cut out of the large one opened. A woman wearing an apron stood there, her arm stretching across the gap in a manner as unwelcoming as the grim appearance of the house.

'Have you missed your way?'

'No. Not if this is Kilcraigie Castle. I'm come to see Mr Andrew Craig.'

'Then you've wasted your journey, for he's not here.'

'I called from America,' said Sara, before remembering that the British phrased things differently. 'On the telephone. Was it you I spoke to? I was told that Mr Craig would be home here tonight. Has he not arrived yet?'

The woman shook her head.

'But you're expecting him still?'

'Aye.'

'Could I wait for him in the house, do you think?'

The woman hesitated and was perhaps about to agree. But a man – her husband, no doubt, suspicious of unexpected callers – appeared protectively at her shoulder. 'We canna let a stranger in with the family away,' he said.

'I'm an old friend of his. I've come all the way from America to see him. There's an emergency. I must speak to him at once.'

'Ye'll still be needing to bide till he comes. We have our instructions.' The man turned away to indicate the end of the conversation, but his wife's expression softened.

'From America is it? Will I make you a cup of tea?'

'That would be kind.' The drink was not to Sara's

taste, but it surely would not be brought to her on the doorstep.

As she had hoped, the door was opened for her to step inside. She found herself in a very large and high hall. The only conventional articles of furniture it contained were two long wooden benches, a refectory table and a long-case clock. But near the entrance door stood three small tricycles of identical size but different colours and, at the further end, standing on a square of carpet, was a climbing frame, wide although not very tall, which incorporated a low slide, three swings and a see-saw.

These objects, inappropriate·in themselves and quite out of scale with the height of the hall, were visually jarring, but their effect upon Sara was devastating in a different way. She hardly noticed the brusqueness with which she was pointed to one of the long benches which stood against a wall and guarded by the man while his wife disappeared. She had been thrown into a state of shock by this reminder that Andrew and Hilary were enjoying a happy family life with their three surviving children – children who were growing up and would continue to grow, secure in their parents' love – while she . . . while she . . . She began to cry, and hardly noticed when a cup and saucer were put into her hands.

The man disappeared through a door and his wife sat down on the facing bench.

'Should you be wanting a bed for the night,' she said, 'there's Mrs Hay at Callander. I could telephone for you.'

Sara dried her eyes. 'No thank you,' she said coldly. She had passed through Callander earlier and could not face the thought of returning along the lonely road. Although Andrew had naturally taken Tony's side during the separation and divorce proceedings, he would understand her feelings during this new emergency and would certainly offer her hospitality as soon as he arrived.

But when would that be? Three hours later she was still sitting on the bench. Across the hall, the woman too sat unmoving, her hands folded on her lap as she made it clear by her silence that no stranger could be trusted to be left alone on the premises. By now Sara had ceased to resent that. Her arms were tightly crossed over her chest and her head was bent low. Moaning faintly, she rocked herself backwards and forwards, just as she had done for hours on end three years earlier, while the whole Italian nation searched for a little boy who was starving to death. But she was not thinking about that time. She was merely waiting for Andrew to come home.

3

Sara had been waiting for almost four hours before a sudden flurry of activity told her that the master of the house had arrived. The woman who had been keeping watch over her moved swiftly towards the kitchen quarters as her husband hurried through the hall, switching on lights before disappearing outside. He returned a few minutes later carrying two suitcases, which he set down near the refectory table. Sara rose to her feet and waited for Andrew to appear.

She had not seen him since he lived as their guest in New York in 1970 while familiarising himself with the range of Tony's business activities. She remembered him as a very tall young man, always well-groomed and neatly dressed and concealing the serious and sharp intelligence for which Tony had hired him beneath an easy-going manner.

What she saw now was not the same person. He even seemed to have shrunk, as though his backbone had given up the effort to support him. His clothes were crumpled and his face was haggard with exhaustion. Tony had looked like this once, she remembered, when . . . but she had promised herself that she would not think about Georgie today.

Andrew moved stiffly; so tired, it seemed, that he could hardly put one foot in front of the other. Even in his present stooped condition he was much taller than Sara, and his eyes were fixed on some distant point above her head. Although she was standing straight in front of him, it appeared that he was not aware of her presence until he was on the point of bumping into her. Even then it took a few seconds before recognition came into his eyes.

He had only known her, of course, as a woman who was always well-dressed and well-groomed. Now she wore her long black hair in a thick Indian pigtail, and her home-sewn dress was made of cotton which had been woven and dyed on the commune.

'Sara! What are you doing here?'

'Waiting to talk to you.'

'Yes, of course; you've heard.' He looked around in a vague manner, as though his eyes could not focus properly. 'Come up.' He led the way upstairs to a drawing room as baronial in scale as the great hall. Like the hall, too, it was underfurnished, containing two sofas and as many chairs as would be needed for a normal family and its friends, but not enough to fill the space. The room was not so much shabby as unfinished. It was perhaps this impression of emptiness which drew Sara's eye at once to an envelope propped up on the mantelpiece above the wide recessed fireplace. She gasped with surprise and made what must surely be the most inappropriate comment in the circumstances.

'That looks like the kind of letter in which a wife tells her husband that she's left him!'

Andrew gave her a curious look. To him, of course, she was the woman who had deserted his friend. He sighed impatiently, indicating that he did not have to explain his movements to her but saw that it would save time to do so.

'Hilary's father is very ill. He's a widower, and he was due to come out of hospital last Saturday. We'd all arranged to go down and live in the house for a week or two, to look after him. When I flew off to Peru – you guessed, I imagine, that that's where I've been – I told Hilary to take Nanny and the girls and go ahead even if I wasn't back in time. Promised I'd join them as soon as I could. This – ' He opened the envelope as he spoke – 'This is just to say that she's done exactly that.'

144

He handed Sara the note as though she had some right to confirm that he was telling the truth. It was an odd thing to do; but neither of them was behaving normally. She had no real interest in Hilary's movements, but glanced at the note out of politeness. With more interest she stared at the four photographs which stood on the massive stone mantelpiece. Andrew and Hilary on their wedding day. Hilary sitting on a sofa holding three babies in long christening robes. An informal snapshot of Hilary with three toddlers crawling all over her. And what must be a recent birthday photograph of three neat little girls in smocked party dresses and white socks and shoes. Lucky Hilary. Lucky Andrew.

'I had to speak to you, Andrew,' she said, turning back to face him. 'To find out . . . You're the only person who can understand . . .'

He nodded: too tired, it seemed, to offer sympathy.

'If you want to get any sense out of me, Sara, you'd better leave it till tomorrow. I'm flaked out. Haven't been to bed for four days and I've never got the hang of sleeping on aeroplanes. Have a seat. What would you like to drink: whisky or coffee?'

'Coffee, please. Black.' Sara had never been much of a drinker, and spirits were taboo in the commune.

He pressed a bell and asked his housekeeper to bring coffee. In the meantime he poured himself a whisky and water.

Sara sank into a sofa. 'I didn't know you'd moved,' she said – not because the subject interested her, but in order to keep to small talk until there was no danger of further interruption from the housekeeper.

'It was Tony's idea. At the time when he set up the Fiori Foundation a couple of years ago. There was no particular reason for its offices to be in London and some quite good arguments for tucking them quietly away. Not much danger here of importunate paupers arriving on the doorstep, or even of charity directors continually inviting me out to lunch.'

Sara nodded her understanding. There had been a good deal of publicity at the time about the arrangement under which Tony had transferred half his fortune to a charitable trust. The endowment had taken the form of shares in Tony's holding company, and the terms of the trust were unusual in that it was allowed to make seed investments in projects thought by the trustees to be worthy of support, however high the risk. It was made clear at the time that Prince Antonio Fiori would personally work to increase the assets of the trust, as well as being a member of the international panel of trustees who decided how its funds should be spent. Andrew Craig had been appointed Director of the Foundation, in charge of administration.

'Don't tell me he picked this part of the world, though. Had he ever been here?'

'His mother's family came originally from Scotland, you know. And yes, he did come once, when he was about ten. He spent a half-term holiday with my mother and me. He'd already started this thing about collecting railway journeys. There was something special about the railway line on Mull. Narrow gauge, perhaps: I don't remember exactly. Mother took him there for a treat. And we stopped off in this area on the way. My father was born in this part of the world: she wanted to show me.'

'This castle?'

'Goodness, no. Nothing so grand. But from that time Tony knew that I had a sentimental feeling for the area. And that Hilary is a great one for country life. So he was the first to suggest it, yes. And when it came to moving, a house in Weybridge proved to be worth rather more than a ruin in Scotland. That meant that I could pay for the domestic part, and the Foundation chipped in enough to restore one wing to act as offices. Ah, coffee. Thank you, Margaret. Is the guest room aired?'

'No. If the lady's staying, I'd best put the clean sheets on Nanny's bed.'

'If you would. Thank you very much. And then don't wait up any later.' He turned to Sara. 'Black, you said.'

'Thank you.'

Now at last they could talk. Sara opened her mouth, ready to pour out her unhappiness, but Andrew spoke first.

'He's dead, I'm afraid, Sara. You probably heard the same kind of news release that I did. "Millionaire missing." That kind of thing. I hoped that perhaps . . . But there were no survivors.'

It was not Tony's death which had brought Sara to Scotland, but she could recognise Andrew's need to talk about it.

'What was he doing in that place?' She had never heard the name Huancayo until three days earlier and had forgotten it already.

'I imagine he just went for the ride. A railway line going up the side of a mountain. An almost impossible piece of engineering. Just the sort of journey that he liked to sort-of collect.'

Sara nodded, knowing this to be true. 'And there was an accident?'

'That's the official story. I don't believe it's true. There's some kind of bandit organisation which hangs out in the mountains and is trying to fight the government on behalf of the peasants. One way they do it is to frighten off the tourists who bring in foreign capital. Not that this was primarily a tourist train, but one of the passengers from the journey up could have told them about the rich gringo who was going straight back down again. A senseless business. I don't suppose anyone will ever prove anything – or even try very hard. Doesn't matter much. The train came off the track and Tony died. I – ' His voice trembled and he stared down at the glass clutched in his hands. 'I saw his body.'

There was a pause in which Andrew was obviously unable to speak. Sara was still longing to raise the subject which had brought her here, but forced herself to give him a moment longer in which to grieve for his friend. She herself had also mourned for Tony until the later and more terrifying news arrived – because after the brief attempt at reconciliation, their marriage had ended in a helpless sadness rather than bitterness, and there had been no further quarrels.

She could restrain herself no longer. 'What's happening, Andrew? I need to know what's going on. I've tried the embassy, the police, and no one would tell me.'

'Going on?' He looked bemused. 'Well, I've arranged for Tony's body to be flown direct to Italy, to be buried in the family mausoleum. There are a lot of formalities, of course, but – '

'I don't mean about Tony. Is – ' Her voice choked over the word, so that only a croak emerged. 'Is – '

'Is what?'

'Isabella? What's happening about Isabella?'

4

For a second time during their conversation Andrew looked perplexed. Then he appeared to understand.

'Isabella will be well looked after. Tony set up a guardianship arrangement a couple of years ago, just in case. For the moment, well, she's only three. There's no need for her to learn yet that her father's dead. I'll fly out in a few days, when I've had a chance to rest.'

'What are you talking about?' Sara could feel her voice rising to a scream. 'Don't you know what's happened?'

'Is there something else? I told you, I've been on the move for days. In the air for thirty-six hours.'

'But surely –' She took a grip on herself and forced her voice to pronounce the words. 'Isabella's been kidnapped.'

'What!' The whisky glass fell from Andrew's hands and spilt its contents on the carpet. He stood up, towering above her. 'Tell me!'

'She's been living at the Villa dell'Isola. I expect you knew: Tony decided that would be healthier for her than New York. She was snatched from her nursery. Together with her nurse. Taken off in a speedboat, the police think. The day after the news came through about Tony being missing. They, the kidnappers, left a ransom note. But the thing is –' Sara began to cry – 'the boat was found smashed at the other end of the lake. So nobody knows . . . The police have got divers down there, but it's very deep, and . . . and they won't tell me more than that.'

'Oh, my God!' Andrew paced up and down the room several times before coming to a halt in front of her. 'Sara, I'm so sorry. And at a time like this, when you must still be upset about Tony.'

'I can't go through it all again. I can't. I can't.' She knew that she was becoming hysterical, but was unable to control herself. 'All that waiting and hoping and fearing and then in the end nothing. I'd rather kill myself now and get it over.'

'Steady. Steady.' Andrew pulled her up into his arms and held her tightly. 'Tony believed that you didn't love Isabella,' he said softly. 'But I always felt – '

'I didn't love her as I ought to have done. I didn't want to watch her growing up. I would have been frightened all the time that what has happened was going to happen. But she was part of my body. Her flesh is my flesh. Whatever is happening to her is happening to me. I can't bear it, Andrew. What am I going to do?'

'You're going to sleep.'

'But there must be something we can do.'

'No. If the police are on the job, we must leave them to it. They'll have been in touch with Tod, John Todhunter, since they couldn't get hold of me. He's another of Isabella's guardians.'

'So you're one as well?'

'Yes. But I'm not going to start interfering now. I must get some sleep, just as you must, otherwise I shan't be fit for anything in the morning. Come on. I'll show you the way.'

Staggering with tiredness and misery, she allowed herself to be led upstairs.

'A bit basic, I'm afraid. We need notice before we can put anyone into a guest room. Everything here gets damp so quickly.' He hesitated for a moment. 'Hilary and I never have much problem getting to sleep when we're at home,' he said. 'All I can offer you in that line is some junior aspirin which we've used at teething time. But perhaps you've got something yourself?'

She nodded as she unzipped the cabin bag which was her only luggage. She had used a prescription sleeping pill for the Atlantic flight. To her surprise, she saw that Andrew was holding out his hand for the bottle.

'Are you afraid I'm going to take an overdose?' she asked. It was a foolish question. Obviously he was.

'I do know that it's easy to take a couple of tablets and then, when you're drowsy, forget that you've had them and take some more.' He read the instructions on the bottle, handed her the correct dose and put the bottle in his pocket.

Sara's sleep that night was full of horrors. Sometimes she was falling through the sky, sometimes sinking through water. Always at the last minute she pulled up with a jerk which should have awakened her: but the sleeping pills were stronger than the nightmares, and the falling and the terror began again. Not until morning did she awaken with a cry to find herself drenched with sweat and shivering with cold or fear.

Groping for her watch, she found that it was six o'clock. She needed still more sleep, but could not find it: perhaps it was her spirit rather than her body which was exhausted. More specifically, though, she wanted a drink of water. Andrew had not noticed the lack of a glass. Quietly, in order not to wake him, she made her way down the cold stone staircase.

She need not have worried about disturbing her host, for he was already downstairs and speaking into the telephone. He spoke in Italian, and automatically she began to translate it as she paused to listen. His command of the language was more fluent and idiomatic than hers, but she could follow what he said well enough. Clearly he was talking to the police, asking what progress they had made, what he could do to help, whether he should travel at once to Italy.

One sentence in particular struck straight to Sara's heart, carrying her back once more to that terrible time when they were negotiating for Georgie's release. Tony had asked her to prepare a list of questions which could be answered by the little boy himself but not by any stranger; questions whose answers would prove that he was still alive. Now Andrew was suggesting similar questions. What was the name of Isabella's kitten, her favourite doll? Sara's grief was increased by guilt as she realised that she could not herself have provided the correct answers.

Did this conversation mean that negotiations for paying the ransom had already begun? That Isabella was certainly alive? With half of her mind Sara longed to know; but the other half had cut itself off. She could not go through all that agony again. There must be some way in which she could pretend that none of this had anything to do with her. Still dry-mouthed, but forgetting her search for a drink of water, she sat down on the stairs and buried her head in her hands.

Isabella is dead. Isabella is dead. She repeated the words silently over and over again. If she could say them often enough, until she believed them, the confirmation, when it came, would be less of a shock. If the statement proved not to be true, there would be a moment of marvellous relief instead; but she did not allow herself to expect that.

As part of the attempt to convince herself that there was no hope, she began to wonder what would happen to Tony's immense fortune now. The Fiori Foundation would presumably keep its generous endowment, but there must still be many millions left. He would undoubtedly have bequeathed them to Isabella, although probably to be tied up in trusts until she came of age. Had his daughter died before him he would have had time to remake his will. But because she had survived him by a few days the money must have become hers, to be distributed as her fortune and not Tony's. Had Tony thought of that and inserted something in the trust deeds to cover every situation? Yes, he must have done. Or at least, it would have been Andrew who would have made the necessary provisions. Trusts were Andrew's speciality.

It was at that moment that a suspicion began to grow in Sara's mind. She was not a grasping woman and knew that she was the one who had destroyed the marriage. Although she could not remarry while Tony was still alive, she had recognised long ago that religion played little part in his life and that he would want to marry again; and so had not been surprised when he obtained a civil divorce a few months earlier. She had signed without hesitation the clause in the settlement in which she renounced all further claim on her husband's estate and agreed that any attempt to contest any will or other disposition of his assets in the future would result in the forfeiture of the generous sum which he had already set aside for her. At the time she had assumed that the chief beneficiaries of her agreement would be Isabella and any children of a future second marriage.

It was Andrew who had drafted that forfeiture clause as well. It was Andrew who must know now into whose hands the Fiori fortune would fall if Isabella's small body was indeed lying at the bottom of the lake. Would those hands be his own?

It was an unworthy thought. She tried to shake it away, but failed. Instead, that one unfounded suspicion gave place to a second and far more terrifying possibility. Suppose that Andrew did believe himself to be Tony's ultimate heir if Isabella were out of the way. Could he have planned all this himself? Could he have arranged for her to be murdered under the guise of a kidnapping? Had he been genuinely surprised when she told him that Isabella had been snatched away, or was he only pretending?

She shivered with horror at the direction her thoughts were taking. This was an impossible scenario. Andrew Craig was an ordinary, upright family man. But then, wasn't that true of many murderers, that no one could believe them capable of their crimes until they were proved beyond doubt?

Stop it, Sara, she told herself. Tony's best friend could not possibly have behaved in such a way. So little did Andrew care for wealth that Hilary had often grumbled affectionately in the past about the stubbornness with which he clung to his Civil Service career when he could have earned so much more as a free-lance consultant.

Ah, but that was when he was first married. Tony had not found much difficulty in cajoling his friend into the acceptance of a higher salary. Had Andrew perhaps felt the first stirrings of envy and greed when he was brought into such close contact with great wealth? Becoming a father made a difference as well. A man might want for his children what he did not consider important for himself.

Impatiently Sara shook away these thoughts, which were galloping out of control without the slightest justification. Emerging from her flight of fantasy, she became aware by a change in Andrew's voice that he must have ended one call and dialled a second number.

'Hilary! Just to say I'm back home, darling. Got back in the middle of the night, but I didn't want to disturb you then. Reckoned I was safe in assuming that our little horrors would have woken you at six o'clock as usual. How's your father?'

As he listened to the answer, Sara stood up and began to make her way slowly back up the stairs, moving far enough round the curve to be out of sight of anyone emerging from the drawing room, but not so far that she could no longer hear. By the time she began to listen again, his voice was sombre.

'I'm afraid so, darling. When I phoned from Lima I'd only got as far as establishing that he wasn't in the wreckage of the train. But they found his body higher up the track. Yes, senseless. When you think of all the precautions he took against being attacked personally, and then this, which doesn't seem to have had anything to do with him as an individual at all! I know it's as bad for you as it is for me. I wish I had something more cheerful to say, but . . . And now there's this business of Isabella. Has it been reported in the papers here? Incidentally, Sara arrived at Kilcraigie last night.'

To Sara, listening furtively, there was something wrong with the inflection of that last statement. Almost as though he knew she were eavesdropping. Almost as though he were giving his wife some kind of warning. But his voice, when he spoke again, was normal enough.

'I'll tell her, yes. As for going to Italy, I'm not sure yet. There's nothing practical I can do there. If there's any question of providing money for a ransom, Tod and I will both have to sign the releases. But of course, unlike the Georgie affair, this has been a police matter from the start, so there'll be no question of using any funds in Italy. It's just as likely that I'll need to go to Liechtenstein. Anyway, I've given the Italian police your father's phone number as well as this one. I'll hope to be over later in the day. I'll phone Tod as soon as the hour is more civilised, and if there's any change after I've spoken to him I'll let you know. But there is one other thing, Hilary.'

This time the pause was of a different kind. He was not listening to the other voice on the line, but marshalling his own thoughts.

'Tony wrote you a letter. No, it was tucked away in his passport. No, I haven't read it. I'll bring it with me. But it will upset you, so I wanted to give you warning. It's – well, it's covered with blood, you see. Yes, well, as soon as I can. Love you, darling. 'Bye.'

Sara hurried upstairs and did not reappear until she was dressed. Andrew, deep in thought, was staring out of the drawing-room window over the ruined castle walls and the loch beyond. He turned, startled, when she greeted him.

'I thought you'd want longer to sleep.'

She shook her head. 'My internal time-clock is ticking the day away. The opposite of jet-lag. Andrew, I must go out to Italy, to be on the spot. Yesterday, when I tried to find out what was happening, no one would tell me. First of all it was only Tony they'd talk to, and when they found out what had happened, it was you.'

'It's a sensible precaution, to have a single name. One might get some rookie policeman giving away information to the actual kidnappers if there wasn't a set of rules.'

'But I'm her mother, for God's sake!' Sara felt her voice sliding upwards again into the high pitch of hysteria and bit her lip in an effort at self-control. 'Andrew, all this time I've tried to pretend that I don't care, that Isabella has nothing to do with me, but it's not true. I brought her into the world. Any pain she's suffering is my fault. I can't just do nothing.'

'But it's the best thing, Sara. You said last night that you couldn't go through the business of hoping and fearing again, and you were right then. Nothing that you do now is going to make the slightest difference. If she's dead already, that's a fact which can't be changed by your fears. If she's alive, we shall get her safely back for money, but your hopes will make no difference. I'm sorry that it's all happened so publicly. It would have been better for you not even to know.'

'But I do know, and I can't pretend that I don't. All I need is an authority from you, so that I can go out to Italy and be told what's going on.'

'It's not a good idea for you to be on the spot, Sara.'

'Why not, for heaven's sake? If they find her – '

'Isabella hasn't seen you for years. She wouldn't recognise you. I even wonder whether you'd recognise her.'

'Oh, for Christ's sake! Are you crazy? My own daughter.'

'How long is it since you last shared a home with her? From what Tony said, you didn't see much of her even then. You've abdicated any right to weep for your daughter, Sara. If she needs to be comforted by someone familiar, one of her nursemaids would be better.'

'You're very cruel.'

'Yes, well, I didn't mean to say all that. Sorry. That wasn't the point I was intending to make. Isabella has presumably been kidnapped by men who didn't know at the time that her father was dead. They would have expected a loving father to rush forward with whatever money they asked. Already they're having to think again and plan a new strategy.'

'That makes it all the more important that they should know there's someone else who cares. Otherwise they might – they might kill her.'

'Why should they do that when they've put so much effort into planning and committing a crime? The child is still a valuable hostage. In a sense, it could be easier for them to get what they want from Tod and me because it isn't our own money that we'll be signing away. They can negotiate with us in an impersonal, business-like way. No emotion. That's why I'm not going to rush off to Italy straightaway, and that's why you must stay out of it as well. You have no rights, Sara.'

The firmness of his voice frightened her, building a wall between them which she could not pass. Until yesterday all her meetings with Andrew had been in Tony's company, and he had always been smiling; but he was not smiling now.

'How can you be so cold?' she asked bitterly. 'If it were your own child – '

'Tony made me promise once that I would do everything I could to protect Isabella's interests,' he told her. 'I've kept that promise and I shall go on keeping it. If Isabella is still alive, I shall do whatever is best for her. And I shall continue to belive that she's alive until somebody proves to me that she isn't. Tony trusted me, Sara. You have to trust me as well. Perhaps I

157

shouldn't remind you of it, but did your intervention help Georgie?'

Her lips trembled as she looked up at him. When Georgie disappeared she had not trusted Ludo, and Ludo had died for her doubts – and Georgie too. She had not even quite trusted Tony to do the right thing, although of course his hopes and intentions were exactly the same as hers; and her moment of mistrust had destroyed their marriage. Now Tony's friend, who owed her no kind of fealty, expected her to accept his decisions without reservation. She shook her head sadly.

'I'm no good at trusting people,' she said. 'Not one of my talents. Well, I won't impose on you any longer. Thanks for the bed.'

'You're not going without a good breakfast. It'll be ready in ten minutes or so. Tell me something about the way you live. I got the impression from Tony that it was in some kind of hippy commune.'

Sara hesitated before answering, reluctant to chatter about unimportant matters. But whether she trusted Andrew or not, it would be necessary to stay in communication with him. She nodded her head – not to express agreement but to accept the change of subject.

'My father gave me a ranch as a wedding present, and I like to have people around to share. But there's nothing hippy about it. It's a creative community. In the old sense of holding things in common.'

'What creativity do you contribute yourself?'

'I pay the bills.' Her support for the community's ideals had not affected her common sense. 'Well, and I paint a little. My psychiatrist told me that I had to learn to make things and then give them away, so I paint bad pictures and find no problem at all in letting them go. It's no good, Andrew. I can't stand here and make small talk. And I've no appetite for breakfast anyway. I'll take myself off.'

'You're flying back to America?'

'No. To Milan.'

Without bothering to repeat his objections, he stared at her gravely. Earlier that morning she had tried to accept the possibility that her daughter was dead, and had failed in the attempt. Only now, as Andrew's dark eyes pierced into her own did she feel her stomach become cold and heavy with certainty. She would never see Isabella again.

5

The visit to Italy proved as futile as Andrew had suggested, and there was no comfort to be found in New Mexico either. On the first day of 1974 Sara rose early, while most members of the commune were still asleep, and drove herself north across the state border into Colorado. She stopped for breakfast at Durango, but found after placing the order that she had no appetite and could do no more than drink a glass of orange juice.

She had been to Durango once before, early in her marriage, when they first took possession of her ranch. Tony had promised her a treat, which proved to be a ride on the narrow gauge railway line to Silverton: the longest of its kind running a scheduled service on the mainland of the United States, he told her. It was her introduction to his passion for riding in trains which were by some definition unique. At the time she had laughed affectionately, and on later expeditions had teased him for indulging such an unproductive hobby. But it had proved to be no laughing matter in the end.

She paid the check and drove on towards one of the huge flat-topped mountains which punctuated the landscape. Passing between the entrance pillars of the Mesa Verde National Park she made her way along the twenty-odd miles of steep, twisting road to the top of the mesa – at first driving cautiously, in case overnight frost should have left the road slippery, but then laughing mockingly at herself. What would it matter if she were to skid down the side of the cliff a few minutes early?

The visitor centres were probably closed for the winter, but there was no need to make the detour and find out, because she knew where she wanted to go. Parking the car at Sun Point, she pulled out the canvas which, still on its stretcher, had been propped against the back seat, and leaned it against the post of an information point before walking towards the edge of the overlook.

The air was cold and thin. In the toy landscape of Scotland, where Andrew Craig lived, they called anything over three thousand feet a mountain. What would he make of scenery like this? Although the table-top of the mesa on which she stood had the appearance of a mere plateau, surrounded by far higher peaks, it was itself over seven thousand feet high. But there would have been no feeling of height had it not been for the sheer drop of the canyons which cut into the mesa. She was standing on the edge of one of them now.

Sara breathed deeply, filling her lungs with the crisp, clean air. She had returned only two days earlier from Europe, which was dirty and wet as well as being inefficient and probably corrupt. For a month she had struggled to clear a way through a fog of words as well as of climate. In the end the police had chosen Christmas Eve to tell her that they had abandoned all hope of finding her daughter alive. The investigation would naturally continue, but now as a hunt for the murderers of Isabella and her nursemaid, Sophia. Merry Christmas.

No, they had not said that. She must resist the temptation to rewrite the conversation which had left her bitter and angry and totally desolate. It was her question about the reward which had produced the most upsetting answer. She knew that a huge sum of money had been offered, but only on Christmas Eve was she told for the first time that thirty-three children had been presented to the police in attempts to claim it. Thirty-three mothers, said the police officer cynically, who were prepared to abandon their own daughters in order to give them – and themselves – a richer life.

161

'Why wasn't I allowed to see them?' Sara replayed the conversation in her head now, on the edge of the canyon. 'I might have recognised – '

'You would have been shown any who were found not to be imposters. But Signor Craig was the only one to know of a mark placed on the child's body at her father's order, so that there should never be any deception of this kind.'

'The tattoo?'

'It is important that this should not be known, in case it should be copied. We did in the end release information that such a distinguishing mark existed, and after that we were not troubled with further frauds.'

'But if Signor Craig is the only one who knows, he might have seen the mark but pretended it wasn't there. Or maybe it doesn't exist at all. He could be using this story just to make sure that Isabella is never recognised.'

Sara would never forget the look which the policeman had given her then.

'I think, principessa, it is your unhappiness and not your reason which makes such a suggestion, and it would not be wise for you ever to repeat it. Signor Craig is a gentleman of the highest integrity who has co-operated fully with our enquiry. I express my most sincere regret for your bereavement, but I suggest that you have nothing to gain by remaining in Italy.'

Andrew had bribed him. That must be the answer. Every time that thought came into her mind – as it came again now in the silence of Mesa Verde – Sara told herself that it was nonsense. The reward had been offered to the police as much as to the public, and no personal bribe could have weighed against the combination of an honestly-earned fortune and professional glory. It was as if, being robbed of anyone to love, she felt the need of someone to hate.

Could Andrew really be a villain? No doubt jealousy was at the heart of her hatred. She was jealous because he had been loyal to Tony and she had not. She was jealous because Tony had found it easier to trust his friend than his wife. In the clear air of the new year she recognised that he had probably been right. Her jealousy was based on guilt. Had she behaved as any normal mother ought to have behaved she would have made a home from which her daughter could not have been snatched. Everything that had happened was her own fault. So perhaps it was herself that she hated. It was odd that she could think so clearly and recognise which of her thoughts were true without being able to free herself of irrational emotions, wild suspicions.

Beneath her feet the night's powdering of snow was melting in the sun, although it would cling for a little longer to the ponderosas growing in the canyon's shade. The sky was as blue as on any summer day. But it was not summer, and there were no other tourists about. Since her arrival she had heard the sound of only one other automobile and that had faded away, presumably taking the road to the other side of the canyon. There was no chattering of human voices, no cries of animals, no rustlings of birds. Only, two or three thousand feet below, the faint rushing of the river which during many centuries had cut its way down through the rock to form this steep ravine.

There was a railing along the edge of the designated overlook to help tourists keep their children safe. But it had been frequently by-passed by photographers looking for a better view at their own risk: well-trodden tracks sloped downwards to the point at which the side of the canyon became a sheer cliff. There was nothing to stop her: no one would see. She paused for a moment only because there was no hurry. Tony had died on a cliff like this. In weeks of nightmares she had seen his body crashing heavily down and down, never coming to rest. Only when the dream changed and she realised that the falling body was her own had she been able to find peace in sleep.

The further side of the canyon was not far away. From

where she stood she could see its flat rock surface, similar to the sandstone platform on which she was standing now. Not far below it was a deep natural cave with a semi-circular roof and smooth floor. From this floor rose one of the sights which the tourists came in summer to see, exclaiming in wonder that something so old should be so well preserved. It was a complex of buildings – perhaps a palace but more probably a village made up of apartments stacked four storeys high.

Even the local Indian tribe, the Navajo, did not know who had constructed these many groups of buildings which were scattered throughout the canyons and had then abandoned them. They spoke only of the Anasazi, the Ancient Ones. There were no signs of attack by enemies. No one had burned or demolished the great towers. It was assumed that years of drought must have forced the once-prosperous inhabitants of these communities to migrate, leaving their homes intact behind them.

Sara had come here with Tony after the Durango railway excursion. She remembered how he had laughed at her fervent denunciation of Americans who travelled thousands of miles to goop at medieval cathedrals in Europe without even acknowledging the existence of older marvels on their own continent.

'It's a tribal thing, sweetheart,' he had argued then. 'We all like to return to our ancestral roots. Ancestral by blood, not by land. Most Americans have European blood rather than Indian, so to Europe they go. As you and I are about to do.' For Sara had been already pregnant for the first time when that conversation took place, and they had returned to Rome not long afterwards in order that Giorgio Fiori might be born in his ancestral palace.

'Oh Georgie!' cried Sara aloud, and the tears streamed down her face. She took a step forward, but then remembered the painting. As she turned back to fetch it, almost tripping over the springy carpet of sage and dwarf cedar near the car, two hands gripped her shoulders.

'Peace,' said Bridget.

'Peace,' said Stephen.

They were both members of her community, using the community's normal form of greeting. It was normal, too, that they should touch her: but not that their grips should be so firm, letting her know that she was a prisoner. She made one attempt to break away, but quickly understood that she would not be allowed to succeed. Sensing the desperate mood in which she had returned from Europe, they must deliberately have followed her.

'The devil takes the high ground for temptation,' said Bridget, a young woman with the thick flaxen hair and pink and white complexion of a china doll. 'Why don't we find ourselves somewhere to sit for a while and meditate?'

They led her away from the canyon edge and gently forced her down to sit, like them, cross-legged on the ground. She made the movements passively, but was unable to relax. Unlike many members of the community, she did not use drugs, and could approach a condition of trance only by emptying her mind of everything but her mantra. In her present over-emotional state such control was impossible and her body continued to tremble as her breath gasped out through her open mouth. It ought all to have been over by now.

The others were waiting for her to become calm before they allowed themselves to start meditating. She must tell them that it was impossible.

'I lost my husband,' she said abruptly. 'Through my own fault. Still loving him, but not enough. I blame myself for the killing of my son. And now I've lost my daughter.'

The words were received in silence at first. It was an unwritten rule of the community that those who joined it left their old lives behind. No one ever asked questions about past crimes or tragedies.

'But you have yourself.' Stephen spoke with the soft voice of a Californian. 'And your own creations. Your paintings.'

'Objects! It's all wrong.' Sara waved a hand in the direction of the cliff dwellings on the far side of the canyon. 'It's wrong that objects like these should survive, objects without souls, when people, who ought to be more important, simply disappear.'

'The objects are important too. Not necessarily to us, looking at them. But to the people who built their own kind of immortality. Every time you paint a picture – '

'I can't paint.' Sara sprang to her feet and Stephen, startled, moved quickly to stand beside her. 'All right, you fetch it,' she said, pointing in the direction of the canvas she had brought with her.

He carried it towards her, propping it up against a rock a little way away. It was a portrait of a young baby, which she had copied from the photograph fastened to the stretcher. It was a terrible painting. Stephen and Bridget stared at it without speaking for a little while.

'I reckon babies are just about *the* most difficult subjects in the world,' said Bridget at last. She was an artist herself. 'They have no necks. No strong features. And the proportion of head to body is all wrong. Something we accept in the living baby but which offends the eye in paint. You'd have found it easier to wait until a year or two later.'

'I have no later photograph.'

For the second time that morning Sara remembered a conversation with the Milan chief of police.

'Have you nothing more recent, principessa?'

'Nothing.' Tony had sent that one early photograph to entice her back from Tokyo when she deserted him for the first time. Not even an informal snapshot existed from the rest of Isabella's brief life. He had made a decision that her likeness should never be publicly known. Sara had had to pay for that decision in the scorn of a policeman unable to believe that a mother could have so little contact with her daughter. 'You make the matter very difficult for us, principessa.'

'You see what I mean,' she said now. 'I can't paint.'

'All that means is that you've chosen the wrong stream of creativity. There will be something else. Sometimes it needs a search, that's all.'

'It was my – ' Sara stopped dead. If past histories were never to be discussed in the community, any mention of a psychiatrist was even more taboo. From the way in which Stephen looked at her, however, it was easy to see that he knew what word she had suppressed. 'I was going to throw that away,' she said feebly.

'Not here, I hope.' Bridget's rosy lips pursed into a smile, as though they had never been discussing a matter of life and death. 'The litter laws in a national monument are very strict.' The atmosphere had changed. They had forced her to converse, and were telling her by their attitudes now that the moment of crisis had passed.

'I have nothing to live for,' she said.

'Then tell yourself that one life has ended and today, with the new year, a new life begins,' said Stephen. 'Why don't you and I walk down the road? I parked opposite the Cliff Palace. Give Bridget your keys and you can come home with me.'

He took her hand and led her away from the painting, away from the canyon's edge, talking as he went.

'Art as therapy isn't true art,' he told her. 'The impulse to create, in any field, has to be an absolute. An attempt at perfection, even if the attempt fails time after time, as it may if the fingers lack the skill to express what is in the soul.'

'I don't feel that impulse. I have neither the skill nor the soul.'

167

'Then you're living the wrong sort of life. What skills do you have?'

She could think of none. 'I have money,' she said bitterly.

He stopped in the middle of the road and turned to face her, still holding her hand.

'Don't mock what is a real asset,' he told her. 'You let us use your land and all of us are grateful, but all that we're creating is a way of life, a spirit of peacefulness. When we disappear, as the Ancient Ones did, we shan't leave even our habitations behind.' By now they were standing opposite the most elaborate of the canyon dwellings, which the archaeologists had named Cliff Palace; a city within a cave. They stopped to look across at it together.

'All over the world,' Stephen went on, speaking quietly, 'there are young men and women who have fire in their bellies but not much else. Artists, writers, composers who know that they have something important to give to society but need help in staying alive while they produce it.'

'So what do you suggest? That I go off and commission an opera?'

'If I were the kind of guy who made practical suggestions I wouldn't be living in the middle of New Mexico making silver ear-rings. I'm a guy who says everyone has to make his own life. Yours has come to an end, in a way. So you have to start a new one, right? I mean – I guess I shouldn't say this – you can kill yourself any time. Why do it now, when you're young and rich and beautiful and anything is possible?'

Against her will, Sara began to laugh. 'You mean that a good reason for staying alive is that you can stop whenever you choose?'

'The very best. So then there's no hurry to choose. If you can't think of anyone to love, think of someone to hate instead. There must be someone who'd like to see you out of the way. Why give them the pleasure? Spit in their eye and live till ninety.'

'I hate Andrew Craig,' said Sara. She made the statement aloud, because the name would mean nothing to her companion. 'Not because I believe he's made himself rich by fraud: I can't prove that. But because he's happy and his wife is happy and his three daughters are happy in a way that I shall never be happy again.'

'That's fine positive talking.' Stephen grinned to show that he was joking. 'Now you have everything you need for your new life. Money to give you purpose and hatred to give you backbone. Happy New Year!'

Sara shook her head in bewilderment, unsure whether she was laughing or crying at the ridiculousness of the cure she had been offered. 'Happy New Year!' she agreed.

PART THREE

1990–1991

1

When she first opened the Princess Fiori Gallery on Park
Avenue in 1977 Sara had positioned a desk for herself
inside a glass cubicle on the showroom floor. Smartly
dressed and with her black hair coiled to add height to
her petite figure, she would emerge from this at the sight
of any casual browser to enthuse about the young artists
and sculptors whose work she showed. It had taken her
a little while to become aware that she was frightening
off potential customers, but when realisation dawned she
moved her office to the open mezzanine at the top of a
spiral staircase. Now any caller who was anxious for her
opinion had to ask for it, and felt a sense of privilege when
she descended.

The same thinking lay behind the decision to use her
title in the gallery's name. She would not have traded on
it had Tony still been alive – nor, indeed, if any member
of his family had inherited it. But for at least a hundred
years there had been too many Fiori deaths and not enough
births, and the dynasty had died with Isabella. At the time
when the gallery was new and unknown, its name, like its
address, had attracted those who thought of art in terms
of European Old Masters. It was Sara's task to persuade
them, once they crossed the threshold, to apply their taste
to contemporary work and pick out the Old Masters of the
future.

The gallery made a loss, of course; but that was how
she chose to spend her income. Long before she acquired
her present expensive premises she had sought out young
artists who seemed to deserve support and had guaranteed
them a monthly cheque for three years so that they could

devote all their time to painting, with the promise of an exhibition at the end of the period. The money she handed over was a gift, not a loan, and she took only the normal gallery fee for sales from the exhibitions. But because she had an eye for talent and used a fierce interview to detect the necessary ambition and determination in her protégés, word had got around that the princess's pictures were likely to be good investments.

Once a year she held a general selling exhibition which she called 'The Privilege of Patronage' and by adroit publicity made the invitation to the private view seem a privilege in itself. The resulting scramble to purchase would have made the gallery self-supporting by the middle of the 1980s had she not as a matter of principle used the increased profits to support still more young artists.

On a June day in 1990 Sara was sitting at her desk, drafting the catalogue notes for the autumn show, when her secretary brought up the morning's batch of letters.

'Two more for the Fiori Foundation,' Karen said cheerfully. 'I'll send them the usual note.'

Sara nodded. The charity which Tony had founded soon after his son's death had been a rich one from the start, and his own death made it one of the best-endowed in the world. Its terms of reference were specific. The Fiori Foundation did not grant scholarships or purchase works of art or send food to the victims of famine. Instead it made what Tony himself had always called seed investments, allotting few grants but large ones in order that some new idea, expensive but potentially beneficial to society, might have a chance to prove itself. It followed that no individual who happened to be in need of a dollar or two had any hope of winning its support, but this did not deter those hopefuls who were aware of its huge resources but not of the restrictions placed on them.

Such individuals, failing to find any address for the Foundation itself in the United States, frequently took the next best thing out of the telephone directory. Sara never bothered to read their appeals. She had prepared a form letter which made it clear that she had no connection with the Foundation and gave the address of its Administrator. Andrew Craig would not wish to receive such applications any more than she did, but she could not be expected to care about that.

Today her session with Karen was interrupted by one of her protégées. Griselda Grier had finished her three-year sponsorship eighteen months earlier. Sara, who loved all her girls and boys, smiled with pleasure as the young woman came running up the spiral staircase.

'Have you got some more work for me to sell?'

Griselda made an apologetic face. 'Well, princess, that's what I've come to ask about. Would it bug you if I were to send just one picture somewhere else?'

'I've always made it clear that you weren't tied to giving me a sole agency. But I'm sorry to hear that you think someone else could do you better.'

'It wouldn't be a regular thing. That's why I came to ask, because I want to stick with you except for this. It's a kinda competition, I guess, though it doesn't say it quite like that. I don't suppose you'd ever have found out about me trying unless I happened to get picked, but I'd feel kinda mean going behind your back.'

'Tell me about it.'

'Well,' said Griselda, 'a guy at art school told me about this poster he'd seen. There's this exhibition which is going to tour round the world for two years. And the thing is, the only pictures they'll consider are by females between their sixteenth and their twenty-fifth birthdays. That's a real narrow category. I figure I might have a chance.'

'What would you get out of it? Of course you can put a picture in as far as I'm concerned. Don't bother yourself about that. How does it work?' Sara was always on the look-out for ways of getting more publicity for her young artists, and Griselda was not the only one who would meet the qualifications.

'There are judges in different countries who take the first look at submissions. Any paintings they pick, the artist gets a thousand dollars and all the insurance and handling charges paid. Then over in Rome, I think it is, sixty'll be put on show to start with, and each of those earns another five thousand.'

'Is it a selling exhibition?'

'Yeah. The reserves go in as the first ones come out at each change of venue. And the artist gets anything over the first six thousand that anyone pays. The other big thing is that some of the painters may get flown to wherever the exhibition is for a time.'

'To get publicity, I suppose.'

'Guess so, but the way they put it is as a special prize. People who go to see the exhibition vote for their favourite picture.'

'Sounds fun,' said Sara. 'You go in and win it. Then we can have another show here with press clippings from all over the world to quote in the catalogue. Just be sure that no one makes you sign away exclusive agency rights. It could be some pushy new gallery trying to get itself on the map. What's the name of the organiser?'

'There's no person's name. Sounds like some kind of aid organisation. The Tantivy Trust, it's called.'

'Never heard of it,' said Sara. 'But like I said, off you go and get yourself picked. Keep me in touch.'

'Sure. Thanks a lot.'

After she had gone, Sara pulled a memo pad towards her. She wrote Tantivy Trust at the head and beneath it began to list those of her girls who were of the right age and whose work might be of the necessary quality. She had thought of four when her forehead creased in a frown and she stared thoughtfully at the heading. It was true that she had never heard of the Tantivy Trust and felt confident

176

that it had no previous standing in the art world. And yet there was something familiar about the word Tantivy. An odd word, but hadn't she heard it somewhere before?

She considered the question for several moments before giving up. But the thought must have lodged in her sub-conscious mind, for early one morning, three days later, her eyes opened wide as the answer presented itself.

Tony, as a little boy, had been to a school called Tantivy. He and Andrew Craig had joked about it once, so Andrew must have been there as well.

It would be interesting, thought Sara, to know more about the Tantivy Trust.

2

Mark Lacey owed Princess Fiori a favour from six years back, when he'd been bumming his way around the Americas in what at the time he'd expected to be the gap year between school and university. This wasn't exactly the way he'd expected her to call it in, but he was happy to oblige if he could – especially since her request was accompanied by a generous cheque 'for expenses'.

The letter which arrived at his studio was straightforward enough. 'Please find out anything you can about the Tantivy Trust. Who runs it, what its address is, how much money it disburses, what the qualifications are for being helped. I enclose details of an art project it's sponsoring – too bad you're a male! Maybe it only operates in this field, but equally this could be part of a wider spread of benefits. You'll see that there's a UK Post Office box number on the leaflet, but don't just write and put the questions to the trustees directly. Get the information without letting them know that you're looking for it. And – this is important – don't mention my name. When you need more money to cover your expenses, call me.'

Playing detective was a new game, but it seemed to Mark that he might enjoy it. More to the point, he expected it to be easy. There was something called the Charity Commission, wasn't there, and presumably its records of all the trusts registered with it were open to public scrutiny. And there must surely be some way of discovering from the Post Office the address hidden behind a box number. 'Should be a doddle,' said Mark to himself cheerfully.

It was not a doddle at all. The Post Office was unhelpful. The register of charities failed to include the name he was seeking. Mark could lay on the charm when he wanted to and persuaded one of the registry clerks to take an interest in his search, but the information which she passed on to him was discouraging. Only trusts registered in England and Wales were filed at this address. The Tantivy Trust might be registered in Scotland, where there was no public access to the records. Or it might – especially if its disbursements were large and international – have its registered office somewhere else in the world. She referred him to reference books and was sorry that she could do nothing more to help.

In the third public library he tried there was a Directory of International Foundations, several years out of date. It did not list the Tantivy Trust.

Using the address on the leaflet which the princess had enclosed with her letter, he applied to enter the Tantivy Trust competition. He was, after all, an artist – and of the right age. If he signed only with initials the organisers would not be able to tell that he was of the wrong gender; and when he found out where paintings had to be delivered and who the assessor was for England, he could take it from there. But instead of being given information, he was asked for it. Not only must he fill up a detailed application form before being told what to do next: he was required to enclose a photo-copy of his birth certificate. Or rather, *her* birth certificate, for the form made it clear that only girls would be considered.

'You might as well have this,' said Mark to Emma, the young woman with whom he shared his studio, although not his life. Two years earlier, in the frantic period after the Chancellor of the Exchequer announced the imminent ending of double mortgage tax relief, they had clubbed together to buy a redundant Victorian school. Both sets of parents, and a good many of their friends, assumed them to be living together; but in fact they had agreed before they signed the contract that it would be a mistake ever to let their college friendship develop into a romantic relationship. A personal quarrel could so easily make the property arrangement unworkable that it was best not to get too involved.

It was their custom to have breakfast together, taking it in turns for a week at a time to prepare it. Both of them were larks rather than owls, anxious to start work at daybreak. It was at breakfast that Mark handed over the Tantivy Trust application form.

'Go in and win!' he said. 'I'd be interested to see any information that you get back.' Emma had already been told about his assignment, though he had obeyed the warning not to mention Princess Fiori's name.

'Are you going to give up now?'

'Well, can you think of anything else I can do?'

'Have you tried the telephone directory?'

'If they're going to so much trouble to keep themselves out of listings, they're not likely to be there.'

'Not the trust, no, but the name might be. It's not a usual sort of name. You might find yourself speaking to a member of the family who originally gave the money.'

It didn't sound a very profitable line of enquiry, but Mark could think of nothing more positive. Next time he went to the public library he made his way to the shelf of directories from all over the country.

It was a daunting sight, but he would only need to consult one page from each. And it was a help, in a way, that Tantivy didn't seem to be a personal surname. In the whole of London the name appeared just once, attached to a publisher. So perhaps the search would not take too long. He moved at speed along the row.

At the end of an hour he had collected about a dozen references, but one stood out as being more promising than the rest. There was a school called Tantivy. He looked up the details in a schools directory while he was in the library and found that it was a smallish prep school in Oxfordshire. Ringing it round, he moved it to the top of his list.

'Are you going to pretend to be a prospective parent?' asked Emma when he reported progress next day.

'At twenty-four? Hardly.'

'People have been known to become parents in their twenties,' she pointed out. 'And Tantivy may be the kind of school where you enter your son eight months before birth.'

'I don't quite see myself acting a part. I was proposing simply to phone up the bursar and ask him.'

'I thought you said you were expected to be more discreet than that.'

'True. Well.' He remained doubtful. Sherlock Holmes had never sneaked around pretending to be somebody quite different. But if the imposture was found out he could suffer nothing more than a moment's embarrassment. He telephoned the same day to make an appointment.

A week later he drove himself to Tantivy. His elderly hatchback would not support any suggestion that he could afford prep school fees, so he left it out of sight of the school buildings and approached on foot.

It was two o'clock in the afternoon: the beginning of a games period. Even if he had not known that September was the start of the school year he could have deduced it from the sight of a group of small boys receiving their first coaching in rugger. Each of them wore a brand new sports jersey which had clearly been bought to last, entirely covering the diminutive shorts beneath. Mark couldn't help smiling as he watched them bouncing around like puppies; but then his expression turned to surprise. Three of the players had pigtails and another, although short-haired, wore a fringe. Girls playing rugger! He was so surprised that it was the first comment he made when the interview began.

'Girls, yes,' agreed Mr Ogilvy, the headmaster. 'We've

been taking them for about fourteen or fifteen years now. I fear that the school's founder may be turning in his grave. But so many of our parents work abroad, and it's a considerable problem to them if they have to make arrangements for their children at different schools. We make it clear that there will be no concessions. They follow precisely the same curriculum as the boys.'

'So I shan't need to wait until my child is born before putting his name down, even if it's a her.'

'You're under a misapprehension, I think, Mr Lacey. This is another change we've made recently. There's such a demand for places here that entry is by competitive examination only. We're happy to put a name on the list when the child is three, if it seems likely that he will thrive in an intensive and competitive atmosphere, but we offer places only to those who show the promise of excellence in one field or another. Not necessarily academic.'

'I see. So there's no hurry. I'd like to ask a question about the payment of fees. It's likely that my parents will wish to make themselves responsible for this.' Until now Mark had merely been giving a false impression, but this was a whopping lie. His father was a wealthy man: a Member of Parliament, a Tory knight. But he had made it clear six years ago that any son of his who was fool enough to turn down the offer of a place at Cambridge was never to think that he could come running home for help. 'Does the school have any special arrangement? I mean, I know that some schools are charities, and others have special trusts.'

'Nothing of that sort, I'm afraid, Mr Lacey. There are various insurance schemes available, of course.'

'Yes. It's just that I felt sure I'd heard of something called the Tantivy Trust, and I wondered . . .'

'You're correct in thinking that such a trust exists, but it has nothing to do with us. Although, as a matter of fact, we have benefited from it on one occasion.'

'How did that happen if there's no connection?'

'I suppose you could say that there is a very tenuous link. We embarked on a considerable building programme about fifteen years ago and sent out an appeal to all the Old Boys. One of them – Andrew Craig, his name was: he was Head of School in 1949 – mentioned this trust to us but said it could only give money for the benefit of girls under ten years of age. This happened to be just when we had decided to become co-educational, so we were able to suggest that the Trust might contribute to the new house which was planned for the girls. In the event the Tantivy Trust was extremely generous. Andrew Craig proved to be a trustee. It was a great pleasure to us that his daughter Victoria was one of the first girls to come here. Now, even though your visit has proved to be a little premature, you'd probably like to see round the school while you're here.'

'Thank you very much.' As Mark embarked on the tour he tried to think how he could discover something about Andrew Craig. The school secretary would have a list of addresses, and there might be an Old Boys' register, but how could he get a look at it?

An alternative possibility presented itself sooner than he could have expected, when he was shown into a computer room in which a group of five boys and two girls were busily engaged.

'Every pupil has four afternoons of organised games in the week,' explained Mr Ogilvy. 'On the other three days there's the choice of individual games, community service or hobbies. All pupils are taught to use computers as part of the syllabus, of course, but at this hour of the day – ?' He looked enquiringly at the nearest boy.

'Magazine team, sir. Writing up the results of the survey.'

'Tell Mr Lacey what you mean.'

'We sent out a questionnaire, sir.' The earnest twelve-year-old addressed himself to Mark. 'To everyone who left Tantivy in the last ten years. Asking them to write down what they were good at while they were here. And what kind of jobs they've got now. And whether there's a connection. I mean, there were other questions as well, but those are the ones that we're trying to put together for a feature.'

'Can you show me?' asked Mark. This was a chance not to be missed. 'What was the name you mentioned, for example?' He looked towards the headmaster but did not wait for an answer. 'Yes. Victoria Craig. What does the computer say about Victoria Craig?'

He waited impatiently while the boy typed in the name. The first section of information came up in coded form, and he was glad of the translation.

'She was good at maths. She won the school maths prize two years running. And she does use maths in her job now because she works for an advertising agency and she's always having to work out percentages and do things with statistics.'

There was no address on the screen. But Mark didn't mind, for something else which could not be encoded – the name of the agency – stared out at him from the screen. He had found the clue for which he had hoped. The Tantivy Trust was somehow connected to Andrew Craig. Andrew Craig was the father of Victoria Craig. And Victoria Craig worked for Trent, Oddy, Palmer and Shaw.

3

'Vicki arrived yet?'

Mark didn't wait for an answer as he strode confidently on up the gang plank of the pleasure boat. He had learned long ago that confidence – plus, of course, the basic information about time and date – was all that was needed to gatecrash a party. It helped, naturally, that he was young and reasonably good-looking and willing to make lively conversation. Even when his hosts suspected that he wasn't on their list they didn't necessarily challenge someone who would help the evening to go with a swing.

Nobody at tonight's bash was likely to be suspicious, though. Trent, Oddy, Palmer and Shaw, better known as TOPS, was entertaining some of its clients. The clients would not know each other and the agency staff would have met only the representatives of the particular accounts they handled.

Punctually at half-past six the *Lady Lucy* cast off from Westminster Pier and set sail for Greenwich. Champagne corks were already popping and the music was not yet loud enough to drown conversation. Mark moved from group to group, asking questions and listening with interest to the answers, before addressing himself to someone who worked for the agency with a casual enquiry.

'Which is Victoria Craig? We've corresponded, but never actually met.'

'Over there. The blonde in the bright green spectacles. Let me introduce you.'

'Don't bother, thanks. There's no hurry, and she can't get away.'

He had noticed the girl as soon as he came aboard. She

was not a natural blonde – and had left her thick eyebrows brown to prove it – but that was a point in her favour. Anyone could wear the hair colour she was born with, but it took someone with a self-critical eye to sum up her own character and create the right look to go with it. She had not chosen the uncombed tangle which was the modern equivalent of the fluffy blonde, nor the long swinging straightness of all the shampoo advertisements. Instead, she had strained the fair hair back and plaited it from the top of her head in a style at once sporting and sophisticated.

Her dress, while suitable to the occasion, carried sophistication over the top and into flamboyance. She was wearing emerald green cuffed shorts over ribbed black tights. A lattice of beads hung round her neck and another round her waist: in between them, a sparkling green and black band of some elasticated material clung tightly, provocatively both concealing and outlining her breasts. Her figure was young and athletic; her skin was perfect. Victoria Craig was not a beauty, but she was a dish.

He gave only the briefest of glances in her direction as she was pointed out to him now, but it was enough to attract her attention. Sensing that she was under discussion, she looked straight at him and their eyes met. That would be enough, Mark reckoned. He accepted a refill of his glass and took it up to the higher, open deck. He was leaning on the rail when he heard her approach.

'Dangerous, crashing a river party.' Her voice was cool and pleasant, with just the faintest touch of a Scottish accent. He turned towards her and smiled.

'Why specially?'

'The obvious way of chucking you out is to make you walk the plank.'

'You wouldn't do that.'

'Why did you come? I mean, why this party rather than any other?'

'How else could I hope to meet you?'

She didn't believe it, but it was the right answer all the same. Her cheek dimpled as she smiled.

'So having come aboard to meet me, you spend your time looking at the scenery.'

'Only while I was waiting for you to join me. I was thinking about the blokes who live here.' The boat had passed under Tower Bridge while he was still below and by now was rounding the great curve of the Docklands developments. 'Working all day in those great towers of the City and coming home in the evening to penthouses with river views. My own age, a lot of them, and earning a couple of hundred thousand a year in the money markets. I was wondering how it feels.'

'Do you envy them?'

'Shuffling money around to make money? Not a bit of it. At the end of the day they must ask each other what they've actually created. What exists that didn't exist before. My name's Mark, by the way.'

'Tory.'

'Tory? That's a name for a political party, not for a girl.'

'I was only two or three when I adopted it. I suppose my political education had been neglected.'

'Do you never answer to your whole name? Victoria.'

'That's a name for a station, not a girl. But no. My parents did one of those crazy things that parents do when they're trying to be clever: they gave all their daughters names beginning with V. It obviously didn't occur to them that when their sweet little babies grew up to be secretive teenagers they might want to know who had the right to open any letter addressed to Miss V. Craig. What do you do?'

'I'm an artist.'

'So what do you do to earn a living?'

He laughed, immediately at ease with her. When preparing in advance for this conversation he had wondered whether to claim to be a journalist, but decided against it. It might excuse any nosiness on his part, but was more likely to close doors in his face than to open them. He had felt uneasy at having to lie during his visit to the school. There was no reason why he should not be completely truthful in this conversation.

'Photography,' he answered. 'The commercial kind, not the arty stuff.'

'Is that why you're stalking me? Hoping I'll get you some agency work? You've picked the wrong person. I work with figures, not portfolios.'

'No, I'm not commercial in that sense. Weddings. Houses for sale. Portraits of people. New graduates, pretty girls who want to be models, that sort of thing. Portraits are what I do best as an artist, so whenever I finish a job with the camera, I suggest that the sitter might like something much classier in paint.'

'Where did you train?'

'It's a complicated story.'

'I'm interested.'

'Well, I was offered a place at Cambridge, on my Greek and Latin A-levels. Got it deferred for a year, to give me a break from exams, and spent the time in America. I had a run-around Greyhound ticket and to pay for bed and food I painted portraits. Knocked on people's doors and asked them, cold.'

'Goodness. Did you get many takers?'

'If I picked right, I could almost always get bed and breakfast for a pencil sketch. And enough bigger jobs to keep me going. Well, one day I was in Newport, working my way along a row of what you and I would call palaces and they call cottages. There was this tiny little woman with black black hair, wearing a fortune in rings on her fingers. She let me have a go. Her face came out like something in a Disney film; you know, Snow White, terrible. But between sittings I sketched her house, and she liked that.

She let me stay for a couple of weeks to work it up into a proper painting and we talked a lot. I'd always wanted to be an artist, but it had never seemed very practical. She thought I had a bit of talent and encouraged me and – well, it finished with me turning down the Cambridge place. My parents and the school were furious.'

'But you didn't go to art college?'

'Not at once. I couldn't get a grant because my father's income was too high and he certainly wasn't going to fork out himself. I had a hairy year doing night classes and picking up what work I could. Then the p – ' He checked himself. Princess Fiori had told him not to mention her name, and he hadn't; but even a reference to her title might be unwise. There could not be too many princesses in the United States. 'The lady from Newport wrote to ask how I was getting on, and when I told her there were problems she said she'd be my patroness for three years. Just like that. She paid my fees and gave me a rent allowance. She was rolling in money, but all the same . . .'

The conversation was running nicely. He needed only a minute or two more to comment on the usefulness of support given to artists while they were young, which would lead on to the unfairness of a male not being allowed to benefit from something he had recently heard of – had she? – called the Tantivy Trust. But he was not given the chance. From one of the lower decks came a sudden burst of loud music. The disco had begun. Tory's eyes brightened and her shoulders moved in time with the beat.

'Come on,' she said, and disappeared without looking to see whether he would follow.

There was no hope of talking in the noisy, crowded saloon. It seemed best to distance himself for the moment. It would be easy enough to rejoin her later. Without being conceited Mark knew that she was interested in him. A lively girl like Tory would not want to waste a party on colleagues whom she could meet any day in the office, and

189

temperamentally she was unlikely to find attractive the sort of businessman who spent his days selling frozen peas or instant coffee. He took the opportunity to get his hands on a full bottle of champagne and secrete it amongst the life rafts. When, an hour later, the buffet opened, he was not surprised that she accepted his gesture of invitation to barge the queue and stand beside him.

They took their plates and glasses up to the open deck again, for the September night was warm and the *Lady Lucy*, on reaching the furthest point of the trip, had moored for half an hour off Greenwich.

'There's a house for you to paint,' suggested Tory, tackling a chicken leg with vigour.

'Marvellous, yes, the whole complex. Although when it comes to painting rather than just looking I prefer more romantic buildings. Idiosyncratic. Gives one more scope.'

'You should see where I live then. I must remember that word, idiosyncratic. I've always thought of the mixture as crazy myself.'

'Whereabouts is that?' He produced the champagne which he had hidden and refilled her glass as she giggled in admiration of his cheek.

'Oh, up in the wilds of Scotland. I'm talking about my parents' home, of course, not my London pad. It's the sort of place which has been going for three hundred years and in every generation somebody's knocked a bit down or built a bit on.'

'What does your father find to do in the wilds of Scotland?'

'Works for a charity. Runs it, in fact. He claims it's easier to get on with the job when there are no social distractions, and I'm sure he's right – although personally I prefer to have the social distractions. The place is bristling with computer terminals and fax machines and what have you, so he's not exactly cut off from the world.'

For the second time that evening Mark was within

touching distance of the question he had come on board to ask, and this time there was no interruption. 'What charity?'

'I don't suppose you'll have heard of it. It's so well endowed that it never has to do any fund-raising like Oxfam and that lot, so it doesn't have much contact with the general public. It's called the Fiori Foundation.'

The unexpectedness of the answer reduced Mark to silence. She had not only failed to give the name for which he was angling but had provided no reasonable excuse for him to press for it. And there was more than that to take him aback. It could not possibly be a coincidence that someone called Fiori had set him to follow a trail which – although still without any obvious connection – had led to a mention of a Fiori charity. This was something he would have to think about. He put the Tantivy Trust on the back burner. For one thing, although it was only his obligation to the princess which had brought him to this party, he would need no such excuse to pursue the acquaintance of such an attractive and lively young woman as Tory Craig. It was only because an immediate change of subject would have seemed too abrupt that he asked one further question. 'Is Fiori a company or a chap?'

'A chap to start with, but he died a long time ago. He set up the Foundation while he was still young and put most of his companies into it. The rest came after his death, because he didn't have any family. The income runs into millions, so it can finance the sort of scheme which everyone agrees ought to happen but which no one can afford. At the moment there's a huge desalination project trying to hold back the Sahara in North Africa. If it works, they'll hand over the project and start again with something new. Probably in South America. Save the rain forest: that sort of thing. My father's mad about trees.'

Mark nodded, signing off the subject. He could almost certainly discover more about the Fiori Foundation from the princess; and although Tory's defences were down as a result of his generous refilling of her glass, she might become suspicious if he pressed an unlikely interest too far. 'Are we going to meet again?' he asked.

'How would I know? Depends on you. I may *look* modern, but I was brought up old-fashioned. I wait to be asked.'

'Then we *are* going to meet again.' So he could move at an easy pace. 'Tell me about your sisters,' he said. 'The two other Miss V. Craigs. Are they older or younger than you?'

'The same age. Give or take half an hour or so.'

'Go on! You mean you're a triplet?'

'Well, strictly speaking' – Tory produced the dimple again as she grinned – 'I'm a quad. The three of us are three-quarters of quads; the fourth one died. But we don't always bother explaining all that.'

'I've never met a quad before. Does it make you feel different from other people?'

'How can anyone tell that sort of thing? It's the identical quads who probably have special feelings, and we're not that. The one who died was a boy.'

'But you're one of a group. Always with playmates your own age.'

'There are cons as well as pros,' she told him. 'Our mother was always terribly keen on the one-of-a-group aspect. You know, dressed us all exactly the same. Same hairstyle as well. Three little girls with fringes. That was my first rebellion, when I started school and didn't want to look the same as someone else. I demanded to wear an Alice band. It was quite a battle, because my hair grew forward just like the others. It took months before it was long enough to stay back and tidy.'

'And you're still a rebel now. The blonde hair.'

'Right.' Tory showed no resentment that he had noticed. 'My fiercest battle, though, was to go to a different school from Ginny and Ness. Father thought it was crazy because it would mean complications of delivering and collecting us from different places. And Mother was hurt because she thought it meant I didn't like my sisters.'

'And do you?'

'Yes. We're great pals, always have been. But I knew that as long as we were together I should never be more than one of the three Craig girls. Never an individual, if you see what I mean.'

'Did you win the battle?'

'Yes. Not bad for a seven-year-old, was it?'

'You must have been a pretty formidable seven-year-old. So where did you go to school?'

'A co-ed prep school in England. You won't have heard of it.'

'Try me.' Although Mark – who of course already knew the answer – was no longer in a hurry to complete his detective work, it seemed foolish to miss this new opportunity of bringing a key word into the conversation. But Tory shook her head.

'Nothing more boring than adults talking about schools. I made a good resolution, after meeting my third Old Harrovian, that no name would ever pass my lips.'

'What about university? Am I allowed to ask about that?'

'You are, because there's no answer. My parents are like yours, dead keen for their little geniuses to pick up degrees. They were both at Oxford themselves, and the pressure was pretty fierce. But only Ness went along with it – and only because that was what she wanted anyway. She's there now, reading Greats. Ginny just announced firmly that she wasn't the academic type and she never wanted to take another exam in her life and she'd like to live at home and make herself useful in the Foundation, thank you very much.'

'And you?'

'I did a few sums. I'm quite good at sums.' She shook her head in a puzzled fashion, as though suddenly aware that she had had too much champagne. Probably she would not have been quite so forthcoming about her family had she been completely sober – but although she might be feeling muzzy, there was nothing confused about her speech.

'I figured that with the cost of sending me to university and the three years of not earning anything it would be twelve years before I caught up on total earnings with what I could get by starting at eighteen, learning on the job and getting promoted on merit. There's nothing I see myself wanting to do for which a degree is a must-have, and I don't think one ought to regard a university course as merely a delightful way of passing one's youth, do you? Well, obviously you don't, since you turned down Cambridge. Anyway, I actually like working. This sort of work, I mean. Talking of which, unless you're prepared to be quizzed by our head of research, I suggest a quick departure.'

'Thanks.' Mark moved briskly away in search of coffee. Only as he reached the lower deck did it occur to him that his own research was incomplete. He had not asked Tory for her telephone number. But no matter; he could ring her at work. Most certainly they were going to meet again.

4

'I wish you didn't have to go.' Ginny Craig, trimly dressed in kilt and sweater, sat on the edge of the bed and watched as her sister packed. The Michaelmas term would not begin until the second week in October, but Ness was returning from Kilcraigie to Oxford a week early to work on a prize essay.

Moving briskly round her bedroom in jeans and a blue checked logging shirt, Ness had the unco-ordinated appearance of a young woman who rarely looked in a mirror. The laces on her Reeboks were untied and her long dark hair was tousled. She paused for a moment to twist it through a ring of twisted velvet so that it hung in a pony tail down her back.

'Well, I wish you were coming with me,' she replied, smiling with affection. 'It was a mistake, you know, not trying for university.'

'If I'd gone to St Andrew's I wouldn't have seen any more of you than I do now. And I couldn't ever have got to Oxford.'

'I don't know why you run yourself down. You speak three languages fluently and two others well enough. You are just in the process of organising, practically single-handed, an exhibition which will visit eleven countries in three continents. Compared with you, the average Oxford undergraduate is still at primary school level. Can you see my other trainers anywhere?'

Ginny found them under the bed and remained sitting on the carpet, with her knees pulled up to her chin.

'But you know very well that I'm not academic,' she said. 'I use my languages to gabble over the telephone, not to read Dante or Cervantes. Anyway, it's all Father's fault. If he hadn't tried to push me so hard . . . When he started talking about crammers, that was the last straw. Why do you think he always picks on me?'

'Because you're his favourite.' Ness, carrying a pile of underwear across to be packed, gave her opinion with confidence.

'Funny way he has of showing it.'

'That pretty well proves my point. He's such a peculiarly fair-minded man that he knows he ought not to have a favourite and so he tries to pretend that he hasn't. Anyway, *I'm* doing what he wanted me to, since it was what I wanted as well; and Tory more or less escaped at the age of seven. So that only leaves you to be bullied. I'm sure that actually he's pleased as punch to have you helping him; someone he can leave in charge here when he and Mother are away, like now.' She began to roll up sweaters and press them into a suitcase already over-full, but paused to glance at her sister. 'Do you really feel that he's extra hard on you?'

Ginny's answer was an oblique one. 'I was doing one of my rock drawings one day,' she said. Drawing and painting were two of her many hobbies, but to the amusement of the family her subject was almost always the same: a piece of rock. Sometimes the cliff of a mountain, more often something small enough to bring indoors. She was fascinated by the subtle shades of grey, the veins and cracks and different planes which could be captured in pencil or, with more difficulty, in watercolour. The others thought that one piece of rock was the same as any other, but to Ginny no two were alike. 'There was a ridge on this one in just the place where a nose might be. I found myself turning the drawing into a kind of portrait. It was still a rock, but it was Father as well. Hard as granite.'

Ness sat on her suitcase and bounced up and down to

press in its contents as she considered this point with interest.

'I know what's part of the trouble,' she suggested. 'He has so many faces. The adoring face when he comes back after a trip and kisses Mother again. The friendly, jolly sort of face when he decides to give time to the three of us on Sundays or holidays. And then his working faces: worried if something seems not quite right, and calm and businesslike when everything's going well – but rather stern either way. I expect that's where you got the rock impression from, because you see more of his business side than I do.'

'Perhaps you're right – about the variety, I mean. Certainly, if anyone asked me "What sort of a man is your father?" I wouldn't exactly know what to say.'

'A man of high standards: that should be your answer. Incredibly broad-minded when it comes to considering ideas which might change the world, and incredibly meticulous over details.' Ness slid off her suitcase and tutted as she found a stack of notebooks which had not yet been packed.

Ginny considered this opinion, testing it out against a variety of problems which had arisen in the past year. It was certainly true that Andrew's standards were high. As a schoolgirl she had found it hard to live up to them. But now that he had accepted her lack of academic ambition, he was appreciative of the time she devoted to the Tantivy Trust. He expected her to work with professional efficiency, but demanded no more of her than of Dorothy, his personal secretary. Perhaps Ginny's doubts about her father's attitude to her were rooted in the knowledge that she ought, like her sisters, to be more enterprising in exploring the world outside her home: but that was not a thought she wished to pursue.

'Let me sit on the case while you close it,' she offered.

'Thanks.' Once the locks were fastened it was Ness's turn

to sit down reflectively. 'I often wonder what we should all be like if Father were still an inspector of taxes instead of an international Father Christmas.'

'He'd be a Permanent Secretary by now, or whatever the top man's called.'

'Maybe. But still a man on a salary, working towards a pension. Different. We might be different as well.'

'I doubt it. I mean, look at the three of us. Father's rolling in money.' Andrew's salary as Administrator of the Fiori Foundation had been fixed for life as a percentage of the Foundation's income. 'He could afford to give us each a huge allowance if we really badgered him for it. We could be planning at this moment to spend half the winter in the West Indies and the other half at the most fashionable ski resort, whichever that is. Instead of that, what have we chosen to do? You're beavering away at Oxford. Tory's beavering away in a London office and I'm beavering away here. It seems to me that we have the Protestant work-ethic so thoroughly bred into us that if we suddenly found ourselves with a million a year each to spend, it wouldn't make the slightest difference to our lifestyle.'

'That's what people who win the pools always say. But it does make a difference, all the same. Well, that's the lot. Everything else is down already.'

'Are you sure you won't let me drive you?'

'Quite sure.' Ness pulled Ginny to her feet and hugged her. 'I love you more than anyone else in the world, but not when you're behind the wheel of a car.'

'I'm a very safe driver,' protested Ginny indignantly. She liked to drive fast, but prided herself on her skill.

'I agree. But one of these days you're going to come face to face with someone who isn't. Anyway, it's all arranged.'

Ginny knew that. One of the permanent members of the household was Gip, an Italian-American who was prepared to turn his hand to any odd jobs in the castle or its grounds but whose primary employment was as a driver. In his youth he had been trained in evasive driving, and it was he who had taught Ginny the tricks of his trade. Not that she ever needed to evade anyone; but her sessions on the skid-pan often came in useful on frozen roads. Gip grumbled almost without stopping that he was worked either too hard or not hard enough; but all that was needed to cheer him up was the request for a journey, at whatever hour of the day or night.

He was waiting now, with most of Ness's luggage already stowed, to take the last suitcase. Outside the mock-baronial door of the castle, the two girls embraced each other for a second time.

'Give my love to David,' said Ginny. She had never met the young man in question, but his name had been frequently on Ness's lips during the long vacation just ending.

'I shall do no such thing. None of my boyfriends is allowed even a hint that I possess a beautiful sister.' Ness laughed, patting Ginny on the shoulders as they drew apart. 'This is what you've *really* missed by not going to Oxford,' she said. 'Not merely a centre of academic excellence and the right to cock a snook at the rest of the world for the rest of your life, but one of the best dating agencies in the United Kingdom. 'Bye now.'

' 'Bye.' Ginny leaned against the balustrade of the stone platform outside the door, watching as her sister ran down one of the two ornate flights of steps which curved widely apart before meeting again at road level. She waved for as long as she could see the car, but her view of it was cut off within a few moments by the hill round which the loch and the road both curved. As always at the beginning of Ness's term she was left feeling flat and a little depressed. She wished that she hadn't mentioned David.

Ginny herself had no serious boyfriends. Friends, certainly: the sons of landed neighbours with whom over the years she had danced reels and enjoyed picnics, fishing expeditions, dinner, ski-ing weekends, car rallies and a host of other activities. Without being conceited, she knew that she had been the belle of the last Gathering Ball, for she had the tall, slim figure of a model and a generous dress allowance on which she made so few demands that she could afford an extravagant ball dress. There were plenty of young men whom she regarded as good company, but she had not yet met one with whom she wanted to spend the rest of her life – or even a single night.

Just recently this had begun to trouble her. She was twenty years old, but felt immature in comparison with her sisters: almost a schoolgirl still. She was ready to fall in love, to have adventures, to take her place in a wider world; but no one had yet appeared to open a door through which she could step.

It was Ness for whom she reserved her whole-hearted love: as a friend as well as a sister. Ginny in her childhood had been the least healthy of the three siblings; always thin and often shooting up in height at a rate which left her pale and tired and susceptible to infection. Her mother, naturally, had done everything necessary to look after her; but it was Ness who had sat beside her bed for hours at a time, reading aloud or playing gramophone records or simply holding her hand. The idea that Ness was bound to love someone else one day more than she loved Ginny was a painful one. Every time they said goodbye she felt sad and anxious: she might never see the old Ness again.

5

Turning back into the great hall after the car had disappeared from sight, Ginny ran up the tapestry-lined staircase. The rooms which comprised the family home were all in the west wing. Between the indoor swimming pool at the bottom and the long gallery at the top which the three girls shared for hobbies and television lay a suite of spacious entertaining rooms and a floor above them which contained six bedrooms. There had been eight once, but two were sacrificed to provide extra bathrooms.

The east wing might almost have been a separate house, and one which Ginny had little reason to enter. The servants lived at the top and worked at the bottom. On the second floor her father had an office suite from which he ran the Foundation and the Trust. On this floor too were guest suites for the use of the Fiori Foundation's trustees whenever they fancied a little stalking or fishing. And on the *piano nobile* was another extensive suite of rooms which was always kept locked.

During their childhood the three girls had never been allowed into this part of the castle, and had made up many horrific stories about the secrets which might be hidden behind the heavy carved doors. On their eighteenth birthday they banded together to demand entry from their father, and were granted the request on the promise that they would never mention what they saw.

What they found was a museum. As the blinds were raised and steel shutters unlocked they gasped at rooms which had become galleries of paintings, tapestries, mirrors in elaborately-carved golden frames, statues, suits of armour, antique furniture, faded but still-beautiful carpets.

There was a moment in which Ginny seriously believed that her father must be an art thief, using the travels which were ostensibly on behalf of the Foundation to spy out works of art and acquire them for himself. As Ness had laughed later, she had always had a vivid imagination.

The truth proved to be only a little less surprising. The suite, their mother told them, had originally been reserved for their godfather, Prince Fiori, who came regularly to stay in the castle in the two years before his death. After the kidnapping and murder of his only son he had leased out the Fiori Palace in Rome for use as an embassy. Some of its contents he sold at that time, but anything directly connected to his family – such as the magnificent portrait of the pope from whom the Fioris were illegitimately descended – had been brought to Kilcraigie for temporary safe keeping.

'He was only thirty-four when he died,' Hilary had told the girls, with a note of sadness in her voice. 'He would have married again, I expect; settled down and gathered all his possessions round him. But after little Georgie's death he became a kind of wanderer. He owned half a dozen homes round the world, but this is where he seemed to be happiest.'

'Since he's dead, what's going to happen to all this?' It had seemed wrong to Ginny that such beautiful objects should be hidden away and never seen by anyone.

'They come under the terms of the Tantivy Trust.' Andrew, standing by the door, had left Hilary to act as guide, but answered this question himself. 'Nothing can be done until twenty-one years after the day of Isabella Fiori's birth, unless of course her body is found before then – and that's hardly likely now. I shall have to remind myself of what's to happen in three years' time. As far as I recall, there's a choice between establishing a museum in her memory or selling all this in aid of the Trust's funds. Anyway, you'll all remember, won't you, that this is not to be talked about to anyone at all. The best form of security is for no one to know that it exists.'

That was the only occasion on which Ginny had seen the door opened. She hurried past it now, climbing to the second floor. At this level, as well as the galleries and corridors leading to the guest rooms on the right and the Craigs' own sleeping quarters on the left, there was a door straight ahead. It led to the office in the tower.

The tower was far older than the rest of the house. It had been built in the fourteenth century and, after acting as a stronghold in its own right, had been used as a watch tower for the castle now lying in ruins beside the loch. Its thick round stone walls completely failed to blend with the straight lines and strong angles of the seventeenth-century building which incorporated it, and the machicolated top with its tiny extra turret rose oddly behind the steeply pitched roofs.

From outside it appeared as an eccentricity, and the interior was hardly more rational. In the original building the only entrance had been at first floor level, presumably by means of a wooden ladder which could be pulled up if an enemy approached. Nowadays the bottom thirty feet of the tower housed nothing but an emergency generator and the cables needed to power the Foundation's computers and other machinery. But an entrance had been broken through on the second floor to give access from the house to a spacious round office.

It was a cheerful room. The walls were white, enlivened by bright posters of Ginny's teenage choice. The well-designed modern desks were black and the various filing cabinets and other office furniture were red if they held the Foundation's papers and yellow if they concerned the Trust. The room was of normal height, because a new ceiling had been installed, cutting off the highest section of the tower to act as an archive room. This could only be approached by a loft ladder extending from a trapdoor; but luckily the space did not need to be visited very often.

Dorothy was already at work when Ginny opened the door. Dorothy Rundle had been Andrew Craig's personal assistant for twelve years and needed no supervision to deal with the Foundation's affairs during her employer's frequent absences abroad. She lived at the castle from Monday to Friday and was regarded as a member of the family.

'Ness has gone and I'm feeling low,' said Ginny, walking over to the fax machine to inspect the night's offerings. Kilcraigie was at the very end of the postman's round and the mail did not usually arrive before ten. 'If there's nothing urgent, I'm going for a walk. Will you field any calls for me?'

'Of course. As long as they're in a civilised language.'

'Thanks.' It was one of the pleasures of working at home and for her own father that she could operate her personal system of flexitime. She was paid a proper salary and she did a proper job, but it was no one's business but her own if she worked until midnight in order to enjoy the morning sunshine.

Her work was exclusively for the Tantivy Trust. Its funds came from the same source as those of the Fiori Foundation, but its income of three million or so pounds a year was smaller and its rules for distributing benefits were very much more tightly drawn. The Fiori Foundation could allocate funds to any purpose approved by the seven eminent trustees, but the income from the Tantivy Trust was allowed to benefit only females born between 1965 and 1974.

Andrew Craig, the Administrator of the Foundation, was also – with his wife – one of the Tantivy trustees, and it was he who had imposed these conditions when he first registered it as a charity. Until then, as far as Ginny could tell, he had enjoyed almost unlimited discretion

204

under the Trust's deeds to spend the money in any way he chose.

She knew now why these particular time limits had been imposed. The capital had originally been set aside by Prince Fiori for the benefit of his daughter Isabella. His first concern was to protect her, as she grew to a marriageable age, from some of the consequences of being a great heiress, so that she would not be like Barbara Hutton or Christina Onassis, rushing from one husband to another without ever finding happiness. For that reason, many of the original conditions of the Trust were designed to prevent her having control of her own income until she was twenty-one, with the capital not being transferred until even later.

But providing a deterrent to fortune-hunters was only part of the prince's strategy. For reasons which Andrew had explained to Ginny, he was paranoid on the subject of security and the possibility of abduction – a fear which proved well-justified when the little girl was in fact kidnapped only a few days after his death. The Trust, which was already in existence then, had made provision for all possible eventualities, including what actually happened. It was ninety-nine per cent certain that Isabella must have died during the kidnapping but, because her body had never been found, the funds were applied for the benefit of anyone who might conceivably have been born the daughter of Prince Fiori. It was as reasonable a restriction as any other, Ginny supposed – although it sometimes amused her to realise that the ban on male beneficiaries did not extend to females of the most unlikely colours.

Much of the money was distributed through existing charities, but every year Hilary thought up one new special project. Since Ginny left school, her task had been first of all to research her mother's ideas, working out their cost and feasibility; and then, if her father approved one, helping to organise it. She enjoyed the work and found that she had an aptitude for it.

Within ten minutes of leaving the office, wearing her walking boots, she stepped out of the door on to the highest terrace. She stood still for a moment, filling her lungs with the clear air.

Of all the months in the year, October was Ginny's favourite. True, she loved the sight of the loch in May, when the low grassy islands which seemed to float on the surface of the dark water were suddenly carpeted with bluebells. She enjoyed her mother's early-summer pride in the woodland garden as wave after wave of azaleas burst into flower. She was awed by the silence which fell in February when the mountains were covered with snow. And she was still as excited as ever she had been as a little girl by the special days which punctuated the year: the Gathering, the Three Corbetts Run, the opening days of the various sporting seasons. But in October the dying bracken and the swaying tips of blow grass turned the glen to a shimmering carpet of gold, spotted only by the blood-red berries of rowan trees.

The trees around the edge of the loch were golden as well, reflecting in the still, clear water. The first gale would bring the leaves down – but, in the past few days, the winds which so often brought rain from the Atlantic had dropped, allowing the sun to shine from a blue and cloudless sky. Even the grey stones of the ruins, which could look dark and sinister in the rain, were mellowed by this golden light. Kilcraigie in October, thought Ginny, was the most beautiful place in the world.

Her hands moved down from her waist, smoothing her kilt. Within a few weeks, as the air grew colder, trousers would once again become the only sensible form of dress, but it was in the kilt that she felt most at home. She liked the smoothness of the front panel across her flat stomach, the tight stitching at the back which gave a trimness to her figure, the swinging of the pleats which fell straight from her narrow hips and allowed her the freedom to run and climb as she would.

In choosing to be tidily and appropriately dressed, Ginny was quite different from both her sisters. Ness didn't care what she looked like, but pulled on the nearest clean garments which came to hand. Tory cared a great deal about her appearance, and dressed to shock – or at least to attract the eye. It would not have occurred to either of them that, as she brushed back her shoulder-length brown hair and fixed it tidily in place with an Alice band each morning, Ginny was making just as firm a claim to her own individuality.

Today, for once, there would be no need to wrap up against the rain. She decided to walk over the hill and then along the side of the loch. There would not be time to go right round, but they kept a dinghy moored at the narrowest point of the long stretch of water; so she could row herself across and return along the opposite bank.

A movement caught her eye as she prepared to set off. On the road which ran along the other side of the loch a car was parked, and not far away from it a young man was in the process of dismantling a tripod. Had he been taking a photograph of Kilcraigie Castle? And if so, why? Scotland was littered with beautiful castles, romantic castles, historic castles; but Kilcraigie – a mish-mash of styles, an architectural mess – was not one of them. Besides, so snugly was it tucked away between the hill and the glen that it was impossible to find a dramatic view. There was no contrast between the darkness of the stone walls and the dark background of the land.

Well, that was not her business. Nevertheless, she continued to watch as the young man returned to his car and drove it the short distance on to the point where the road came to an end. He looked up at the castle for a moment and then began to climb the steps which led up through the terraces.

Ginny met him half-way, and for a moment they stared at each other without speaking. He was a good-looking young man with thick fair hair. The brightness of his blue eyes gave him a forceful expression which was softened by the creases in his face and the half-smile which turned up the corners of his mouth. He was the first to break the silence.

'Good morning,' he said. 'My name's Mark Lacey. You must be Ginny.'

6

Mark's first glimpse of Ginny Craig was through the view-finder. He had been on the point of taking a photograph of Kilcraigie Castle when she stepped into the picture: a tall, slender girl who moved with a graceful ease, her kilt swinging.

From the distance it was impossible to see her face clearly; but within a few moments – moving fast in order to intercept her before she took off for a country walk – he confronted her half-way up the elaborate stone staircase which led from the ruined castle to its successor.

She was a beauty. A classical beauty. On her oval face every feature was in perfect proportion. Applying his portrait-painter's eye, Mark recognised that there was little difference between her bone structure and Tory's; but Tory used colour to give prominence to her eyes and lips and to shade away any plumpness in her cheeks. Ginny, by contrast, wore no make-up and was perfect without it.

At this moment, not unnaturally, she looked startled by the abruptness of his self-introduction. Mark smiled as he added, 'I'm a friend of your sister.'

This was a true statement. Although he had met Tory less than three weeks earlier, they had seen each other almost every day since then. He had been to dinner in her flat and she had spent a Sunday in his converted school, but most of their dates had been for parties or discos. It was not a friendship which was likely to lead anywhere. Mark had recognised quickly that Tory was attracted by new acquaintances and that before long she would give her time to someone newer. Probably he had brought that stage of their relationship to an end merely by leaving

London. But they had enjoyed each other's company. To claim friendship was not too much of an exaggeration.

Ginny seemed to be considering whether or not to believe him. 'My older sister or my younger sister?' she asked.

It took him a second to realise what she was doing; then he laughed.

'Is this some kind of code you operate between you? Do you only explain the situation to people you like, so that anyone who knows is by definition approved? Well, I don't mind playing. I'm a friend of your sister Tory, who is a third of three-quarters of quads.'

Ginny's grin as she held out a hand transformed her from a mere beauty to an attractive, intelligent girl. 'Well done,' she said, accepting him. 'How did you know I was Ginny, though? I might have been Ness.'

'From what Tory told me. "Ness is the clever one and Ginny is the beautiful one."'

She showed no reaction to the quotation, which doubtless she had heard before. 'You weren't expecting to find Tory here though, were you?'

'Oh no. I left her working hard in London. Nor had I better pretend that I was just passing. Nobody can exactly pass by Kilcraigie Castle, can they? Were you just setting off for a walk? And if so, may I come with you? I've been driving for a couple of hours and need a bit of exercise.'

He was conscious of her hesitating, although she tried to disguise her doubt by looking down at his feet as if to make sure that they were stoutly clad. 'Hold on just a moment,' she said, and ran up the steps again before he had time to ask her why.

Her absence extended itself for longer than seemed necessary. What was she doing? Perhaps, he thought hopefully, she was alerting her mother or the servants to the fact that on her return she would be inviting someone in for a meal, or even to stay. But her expression when she returned afforded no clues.

'Am I clean?' he asked. 'Have Scotland Yard and Interpol checked my description and car number and felt able to assure you that I'm not a known criminal?'

Her pale skin flushed and she did not meet his eyes as she indicated the direction in which they should walk.

'My God, don't say I've hit the bullseye!' exclaimed Mark. 'Were you really checking on me?'

Still blushing, she turned back to face him.

'We keep a book next to the telephone,' she told him. 'It's a rule of the household that whenever we go for a walk or a sail we have to make a note of direction and expected time of return. So that my mother or the housekeeper will know when to start worrying if there's any sort of accident; and where to look.'

'You would have done that before you set out: before you met me.'

'So I went back to add "in the company of Mark Lacey, a friend of Tory's". And then' – Ginny's blush deepened – 'Yes, I did phone Tory to check that you were who you said you were.'

'And now you're telling me what you've done.'

'That's part of the system as well. Standing orders from my father. Because if a burglar or something does turn up, it's better to put him off before he starts than to catch him afterwards.'

'Not many parents carry security to such lengths.' He moved to walk side by side with her as they left the terraced garden and began to climb the hill.

'Well, a long time ago they got involved in a kidnapping. Involved only in the sense of knowing the parents whose child was snatched, but I suppose that was enough to show them what an awful experience it can be. Most people probably think that kind of thing never happens. My parents know that occasionally it does. Taking precautions is just a matter of habit. Nothing personal.' She turned her head to smile at him in a friendly way, but her next question suggested that her upbringing might have made her as suspicious as her parents.

'You said you weren't simply passing by. So why have you come here? Who did you hope to see, since you know that Tory's in London?'

'I've been spending a long weekend with a schoolfriend of mine; John Lindsay of Invertay House. Perhaps you know him?'

'I know his younger brother.'

'A Sassenach like me assumes that anywhere in Scotland must be near anywhere else. That was before I found out about the roads! Tory had told me about Kilcraigie, and put an idea into my head. I suppose it's your parents I really need to see, but I'd like to get you on my side first.' Tory had also, as it happened, told him that her parents were in Brazil at the moment, and it was that information which had sent Mark north in a hurry.

'On your side about what?' asked Ginny.

'About painting a family picture. I'm an artist, you see. An old-fashioned kind of artist. I mean, I don't paint huge panels in three shades of black, or covered with blots. I have a very clear idea of what I'd like to become well known for. Large oil paintings of complete families in or outside their own houses.'

'I see what you mean by old-fashioned! I've seen some of those eighteenth-century groups. Children looking like dwarf adults and their parents showing off their best clothes. Incredibly wooden.'

He was pleased to discover that she was a girl who looked at pictures and was prepared to talk about them. 'I don't reckon to be as formal as that,' he told her. 'Some people, obviously, just happen to be living in a house for a few years before they move on: no real connection. That's not interesting. But I have this theory that some people are

212

in tune with their homes, almost part of the architecture. Those are the ones I want to paint. Some of them are indoor people and need to be shown in a drawing room or library or whatever. Others are outdoor people. The sort of picture for them is with the house and grounds as a background.'

'And how do you know which group the Craig family fits into?'

'I don't, of course, not till I've met you all. But *you* fit. As an outdoor person. I saw you from across the loch, and I knew at once.'

'I don't believe it!' Ginny was laughing as though she would never stop. 'Are you telling me that you spend your life driving round the countryside, knocking on people's door and asking a whole family to assemble in its garden to be put on canvas?'

'Of course it's not like that,' he protested. 'Although as a matter of fact I did just that sort of thing for a year in the States. People didn't seem to find it odd. Partly because they have a more encouraging attitude there to a young guy who wants to get on in life and has an idea to sell. But mostly because there's a tradition left over from the early days. There were primitive painters who'd go from door to door with a selection of canvases already painted except for the heads. Do you fancy little Johnnie in pink satin or green velvet, madam?'

'And have you had many commissions since you've been back from America?'

'No,' he admitted honestly. 'It's not easy, getting started. You're asking people to commit a lot of time as well as money. I have to work on a no-like-no-pay basis for the time being, just so that I can collect a portfolio to show. So to answer your question, I'm here because Tory told me about the castle, and your parents sounded as though they were the sort of people who'd be encouraging, and having three daughters of the same age would make for an interesting picture. I mean, suggesting the resemblances and the differences at the same time.'

This was not exactly the approach he had planned in advance. During his dates with Tory he had confirmed the connection between Andrew Craig and the Tantivy Trust. His earlier problems in tracking down the Trust proved to be mainly because it was registered in Scotland. Keeping the conversation casual, he had gained the impression that there was nothing secret about its existence; but Tory personally had never been involved with it. She knew in a general way how it spent its money, but nothing about the way it had been set up. If he wanted to ask questions he would need to meet Ginny.

He had driven north with the intention of being straightforward in his enquiries. What had thrown him off the track was Ginny's beauty and the sparkle with which her expression flickered between peaceful calm and intelligent vivacity. He didn't want her to think of him as a kind of detective who was seeking her company merely because a stranger in America had instructed him to do so. The longer it took to discover what he needed to know, the more of her company he could enjoy.

Nevertheless, he could not afford to let any opportunity slip – and the first chance to raise the subject came an hour later, as they slithered down the slippery side of the hill towards the loch. Ginny was telling him what he already knew.

'You'll have to wait a bit if you want to enrol my father as one of your patrons. He's in Brazil with my mother at the moment, trying to set up a scheme to save a few thousand acres of rain forest. The World Bank has failed. The United Nations has failed. But Andrew Craig thinks he has something to offer which can't be refused.'

Mark looked at her in surprise. Why did she want to run her father down? It sounded as though he was doing useful work. Perhaps Ginny misinterpreted his glance, for she answered a question he had not asked.

'He hasn't got that kind of money personally, of course,' she said. 'But he has funds at his disposal from a kind of charity.'

It was a lead which could not be ignored, even though it might put the pleasure of their walk together at risk.

'Which one would that be?' he asked her. 'The Fiori Foundation? Or the Tantivy Trust?'

Ginny gave him a glance which was suspicious rather than merely curious. 'How do you know about the Tantivy Trust?' she asked.

'Nothing secret about it, is there?'

'No. But not many people have heard of it, all the same.'

'Artists and art students have. If they're female, at least.'

'But how – ?'

'Tory came to lunch with me one Sunday and met a friend of mine. Emma Tallant. She paints as well. She'd wanted to enter for some competition and was moaning because she'd left it too late. Tory told her that it was probably you who'd turned her down. Speaking as a male chauvinist pig, I reckon your trust ought to be investigated by the Equal Opportunities Commission or whatever it's called.' He smiled to show that he was joking. 'I suppose it was set up by a woman, was it?'

'No.' It seemed that his explanation had satisfied Ginny, who answered in a straightforward manner. 'By the same man who established the Fiori Foundation. A friend of my father's. I never knew him – or at least, I don't remember him.'

She must be talking about Prince Fiori. In a recent telephone conversation, the princess had confirmed that she knew about the existence of the Fiori Foundation and had told him a little about her ex-husband. It had never seemed likely that two wealthy men should each independently choose Andrew Craig to administer their estates, so this corroboration came as no surprise.

'So there was no female involved in it at all?'

'There was in a way. Prince Fiori had a daughter, Isabella, who was kidnapped. The trust fund was set up for her originally. The details don't matter, but the money has to benefit girls.'

To Mark, the details *did* matter, but he had no chance to press the point immediately, for Ginny was pointing to a small rowing boat tied to a tree stump at the edge of the loch.

'We'll row across,' she said. 'You get in and I'll push off.'

She jumped gracefully in as the boat began to move, settled the oars in the rowlocks and rowed across the smooth water towards the village on the further shore.

'I ought to be doing that,' suggested Mark.

'I'm used to it.'

'Is it safe, leaving a boat unguarded like that? Do you keep it there all the time?'

'There or on the other side. People roundabout are honest. And observant. No one would steal or vandalise it. We don't mind anyone using the boat as long as they return it to where they find it.'

'This Trust, though.' Mark returned to the subject which interested him. 'Why are its benefits restricted not just to women, but to women of a particular generation? I mean, it's quite usual for a charity to specify a certain age to help: children under five, or whatever. But this one, as far as I can gather, will always be helping the same band, as they grow older and older. This year you're putting young artists on exhibition. In sixty years' time you'll be building retirement homes for the same artists grown old.'

'That's right, more or less.' Ginny rested on her oars – not because she was tired, but because she seemed to relish the peaceful silence of floating on the water: there was a pause before she explained.

'It's complicated. I told you, Isabella Fiori was kidnapped. She lived on a private island in the middle of a lake. There was an alarm system all round. But at some point in the previous couple of hundred years someone had constructed a terrace over what was originally a watergate. The watergate was still there – they found it when the police search was going on. The kidnappers swam in one night and got access to an old cellar which eventually connected with the kitchens. They were inside the alarm system by then and no one heard them get to the nursery. Except probably Sophia, the nurse. When I first heard the story it seemed most likely that she was one of the gang; but my father never believed that. He assumed that she was killed to stop her raising the alarm.'

'Assumed? Were the kidnappers never caught?'

'It was worse than that. Isabella was never found. There was a crashed speedboat at the other end of the lake next morning. The police concluded that she must have drowned in the accident. She was very young at the time.'

'So your father spends her fortune in the hope that one of the people helped will be the missing Isabella? A long shot!'

'Yes, of course. But there were all sorts of conditions set down according to whether she was alive or dead after her father's death, or whether the situation was uncertain.' Ginny began to row again, while Mark was silent for a little while. She had given him plenty of food for thought.

There was something fishy about the story of the kidnapping. Drowned bodies usually rose to the surface eventually. Although of course the kidnappers might have retrieved the body and taken it away in order that they could still negotiate for a ransom. It would be interesting to learn how such negotiations had gone – but Ginny was unlikely to know that. Andrew Craig was the man to tackle; this mysterious figure with millions of other people's money at his disposal.

None of this, in a sense, was any of Mark's business, but gratitude and sympathy made him determined to press on with his enquiry. Princess Fiori was presumably Isabella's mother – although she had not volunteered that information during their telephone conversations. Did she believe that her daughter was certainly dead or was she aware of the uncertainty which Andrew Craig appeared to feel? Even though she had been divorced before Prince Fiori died, might she not have expected to have some control over her daughter's fortune? Well, perhaps she was rich enough not to worry about that, but the question of Isabella's life or death must certainly be of importance. Besides, the more closely he kept on the trail, the more time he could spend with Ginny Craig.

7

Ginny was not surprised by Mark's interest in the origins of the trust for which she worked. The story of little Isabella Fiori was unusual and sad and mysterious: she often wondered about it herself. But she was glad when he indicated that he had heard enough of the subject by asking a different kind of question.

'Don't you get bored, stuck away up here?'

Ginny gave one last strong pull on the oars and then shipped them neatly as the boat glided towards the landing jetty. They had arrived at the other side of the loch, where a group of stone cottages clustered round the tiny church on a rocky platform which gave Kilcraigie its name. As she tied up, she considered what to say.

The short answer to the question was that she did not by any means consider herself 'stuck away'. Although she had been too happy at home to join in Tory's demand for independence at the age of seven, she and Ness had also gone to boarding school when they were eleven. From as early as she could remember the whole family had spent the long summer holiday each year in Italy. Every Easter they visited either London or Paris. For twelve weeks after leaving school she had toured the United States, treated as a VIP in each of the Fiori hotels whose profits still swelled the funds of the Foundation; and on her return had lived for another three months in Edinburgh while she learned typing and bookkeeping and office administration. Within the past few months she had travelled round Europe to make arrangements for the forthcoming exhibition, and when the tour started she would visit each gallery again, making sure that all was well. Although she was not as sophisticated in her personal relationships as Tory, nor as academically clever as Ness, her self-confidence in travelling and doing business abroad would have let her put up a good case for denying that she was a stay-at-home. If she hesitated now, it was because she had recently begun to wonder whether it was time to spread her wings further.

None of this was any of Mark Lacey's business. But the silence had lasted too long. He rephrased his question as they began to walk back towards the castle at a brisk pace.

'What I mean is, don't you find it lonely, living here?'

'The loneliness is what I like about it. My mother has a theory about how it's good for children to be brought up in the depths of the country. She thinks that a country girl can always get used to living in a crowd and doing city things if she has to, but town children feel completely lost if they're stuck away miles from anywhere. I agree with that. When I go to London or Paris or Rome or New York' – she could not after all refrain from a little showing off – 'I find it exciting, not bewildering. But Tory brought some of her London friends here once and it was terribly hard work keeping them amused. Do you realise, Mark, that every single thing you say has a question mark at the end?'

'Sorry,' he said. 'Well, almost sorry. Just one more question and then I really will stop. May I paint you?'

'Why should you want to?'

'Because you're beautiful. A young artist like me doesn't often get the chance of a beauty. You wouldn't need to keep the painting if you didn't like it, because it would be the sort of thing I could show to other prospects, to make them hope that they'd turn out beautiful as well. Even before I met you, I'd planned to ask if I could make a sketch to fit into a family group. But now I'm feeling more ambitious. This could be something special. It's a matter of chemistry, you see. Almost like falling in love, but different. I mean, I can produce a likeness of anybody who cares to sit down in front of me because that's what my talent is. But very occasionally I look at someone and see a whole picture complete in my mind. Not just the features, but with a personality shining through. I'm not expressing myself very well, I'm afraid. But I really would like . . .'

Ginny continued to walk steadily ahead as she considered the request. She had told the truth when she claimed not to mind the loneliness of her life, but that didn't mean that distractions weren't welcome. She found Mark attractive. She liked talking to him. And to have her portrait painted would be an interesting experience. He was a proper, trained artist, who could give her some tips on how to improve her own amateur efforts. There was only one snag.

'How long would you need?' she asked.

'Actually with you? About half an hour today to find the right background and take some photographs. After that, I could probably manage with three two-hour sessions if I had to, though I'd like more if possible for the pleasure of staring at you. I can work on the background and your clothes when you aren't there.'

'The trouble is that I'm afraid I can't ask you to stay.' It was ridiculous, thought Ginny resentfully. She was twenty years old. It was time that her father stopped treating her like a child. Margaret and Donald both lived in the house, with Dorothy there as well from Mondays to Fridays; and Gip had a flat in the stables. Nothing could possibly happen. But a rule was a rule. 'My mother's immensely hospitable, and if she were at home there'd be no problem. But . . .'

'You mean that you aren't allowed to ask friends to stay if your parents happen to be abroad!'

'Of course I can invite my friends. But I've only known you for two hours.'

'Snubbed! First you have to check up on me and now you have to keep me out of the house. You certainly take security seriously in your family. Makes me wonder what guilty secrets are tucked away behind those forbidding walls.'

Fortunately Ginny was walking a little ahead of her companion, so that he could not see her flush. The secret lay behind the heavy wooden door of the Fiori suite: the treasures whose very existence must not be suspected. But although Mark had spoken as though his feelings were genuinely hurt, his next question came cheerfully enough.

'One thing I know about Scotland is that their bed and breakfast system is magnificent. Could you fix me up somewhere locally?'

'Yes. Yes, certainly I could do that.'

'So you'll let me try a portrait?'

Conscious that she had been behaving ungraciously, she turned her head to smile at him in a more friendly way as she nodded. Mark grinned back, his blue eyes delighted by this success. The impact of his smile seemed momentarily to rob Ginny of breath. Was this what he meant by chemistry? Those eyes told her that he was not now admiring a face as it might appear on canvas, but a real one. Swallowing the lump in her throat, she turned her head forward again and increased her pace until they reached the end of the road.

'This is the right place for me to paint you.' Mark was unlocking his car as he spoke. 'Amongst the ruins, with the water at your feet and the golden glen behind.'

'I'm a working girl,' said Ginny. 'I can't spend all day shivering out here.'

'Let me just take some photographs.' A camera was already in his hand. 'Would you mind slipping off your anorak? Just lean against that bit of wall, will you? I'll get the composition right in my head and then if you could come out again this afternoon for half an hour I can block out the general shapes. That will leave me plenty to do by myself for a bit. And even when I need you, it could be inside for some of the time. As long as we can come back towards the end to catch this marvellous light.'

'Am I allowed to comb my hair before you start?' she asked smilingly, inspecting the first of the instant photographs.

'I'm not sure. You may think of yourself as a tidy, conventional girl, but I may see you as wild and passionate. I can't tell till I start.'

'Don't I have any choice in the matter?'

'No. Just turn that way. That's it. No, the painting is mine unless you choose to buy it, so I shall paint what I see. I strongly suspect that behind that beautiful face lies a determined character. If so, it will make itself known, and neither of us will be able to stop it.'

'It all sounds most alarming.' But Ginny allowed herself to be moved about, sitting or standing as she was told.

Later that day, as she settled down to her work in the office at last, she found herself smiling at the prospect of his companionship, and hurried through her tasks so that she could see how he was getting on.

The next ten days passed happily. Mark spoke little while he was painting, but at other times proved to be good company. She was almost sure that he could have finished the portrait more quickly if he had tried, but was glad of the length of time it took. In any case, it was partly her fault that the period extended itself: it was by her invitation that they swam together in the heated pool, walked together over the hills, ate and chatted together. Each night, as she watched him leave on the ten-mile drive to his lodgings – for none of the tiny group of houses at Kilcraigie itself had a spare room for a guest – she felt both apologetic and guilty. She was obeying the letter of her father's instructions, but certainly not their spirit; for although Mark worked out of doors for most of the time, she had invited him to use the great hall whenever it rained

– and in practice he had the run of the family half of the castle while she was in her office.

Overcoming her shyness, she produced some of her own drawings and paintings for him to criticise. She was pleased by his praise and grateful for the technical hints he offered. He made a sketch of her whilst she in turn was painting one of her favourite rocks under his supervision.

'This isn't connected with the portrait,' he said, showing her the result. 'But if I were to do a family picture, obviously this is what you'd be doing in it. I've already tried one of Tory.' He found it in his portfolio and showed it to her. 'It's interesting, don't you think, to see the basic resemblances under the differences of presentation?'

'Interesting but hardly surprising, with the same parents. We may not have been identical quads, but we're still sisters.' Her attention was caught by a sudden rustling as the bronze tips of the long blow grass of the glen began to bend and dance like a piece of fluttering silk.

'Wind's changing,' she told him. 'You may not be able to have many more outdoor sessions. A week without any serious rain is good going in this part of the world.'

She gave the warning regretfully. There was no longer any reason for Mark to stay on. And she had enjoyed his company. She would be sorry to see him go. Very sorry indeed.

8

Ginny's guess was right. Next morning the weather forecast on the radio promised a westerly gale with winds gusting at more than ninety miles an hour. Mark hurried her out to the ruins as soon as he arrived, but when he began to fix the canvas to his travelling easel it tried to take off like a land yacht. Hastily he packed it away but then paused as he saw the attitude in which Ginny was waiting for him. She was leaning against the wind with one arm bent over the top of her head as if to prevent her hair from flying away and the other hand holding down her kilt.

'Hang on a minute!' he said, and took out his sketch book. She laughed aloud, exhilarated as always by the bluster of the wind, and allowed him only a few minutes.

'I must send Dorothy home early for the weekend,' she told him. 'If she leaves it until later, she'll be blown off the road. And that means that I shall have to spend all day in the office, to answer the telephone.' She ran into the house and up the stairs. Mark followed her into the tower.

'May I stay here and distract you?' he asked after Dorothy had left.

'Well, I really must work. I've been slacking, this past week.' She sat down at the computer.

'Is this still the exhibition?'

'No. That's all pretty well set up. I shall go off to Rome for the launch, but not quite yet. I'm working on another Trust project now.'

'And what's that?'

'It's an idea of my mother's. To help what *she* still calls the mothers of illegitimate babies and everyone else nowadays calls single parents. You probably know, a lot of councils will allocate flats or even houses straightaway to girls who have babies. Both my parents disapprove strongly of this. My father thinks it's disgraceful that a lack of self-control should be in a sort of way rewarded, and suspects that the policy may even encourage immorality. My mother believes that it's terrible for a girl who probably knows nothing at all about bringing up children to find herself suddenly shut up twenty-four hours a day with nothing but a baby for company. They're both incredibly old-fashioned, my parents, but what they say often makes a lot of sense.'

'So what's their solution?'

'Well, keeping inside the age boundaries of the Tantivy Trust – girls born between 1965 and 1975 – they're thinking of setting up a housing association. To build or convert houses that would accommodate four girls at a time. Father's theory is that the girls wouldn't like sharing and so they might lean on their boyfriends to get married and start a proper family life. Mother's idea is that they would enjoy each other's company and support each other on the child-care front. They might even organise a child-minding scheme amongst themselves so that one or two of the four could go out to work and come off benefit.'

'And what's your role in all this?'

'We're going to have a couple of trial runs in two different areas. I've got a lot of estimates of different ways of doing things. I'm putting everything on to the computer so that I can produce graphs of comparative starting-up and running costs. So now I shall need to concentrate.'

Mark took the hint only in the sense of remaining silent for a little while. He did not, as she had expected, retreat to work on his painting, but instead remained in the office. Even though he did not move, she was aware of his increasing restlessness.

'A week ago you mentioned scrapbooks,' he said abruptly. 'About the Fioris. May I look at them?'

She hesitated for a moment, but could think of no objection. The newspapers from which the cuttings had been collected were all available to researchers in libraries, and they contained no reference to the Fiori treasures in the locked suite of rooms.

'Just a minute.' She tapped the keyboard to start a printout and then moved across to the corner of the room near Dorothy's desk and pressed a button. The trapdoor in the ceiling was electrically controlled. Mark watched with interest as it swung open and a ladder slowly stretched itself to the floor.

'Can I – ?'

'No. You wouldn't know where to look.' It took her only a moment to find what he wanted. Up here at the top of the tower, in what was officially the archive room, the sound of the wind was much stronger – alarmingly strong, in fact, as it beat against the tiny turret above her head and howled round the flagpole. She wasted no time in collecting the scrapbooks. Most of the cuttings were in Italian, but there were probably enough English items to satisfy his curiosity.

It was some time before he spoke again. She could tell that he was longing to ask a question, but he waited until she raised her head to look at him, implicitly permitting him to interrupt.

'I find it odd,' he said. 'The theory behind your Trust is that it should benefit women who might conceivably be Isabella Fiori, right? But there's no possible way, surely, that she could be in England, living as an un-married mother. Wouldn't it be more logical to concentrate your benefits in Italy, on the assumption that if she survived a botched kidnapping, that's where she'd still be?'

'We do operate in Italy from time to time, and other

countries. Our income is so enormous that making donations to local charities is a good way of disposing of some of it. I don't really believe that Isabella is anywhere. It's just that the money has to be spent on someone, and the rules say – '

'But who made up the rules?' He stood up and began to pace around the office. 'Doesn't it seem to you, Ginny, that there's something not quite straight about this whole set-up? I don't mean dishonest, necessarily, but not straightforward. The nurse, for example: Sophia. Didn't her family make a fuss about what had happened to her? Or if they didn't, wouldn't that suggest to the police that she was implicated in some way? It seems odd that there's hardly any reference to her after the first few days. And as far as Isabella herself was concerned, this wasn't just any ordinary little girl who went missing. An heiress to immense wealth – and, in fact, an heiress who had inherited only a few days earlier. In the glare of the public eye even before she disappeared, because it had just become known that her father was dead. It's hard to believe that the police couldn't have found her in the end, if she was still alive. If they gave up, it must surely mean that she was dead.'

'But there was no body.'

'Suppose there had been. You said the Trust deed dealt with various possibilities. If Isabella had been certified dead without any doubt seventeen years ago, would your father still be distributing the funds as he does today?'

'I don't know. I've never read the original deed. What are you getting at, Mark?'

'Just wondering aloud. I suspect that there'll be some written provision for what should happen to all the money if Isabella were known for certain to be dead. On the other hand, if she were known for certain to be alive, she'd now be looking forward to the day when she would take over her inheritance. What would appear to suit your father best is uncertainty, and that's what he's got. A good life in a grand home. Money enough and plenty of excuse to do whatever he wants and go wherever he chooses.'

'Now look here!' exclaimed Ginny indignantly. It was in fact the Foundation, not the Trust, which contributed to the expenses of running a home which was also an office and which paid for its administrator's travelling expenses; but that was none of Mark's business. 'You make it sound – '

'Sorry, sorry, sorry,' said Mark.

'You're not sorry at all. You're suggesting – '

'Another question, then,' he said. 'You and your sisters all come into the Tantivy age band. Is there a special Trust project for you?'

'Oh, for heaven's sake!' Ginny exclaimed. 'I wish I'd never answered any of your questions. If I'd known you were going to go on nosing around like this . . .' Her annoyance stemmed partly from a sincere wish to get on with her work without further interruption, but partly also because he had touched a tender spot.

On their eighteenth birthday Ness and Tory and Ginny herself had been told that they could each choose what they would like as a coming-of-age present, which would be paid for out of the funds of the Tantivy Trust. Had Prince Fiori – who was one of their godfathers – been alive, said Andrew, he would undoubtedly have given them a generous birthday present every year, and he had told their parents that when they attained their majority they were to ask for whatever was their hearts' desire. That was the specific phrase that was used: 'their hearts' desire'.

At the time the three girls had been too thrilled by the possibilities to feel surprised by such a bequest. Only later, after she had begun to work for the Trust, did Ginny feel uneasy, wondering whether Prince Fiori had really intended such generosity.

Ginny's choice had been to have a car of her own; but it turned out that her parents had already ordered one as a gift from themselves. As for Ness, she had asked for the cost of going to university but was told that Oxford was part of her education and not to be thought of as anything special. So it had been agreed that the two of them could choose again when they were twenty-one – the age which their godfather would in any case have had in mind when he set down the offer. Tory, however, got what she wanted straightaway – a flat in London – and such things did not come cheaply. It was almost certain that the arrangement was above board: almost, but not quite. She was relieved now when Mark, realising that he was irritating her, stood up and left the office without asking any further questions.

She found it difficult, nevertheless, to settle back to work, for the conversation had disturbed her. She had never given much thought to the circumstances under which the Trust had been set up. It was all so long ago; and her father had told her as much as she needed to know. Now she found herself fretting about the details. It was clear that Mark suspected something underhand. Well, Mark's opinion was of no importance. He had never met her parents. Would he be reassured, she asked herself, when he did?

No one could possibly fail to like and admire Hilary Craig, who was hard-working, efficient and cheerful. More demonstrative than her husband, she showed her love for the three girls in hugs and kisses and was always ready to understand and sympathise with their problems. It was impossible to think of her as anything but completely honest.

Andrew was different: a man accustomed to keeping other people's secrets; naturally discreet. Ginny often wondered how well she knew her father. Was he a man greedy for wealth? Could he ever have been guilty of any crime? No: surely not. And yet in her heart Ginny was not quite sure.

These disloyal suspicions were interrupted by Dorothy's unexpected return in an unusually flustered and wind-blown state.

'Road's blocked,' she announced. 'There's the father and mother of a gale blowing outside. Three trees across the road, all tangled up with each other. I might have been able to climb round on foot, but there's no hope of getting a car through.'

'Have you reported it?'

'Yes. I phoned the police from Mrs Barrie's on the way back, but they made it clear that they'd got enough on their hands with main road blockages. No hope of clearing a way for just one person to use. I'll call Mother from here and tell her I can't make it this weekend.'

'What a shame. You must make up for it some other time.' As Ginny sympathised, it occurred to her that there were two people, not just one, who would have expected to use the only road out of Kilcraigie. 'So Mark won't be able to get out either.'

'Not unless he fancies a little mountaineering.'

'He'll have to stay the night. Would you tell him?'

It would make it all right, in a way, if Dorothy rather than herself offered the invitation. Ginny had found it humiliating to banish her visitor every evening, without feeling that she could use her discretion to judge him a suitable visitor. She was glad of the chance to welcome him as a guest. In circumstances like this, how could her parents possibly object?

9

That night, long after she had gone to bed, Ginny was kept awake by the sound of the gale which had been growing stronger throughout the evening and by now was screaming around the chimney pots. Since she couldn't sleep, she decided that there was one simple way in which to arm herself against any further arguments with Mark. She would go and read the deed which had established the Tantivy Trust.

This proved not to be a very well-timed idea. The archive room at the top of the tower was taking the full force of the wind, which hurled itself against the thick walls with a sound like thunder and shrieked round and through the little turret above. Still, if the tower had stood for more than five hundred years, it ought to be good for a few hours more. She unlocked the filing cabinet and pulled out the drawer which was labelled Tantivy.

There was nothing secret about the deed. She could have inspected it at any time she wished; but her parents had told her everything she needed to know when she first started working in the office. It had never seemed necessary to find out more.

It took her only a few seconds to find the long, narrow legal document. It was only a photocopy; no doubt the original, with its array of stamps and seals, was in John Todhunter's strong room. Its easy accessibility to the casual reader was in marked contrast to the other documents in the same drawer. These were large lawyers' envelopes, strengthened with a linen weave and sealed against prying eyes in an old-fashioned way with red sealing wax. Out of curiosity she flicked through them, recognising the names of projects which the Trust had funded before her time. Presumably these were the contracts or articles which had established the projects, as distinct from the day-to-day accounts and correspondence kept in the lower office.

One of the envelopes, less bulky than the rest, caught her eye. On it, in her father's neat handwriting, was written the single word 'Sophia'. A week earlier the name might not have conveyed much to Ginny, but it had come spontaneously to her lips when she was describing the kidnap to Mark. The name of Isabella's nurse – the other missing person – had been Sophia.

The temptation to look inside the envelope was very great, but she managed to resist it. She was about to start reading the trust deed instead when the tower was hit by a particularly spiteful gust of wind, forceful enough to make even the thick stone walls shudder and feel as though they were swaying. It seemed prudent to retreat to the lower office before beginning to turn the pages.

She had just read the preamble and was absorbing the details of how the Tantivy Trust was to be funded and invested, when the wind struck again, battering against the walls with all the force of a rival clan bringing cannon into play. It must have been swirling, for the next pummelling came from the opposite direction. Without any further warning, the turret at the top of the tower came crashing down.

Seen from a distance, the turret was tiny in proportion to the rest of the castle, but it was heavy enough to hurtle like a rocket through the roof and into the archive room. As the ceiling of the office shook and cracked, Ginny jumped from her chair with a cry of alarm and twisted herself away from the desk, pressing her body against the wall and covering her head with her arms as though preparing for the crash landing of an aeroplane. She had left the ladder down, so that a shower of debris crashed through the open trapdoor and into the office. The air thickened with dust.

233

It was a little while before she dared to open her eyes. Pieces of stone and plaster were still falling, but now in slow motion, like the dripping of a tap which had just been turned off. Ginny found herself shivering with shock. One arm was bleeding where a splinter of stone must have cut it – but if she had decided to remain on the higher level whilst she read the deed, she would not have escaped so lightly.

The room filled with a new sound as the wind swirled down through the hole in the roof above and began to tug at its edges as though pulling at a loose tooth. It was no time to hang around.

The sound of the crash had awakened the whole household. Margaret and Donald, who slept on the top storey of the Fiori wing, were the first to arrive – realising that there had been an accident but startled and alarmed to discover Ginny's presence.

'I'm not hurt,' Ginny assured them. 'But it'll start to rain as soon as the wind drops and everything will get soaked. Could you find a tarpaulin or something of the sort, Donald? And a ladder. If we put any weight on this one, it will bring the whole frame of the trapdoor down.'

He nodded and moved towards the door of the office, where he was almost knocked down as Mark came running in.

'Ginny! Ginny, are you all right?' He took her into his arms. 'God, I was scared. I heard all the racket and went to your room to make sure you were all right, and you weren't there. I knew somehow, I was sure, that I'd find you here. Oh Ginny, darling Ginny, I love you. If you'd been killed, if you'd been hurt . . .' He began to kiss her, holding her so tightly that she could hardly breathe.

Little by little Ginny stopped shivering and relaxed in the comfort of his embrace until at last, smiling with relief, he let her go. Margaret, the housekeeper, was waiting anxiously to tell her that her bleeding arm must be disinfected and dressed.

'Could you give Donald a hand with covering things up?' Ginny asked Mark, who willingly agreed. 'But be careful. I don't imagine that the floor is very safe.'

'I'll be careful all right. I intend to be around tomorrow.' He squeezed her hand as she allowed herself to be led away towards the first-aid box.

Next morning she slept through the sound of her alarm clock. By the time she went down for breakfast the gale had abated slightly. Now, though, it carried a driving rain which whipped against the windows with a forcefulness very different from the usual gentle mist of the area.

'No more outdoor painting,' she said to Mark, who had finished eating but was sipping coffee as he waited for her. She felt shy of him, as if they had both revealed more of their feelings than they intended on the previous evening. 'And for the next few days we shall have workmen all over the place.'

'You're telling me that it's time to go.'

'Yes, I think so, don't you? As soon as the road's open.'

'Judging by the radio news, the whole island has blown over in the past twenty-four hours. Everyone is searching for men with chainsaws.'

'There are more up here than in most places.' Dorothy had telephoned the owner of the fallen trees on the previous afternoon, and before lunch the news came through that the way was open.

Ginny could not explain even to herself why she wanted Mark to leave. It seemed to her that she had suddenly fallen in love – but because it was the first time, she was not quite sure. What she did know was that she wanted to be touched, kissed, embraced again – wanted it so passionately that she was aware of danger and needed time to think. To soften her decision, to make him aware that she loved him, she would not let him go without arranging another visit, when her parents would

235

be at home to study the finished portrait and perhaps commission a family group: a visit to make sure that they would meet again.

After he had left she moved her current papers temporarily to her father's office so that the work of repairing the ceiling and floor of the archive room, and making safe the top of the tower, could proceed without disturbing her. The archives themselves, of course, had to be moved while the repairs were in progress. Most of the documents were still locked into place; but Ginny had left the Tantivy drawer open when she retreated to the lower office, and this had caused the whole filing cabinet to topple over as a lump of stone hit it. Donald, when he first climbed up, had found the contents of the drawer on the floor and covered by debris; as an immediate measure he and Mark had bundled them into a plastic bin-liner to protect them against the rain.

Only after the builders had left did she and Dorothy devote an afternoon to putting everything back in place. The envelopes in the plastic sack were dirty now, but had proved strong enough not to tear. One or two of the bright red seals had cracked or broken. That was hardly surprising in view of the buffeting they had received. Ginny made a note to ask her father, when he returned, whether this mattered – whether it was legally necessary for them to have new seals affixed.

The envelope labelled 'Sophia' was one of the damaged ones. Ginny was just about to slot it back into the drawer when she paused to inspect it more closely. The flap of the envelope was not closely sealed along its whole width. Instead, both ends were slightly raised. She ran her finger underneath as far as it would go and confirmed that, as she had immediately suspected, glue had been applied in the centre.

Someone had been snooping. The sealing wax could have been broken by the falling turret and it was just conceivable that dampness could have caused the flap to peel open. But only someone who knew that he ought not to be looking would try to conceal the fact that the envelope had been opened.

It had to be Mark. Only he and Donald would have handled the spilled documents, and Donald was not a man to pry. Mark, though, had already revealed an inexplicable curiosity about the Tantivy Trust, and he would have remembered the mention of Sophia's name.

What possible interest could he have in the circumstances which had led to the founding of the Trust? Was it conceivable that he had met someone who, rightly or wrongly, believed herself to be the missing heiress, Isabella? Or perhaps he had made the identification himself, attaching it to a girl who had no suspicion of this possible identity. Had he come to Kilcraigie solely for the purpose of finding out whatever he could? Was his enthusiasm for the idea of painting her portrait nothing but a cover for his real intentions? Sick with disappointment, Ginny continued to stare at the envelope.

There was one more question to ask herself. What had he managed to discover? And the quickest way to find the answer was to read the Sophia file herself. She could explain to her father when he returned why she had felt it necessary to open the envelope.

The short contract inside was written in Italian. Had Mark, she wondered, been able to understand it? Ginny herself was fluent in the language and read it through quickly. Andrew Craig contracted to pay a monthly sum to Sophia Moro until her daughter Maria should reach the age of twenty-one, and then to provide Maria with a dowry. In return, Sophia Moro contracted to observe silence.

Silence. Not *silentia*, the silence of the library, but *omertà*, the silence of the mafia. A sinister word, used without explanation. Silence about what? And why? Uneasily

Ginny remembered Mark's comment that there was something not straightforward about the kidnapping of Isabella Fiori. Ginny herself had believed once that the nurse was probably part of the plot; but it had never occurred to her that her father might be in some way involved.

As soon as Dorothy had finished work for the day and gone to her room, Ginny searched for the Trust's earliest accounts, which were stored in an unlocked cabinet. Yes, there were the contracted payments to Moro. After only a few months the name, but not the details of the standing order, was changed: Moro became Strangio. Perhaps Sophia had married. The payments continued up to the present day. Ginny remembered asking her father about them once when she first started keeping the Trust's books, and was told that the recipient was an old retainer of the Fiori family. She had believed it: why should she not? She did not believe it now.

And Mark: if he had managed to understand the contract, what must he be thinking now? What did he plan to do with the information? Ginny had thought, she had honestly thought when he took her into his arms on the night of the storm that he was in love with her. How impossibly naïve she had been! He had picked his time well, when her parents were away, to charm her into inviting him to stay and to pump her about her work. And she had fallen for it.

On his honour he had sworn that he was not a journalist, but perhaps the truth was worse than that. Was he a detective? If so, who was his employer? Who was it who was so anxious to learn the fate of Isabella Fiori?

The answer arrived on her desk a few days later, in the form of a telephone bill. The Trust and the Foundation each had their own telephone numbers, separate from the Craigs' family line, and it was the Trust's itemised bill which Ginny checked now. Although she was not as adept at juggling figures as her father and Tory, she had a

238

good memory for numbers. As her pencil paused against each set of digits, she knew who would have answered that particular call.

Except in one case. On the last day of Mark Lacey's stay, someone had telephoned New York. That was the chaotic day on which she had moved out of the office ready to let the builders move in, so she took the precaution of checking casually that Dorothy had not been forced to use the wrong telephone for once. Only then, when she was alone, did she look at the rows of clocks which indicated the time all over the world and call the unfamiliar number herself.

After only three rings a young woman's voice answered.

'This is the Princess Fiori Gallery,' she said. 'Can I help you?'

Without speaking, Ginny put down the receiver.

10

'Don't be such a bloody fool!' exploded Ness. 'You're never likely to get a chance like this again. It's the whole of your future that's at stake. What's more important, there are a lot of other people's futures at stake as well. People you may be able to keep alive. For God's sake, get your finger out and go.'

'I don't want to lose you.' Although Ness had been battering David with her tongue for some time already, he was proving surprisingly stubborn, not enjoying what she thought of as an argument but he perhaps saw as a quarrel.

She had known David Goodman for almost eighteen months and was well acquainted with the many different sides to his character. In his work – he was a graduate geneticist – he combined brilliant intuition with extreme concentration; and as though to release the intellectual pressure, in his spare time he played rugger. Ness had long given up going to watch him play, because she didn't want to be present at the moment when he was carried off the field with a broken neck. He was a big man, with hard muscles and a bony face. A strong man in every sense: and yet at this moment he was near to tears.

He should have been excited by the offer which had arrived from America – but had realised that there was a price to be paid for it. Ness, younger than he, was still an undergraduate. Unlike most Oxford first degrees, Greats was a four-year course and she was only a little more than half way through.

'You haven't got me to lose,' she pointed out forcefully now. 'I've got work to do, exams to take, a job to find eventually. Suppose I'm offered something in Australia, you'd look pretty silly, wouldn't you, hanging on here in England, trying to make ends meet on a ludicrous grant that's only for two years, with no prospects. There's no contest. You've bloody well *got* to go. You can't give up the promise of a brilliant career, a *useful* career, for the sake of a girl.'

'Yes I can, if the girl is you. I love you, Ness. It's simply not possible just to – '

'I'll tell you what's simply not possible,' she said. She ran her hands so vigorously through her hair that it broke loose from its pony tail and fell untidily on to her shoulders. 'You're trying to put too much responsibility on me. In twenty years' time you'll be middle-aged and bitter, thinking of all the people you could have helped if you'd only had the resources, and it's going to be all my fault. I won't have it, David. I bloody well won't have it.'

As a general rule, Ness swore only when she was alone and searching an untidy room for some object which was maliciously concealing itself, but she was deliberately now working herself up so that David should be left in no doubt about her feelings – or, at least, the version of her feelings that she wished to project.

'If only you'd promise – '

'Well, I won't.' They had been over this ground before. He was pretending that if she would agree to bind herself to him in some way, it would give him the confidence to leave her; but she was sure that in fact he would take it as encouragement to stay. 'I'm only twenty. It's too soon. I've got to sort myself out, decide what I want to do with my life.'

A year earlier this would have been a true statement. Ness, in her last year at school, had considered her future as carefully as Ginny and Tory had planned theirs, but had come to an opposite conclusion. Before settling down to a forty-year slog she didn't see why she shouldn't enjoy herself for a bit. Although her teachers had assured her that the study of the classics was the best possible discipline for training the mind, her real reason for choosing the subject was that it seemed unlikely ever to be of the slightest practical use. She envisaged her years at Oxford as a time out of life, with no responsibilities; a time when she could enjoy a variety of new experiences and make a variety of new friends, both men and women, without making any single commitment.

On one level, Ness was angry with David for leading her off the path she had chosen. It was more than a year since she had fallen in love with him. Even now, while she was so determinedly banishing him, her body ached for his. As soon as he surrendered and went away, she would be so miserable that she was almost crying with the pain of it already. But she knew her own character. She wanted to be her own woman for a little while – perhaps for a long while – before becoming someone else's. The fact that she was genuinely, hopelessly in love with David Goodman at the moment didn't mean that she would love him for ever.

So for David's sake, as well as her own, she felt sure that what she was doing was right. David's research into hereditary disease held out hope to men and women who longed to have children but could not face the pain and guilt of watching them die – and it was a Texan university, not a British one, which had offered him tenure and laboratory facilities free of economic constraints. 'It's too soon for you, as well,' she said. 'I mean, we're not going to lose touch, I hope. In three or four years' time, if we both feel the same, well . . . But you don't want to tie yourself down now.'

Angry now, David stood up, towering over her as she sat on the floor. 'Don't tell me what I want or don't want. I know what I want, and you say I can't have it.'

'All right then, *I* don't want to tie myself down. Oh, do come in!'

She had heard a tap at the door a few moments earlier and had ignored it. If it was a friend from her own college, Christ Church, he would go away. But the tap had been repeated. Now the door was opened by a stranger: a fair-haired young man of about David's age; in his early twenties but too old to be an undergraduate.

The expression on his face was one of uncertainty, as though he recognised that he was intruding in spite of the invitation to enter. Ness didn't have the foggiest idea who he was or what he wanted, but seized on his arrival to emphasise the point she was trying to make to David. She greeted him as though he were an old and close friend.

'Did you knock before? I *am* sorry to have kept you waiting. Come in. Sit down. David's just going.' She hauled herself to her feet and fixed her hair back into place without bothering to look in a mirror.

'Yes,' said David, ignoring the visitor. 'I am just going, but not very far. We haven't finished this conversation yet.'

'I'm sorry,' said the stranger as the door closed. 'I interrupted you.'

'Just as well, probably. But were you looking for me, or for someone else?'

'You, if you're Ness. My name's Mark Lacey, and – '

'Oh yes, I've heard about you.' Ness did not specify who had been the source of her information. She phoned home regularly, and there had been an odd change of gear in her conversations with her sister. At one moment it sounded as though Ginny had been swept off her feet by the young man who had arrived completely out of the blue. But a week or two later, after he had left, she seemed reluctant to talk about him, as though regretting her earlier enthusiasm. 'He's very inquisitive,' she had said. 'If he turns up to see you in Oxford, don't answer questions about me or Father or the Trust or the Foundation. Just keep asking him back why he wants to know.'

This instruction had left Ness feeling curious. In other circumstances she wouldn't have bothered to waste time on him; but as it was she made a cautious check. 'The artist, right?'

'Yes. So probably you can guess why I've come here. To ask if I can make a quick sketch of you – something that I can show your parents when I try to persuade them that they'd like a family group.'

'My impression was that you'd been attempting something rather more permanent than quick sketches while you were up at Kilcraigie.'

'I did a couple of portraits, yes.'

'Where are they?' demanded Ness. 'I presume you've brought some of your work to Oxford so that you can show it to me if I need persuading.'

'Yes. They're in the car outside. I didn't want to lug them into the college without knowing . . .'

'Show me.' Ness pulled on an anorak and led the way out. 'Risky,' she commented, as he indicated an elderly hatchback parked on a double yellow line: but there was no warden in sight. The back seat of the car had been removed and in its place was a wooden construction which allowed two canvases, still on their stretchers, to be fastened between double frames by pieces of cork. Mark undid the first and leaned it against the side of the car.

He had made a good job of the ruins. Left as a landscape of water, grass and rock, it would have been an interesting painting. But the impact was diminished by the central position of a recognisable but lifeless Ginny. Ness could think of nothing to say about it. Though reluctant to express criticism, she was not prepared to praise.

'You don't like it.'

'It's a good likeness, in a way. But only of a beautiful face. There's more to Ginny than that.'

'I know. I overworked it. Just so that I could have the pleasure of staring at her for as long as possible. You may

prefer this. She only allowed me ten minutes for the pose.'
He brought out the second painting.

Like the first, it was a full-length portrait of Ginny, but
this time seen close up, with little room left for background.
There must have been a gale blowing. Ness could see the
wind in the long, thick lines made by the palette knife.
Ginny was not holding a polite smile, but laughing aloud
as she tried to hold her flying hair down with one hand and
her kilt with the other. In spite of the wind, the picture was
infused with sunshine. It was the portrait of a golden girl; a
laughing, living girl on a golden day. 'Now that,' said Ness,
'is something else entirely.'

'I painted it back in the studio. From memory and from
the photographs I'd taken. I suppose the difference is that
by that time I'd fallen in love with her.'

He looked at Ness with an expression at once shy and
challenging: making a confession and waiting to hear her
comment on it.

She made no direct answer. She knew that she was
Ginny's only confidante; always had been. Tory was too
unsympathetic and their parents too often absent. For as
long as she could remember she had felt protective of the
sister who had never seemed completely confident in her
own abilities; and it might well be that she needed to be
protected against Mark Lacey. This was not the moment
to take the easy course and send him away.

'You make it difficult for me,' she said. 'I wouldn't want
to be painted like that.' She pointed to the chocolate-boxy
example. 'Not me at all. But on the other hand, we
can't expect you to fall in love with each member of
the family in turn just so that you can produce the right
effect.'

'Oh, I can do any style you like. I'll show you the
sketches I did of Tory.'

These were different again: quick and lively – some of
them almost like caricatures in their economy of line. Ness

smiled at one in particular, of Tory holding her spectacles and jabbing them forward to illustrate a point. Yes, that had caught her perfectly. 'What would you want of me?' she asked.

'A few photographs. And then half an hour with a pencil would be enough for what I can see. Ideally, I'd like a little time to talk to you first, to find out what kind of person you are.' He began to pack his work back into the car.

'I can tell you what kind of person I am. I'm an impatient person with a great deal of work to get through. I can't afford the time just to sit and be stared at.'

'I can draw you while you're working. That would be good. You could just forget about me.'

'Are you a warts-and-all painter? I mean, I'm not prepared to dress up.'

'I want you as you are. Your choice. May I take you out to dinner tonight, just to chat? And then come back tomorrow.'

'Dinner? Well, "Le Manoir aux Quat' Saisons" would be very nice.' She laughed as she saw from his expression that he had heard of the restaurant – and its prices. 'No, I'm dining in Hall tonight, thanks very much. But I could offer you a cup of tea at four o'clock tomorrow. And half an hour afterwards for your sketch.'

'There's a degree-giving ceremony in the afternoon. I thought I'd hang about outside the Sheldonian with my camera and catch people wearing their new gowns. I'll be along after that, then.'

He was carrying his camera when he arrived next day, and took her straight out into Peckwater Quad to be photographed.

'I'm surprised to see you looking unbattered,' Ness laughed. 'I'd expect the usual Oxford photographers to put the knife in when a stranger arrives on their patch.'

'I tried to look like everybody's elder brother. And I'm

fast.' His grin suggested that he had had a profitable afternoon. 'Do you always wear your hair like that?'

'Is that a criticism?'

'Heavens, no. I just want to have you with your usual look. And it was loose when I arrived yesterday.'

'Only by accident. I prefer it out of the way. Right. Tea, then.'

'You've got a marvellous set of rooms,' he said after they had climbed the staircase. He was looking out of the window at the quadrangle as she switched on the electric kettle.

'Having a separate bedroom is an advantage of being in what was once a men's college. The original women's colleges can only offer bedsitters. I'm madly untidy, but I have just enough discipline to confine the mess to the bedroom and shut the door on it. Next year, alas, I shall have to go out of college and rent some scruffy room in the city. Help yourself to sugar. And then tell me, do you always invest as much time and effort as this in what must be a speculation? I mean, you can't have more than a fifty per cent chance that my parents will commission you. And I don't suppose you're exactly in the Van Gogh class as far as price is concerned.'

'Naturally not. I'm still alive.' He smiled, but almost at once spoke more earnestly. 'But no one paid Van Gogh anything in his lifetime; no one except his brother. I have to build a reputation for myself. You used exactly the right word: it's an investment. Would you mind taking your sweater off for a moment?'

She gave him a mischievous, questioning look. 'Are we playing strip poker without cards?'

'It's quite difficult to tell whether there's a fat body or a slim one inside something so bulky,' he explained earnestly. 'Now that I can see how slim you are, I can indicate that.' His pencil moved quickly. 'You can put it back on now if you want to.'

'No need.' It had not occurred to Ness that a stranger might think her fat. The Arran sweater, with its heavy knitted pattern, was one of her favourite garments because Oxford was so often cold and damp, but she had never before considered what impression it made. She was in fact just as slightly built as Ginny – although not quite as tall. She decided not to put the sweater back on.

'How do you usually sit when you're working?' Mark asked.

'I'll show you.' She put her mug down on the floor, picked up a book and a notebook and settled herself on a floor cushion, with another cushion to soften the wall against which she leant. He moved so that he could see her in profile, and began to sketch again.

'Are your parents back from Brazil yet?' he asked.

'Two days ago, yes.'

'I thought I might go back up there next week, now that I've got all three of you to show them. With a rough of what a picture might look like.'

Ness turned her head to grin at him. 'Perhaps I should warn you that Ginny won't be there.'

'Oh.' He looked surprised. 'She told me . . . Well, yes, that might make a difference to the timing. Where is she?'

'Italy.'

'Italy!' The sound of his scribbling pencil stopped.

Ness raised her eyebrows in comment on his startled expression. 'She must have told you about this touring exhibition of hers.'

'Yes, of course. I thought she wasn't going out again until after Christmas, though. She's in Rome, then?'

'Rome to start with. She said something about taking a few days' holiday after she'd finished her business, and going further south.'

Now he looked not so much startled as alarmed. 'She oughtn't to do that. Not by herself. It isn't safe.'

Ness put down her mug and stared at him. Why on earth should he seem to be suddenly so upset?

'What are you talking about?' she asked. 'Ginny's been taking holidays in Italy ever since she was a toddler: we all have.'

'But in November? And not in the south, surely. I've been reading . . . It's bandit country. A young girl on her own . . .'

'You're probably thinking of Calabria, that sort of area. When I said "south" I didn't necessarily mean deep south.' Too late she remembered that she had been asked not to pass on any information to her visitor, and did her best to add a misleading note. 'She's got friends in Ischia. I expect she's going there.'

Mark made no further comment, but continued to draw her whilst she, in turn, became engrossed in the book which she had picked up originally just to create the pose. Only after he had thanked her and left did his obvious and inexplicable anxiety prove infectious. She frowned to herself as she tried without success to remember Ginny's exact words. If she were indeed going to stay with friends, it was odd, certainly, that she hadn't mentioned their name to her sister, who would probably have been acquainted with them as well. But odder still was the fact that Mark Lacey, who had known Ginny for only a short time, should be so greatly put out by the news of her travels.

'You're jealous!' said Ness to herself aloud. Jealous because for years she had regarded it as her personal responsibility to protect this one of her sisters: Tory had always been able to look after herself. It couldn't be expected that such a state of affairs should continue. Someone like Mark Lacey was bound to come along sooner or later. And Mark Lacey, on first acquaintance, seemed like a nice guy – and Ginny, for all that she looked so quiet and neat, was a sensible and well-organised girl. She was well able to make her own judgements about young men and to look after herself in foreign parts. She had work to do in Rome and it was reasonable that she should take advantage of the journey to relax afterwards. There could be no mystery about her visit to Italy. No mystery at all.

11

The Fiori Foundation still owned five-star hotels in the best central areas of capital cities – often historic buildings in their own right – and over the past twenty years its managers had added modern conference centres to the chain. It was in an exhibition hall attached to one of these newer hotels that the Tantivy exhibition was scheduled to open. Just as well, thought Ginny as she inspected the first batch of paintings to have been selected, for their great size and stark character would have been out of place in any of the small and expensive galleries of fashionable Rome.

The choice of paintings had nothing to do with her. She had asked to look at them only to make her journey seem worth while, since the final arrangements for the opening could easily have been settled by telephone and telex. Even after her inspection was finished, it was still light. She could probably make Naples for the night, if she stepped on it. Or could relax here and make an early start next day. She was still absorbed in the decision as, returning to the reception area of the hotel, she became aware of someone standing in her way. It was Mark Lacey.

'What on earth – ?' She started to ask what he was doing here, but did not finish the question because she knew the answer.

'I've been waiting an hour for you to emerge,' he told her. 'Practising exclamations of astonishment at running into you. But really, of course, I'm here because you're here.'

'How did you know?'

'Ness told me. She doesn't know what you have in mind to do next, but I can guess.'

'How?' Once again she knew the answer, but this time chose to force him into a confession.

'The night of the gale, when I was helping Donald to spread covers in your archive room. One of the filing cabinets had been knocked over. I was shoving back papers which had fallen out, just to keep them dry, and I saw the one labelled Sophia. A name you'd mentioned when you were talking about the kidnapping. It had been torn open in the crash.'

Ginny felt sure that this last sentence was a lie; but a little of her suspiciousness was eased by his willingness to confess that he had been prying.

'So you took it away to read and then glued it up again and hoped no one would notice. Were you able to understand it?'

'I took a copy and read it out to someone who did. Ginny, you mustn't go there. It's a dangerous part of the world, and you'd be asking dangerous questions. Let me do it for you.'

'How good are you at conducting an interrogation in Italian and understanding the answers?' asked Ginny – asking that question in Italian herself and not bothering to wait for any reaction. 'It's not the sort of situation to be resolved in sign language. Besides, the dangerous area you're thinking of is further south, in the toe of Italy. That's where that gang of kidnappers was cornered last year, and where the hostages were hidden. Metaponto isn't in Calabria.'

'It's near enough. I don't imagine the inhabitants change character within a few miles.'

'Well, I shan't appear as myself, so to speak, but as a secretary. A poor little underpaid wage slave. In other words, not worth anyone's while to kidnap.' She had other deceptions in mind as well, but saw no reason to show her hand.

'All the same, I'm coming with you. You're quite right

252

that I couldn't do anything on my own without the language, but at least it's got to be made clear that you have a protector.'

Ginny sat down on one of the sofas in the reception hall to think about it and gestured that Mark should join her.

'Seems to me that I need to be clear about where the danger lies,' she said. 'It's time you came clean about your interest in all this. You didn't come up to Kilcraigie just by chance, did you, Mark? You came to dig for dirt – in the hope of finding very much the sort of thing that you actually did find. Why?'

'I've felt bad about that,' he confessed. 'I said I wasn't a journalist, and I'm not. And I said I wasn't a detective and it's true that I'm not that either in any professional sense. But I *was* asked to investigate. By Princess Fiori, the mother of Isabella. She was told, long ago, that her daughter was certainly dead. Now she suddenly discovers that there's an element of doubt – that your father, for one, is acting on the principle that Isabella still might be alive somewhere. You can imagine, the princess wants to know what's going on.'

'So she's paying you to snoop.'

'She's covering my expenses because otherwise I couldn't afford, for example, to fly out here at a moment's notice. But not more than that. I owe her a favour, and I sympathise with her anxiety. I mean to say, any mother would be upset to suspect that people might have been telling her lies about her own daughter. Besides' – Mark's expression changed to one of dreamy pleasure – 'how else would I ever get the chance to visit Magna Graecia? Pythagoras died at Metaponto: did you know that?'

Startled by the change of subject, Ginny couldn't help laughing at such an unlikely cause of enthusiasm. 'The square on the hypotenuse chap, you mean?'

'The same. And Sybaris is only just down the coast. Where the Sybarites disported themselves and gave a name for ever to happy hedonists. I was due to be a classicist before I came off the tracks, and some of the excitement lingers. When names fly off the pages of text books and become real places. Are you planning to drive down? I've been looking at the map. If we kept on the E1 right down to the edge of Calabria we'd actually be in Sybarite territory. It would be further in miles, but much faster using the autostrada than driving through the mountains.'

'Miles further. I've been looking at the map as well. There's a perfectly good road further north. And my interest in Sybaris is minimal. I failed O-level Latin.'

Ginny was thinking as she spoke. It might be foolish to accept the company of someone whose interest in the subject sprang from such a different source; but he knew where to go by himself if he chose. It would be easier to keep tabs on him if they travelled together. Although she was still made uneasy by the realisation that she and her father were under investigation, she had no reason to think that Mark would do her any harm.

'Okay,' he said cheerfully. 'Obviously the choice of route is yours. But you can't actually keep me away, and it will make a lot more sense if we go together.'

'Right,' said Ginny. It had already occurred to her that he could only learn as much as she cared to translate for him. 'Thank you very much. We'll leave at six tomorrow. Stop for breakfast the other side of Naples.'

The Italian trustee of the Fiori Foundation, a friend of her father's and a regular visit to Kilcraigie, knew how much she enjoyed driving fast and had lent her a Ferrari. At a speed never possible in England they ate up the miles next day. On the way back they could dawdle, if they wished, to enjoy the scenery, but now she was anxious to cover the ground as fast as possible, stopping only to eat and stretch her legs. As they approached Metaponto, though, she was forced to slow down.

She had meant to enquire about their destination at the bank to which Sophia's money came each month, but it was closed; so she halted instead in front of the railway station. For a moment, as the excitement of fast driving faded, she was too tired to move. She flexed her fingers and circled her shoulder muscles until some of her energy returned.

The railway clerk was helpful and she returned to the car with some clear directions.

'We have to get back on the road, drive through the old city and turn left for Matera and then right for Ginosa. The Massaria Bradana is on the other side of the river. There's a rough track, but it sounds as though I'd better not risk the Ferrari on it. We'll walk the last part.'

'Just as well. This is definitely not the sort of car that an underpaid secretary should be seen driving. Oh, just look at that!' He had caught sight of a ruined temple. 'Have we got time? The Antiquarium should be interesting as well.'

'Afterwards.' She was anxious to get the encounter over.

'The city backed Hannibal,' Mark told her as though two thousand years were not enough in itself to explain the temple's collapse. 'So the whole place was sacked by the Romans later.' He looked around eagerly as they drove at a sedate pace through the ruins before turning into the river valley.

When the time came for them to leave the car and walk, they soon found themselves on a ridge from which they could stare down at the massaria. It seemed too large to be a farmhouse, too small to be a village. The main building was constructed from huge blocks of stone, which Mark instantly guessed to have been taken from the ruined walls of the city. It was surrounded by a dozen or more habitations so small that it was hard to be sure whether they provided homes for men or pigs. There was no movement to be seen: no sign of life at all. Ginny was used to those

255

parts of Italy where life was lived largely on the street, where there was always bustle and shouting. Even from a distance she felt chilled by the silence below.

'Let me take your shoulder bag for you before we start scrambling,' offered Mark – and then laughed teasingly as he pretended to drop it. 'Heavens, what are you carrying in here? A couple of bricks?'

'It's the guide book that weighs heavy.' But it hardly seemed worth while unlocking the car to put the book away. Ginny stepped forward to begin the steep descent but, before he followed her, Mark had a suggestion to make.

'I know your Italian's good,' he said. 'But it might be worth your while not to make that too obvious. If you ask your questions as though you've had to prepare them carefully and need the simplest of answers, you might persuade people to jabber away behind your back, thinking you won't understand.'

Ginny nodded without expressing agreement in words. She was nervous now, and glad to feel Mark's hand holding hers as they made their way down the slippery track. From the moment they came near to the buildings they were under observation. Not that they could see their watchers, but she felt her skin prickling under the gaze of invisible eyes peering through small dark windows. Shivering in a wind which seemed to be howling straight down from the mountains, she led the way with a show of confidence to the large central building. The sturdy walls were black with age and dirt and the mean windows were crossed with iron bars for security. It looked like a fortress from outside, but from within might well have the atmosphere of a prison.

To judge from its size, the main entrance must have been designed to admit farm carts pulled by horses or donkeys, but it was firmly closed, with no bell or knocker. Mark, exploring, discovered a smaller door at one side.

They stepped inside and found themselves in a large

courtyard. Here at last were signs of life. Hens scuttled busily about, dogs barked, small children played in the dirt. Around the courtyard a covered cloister softened the first prison-like impression. Part of it was used as a shelter for hay and firewood, but chairs were scattered around other sections, and in some of them women sat preparing vegetables. The barking of the dogs drew their attention and brought others to windows or out through doors. The number of inhabitants so quickly appearing suggested that the original massive house must now be divided amongst several families.

Ginny approached the first person she saw – an old woman so bent that she could not have been more than four feet tall, wearing a heavy black dress which swept the floor. As Mark had suggested, she made her first remark in the stilted phrasing of a holiday-maker.

'I am looking for Signora Strangio.'

The old woman scuttled away with surprising speed, leaving Ginny to wonder whether or not a message was being transmitted. The pause gave time to consider whether to continue taking Mark's advice. Speaking basic Italian might fool Sophia, but it would also give Mark himself, with his A-level Latin, more chance of understanding what was going on, and she was not sure that she wanted that.

It was not the old woman who returned but an unshaven middle-aged man with the build of a wrestler, wearing a waistcoat over a collarless and partly unbuttoned shirt. He stood aggressively close to Ginny as he mumbled a question which she pretended not to understand.

'I beg your pardon?'

He swallowed whatever he had been chewing and repeated the words. 'What's your business?'

'Private business with Signora Strangio. I've come from Great Britain.'

The big man looked from her to Mark and turned his

head to one side to spit. But the answer appeared to be acceptable. He disappeared again into the building.

Ginny reclaimed her shoulder bag from Mark and spoke quickly before the man returned.

'I'd like you to stay outside. No point in having both of us shut in here if anything should go wrong.'

'But – '

'Quick,' she said urgently. 'Go back to the place where we stopped to look down. Even if I'm not finished here, I'll come outside within an hour and wave to you, right? If I don't, it means there's a problem.'

Until a few minutes earlier she had not taken Mark's warnings seriously, believing that he was being melodramatic in order to find out as much as she did about the events of seventeen years earlier. But would she have made the journey at all if she hadn't had her own suspicions about what might prove to be an old crime? Even now she was not sure whether her instructions were designed to exclude her companion or to assure herself of protection, but her forcefulness had the desired effect. Although still reluctant to go, he shrugged his shoulders, gave her a quick squeeze round the waist and disappeared.

It was the old woman who returned, making a gesture which appeared to be telling Ginny to stay where she was but proved, when repeated, to mean 'Follow me'. She led the way across the courtyard and indicated an open door.

Ginny stepped inside and found herself in a warm and smoky room, very large and inadequately lit, which obviously served as both kitchen and living room. The big man, slurping noisily, had returned to his interrupted meal, but with a flick of his fingers he sent the two boys who had been sharing the table with him out of the room. A woman stood beside the cooking range, a ladle in her hand. This was presumably Sophia.

She must be about forty, and the odd thing about her was that she looked no older than that. It was something

258

that Ginny had noticed as she drove through the town: there were young women and there were old women, but there were very few who looked middle-aged – they all seemed to have moved straight from twenty to sixty. Also, all except the young wore black, but Sophia did not. Her apron and shawl covered most of her dress, but what could be seen was brown. Her hair was coiled on the nape of the neck in a style which was old-fashioned – but neat enough to indicate someone who took pains with her appearance. As she walked down to the massaria Ginny had expected to meet a peasant. She should have known better. Sophia had worked in Rome, had travelled to New York, had been employed by a millionaire. She would have returned to her home as a woman who had done well for herself, and the regular payments which Ginny had come to investigate would have helped her to keep up appearances. In a community like this, she probably ranked as a prosperous woman.

'Signora Strangio?'

'Yes.' The answer, naturally, was spoken in Italian.

'My name is Virginia Lacey.' Not wishing to acknowledge the surname which Sophia might recognise, Ginny used the first name which came to mind. 'I'm sorry to interrupt your meal.'

'I eat afterwards. What do you want?'

'I've been sent here by the Fiori Foundation.' Before leaving England she had typed a letter of authority for herself on the Foundation's notepaper and signed it with her father's name. She handed this over and then, when Sophia had read it, turned her head to look at the man at the table, not wanting to say more without encouragement.

'This is my husband,' said Sophia. 'He knows everything. You can speak.' She put down the spoon and sat down at the table, indicating that Ginny should also take a chair. 'Is there some problem?'

'No. No problem at all.' Ginny smiled. She had prepared

the best approach to take and was suddenly sure that it would be all right. 'It's a question of the – ' What was the right word? Pension? Monthly payment? 'The money,' she said. 'I have to make sure that you have received it every month, as arranged.'

Sophia nodded her head, her eyes still wary. 'I sign the paper every time at the bank.'

'Of course. But then, you see, there is the other thing. I have to make sure that Sophia Strangio is still alive.'

For a moment the woman looked puzzled, but then threw back her head and began to laugh loudly. This, without doubt, was something she understood.

'I understand,' she said, and the atmosphere lightened with her smile. 'Shall I bring in ten, twenty people to swear that no imposter is robbing me of my rights? Or have you brought questions to ask that only Sophia Strangio can answer?'

'There is one.' Ginny threw up her hands in a gesture of apology. 'You will forgive me, signora, but I speak for my employer. I am to ask, from many years ago, how you left the Villa dell'Isola and on whose instructions.'

'In a rowing boat with the child,' she said. 'Very quietly, while the speedboat roared to the other end of the lake. I think you know that that's the right answer.'

'And the instructions?'

'From my employer, naturally. The Prince Fiori. Well, it was the Englishman who sent the message to say that the time was coming.'

'Thank you very much.' Ginny bit her lip uncertainly. 'There's something else?'

'Yes. About the little girl.'

The man looked up from his meal to stare at her and the suspicious expression returned to the woman's eyes.

'There is nothing that needs to be said about that. I don't talk to her about those days, and she doesn't remember.'

'But you see,' pointed out Ginny, her mouth suddenly

260

dry. 'There was a promise that she should be given a dowry, yes? When she reached the age of twenty-one.'

'Ah, yes. In three months' time.'

'So I must assure myself that she also is alive.'

There was a moment of silence. Then the man nodded, and Sophia went to the door through which the two teenage boys had left. 'Antonio! Go and fetch Bella here. At once.'

Ginny felt a cold lump form in her stomach. She buried her head in her hands, trying to prevent herself from being sick. Bella! Isabella, that must be. Sophia had been paid all these years to keep an heiress concealed. A girl who should have been one of the richest women in the world was living the life of a peasant in a dump like this. And the Englishman had arranged it. The same Englishman, presumably, who – not quite ruthless enough to kill – had been paying her to keep silence all these years while he continued to spend money to which he had no right. The Englishman who was Ginny's own father.

12

'Bella?' repeated Ginny. She could still hardly believe what she had heard. If the arrangement had been made by Prince Fiori himself . . . Could that be true? Why should he do such a thing? There must have been some second half to the plan. But then, of course, by the time the faked kidnapping took place, the prince was already dead, perhaps leaving only one person who knew the truth of what had happened and knew, too, what was supposed to happen next.

Sophia misinterpreted her shock as doubt.

'Bella, Isabella, is all the same thing,' she said – and then, as Ginny shook her head unhappily, her face was lightened by understanding. 'Ah, you need to hear the name on the certificate perhaps. Maria. But by the time we left the island she was already three and a half years old. Talking, understanding, knowing herself as Isabella. It's not good to change a child's name. We told her only two years ago that she was christened Maria – and that we call her Bella because she was beautiful.'

'But – ' Before Ginny had time to work out the significance of what she had been told, a young woman came into the kitchen. A small boy clutched at her skirt, which was tightly stretched to show the swelling of pregnancy. She raised her eyes questioningly at the sight of the stranger.

Ginny looked from Maria to Sophia and back again. The same narrow forehead, the same slightly receding chin, the same heavy eyebrows, the same straight dark hair. There was no doubt in her mind: she checked only for form's sake.

'This is your daughter? Your true daughter?'

'Of course.' Again Sophia misunderstood Ginny's expression, in which relief mingled with incomprehension. 'About the dowry, it was ridiculous that she should wait so long. Twenty-one is far too old. But her husband has been promised that the money will come.'

'Yes,' said Ginny faintly. 'Yes. I can tell my employer. Thank you.' She stood up, smiling at Maria, who disappeared as silently as she had come. 'So what,' she asked, 'happened to the real Isabella?'

The question was a mistake. The man at the table growled something in what must have been a local dialect. Even had Ginny been able to distinguish the words, she would not have understood them, but the hostility of his tone needed no translation: either the visitor ought to know the answer already or else she had no right to any more information. Sophia, however – no doubt relieved that the interview had proved satisfactory – gestured at him with one hand to indicate that she was in control.

'How should I know?' she asked. 'I went with my baby from New York to Italy as I was told. The Fiori child remained with her father. I was promised that the arrangement was for two years only, and the promise was kept. It was not my business to ask questions. Now that you have satisfied yourself that all is in order, will you eat?'

'No, thank you,' said Ginny. 'You're very kind, but I have a friend waiting for me.' Although etiquette probably required that she should accept the invitation, she felt drained by the conversation and anxious to sort out her thoughts. With many expressions of thanks and farewell, she shook hands and hurried away.

She had expected Mark to be waiting on the ridge, as they had arranged; but instead he sprang on her – there was no other word for it – as soon as she had passed the corner of the massaria's great wall. She gasped with shock before recognising who it was and relaxing in his arms. He kissed her with the same urgency of relief that she remembered from the night of the storm.

'Do you only kiss girls when they're frightened?' she asked, smiling.

'In your case it's when *I'm* frightened,' he told her. 'You should have let me stay. I've been having kittens out here, knowing that I shouldn't have left you alone.' He took the heavy bag back from her and slung it over his own shoulder.

'There was nothing to worry about. A perfectly pleasant conversation.' All the same she found comfort in feeling his arm round her waist as they climbed the track together.

'So what – ?'

Ginny did not answer at once. She needed time to think about what she had learned. Part of it now appeared to be straightforward enough. Prince Fiori, anxious lest his daughter should be kidnapped like her elder brother, had set a decoy in place. Had Sophia realised the danger to which she was exposing her own child and even herself? Well, there was no longer any need to consider that question. The arrangement had been given a time limit, presumably because little Maria as she grew older could not be allowed to consider herself an heiress. Nor would the prince have wished to act the part of her father.

So the real Isabella had stayed with Prince Fiori, who must have made some secret arrangement for her upbringing. The mock kidnapping would have enabled him to conceal her hiding place for a little longer if he had lived. But he had died just before it took place. Had the secret of his daughter's whereabouts died with him? That was inconceivable. Someone must have known: a nurse, at the very least. And even those who were not aware of the precise situation – perhaps because an assumed name was being used – must have become worried when the little girl was no longer visited.

Everything pointed in one direction. An hour earlier

Ginny's heart had been pierced by the suspicion that her father had condemned an heiress to a life of hardship. She had been wrong in detail, but now that suspicion was replaced by another. Andrew Craig, she knew, had been the prince's closest confidant. If anyone knew the truth of Isabella's whereabouts, it would be he. He could have had no premeditated plan to keep her hidden, but the opportunity would have presented itself when his friend died so unexpectedly only a few days before some second step was due to be taken. In one sense Ginny realised that she had not progressed very far with her investigation; but it was far enough to worry her.

'I can't bear the suspense,' said Mark.

'I'm not sure that I ought to discuss it with you,' Ginny told him. 'I feel mean about saying that when you've come all this way, but – '

'You think it's none of my business. True enough. But you'll agree, I imagine, that Isabella's mother has an interest in the matter. Just think of her situation, not knowing whether her daughter is still alive after all. At least you can tell me if you know that Isabella is dead.'

Ginny was torn between the wish to share her discovery and discuss it and the conviction that she could be putting her father at risk by saying too much. The obvious course of action would be to remain silent until she had the chance to discuss the whole matter with Andrew – but could she be sure of learning the truth from him if he were the one who had acted criminally? To distrust her own father was a terrible thing to do, but she could not manage to shake away her doubts. Feebly now she compromised.

'I can't say that with any certainty,' she admitted. 'I think it's quite possible that she *is* alive somewhere. But I don't know where.'

'So the kidnapping – ?'

'Was set up, presumably as a means of making it impossible for any real kidnapping to be planned. Sophia was warned when it was going to take place, and bundled off here with her own daughter. That was what she was to keep quiet about all these years. But *she* doesn't know what happened to the real Isabella any more than I do.'

'She can't simply have disappeared off the face of the earth.'

'No. Maybe she's going to appear on her twenty-first birthday. Brought up, perhaps, by some rich South American family. That's where her father died, in South America. If we could track through the last few weeks of his life, perhaps we'd find some unexplained visit, something that had nothing to do with his business interests.'

'People get kidnapped in South America as well as in Italy. If I were going to hide an heiress, I'd look for somewhere a lot safer than that.'

'Well, that's only an idea. Off the top of my head. I don't know any more than you do.'

By now they had reached the car again. Mark stretched out his hand for the keys. 'Let me drive now. No further need to go at a hundred miles an hour. I suggest we spend the night here.'

'So that you can look at your precious ruins in the morning?'

'Why not? You were telling the truth, weren't you, when you said your conversation here went well? I mean, you're not expecting anyone to creep in during the night and stick a knife between your ribs?'

'Of course not.'

'Right, then. We passed something called the Kennedy Hotel that looked open.'

'Okay.' There was another doubt in Ginny's mind now, more personal than anything to do with Isabella; but the choice of any particular hotel was not relevant to it. Mark was hoping – probably expecting – to spend the night with her. She had felt his excitement when they kissed and he pressed his body hard against hers. She was even more strongly aware of it now, even though he neither touched nor even looked at her as he drove. And what he wanted was what she wanted as well, in a sense – but only in one sense out of many.

She had fallen in love with Mark at Kilcraigie; but the discovery that he had made her acquaintance deliberately and deceitfully for the purpose of snooping had put a quick stop to that. Indeed, her journey to Rome had deliberately been rescheduled so that she would be away from home when he returned to meet her parents.

But with his sudden appearance in Italy she had fallen in love with him all over again, and this time the urge to tell him so was stronger. Sophia's comment on Maria had struck a personal note. For a girl to be unmarried in Italy at twenty-one was obviously to be thought a failure. For a girl in Scotland to be still a virgin at twenty might be thought pretty odd as well. Although her parents were old-fashioned, a strict upbringing had not prevented Tory from having several boyfriends, while Ness had a more single-minded but equally passionate relationship with David. If Ginny had so far resisted temptation, it was only partly because she was shy. More to the point, no temptation had ever been strong enough. Until now.

And yet it seemed to her, as they drove bumpily but sedately back into town, that she must keep her distance. There was a mystery still unsolved, and it could yet prove true that her father was responsible for an injustice, even a crime. What she would do should that suspicion prove true was something she didn't want to think about yet. But to sleep with Mark without confiding in him, to share her body but not her thoughts, would be as deceitful on her part as if he, on his, were only pretending desire in order to pump her. Which of course, she told herself severely, might very well be the case. She didn't believe it, but it would be unwise to dismiss the possibility out of hand.

So caution was the best policy. What reason should she

give? She could tell him, truthfully, that she was not on the pill, but probably he had stocked up with condoms. She could claim to have the curse, but that could only be a temporary excuse. Or she could – and how extraordinary it was that she should only just have remembered this! – she could remind him that he had a girl already. Tory had mentioned, in that quick telephone call when Ginny made her first check, that Mark had painted a fine portrait of the girl he lived with. At the time Ginny had had no personal interest in the unexpected visitor, and had remembered only the part of her sister's information which confirmed that he was indeed an artist, but now the memory made her suddenly indignant. Why had he never mentioned the girl to her? Well, it was obvious enough why. Because he was not in love with Ginny at all, but merely using her inside information to spearhead his own enquiries.

She could have accosted him with her knowledge and accused him of playing around, but instead forced herself to keep calm. After all, she was under no obligation to provide excuses or reasons or challenges. All she had to do was to say No. He would be disappointed, and to a degree she was disappointed herself; but the decision was hers.

'I'll go and ask,' she said as the car drew up in front of the hotel. Mark followed her in, but she was first at the reception desk.

'We'd like two rooms for the night,' she said.

13

The flight back to England allowed Ginny time to consider seriously what might have happened to Isabella Fiori. It had been too difficult to concentrate on the subject whilst still in Mark's company. He had been puzzled and hurt at finding her bedroom door closed to him only a few hours after she had kissed him so passionately. But overnight he appeared to have formulated an explanation of his own: that Ginny was an old-fashioned girl who wanted to be courted and wed.

It amused her to observe the change in his behaviour. He still touched and kissed her like a lover, but took pains to be polite and unthreatening. He had talked more freely as well – about the ruins which they visited together and the people who had once inhabited them, but also about himself, as though recognising that they needed to get to know each other on a more intimate level than that of merely falling in love. He asked about her own childhood and family life. It was a deliberate strengthening of the element of friendship in their relationship; and Ginny, relieved that there had been no angry or pained confrontation, found herself able to relax in the enjoyment of his company during the three days before they arrived back in Rome.

His closeness, though, had prevented her from sorting out her ideas – because she had no intention of sharing any conclusions with him and was afraid that he would be able to sense this. Certainly he had not put the Isabella affair out of his mind. His last words, as he saw her off on a flight which had no room for him, were a laughing suggestion that her next expedition would be to South America.

Ginny had no such trip in mind. If Princess Fiori wanted to investigate the travels of her late ex-husband after so much time had passed, good luck to her. A more sensible approach from Ginny's own point of view was simply to ask her father what he knew about the events of that period – and sooner or later she would do exactly that. But not just yet. She did not quite trust him to tell her the truth, and so the more she found out for herself first, the better.

As the plane flew over the jagged black teeth of mountains still awaiting their first snowfall of the winter, she checked systematically through all the different possibilities. Earlier on she had been unable to prevent the question of whether her father had some involvement in the death of Isabella Fiori from entering her mind: but she had dismissed it at once. He was not that kind of person. She had briefly suspected him of banishing Isabella to a life as Sophia's presumed daughter; but now that hypothesis too could be dismissed, thank goodness. What remained?

It was possible that Isabella had disappeared in exactly the way she had postulated to Mark; so that Andrew Craig had good reason to suspect that she might be alive somewhere but genuinely did not know where. That was what he would probably say if she asked him – and it was what she wanted to be true. But in such a case he would surely have devoted far more of the Trust's income to a search for the missing heiress.

So she was left with the most likely scenario of all: that Isabella was alive and that Andrew Craig knew where she was but – for good or bad reasons – was concealing the fact. If the reasons were bad, it must be assumed that Isabella did not know her true identity. If they were good, it was more difficult to guess whether the same would hold true. An adult might agree to keep a secret of that sort, but Andrew could well have felt that a child or adolescent would succumb to the desire to boast and spend.

There was no doubt that Andrew – and, indeed, the whole Craig family – had profited from the uncertainty. Yet Ginny did not believe her father to be a greedy man. His salary from the Fiori Foundation was linked to the amount distributed each year. Generous to start with, it had increased as interest on the invested capital rose and was compounded to provide an even higher income. And the arrangement was for life: he had told Ginny that once. The Craigs were rich – not as Prince Fiori had been rich, but compared with almost anyone else. Andrew would have had no need to hide away someone who at any moment might stumble on a clue to her own birth and emerge from obscurity to challenge his stewardship.

Nor did he behave like a man who had something to his discredit to hide. Although he applied himself to his work with unusual seriousness and had at times been a stern father, he had always been able to relax and play in a light-hearted manner on holiday and on Sundays. There had never been a time when she could have suspected him of living under the shadow of a guilty secret.

So the next possible assumption was that he did know where Isabella was but that he had no bad conscience about it. How, in that case – and at that moment Ginny gave such a gasp that the man in the next seat looked up from his newspaper, thinking that she must be ill. She gave him a quick smile of reassurance without allowing her train of thought to be interrupted. As though she had taken off dark glasses on a day of bright sunlight she found herself for the first time able to see clearly a possible scene whilst being forced by the glare to blink in disbelief. She had found the answer.

Prince Fiori, nineteen years ago, had divorced his wife and was left with the custody of a baby. He had grave fears about her security and perhaps also some doubts about whether he could give such a young child the care she needed. What could be more natural than that he

271

should ask his best friend to look after her for a couple of years! Baby Isabella would be mothered by Hilary Craig and would have companions of her own age. Her father would have a personal suite in the house where she lived so that he could visit her under the guise of discussing Fiori Foundation business. Of *course*!

One awkward consequence of that theory was that the story about the birth of quads, and the little boy who died, must be a lie. Hilary had had twins – and had moved away from the area in which they were born so that no questions would be asked when a third little girl appeared in the family. This idea caused Ginny some uneasiness, for she knew her mother to be exceptionally open and honest. It was difficult to believe that she would have kept such a secret from her own daughters when so much deception was involved. But at least to start with, it would all have been organised from the best of motives, for the good of the little Isabella.

Probably the arrangement was never intended to be permanent, but to last only for the two years agreed with Sophia – the two years during which Isabella was doubly protected by the presence of a decoy at the Villa dell'Isola and by the heiress's use of a false name. When Prince Fiori died, what could Andrew do but continue the deception? He might have considered handing the child to her mother, but perhaps he had been specifically instructed not to do this, if the divorce had been a bitter one. Or, of course, he could have made the true position public and set up some kind of guardianship arrangement. But what sort of life would that be for a little girl with an income of millions of pounds a year? How much better it was to believe that by that time Hilary and Andrew had grown so fond of their little ward that they couldn't bear to part with her. Perhaps they had even quietly adopted her.

None of these possibilities would absolve Andrew from the charge that he had deprived an heiress of her status and income, but it was easy to argue that his motives throughout could have been unselfish. Regardless of her neighbour's curiosity, Ginny gave a deep sigh of relief. If her reasoning was correct, there was only one more question to be answered: but it was the most important question of all. If it were true that one of the three Craig girls had been born Isabella Fiori, which one was it?

14

It may be me!

How long had that possibility been simmering at the bottom of Ginny's mind before bubbling its way to the surface? Once there, it could not be ignored, and she was tugged in two directions at once by conflicting currents of thought. Was she or was she not Isabella? Did she or did she not hope that she was Isabella?

The first question could not be answered yet, but the second should have been simple. Wasn't it everyone's dream to be a millionaire? Why else did people fill in their pools coupons or hope for the bingo jackpot? But they would be thinking about a million pounds in capital. Peanuts.

Even Ginny, although she worked for the Tantivy Trust, did not know the full extent of the fortune that had been settled on Isabella Fiori when she was only one year old. The unusual discretion allowed to her trustees meant that after Prince Fiori's death Andrew Craig had been empowered to do anything he liked with the income until twenty-one years after Isabella's birth, although the capital was to be preserved for much longer. When he had decided – by his own choice – to set up a charity, he had allocated only part of the income to that purpose. That was the part which Ginny knew about, and it came to almost three million pounds a year. If the rest had been re-invested over the years, it must by now have grown to an unimaginable sum, producing in turn an unimaginable income.

Even the three million was too much. What could one possibly do with it all? There would be a temptation to spend. To buy a palace when one might be happier in a cottage. To hang Old Masters on the wall when there could be more satisfaction in painting one's own pictures. To employ servants because the house was too big and install burglar alarms because the contents were too valuable – it was easy to see how money could take control of one's life. It might come to seem ridiculous to have a job, but how would the time be passed without one? Ginny had been brought up to take it for granted that she would work for her living. The whole question of whether work was a virtue as well as a necessity was another stone to be tossed into the whirlpool.

She was going too fast. It was crazy to build a whole house of hypotheses on a foundation of guesswork. Facts must come first.

Her car was waiting at Heathrow, but instead of starting at once on the drive home she telephoned to say that she would spend a day or two in London. Her parents by now were back from Brazil, but there was some research to be done before she began to ask questions directly of them.

First call was at St Catherine's House to inspect the Registers of Births and Deaths. She couldn't remember that she had ever seen her own birth certificate. There was no sinister reason for this: there had never been any need for it. Her mother, almost certainly, would produce it if she were asked. But for the moment, since she knew the place as well as the date of her birth, there was no difficulty in finding the entry.

It seemed that this first call would also be the last. There, neatly listed, were the names of the four babies to whom Hilary Craig had given birth in June 1969: Vivian, Victoria, Vanessa, Virginia. So there had been no lies about that. There were, as there had always appeared to be, three Craig daughters.

'How do I check on someone's death?' she enquired.

'You need to know the date and the area.'

The little boy had died within his first few hours of life. It was easy enough to confirm this. But suppose one of the girls had died as well: not at once, but later? There was no simple way to look this up without any information. Ginny searched in vain through the lists for the month after Vivian's death. It was too late in the day to do anything more then; but next morning she made her way through a November drizzle to the hospital in which she had been born.

Offering her passport as proof of identity, she pleaded to see her own earliest record. The registrar pulled a face at the thought of looking for twenty-year-old information, but allowed her assistant to climb a ladder and pull down the relevant file. Ginny offered to search it herself, but this was apparently not allowed.

'Craig. Four babies born prematurely by Caesarean section on June 21, 1969: three girls and a boy. The boy died on the same day. Two girls discharged on September 30.'

'Why so late?' asked Ginny.

'I haven't got the medical notes here; only dates. But quads would certainly have a low birth weight, and the policy is to keep them in until they reach a normal weight, six or seven pounds. The third one must have taken longer to do that, for some reason. She wasn't discharged until December 23rd. Home for her first Christmas!'

'Which was which, do you know? I mean, what was the name of the third one?'

'The names aren't here. Baby One, Baby Two, Baby Three. The boy was Vivian. That suggests that he had an emergency christening when it was clear he was going to die. I'm afraid that's all we can tell you.'

'Thanks very much for your help.' Ginny was just about to leave, but turned back to put one further question. 'If

276

someone in Weybridge was looking for a nanny in 1970, who d'you think she'd ask?'

'A lot of mothers prefer word-of-mouth recommendation. I can tell you the names of some current agencies, but I can't promise that they were necessarily going strong then.' The registrar scribbled down a few names and underlined the three oldest-established. Ginny struck lucky with her first choice.

'We keep very precise records,' said the Norland secretary. 'All our nurses have our own qualification and naturally it's of concern to us that they shan't bring it into disrepute. They can use us as an employment agency, and so we preserve whatever information is necessary for references. You're hoping to contact your own one-time nurse, are you? How nice!'

'I don't actually know – '

'We cross-reference by the names of employers. Yes, here we are. Mrs Andrew Craig. Asked for someone experienced. First babies. Triplets, although only two at home to start with. Nurse Godwin. No longer working. She married twelve years ago and emigrated to Australia. Mrs Saunders now.'

'Australia!' Ginny had hoped to call on her. 'Oh. Do you have her address?'

'It's not our policy to give that out directly. But if you write a letter and send it here, I'll see that it's forwarded at once.'

'One more question then, if I may. I'd meant to ask her. Do you know when and why she left?'

'She had a one-year engagement from September 1970. Most nurses have favourite ages. Nurse Godwin specialised in young babies. That was why she was recommended in this case. She seems in fact to have stayed on for a few weeks longer than the year. Until December 1971. Perhaps there was difficulty in finding a replacement.'

'And did Norland supply the replacement?'

'No.'

'Well, thanks very much,' said Ginny. 'I'll write to Mrs Saunders.'

The rain was heavier now. She made a dash for the car and sat in its shelter without moving for a few minutes, trying without success to think of any other calls which could usefully be made; but it was not long before she gave up and pointed the bonnet towards Scotland. By starting home at once she could have three hours' driving before dark, and then break the long journey with an overnight stop.

There was one more person who might be useful, she thought – though without much conviction – as she made her way to the motorway and began to pick up speed. Nanny Mackay had joined the Craig family when it first moved to Kilcraigie Castle and had stayed until the girls were seven. She had kept in touch with them when she moved on to live with other families in Scotland, so it would be easy to contact her and ask questions. But she was not likely to provide any surprise information. The family photograph albums were full of snapshots of three little girls from the toddler age upwards. If any stranger had been introduced into the family it must have been before the move to Kilcraigie, and nothing that Ginny had been told made such an arrangement seem likely. Hilary Craig had given birth to three daughters and she had three daughters still.

So there was no need for any further self-questioning about the delights or disadvantages of finding herself a millionairess. She was thrown back to the earlier question: what had happened to Isabella? Trying to concentrate on this as she drove, she found her mind continually drawn down the side-track of Nurse Godwin. What information might she be able to supply? Had she personally handed over three babies to her successor? Wasn't it an odd coincidence that the Craigs had moved and employed a new nanny at just about the time that Sophia and her baby had gone to live at the Villa dell'Isola? Yes, it was. The mystery was not solved yet.

The Audi had a mind of its own, a natural cruising rate of its own. It never needed to be pressed on, but only to be reined in. Fresh from the pleasures of driving along the autostrada, Ginny allowed her speed to creep up. She was accustomed to drive fast – but she was also accustomed to concentrate on her driving. Today, her attention continually flickered, like the rear light of the coach which had pulled into the fast lane without signalling and was now roaring northwards in front of her, spraying the windscreen with dirty water faster than the wipers could clear it away. The physical flicker was as distracting as the mental one. When the coach driver, approaching the queue for a contraflow system at an illegal speed, put his foot on the brake, it took Ginny half a second too long to react.

15

'You're lucky to be alive.' Ness squeezed Ginny's hand so hard that it hurt. 'When Mother first phoned . . . ! You've got to look after yourself, Ginny. I can't do without you.'

'Nice of you not to say that you told me so.' In her pleasure at seeing her sister, Ginny managed a smile. Her mouth was almost the only part of her body that could be moved without pain. Both her legs were badly bruised and her right arm was broken; but the greatest discomfort came from her chest. Although the seat belt had prevented her from flying through the windscreen, it had not saved her from a bang on the head, and her ribs had been fractured when she jerked forward against the steering wheel. For over an hour she had been trapped, unconscious, in the wreckage and, as Ness was reminding her, she was fortunate that the consequences had not been even more serious. Hers had been the fifth vehicle involved in a concertina collision, and three of the other drivers had died.

'Is it very painful?'

'It would be better if I were allowed to stop breathing.' She was forced to pause for a moment between sentences. 'Some sadist turns up every couple of hours and makes me cough, and that's not too funny. You do the talking.'

'Right. I'll tell you the latest instalment of the Ness-and-David saga. The idiot has turned down a dream offer from Texas in order to go on slumming it in Oxford.'

'You should be glad.' Another pause for breath. 'You love him, don't you?'

'I adore him. But the way things are going, I shall feel obliged to go on adoring him, no matter what. I'd rather really – honestly – that we both went our own ways, worked out what we wanted from our own lives, and only then decided how we could make them mesh. What he wants is to get married. Quite apart from the fact that I'd be crazy to do that before I've taken Finals, I have the feeling that what he's after is to be settled for life in order that he can concentrate on his work without emotional distractions.'

'Sounds a bit dull for you.'

'That's putting it mildly. To turn one's back on excitement at the age of twenty! And yet, of course, if he *is* Mr Right I ought to recognise my luck in finding him early. All very tricky, and slightly worrying. I'm not like Tory, able to juggle with half a dozen adoring swains. She's coming to visit you on Sunday, by the way.'

'Great. The car. Write-off, I suppose?'

''Fraid so. Father may suggest that you get something more sedate next time.'

'If I can afford a next time.' Although there was no shortage of money in the family – and Hilary and Andrew were generous – the three girls had been brought up on the principle that anyone who broke or lost a possession must take the responsibility for replacing it herself.

'There's insurance. And you never know, your godfather might stump up.'

'Godfather?' Ginny couldn't think what she meant.

'The late Prince Fiori of blessed memory. Don't you remember, he bought Tory a flat on her eighteenth birthday and promised that you and I could catch up on our twenty-firsts.'

'Fiori! Ness, I – ' Until that moment Ginny had been unable to remember what it was that had been on her mind as she drove north immediately before the accident. She was sure that it was something important, but it had vanished as completely as any memory of the crash itself. Now she remembered.

Her exclamation, though, was too abrupt to be wise.

She began to cough, but was lying too flat in the bed to do so comfortably and began to groan with the struggle to control it. Ness, alarmed, rang for a nurse and there was no further private conversation between the two sisters before Ness had to return to Oxford.

Perhaps it was just as well, thought Ginny when, later, she lay back, comfortable again but exhausted. What was the point of discussing her suspicions when they were so unsubstantiated – indeed, when she was not sure what it was that she suspected? They would only be a distraction from Ness's work, as they had been from Ginny's own driving. She was not even clear in her mind what conclusion she had come to before the accident.

A later visitor helped her to remember. Mark arrived as soon as she was judged fit enough to receive visitors outside the family. Like Ness, he clutched her hand fiercely.

'Twice you've frightened me – and the third time, when it really mattered, I wasn't there.'

'Just as well. Might have killed you.' By now Ginny could breathe and speak in a more regular fashion as long as she didn't say too much at a time. 'Who told you?'

'Your housekeeper. I phoned Kilcraigie Castle, thinking you'd be home by then. And hoping that I could come up and have a word with your parents about the painting.'

'Oh yes. The painting.' Ginny didn't believe in the painting as anything more than an excuse, but it was enough to remind her that Mark was following the trail of Isabella Fiori with as much determination as herself. She was initially relieved when a second visitor arrived; but her relief did not last long.

It was Nanny Mackay who arrived, bearing books to read and chocolates to eat. Mark needed only a few seconds to realise that he was talking to someone who had known Ginny since she was eighteen months old, and showed no shame at pumping her directly. Ginny was equally quick to realise what he was after. In subtle requests for anecdotes he was able to establish that when Nanny Mackay took up her duties at Kilcraigie Castle, at the time when the Craig family moved in from England, there were three little girls in the family.

Ginny kept quiet, not wanting to ask questions of her own while Mark was there to listen to the answers. She guessed what he was trying to prove and suspected that he had got it wrong. It was easy to understand why he might believe that Isabella must have been taken to a new home at the time of the mock-kidnapping from the Villa dell'Isola. He had not been present at the interview with Sophia which made it clear that the period to investigate came two years earlier. Ginny had not passed on that information while they were in Italy, and she said nothing now. It would be some weeks before she could take up the role of detective again. At the moment she was unable even to write a letter, and she had no wish to reveal her suspicions by asking anyone to take dictation. So she was glad to feel that Mark was unlikely to catch up with her in any enquiries he might be making.

For the same reason she discouraged him from any plans to visit her again. She had been taken to the hospital nearest to the accident as an emergency case, but now that her life was no longer in danger Andrew was arranging for her to be moved to a private hospital nearer to home; and she hoped to be back at Kilcraigie for Christmas. Until she was fit enough to pick up the threads of her own life again, the quest for Isabella could be put on hold.

16

The excitements of Christmas were over. Ness had begun a new term at Oxford and a temporary secretary had been engaged for the Tantivy Trust so that Ginny need not sit uncomfortably in an office chair or attempt to type until her right arm was back to normal action. By now her headaches had abated, but her balance was still uncertain and she was not yet able to walk easily or for long at a time.

'This is the boring part of convalescence,' she sighed to Tory. 'The arrival of the physio is the biggest event of the week, except when you turn up. And my hour of doing exercises in the pool is the highlight of any day. When I knew I was in a bad way, it didn't worry me just to lie and do nothing all the time, but now –'

'You didn't have much choice before, did you?' suggested Tory, who had flown home for a weekend to keep her sister company.

'True. But now I feel I ought to be able to do more and it makes me cross when I suddenly flop.'

'I'll take you for a walk this afternoon. You shall stride out for as long as you're able, and I'll crawl behind in the Range Rover ready to pick you up when you drop.' Tory wandered over to the window as though to plan the walk, and exclaimed in surprise. 'What's Ness doing here?'

'Ness! It can't be. She only went back to Oxford eight days ago.' Moving carefully, Ginny joined her sister at the window. Ness waved vigorously as she ran up the steps, and within a few minutes joined the others in the long gallery which had always acted as a private sitting room for the younger members of the family.

'Why have you come home?' asked Ginny when they had hugged each other in surprise and pleasure. 'And why didn't Mother say anything?'

'Because I didn't tell her I was coming. I shall have to go back tomorrow. But I've got something important to discuss. Too big just to ask over the telephone.'

'Tell us.' Tory and Ness sat down, as usual, on the floor. Only Ginny, who would have had difficulty getting up, lowered herself on to a sofa.

'It's the question of the twenty-first birthday present from our generous late godfather.'

'Five months still to go,' Ginny reminded her.

'I know. But I've got the chance of something which won't wait till then. I shall have to spend next year out of college. They don't have enough rooms for all of us all the time. There used to be landladies in Oxford to deal with this situation, but the breed seems to have disappeared years ago. What most people do now is to make up groups of five or six and rent a house. I've been looking, and they're so squalid, these houses! Small builders buy them up and put bits of cardboard to divide the bedrooms and slap some paint over the dry rot and charge the earth. And with six people sharing a bathroom and kitchen and having to agree on how to split the bills, it's a recipe for losing your best friends.'

'So?'

'Well, I don't know how much cash is on offer, but I've found quite a decent place that I could buy, not rent. I could still have people to live there with me, but I could charge them a fixed sum a month instead of haggling over shares. I'd be the landlady, in effect, so I could lay down the law. It's a nice place, in good repair, and I could make sure it stayed looking nice.'

'You won't be in Oxford for ever,' Tory pointed out.

'Then it can be sold again. That's the point of having something respectable.'

'Sounds sensible,' Tory said. 'Father reckoned that my flat was a good investment, quite apart from giving me somewhere to live. I should think he'll take the same line with you. He'd probably have agreed over the telephone.'

'Perhaps. But there is one other thing.' Ness hesitated for a moment. 'One of the people I'll be sharing with is David. Since he's given up the chance of living in luxury for my sake, the least I can do is offer him a roof over his head. I can't tell you how mean the research grants are in England. Anyway, I wouldn't want Mother and Father to find out accidentally afterwards that we were living together, and feel that they should have been told.'

Ginny and Tory considered this in silence. Their parents were so happy in their own marriage that their views on divorce and extra-marital relationships were old-fashioned. But they had enough knowledge of the ways in which other people lived to realise that not everyone these days conformed to their own pattern of family life. Ginny herself, in the course of her research for the Trust's hostel idea, had recently prepared a file whose graphs showed how many couples co-habited before marriage, how many children each year were born out of wedlock, and how many parents married subsequently. Hilary had found the figures startling at first sight, but was enough of a realist to come speedily to terms with them.

'So they're not expecting to see you.'

'No. But I got Dorothy to guarantee me an hour with Father. Starting now, so I'd better go. I'll come back afterwards to find out how you are, Ginny, and all that sort of thing.'

'How very honest of Ness,' said Tory after the door closed. 'I wouldn't dream of disclosing what goes on in my flat. I reckon parents don't want to know. She may be sorry.'

'They can't precisely say No, can they? After all, it's Prince Fiori's money, not theirs.'

'Not sure. Whether they can say No, I mean. It's their signatures that have to go on the cheque. I wish we'd known the prince. How about a game of backgammon? Your rest period isn't over yet.'

They played almost in silence, but Ginny's mind was not on the game. She had known about Ness and David for a long time, but when they moved in together something important would change. For years Ginny had come first with Ness, but that would not be true any longer. She was not precisely jealous, but – yes, she was. She was upset because she was alone; and it was Ness's withdrawal which would leave her lonely. It was tempting to think that she could use Mark to fill the empty space – but Mark was someone who could not be trusted. He claimed to love her, and she wanted to believe him; but she couldn't. None of this could she explain to her sister. It was all too complicated.

A door slammed on the other side of the house. It must have been a huge slam for the sound to have penetrated so far. Tory and Ginny looked at each other. 'Sounds like No,' said Tory.

They waited impatiently, but it was their mother who was the first to appear. With an anxious expression on her face she hurried into the room, looked quickly round and disappeared again. Clearly she was searching for Ness: to make up a quarrel, perhaps. Hilary had never been able to bear that anyone should sulk or be angry even for a moment.

Another hour passed before Ness came in. Her face was pale and Ginny suspected that she had been crying, although now her expression showed no emotion except for the anger in her eyes.

'I should have got the taxi to stay,' she said. 'Tory, would you mind driving me to the station? Or I'll drive, if you'll bring the car back.'

'You said you were going to stay till tomorrow.' Ginny

was upset to think that they would have no chance to talk.

'Changed my mind. I'm not supposed to leave Oxford during term anyway. Okay, Tory?'

'Right.'

Ginny was left to wait impatiently till Tory returned.

'What happened?' she asked.

'She's not saying. Not a word. But she's steaming. There must have been the hell of a row. I suppose they said No to David and she reminded them that she was an adult. If she'd been willing to hang on here instead of rushing off, I'd have shown her the letters. It would have given her a weapon against Mother. A quiet reminder that people do from time to time fall in love without getting married.'

'Mother! What letters? What are you talking about?'

'Love letters. The sort of thing that every wife keeps under the lining of her handkerchief drawer without ever considering that every husband must think of looking there from time to time.'

'You didn't read them!?'

'Of course I read them. I didn't go looking for them. All I wanted was to borrow a handkerchief. But they hardly rank as current affairs. More than twenty years old and besides, the man is dead.'

'Then they can't be very important.'

'But she kept them. Could have been out of conceit, to remind herself that she was once loved by someone besides Father; but I don't believe she has a scrap of that sort of feeling. I reckon she kept them because she loved him too. A reminder wouldn't have done any harm, to stop her coming down so hard on poor old Ness.'

'Who were they from?'

'Our godfather the prince. Well, signed Tony, but they identify him clearly enough. You *are* curious, aren't you? Hang on. I'll see if they're still there.'

'No, I – '

'Oh, don't be such a goody-goody. You're dying to see them. Hold on.'

'Goody-goody' was the right word for Ginny. Jealous of her own privacy, she knew that it was wrong to intrude on anyone else's. She had had a bad conscience for weeks about the sealed envelope which Mark had opened and which, seizing the opportunity, she had read. It had been her intention at the time to confess to Andrew as soon as he returned – and, indeed, to warn him that he was apparently under investigation. But when her own doubts and suspicions began to grow, she had felt the need to find out more about the events of twenty years earlier before hearing her father's version of them.

Tory's act of espionage served as a reminder that since her accident she had done nothing to pursue her enquiries into the whereabouts of Isabella Fiori. The blow to her head had affected her concentration: she found it difficult to sit down for any length of time to plan out a course of action in any sustained manner. She was just in the process of telling herself that she must pull herself together and get cracking on the investigation when Tory returned with a bundle of letters and threw them on her lap.

For a moment Ginny refused to look down. She loved her mother and would be ashamed to be caught prying into her past life. But there was a special temptation here.

Hilary Craig had just celebrated her fifty-first birthday. She was a cheerful, businesslike woman who had run the Tantivy Trust almost single-handed, with only secretarial support, until Ginny started to take over some of the responsibility; and who also helped her husband with the affairs of the Fiori Foundation. While the girls were young she had stayed at home with them, but nowadays she accompanied Andrew on all his travels.

In addition to this family business, she played her part in the life of the community – which had accepted her in spite of her English birth. She had been a Commissioner of what at the time were still called Girl Guides, she sat on committees which prepared for disasters or organised balls or appointed teachers to schools and she was actively involved in the Duke of Edinburgh Awards. In Scotland she wore cashmere and tweeds in the winter and tailored dresses in summer, with two pairs of elderly baggy trousers taking turns as gardening wear. Only on the family holidays in Italy did the impression of neat efficiency disappear. Her slim, straight-backed body still looked good in a swimsuit or sun-dress and the years fell away as she relaxed in light-hearted laziness.

Even then, though, at her most carefree, she was still a responsible middle-aged wife and mother. Ginny found it impossible to imagine her as she would have been in her twenties, before her children were born. Had she then, like Ginny now, felt unsure of herself, worried about making mistakes, a little lonely but at the same time approaching new relationships only with hesitation? The letters which Tory had so disgracefully borrowed might throw a light on Hilary when young. Almost against her will Ginny allowed her eyes to rest on the letter at the top of the pile. It had been written in Rome in 1962. The first few lines were enough to banish her qualms.

> *Dear Hilary,*
> *It's important for anyone who's granted a privilege to take advantage of it at once, in case it lapses through disuse. So I'm writing to you just because you told me I might, without having anything to say. Except of course that it was a great pleasure to meet you and that old Andrew's a lucky dog.*

'I don't call these love letters,' said Ginny. 'They're just friendly.'

'Wait till you get to the last one. It positively sizzles.'

The innocuous start to the letters had banished Ginny's

feeling of guilt and she read on through the one-sided correspondence. If it revealed anything at all, it was the loyalty which both Tony and Hilary felt towards Andrew – until the very end.

The last letter, unlike the others, was still in its envelope: an air mail envelope edged in red and blue. It bore no stamp. There was another, more sinister, difference between it and the rest of the pile. It had been soaked in blood.

The pages inside had at one time been stuck together with the blood, but had been eased or torn apart. Now Ginny's sense of trespass returned. Tony Fiori was writing out of loneliness. His marriage had ended in divorce and he expressed his bitter regret that he had not met Hilary before her engagement to Andrew. In a flight of make-believe he imagined that such a meeting had taken place, that they were married. The words flooded more and more passionately over the page as he described how he would return to Kilcraigie Castle and carry her up to bed. As Tory had promised, it sizzled with his desire. Nevertheless, Ginny frowned doubtfully as she carefully folded it back into its original creases.

'He didn't post it. Didn't even sign it.'

'It was written on the day he died, or the day before. I checked the date.'

'It's odd that it should be so different from all the rest.'

'Maybe there were others like that, but she was frightened to keep them. She wouldn't have wanted to throw this one away because of it being his last. He may even have written it when he was dying.'

Ginny shook her head. 'The handwriting's far too neat and regular. And if he knew he was dying, it would be a different sort of letter. A "Remember me" sort of thing. I suspect that he never meant to post it. And that's why she's kept it, because she hadn't known before how he felt.'

'Maybe.' Tory patted the letters neatly together and

went upstairs to return them to their hiding place. 'Exercise time,' she said briskly when she returned. 'Glen or loch?'

'Loch. I may need a bit of help up the steps coming back.' Together they changed their shoes and put on anoraks. Ginny's legs and body still ached when she walked up and down steps; but she no longer had any problem on level ground except for a general weakness which was liable to overcome her without warning. 'There was one thing that was mentioned in those letters,' she said as they set off for their walk. 'AIH. He seemed to know what it implied, but I'm not sure that I do.'

'Artificial Insemination by Husband. I asked around after I first read that, and I think I sorted it out. It sounds as though that baby trouble they had probably started when Father had mumps.'

Ginny nodded. All the family knew the story of the honeymoon.

'That sort of thing in adult life can sometimes make a man completely infertile, but more often it's less dramatic than that. Just that not enough of his sperms are strong enough to make the journey and do their job of fertilisation.'

Only Ginny's genuine wish to know prevented her from finding the conversation distasteful. Both Tory and Ness were uninhibited in their vocabulary, happy to call any kind of spade a spade, but she had always been more squeamish about discussing bodily functions. It went, no doubt, with being a goody-goody.

'So?'

'Well, it's all different nowadays, because doctors know how to do the actual fertilisation in a test-tube. The best they could do in the 1960s was to sort of collect the strongest sperms and send them on their way at the optimum time of the month. Using masturbation, I suppose. It must have been rather horrid.'

'Yes. But it seems to have worked.'

'I suppose so.'

'What do you mean, you suppose so?' asked Ginny.

'Doesn't it sometimes occur to you that none of us look much like Father?' Tory asked. 'I mean, you and I are both tall, and I've got his stupid short-sightedness, and Ness I suppose has got his black hair, although it's wavier, and his pale skin, but none of us actually resembles him.'

'We're all good at maths,' Ginny pointed out. 'Keeping accounts and being businesslike.'

'True. But that could be environment, not heredity. Simply because we've been brought up not to be afraid of figures.'

'So what are you getting at? Are you suggesting that Mother and Prince Fiori . . . !'

'No, not necessarily. Although . . . Well, no. But put yourself back twenty-one years. Mother is desperate to have a baby. She's attending a fertility clinic run by someone who owes a favour to her husband's best friend, her own secret lover. There must be all sorts of ethical rules which apply to that kind of situation, but suppose the doctor agreed to bend one of them. Telling himself, no doubt, that it was all for the best. Trying to make it work just with Father to start with, but then, well, giving that contribution a helping hand. A touch of Artificial Insemination by Donor. Mother herself need never have been aware of it.'

Ginny found herself startled by the suggestion, and initially disbelieving. And yet she had often wondered in daydreams whether she might have some other, more romantic, father than the one she knew. Why should she be disturbed to think that she could be genetically linked to a stranger, someone she would never meet?

Tory meanwhile was continuing to think aloud.

'So suppose that loyalty to his friend made it out of the question for the prince to seduce the said friend's wife but the same kind of loyalty made it possible to provide the two of them with a family in a different way. Don't you think that might stir up a volcanic eruption of frustration?'

'You don't seem very worried by the possibility.'

'As far as I'm concerned, what has always been assumed to be true is a fact. Anything else is worthless speculation. Philosophy of Tory Craig, proposition one.'

'There are ways of finding out nowadays,' suggested Ginny slowly. 'We could ask to have our DNAs done. Ness told me once that scientists always like experimenting on twins and triplets and quads. And with Mother and Father still alive – '

'Out of the question!' said Tory firmly. 'Mother and Father would have to provide specimens as well as us. Just think what a slap in the face it would be for them if anything unexpected emerged. Especially if it was only unexpected to one of them. Simply asking the question in the first place would be bad enough. I don't think we ought to mention this to Ness. Not while she's all het up, at least. You're flagging.'

'Yes,' agreed Ginny. 'Sorry. I hate it, being so feeble. But I think perhaps . . .'

They turned back towards the castle, walking more slowly, and arrived home to find their mother waiting to greet them.

'Drawing room tea,' she said as cheerfully as though nothing unusual had occurred. 'A touch of gracious living.'

'What have we done to deserve this?' asked Ginny. Tea was a Sunday treat and this was a Saturday. Up in the office there was an electric kettle with whose help she and Dorothy brewed themselves tea and coffee whenever they wished, but that was quite different from this array of scones and cakes.

'It's a welcome to Tory. A bribe to make her come and see us more often.'

'You should have told Ness that Margaret's Dundee cake was on offer. She wouldn't have gone off in such a rush

294

then. Did you have a row?' Ginny asked the question as casually as she could, knowing that Tory was as interested as herself to hear the answer.

'Not precisely a row. A difference of viewpoints, perhaps. Scone?'

'Lovely. What about?' The answer, presumably, was David.

Hilary put down the plate and began to pour from the silver teapot.

'It's up to Ness to tell you if she wants to. I wouldn't like her to think that we'd tried to brainwash you both in advance into agreeing with our point of view.' The ringing of the telephone saved her from being pressed further; but she did no more than give the number before handing it to Ginny.

'Hello, Ginny,' said Mark's voice. 'It's me.'

17

'Was that your young man?' asked Hilary when the telephone conversation was over. 'I recognised the voice. He
phoned here once before, when you were in hospital.'

'He's not my young man,' Ginny protested.

'Have it your own way. The young man who would
obviously *like* to be your young man. The artist. Ness
told me a bit about him.'

'Yes. Did she tell you about the painting he wants to do?
He was ringing to ask if you and Father could spare him a
little time next week. I said I'd call him back.'

'Certainly he can come. I'll look in the book. And he'll
stay here for a few days, I hope. Company for you.'

'Thanks.' Ginny had taken the offer of hospitality for
granted. It was automatically assumed by her mother
that anyone arriving from outside Scotland would need
to recuperate after the journey.

'Sit down and finish your tea, then.'

But Ginny's attention had been caught by the cluster
of photographs which stood on the grand piano. All
three girls had been forced to practise on it when they
were young, but none of them had shown the talent
or the inclination to continue, and the lid was rarely
raised nowadays. She stretched out a hand to pick up
a formally posed group in black and white. It showed a
young, smiling Hilary, seated with three babies carefully
arranged on her lap.

'Which is which of us?' Ginny asked.

'To be honest, I've never been quite sure. It was such
a fuss getting you all into position – the only time that I
ever tried holding all of you at once. I was terrified that

one of you would wriggle at the wrong moment and fall off. You were six months old when that was taken. It would have been easier if we'd had you christened when you were younger.'

'Which is the smallest one?' Only the faces of the babies could be seen, for each was wearing a long christening robe.

'What do you mean?'

Ginny had asked the question without thinking. Too late she realised that her mother had never mentioned the anxiety that one of her three daughters must have caused her all those years ago. It was only from her visit to the hospital that Ginny had learned of the need to keep one tiny baby in care for a considerable time; and that memory, pushed out of her mind by the subsequent accident, had been revived by the reading of a letter she had no right to see. All she could do now was to fib her way out of it.

'You told us once that one of us was much smaller than the other two when we were born.'

'I can't have done.'

Even as she struggled to escape from her own mistake, Ginny recognised how carefully her mother was choosing words which did not exactly tell a lie.

'It was ages ago. When you were explaining that we weren't identical. And telling us about the little boy who died.' That part at least was true; but when Hilary shrugged the original question away it was impossible to press it further.

There was someone else who could provide an answer, though. The trauma of the accident had for some time caused Ginny completely to forget the subject which had been engrossing her at the time it occurred; and even after her discharge from hospital she had felt mentally as well as physically lethargic. The whole Isabella question had evaporated from her mind until earlier that day. Now it returned with a new urgency. That night she wrote a letter to Mrs Saunders – using the Norland address, as she had been instructed. Instead of putting it on the tray in the hall, she gave it to her sister.

'Post this in London for me, will you?'

'Okay.' The name meant nothing to Tory, but she was surprised by the address. 'What do you want a Norland nanny for? Is there something you haven't been telling us?'

'Don't be an idiot. It's to be forwarded. Someone whose address I've lost, that's all.'

There was bound to be a long wait. Two days must pass before the letter was sent on its way to Australia. It would take perhaps ten days to arrive, with another ten days for an answer to come back; and Mrs Saunders – married, and with a family of her own to bring up – might not bother to write immediately. The only sensible thing was to put the matter out of her mind for a month. In the meantime, she must get back to work – and she could look forward to Mark's arrival.

He came, a few days later, in a new car. Not the sort of car that Ginny herself enjoyed driving. A sensible, useful estate car – but a considerable improvement on the rusting hatchback which had been all he could afford before. He was anxious to show it off to her. 'Can you manage the steps?' he asked.

'Of course. I'm pretty well back to normal now.' All the same, after she had admired its neat lines and generous capacity she did not accompany him on each journey up to the house. He was happy for Donald to take his personal bag, but insisted on carrying each of the paintings he had brought to show her parents up the steps himself.

She sat in the car while she waited, guessing that he would suggest a stroll by the loch to stretch his legs as soon as the unloading was finished. To amuse herself, she turned the ignition key and tested every control in turn as though she were considering a purchase herself. Lights flashed on and off, the doors clicked fast as she pressed the central locking button, the radio offered a shipping forecast. There was a cassette player as well: she searched for a cassette with which to test it. None of the stack had been commercially recorded: he had bought blank tapes and compiled his own concert. The marks which identified each work presumably meant something to him, but nothing to Ginny. She picked a tape at random and pressed it home.

After a moment of confused noise it proved to be not music but speech, and Italian speech at that. She smiled briefly, thinking that perhaps Mark had decided to teach himself Italian in order to keep up with her if they ever visited the country together again. Then the smile faded from her eyes. What she was hearing was her own conversation with Sophia.

It was muffled and indistinct, from time to time interrupted by bangs or the loud scraping of a chair on the floor, but enough could be heard to assure her that she was not mistaken. For a little while she listened incredulously. Then, as Mark appeared once more at the top of the steps, she hastily rewound the tape and turned on the radio instead. 'Woman's Hour' now.

'One more journey,' he said, carefully extracting another of his paintings through the back of the car. It gave her time to put the cassette back where she had found it. There was even time to think.

On the day of that conversation in Metaponto she had sent him back to wait a little way away, but he had not gone so far. Instead, when she emerged, she had encountered him not far from the massaria. Had he lingered throughout her visit somewhere near the door, where voices could be heard although he could not be seen? No, that wasn't likely. There would have been too many other people around, curious about the visit themselves but unlikely to tolerate curiosity in others.

So she herself must have been carrying a recorder of some kind. Her anorak had large pockets, but she would have noticed, surely, if a hard weight had been slipped inside. Her shoulder bag, though – that was a different matter entirely. She was always being teased about the unnecessary load which she carried about with her – a purse full of money, keys, notebook, a collection of pens, comb and lipstick, quite probably a paperback – and on this occasion a passport and guide book as well. Yes, she might well not have noticed if Mark had surreptitiously added a recorder. And he could have done it easily, for she remembered now that he had carried the bag for her while they scrambled down a steep slope.

So that great hug he gave her when she emerged safely had not been prompted by love and relief, as she had thought. He had needed to reclaim his property without making her aware of it. He didn't care about her at all. He was simply a spy. Sick with disappointment, Ginny got out of the car.

Later that day, while Mark was making his presentation to her parents, Ginny had time to work out the consequences of what had happened. Mark himself might not have been able to understand the recorded conversation, but it would not be hard to find someone who would translate it for him – or he could simply have made a copy to send to his patroness. Princess Fiori must have lived in Italy for long enough to become fluent in the language.

So she would at last have learned that the child abducted from the Villa dell'Isola was not her daughter; that Isabella had disappeared from sight some two years earlier and therefore was probably still alive. Mark, almost certainly, would have been aware of that as well on the day when he paid his hospital visit. The conversation with Nanny Mackay, which ought to have soothed his suspicions, must instead have fuelled them. He had discovered as much as Ginny herself had now – and, like Ginny, he must

300

be wondering whether Isabella's identity was concealed beneath that of one of the three Craig girls. But he had no way of proving it, and certainly no way of finding out which one it might be. He didn't know about Mrs Saunders.

Ginny found it hard now to know how to feel about him, how to behave. Common sense told her that she ought to send him packing – and tell her parents at once that he was spying on them. Why was she so reluctant to take that decisive step? Was it only because of the excitement which stirred her body when he kissed her, and the ache of loneliness every time he said goodbye? She ought to be ashamed to let her feelings overwhelm her reason in such a way.

But the situation was not straightforward. It was possible to sympathise with Mark's view that Princess Fiori had a right to learn exactly what had happened to her daughter. And the moment she put the question directly to her father she would lose any further opportunity of coming at the truth by a sideways path. If Andrew had done nothing to be ashamed of, then the facts of the case, when they emerged, would do him no harm.

As for Mark, Ginny told herself that she was a fool to love someone who was behaving so deceitfully; but he was the first man with whom she had fallen in love and it was impossibly hard to stop. After all, she told herself, he had made an earlier confession of what he was doing. Probably he would tell her about the recording when the right opportunity arose. Although she recognised his motive for making her acquaintance in the first place, she had felt sure since then that he had grown to love her, as she loved him. But was her certainty mistaken? Was he still using her only as a key which would open the door to the mystery?

Her parents, of course – thanks to Ginny's own secrecy – knew nothing of his connection with Princess Fiori or his unusual interest in the Craig family. They took him at

301

face value – as a young artist struggling to make his way. Acting as a patron of the arts was one of their pleasures, and giving a helping hand to young people at the start of their careers was another; so it was not surprising that his sales pitch should prove successful.

Hilary waited until Ginny was on her own before announcing a decision.

'We've had a look at Mark's portfolio,' she said. 'I must say, we were impressed. We've bought one of the two that he did of you.'

'Two?'

'Yes. You haven't seen the second one, he said. He did it after he left here before. It's much more exciting than the one you did see – he brought them both, so that we could compare. We've commissioned him to paint Ness and Tory, separately, in the same style; and frame all three of them in a uniform way. I warned him that Ness probably wouldn't be prepared to sit for him until the vacation, but there's no hurry.'

'So you're not going to let him do the castle?'

'No. I love it dearly, but it's an ugly old thing. And I must say, I do find these whole-family paintings a bit contrived. To tell you the truth, I think he does as well. The relief in his eyes when we said we'd prefer just single portraits . . . ! I suspect that he's plugging the house-and-family idea because it gives an excuse for cold-calling; but portraits are what really excite him. As well as the three individual portraits he's going to have a go at doing a painting of the three of you together. In a mixed-up sort of way. Three heads emerging from a sort of swirl. Sounds confused when I say it, but he showed us a pencil sketch of what he has in mind, and it really could be something quite special.'

Twenty-four hours earlier Ginny would have been delighted on Mark's behalf and also on her own, since it meant that she would see more of him. But the discovery of the cassette had left her unsure of herself. Her body longed for his touch, but caution warned her to hold herself aloof. Instead of looking forward to every moment when they could be alone together, she went out of her way to make sure that within the castle they were always in company. She could tell that her withdrawal puzzled him; and he in turn appeared more tentative than before.

In the open air, though, she was more relaxed. No snow had yet fallen to make walking difficult. With every day that passed Ginny felt fitter, and her spirits rose as her strength increased. Mark's conversation was stimulating, enlarging her horizons, and – illogical though it might be – outside in the clean, crisp January air she found it impossible to maintain her resentment that he had spied on her. Little by little their friendship began to steady again – until the day when they made their way down from the head of the glen in time to see an unexpected visitor dismounting from a taxi. She was a small woman, elegantly dressed: a stranger to Ginny, who turned in surprise to Mark as he gasped with annoyance.

'Who's that? Do you know?'

'Yes, I do. It's the princess. Princess Fiori. And she shouldn't have come.'

18

He could say that again! Ginny was tempted to laugh at the dismay on Mark's face. It would be the last thing he wanted, that his spymistress should appear in person and reveal to Hilary and Andrew Craig that they were under observation. Worse than that – she would probably accuse them of abducting her daughter. The desire to laugh faded. This could be serious.

Mark obviously thought so too. 'Ginny, do you mind . . . ? I must have a word with her.'

He ran ahead without waiting for an answer and caught up with the princess as she was studying the unfamiliar currency in her hand and deciding how much of her change should be returned to the driver as a tip. She greeted Mark enthusiastically and handed the problem to him. But he must have made some comment as he paid, for the taxi did not move away.

Ginny made no attempt to conceal herself at first as she continued on her slower way towards the lower ground; but it seemed that Mark had forgotten her existence and the princess had not noticed her presence; for the two of them, talking earnestly, made their way on to the grassy promontory on which the original castle had once stood. Its ruined walls offered perfect hiding places. Ginny didn't think twice before taking advantage of them. Mark had spied on her in Italy: it was her turn now.

By the time she had made her way quietly into an eavesdropping position, their discussion was in full spate.

'No doubt at all.' It was Mark talking. 'Brain damage, blindness and imperfect lung development. Caused by a combination of lack of oxygen before and during the birth, and an overdose after it. The baby wasn't expected to live for more than a maximum of five years, probably much less. And only a vegetable kind of living at that; lying on a bed. She was moved from the hospital to a nursing home at the age of six months, but nobody could do more than keep her comfortable.'

'You said you found the record of her death?'

'Well, I reckoned that the Craigs were a caring kind of family. They wouldn't move up here and just abandon a baby down in England. Even though visits wouldn't mean a thing, they'd visit. So there seemed a good chance that they'd brought her to be cared for somewhere near here and that she'd died in Scotland within the next four years. It's easier to find out about this sort of thing in Scotland than England, when you don't really know what you're looking for. There's an office in Edinburgh where they'll do a search covering two years before and two years after the date you give them. The people there did the work, not me.'

'Just one thing you forgot to tell me. Which was the one who died?'

Ginny strained her ears to be sure of hearing the answer. She was angry with herself at letting Mark get ahead in his researches, but she had come to the same theoretical conclusion even if she couldn't prove it. Now she was going to learn the only fact that mattered.

Or so she hoped; but Mark's voice was apologetic.

'They fudged it,' he said. 'Afraid that someone might stumble on it by accident, perhaps. The name in the death registration is Vee Craig. But I checked with the place where she was nursed after the move to Scotland, and where she died. That's the name she was called by, and there's no doubt, from the symptoms, that it was the same child.'

'So it's one of the three, but you don't know which one. Right?'

'Yes. But listen, princess, you can't just barge in and demand to know all about it.'

'Why not? One of those girls is my daughter. I guess that gives me right enough. And Andrew Craig has been sitting on her fortune for twenty years. Don't expect me to have any sympathy for him.'

'He's given your daughter, whoever she is, a happy home for twenty years. But the thing is, they – the girls – don't know anything about it. Well, Ginny has a kind of suspicion that something's wrong, but she certainly doesn't know exactly what. You're going to throw the hell of a spanner into the works if you just storm up and make an announcement. Think what a shock it will be – for your daughter more than any of the others, discovering that she isn't what she always thought she was. You can't expect her to fall into a stranger's arms and shout "Mother, I love you." She needs a chance to get to know you before it all comes out. To meet you, at the very least.'

There was a long silence before the American reluctantly agreed.

'Maybe you're right. But you can let the cab go. I haven't come all this way just to sneak off again. And I intend to force Andrew's hand. Whether he tells his kids or not, whether he makes an announcement to the world at large or not, he is about to tell the truth to *me*.'

'How can you get him to do that?' Mark's voice sounded apprehensive.

'I have a candidate for the role of Isabella Fiori. A girl I'm prepared to recognise publicly as my daughter. Andrew Craig lost Isabella and I found her. If he's not prepared to believe me, he'll have to produce a better candidate of his own. And some water-tight proof. And a damn good explanation. Get rid of the cab and bring my bags up for me.'

'Right.'

Ginny kept very still until the two conspirators had

stepped inside the castle door. Then, before they had time to reach and glance out of any window, she hurried up the steps as fast as she could manage and made her way to her office desk. There was no time to warn her parents of the impending confrontation – and anyway, why should they need a warning? Unlike herself, they presumably knew the truth of what had happened and must be prepared to take responsibility for their past actions.

The fact that she could argue in such a way suggested that Ginny's own conscience was not entirely clear. She ought to have spoken to her father as soon as he returned from Brazil. But would he have told her the truth then, when she could have confronted him only with vague doubts? Well, it was too late for regrets. A pretence of business was for the moment her best defence against disturbance. But although she pulled a file towards her and opened it, she did not look down.

She had missed a trick in London by not getting hold of the medical records. It hadn't occurred to her that they might still exist – or that, if they did, a casual enquirer would be allowed to see them. Mark must have chatted someone up to good effect. His version of that part of the story had the ring of truth to it. Prince Fiori's letter had made it clear that one of the girl babies was indeed small and frail and might not survive. And the christening photograph, taken at the time when the third baby left hospital, might have recorded a home visit only for a single day, before a permanent bed was found in some other institution.

She was equally prepared to believe that the General Register Office in Edinburgh had produced details of the particular death in which she was interested. But did she believe that Mark didn't know which of the three had died? No, she didn't. No doubt he had his own reasons for not revealing the truth just yet to Princess Fiori. What could they be?

307

The answer came more quickly than she liked. Mark had met all three of the Craig girls, and now he knew which of them was an heiress. He could set his cap at her, insinuating himself into her affections so that she – whoever she was – would not want to let him go when the truth eventually emerged; whilst he for his part could pretend amazement. If Ginny herself was his target, he probably thought that he need only lean a little harder on a relationship which he had already established. If it was one of the other two, Ginny would soon notice him beginning to cool off.

Slamming the file back into a drawer, she decided to go down to the pool. The corridor leading to her father's office offered a new temptation to eavesdrop on Sara Fiori's accusations, but the walls and doors of the castle were thick. Although the sound of raised voices could be faintly heard, she could not distinguish the words. Continuing on her way to the lowest floor of the building, she changed into a swimsuit. Mark was practising his diving when she emerged.

'I hoped you'd come.' He hauled himself out and came smilingly towards her. It was not the smile of someone whose plan was to cool off towards Ginny and transfer his affections to one of her sisters. It was the smile of a man who knew what he wanted and thought himself well on the way to getting it. That must mean . . . but Ginny hastily stepped aside as she detected a new element of mischief in his grin, as though he planned to push her into the water.

'I more or less have to have a session every day,' she reminded him. 'Part of the physiotherapy.'

'Oh yes, of course.' He took the comment, as she had intended it, as a hint that her body was still fragile from the accident, so that there must be no horseplay. That implication was not justified, but her words were literally true. Swimming, she had been told, was the best form of exercise. She lowered herself into the water and began a steady progress up and down the length of the pool. Mark swam beside her, not liking to interrupt but hoping for a sociable period when she had finished her stint.

He was to be disappointed. As soon as Ginny had completed her forty lengths she climbed out of the pool and rubbed herself dry.

'See you at dinner.' She could tell that he was puzzled by her off-handedness – and probably surprised as well that there had been no questions about Princess Fiori; but she offered no explanation.

Back in her own room, she studied the contents of her wardrobe with unusual indecision. It was the custom of the Craigs – even when there were no visitors – to change for dinner. Not into evening dress; merely out of their working clothes. What should she wear tonight?

Was this an occasion on which to look smart and sophisticated? Although she did not normally wear them for family dinners at home, she possessed two or three informal evening outfits which both looked and were expensive. By choosing one of them she could show that she had been brought up on a good allowance and taught how to look and behave in society. Ginny herself didn't care a fig for that kind of thing, but it seemed important to demonstrate that Andrew and Hilary had behaved generously to the three girls they had brought up.

Still undecided, she slipped one of the dresses on. It had a low sweetheart neckline and a brief cape top which showed her slender arms to advantage. The skirt fitted tightly round her slim hips before flaring out into fullness above the knee. Ginny had good legs, a perfect skin and the measurements of a model; as she studied herself in the glass, she was satisfied with her appearance. Andrew and Hilary would raise their eyebrows when they saw her, but she didn't care. By being over-dressed she would register the fact that she was an outsider. Assuming that Princess Fiori had succeeded in forcing Andrew into a confession, everyone else at the table would know more than she did about her own family, perhaps about herself.

Was this then a gesture of independence? Or was she trying to present herself as a prize and waiting to see who would be the first to claim her? Did she secretly wish for Princess Fiori to take one look at her and hope that she had found her long-lost daughter?

The question filled Ginny with such alarm that she was forced to sit down for a moment. On each earlier occasion when she had wondered privately whether she might be Isabella Fiori she had considered the possible consequences in terms of money. This was the first moment at which the true cost of being an heiress came home to her. The thought that Andrew and Hilary Craig were not her parents, that this stranger might be her mother, was unbearable.

Throughout the evening which followed, however, she had to bear it. She could never remember a more uncomfortable meal. Andrew and Hilary barely managed by good manners to conceal their anger at Sara Fiori's arrival – although their attitude to Mark was unchanged, suggesting that the princess had not yet revealed his part in the sleuthing. Mark must have been nervous lest the extent of his involvement with the uninvited visitor should emerge, but he continued to behave in his usual light-heartedly friendly manner towards Ginny. Her lack of response disappointed him and he was unable to take his eyes off her.

As for the princess, she appeared to be thick-skinned; either not knowing or not caring that she was unwelcome. She directed all her attention to Ginny, but although her conversation was warm and interested, there was no sign of hope or delight in her eyes. If she had expected some kind of maternal chemistry to reveal to her that she had discovered her daughter, it seemed that she had been disappointed.

Once she learned that Ginny worked for the Tantivy Trust, she concentrated her questions on this.

Ginny replied with a question of her own. 'How did you come into contact with it?'

'I like to help young artists get started. They show in my gallery. One of them asked me if I'd object to her putting in for your competition.'

It was a suitable cue to divert the subject from the origin of the Trust to its present activities. Ginny talked at length about the success of the exhibition she had organised: its itinerary and the unexpectedly high level of sales. She could see her mother's mouth twitching with amusement at the determined way in which her daughter was directing the course of the conversation. If Hilary *was* her mother, of course; if Ginny *was* Hilary's daughter.

At the end of the meal, when Andrew led Sara towards the drawing room for coffee, Ginny put out a hand to hold Hilary back.

'What is it, darling?'

'Nothing really. Just that – I do love you.'

'Love you too.' Hilary gathered her into a hug and kept an arm round her waist as they moved out of the dining room. 'Any special reason, though?'

'Just general affection.' What did Mark, waiting politely behind, make of that, she wondered?

Princess Fiori, thank goodness, was sufficiently tired after her flight across time zones to retire early to bed and Andrew, relieved, murmured about the need to return to his office for an hour.

'Excuse me,' said Ginny to Mark and Hilary. She caught up with her father on the stairs. 'Can I have a word?'

'Of course.' He opened the door for her and gestured towards a seat. But instead of taking it she wandered across to a wall lined with books on all the subjects with which the Fiori Foundation had ever concerned itself. Desalination, birth control, blindness, afforestation, tidal electricity generation – she ran her fingers over the covers without being aware of their contents.

'Something wrong?' asked Andrew.

She turned to face him. Would it be the last time that she looked at him as daughter to father? It seemed more like the first time as she stared, studying his face as though she had never seen it before. The first signs of grey were appearing in his dark hair, and the creases of concentration in his forehead were no longer smoothed away when he smiled. Strangers had always found his natural expression stern, and his height intimidating; but Ginny had never been frightened of him.

'I just wanted to ask you,' she said, fighting to keep her voice steady, 'whether you're really my father?'

19

Andrew stared at her across the room as he lowered himself into the swivel chair behind his desk.

'Of course I'm your father, pet. Why on earth – ?'

He was pretending to be startled, but she could tell that there was alarm behind the pretence.

'I don't want you to answer as though it doesn't matter. I want to know the truth.'

'What has that woman been saying to you?'

'Nothing. Nothing at all. I haven't spoken to her except when you were in the room. But I've been wondering for some time . . . She's looking for her daughter, isn't she; for Isabella? And her search has brought her here. What is it that you're afraid she *might* have said to me?'

'Sit down,' said Andrew; but even after Ginny had done so he did not answer directly.

'She claims to have found Isabella in America,' he said.

'But you don't believe that, do you?'

'There's a tattoo,' Andrew told her. 'It's only tiny. Sara may remember approximately where it is and may have tried to get it copied. But a doctor would be able to tell if a mark had been made recently and not in babyhood. I've told Sara that I'll be happy to set up a test. But she won't dare to attempt it. It would lay her open to a charge of attempted fraud.'

'If she knows she can't get away with it, then why – ?'

'She had no right to come here,' said Andrew, suddenly angry. 'And she has no right to her daughter.'

'How can you say such a thing? Any mother – '

'No.' He shook his head vigorously. 'There's more to

being a mother than the act of giving birth. Sara made a decision a long time ago that she didn't want to be a mother. It was a wrong decision and I've no doubt she regrets it now; but it's too late for her to pretend it never happened.'

'What did happen?'

'She had a very rough time. When her son was kidnapped, when he died. You know all about that.'

Ginny nodded.

'It was unfortunate that her second baby was born in the middle of that terrible period. She rejected it. If that had been just an instinctive reaction, perhaps it would have been understandable. But it was more sustained than that. She abandoned her daughter, abandoned her husband. She still loved Tony, I think. She came back to try again. But only as a wife, not as a mother. She refused to hold Isabella. She hardly even looked at her.'

'She should have had help. A psychiatrist or something.'

'They tried that. But she didn't want to be helped. When she and Tony divorced, she didn't ask for custody. Not even for access. She doesn't want a daughter as a person, a human being to love and be loved – and she must know that if she ever finds her, that daughter could reasonably reject her as she was once rejected herself. There's no link. They'd be strangers. No, worse than strangers, because what ought to have been a natural bond was deliberately broken.'

'So why has she come here?'

'For twenty years she's genuinely believed that Isabella was dead – without apparently needing any proof of it. It may have been a fear-induced wish. That was what she expected to happen from the moment the child was born, therefore that must have been what did happen. My own position has always been different. The terms of the original trust for Isabella have forced me to act on the assumption that she could be still alive somewhere, whether I believe it to be true or not. Somehow or other Sara has got wind of that and misinterpreted it.'

'Does she feel that she's been swindled out of a fortune?'

'It would always have been Isabella's, not hers. But no, as a matter of fact I don't think that. She was a very wealthy woman in her own right when she married Tony. He made a generous divorce settlement on her, and since then her father has died and left her another fortune. What she does seem to want to prove is that I've been living well myself on money that should have been Isabella's. She's never forgiven me for the fact that Tony trusted me more than he trusted her, years ago.'

'He really did, did he?'

'I found something to show her.' Andrew opened a drawer of his desk and pulled out a legal document, typed on a long sheet of paper and covered with official stamps. 'Take a look.'

Although she was unwilling to be diverted from the main stream of her questioning, Ginny could not resist glancing down.

'It's a power of attorney,' Andrew explained. 'Very short, very simple, because it gives absolute power with no safeguards. This is something quite separate from the document which established the Fiori Foundation and the Tantivy Trust, and quite separate again from the arrangements set down in his will. The will was only to come into effect when he died. This power of attorney was to apply if he was still alive but for some reason unable to deal with his own affairs.' He pointed a long finger at the list of possibilities. 'If he was physically incapacitated, for example, or certified mad, or under any form of duress, or simply missing. The circumstances that this envisages were extreme and unlikely; but the point about the document was that if it did come into effect I could do absolutely anything with his property which I considered to be in his best interests – not much of a restriction. So yes, he trusted me. Sara simply couldn't understand the value that Tony put on friendship. She'd like to hurt me if she can, and the Isabella business seems to be offering her an opportunity. I can hardly expect her to trust me to have acted for the best. But I can ask it of you.'

'It seems to me that you're asking for a good deal more than trust,' exclaimed Ginny. 'You're expecting faith. It's different. You're the only person who knows what's really been going on and you're not going to tell, are you? You're leaving me to struggle with a situation which I don't understand, which doesn't make sense, and expecting me to make up for myself whatever explanation is most favourable to you and then to believe it.'

'And that's too much to ask?'

'Yes,' she said. 'It is.'

Andrew swivelled round in his office chair and stood up behind the desk. He walked across the room and pulled Ginny up into his arms.

'I love you, Ginny,' he said. 'No father has ever loved a daughter more. And I *am* your father. I've never lied to you and I'm not lying now. Do you believe me?'

She had asked for a considered, unambiguous statement and she had been given it; yet still she hesitated. He might argue later that he regarded himself as her father because he had adopted her, or because he had loved her and brought her up. 'I want to hear the whole story,' she said.

Disappointed, he allowed his arms to drop.

'I can't tell you that.'

'Why not?'

'You can take your choice of reasons. Perhaps I don't know the whole story. Perhaps there are secrets which are not mine to tell.'

'So *you* don't trust *me*. Well, it doesn't matter. I know how to find out for myself. It won't take long.' She, like Mark, could trace the home where a handicapped baby had

316

lived, could discover the name on the death certificate. Or a letter would arrive from Mrs Saunders, naming the baby who had not lived at home for more than a day. For the moment, angry with disappointment, she moved towards the door.

'Ginny!'

'Is Ginny really my name?' she asked, turning back. 'I don't even know something as important as that. For all I can tell, nothing, nothing at all, is what it seems.' She was tempted to slam the door, but instead closed it with careful quietness, as though to emphasise the barrier between them.

It was earlier than she usually went to bed, but she had no wish to prolong the evening, nor to return to company. Deep in thought, she made her way round the gallery and along the corridor to her bedroom. She switched on the light – and then gasped in shock. Mark was standing beside the bed.

'What are you doing here?' She closed the door quickly, lest anyone should see him.

'Waiting to talk to you. You've been so – so distant all evening. Holding me off. And looking so beautiful.' He moved towards her; but she put out a hand to stop him.

'Don't touch me. I don't want to be touched.'

'But I love you. I love you so much.' Her command had checked his intention to embrace her, but he could not keep his hands away. His fingers stroked the smooth skin of her arms. 'Ginny, please. I adore you. I want to marry you.'

'You've never said that before.'

'No. Well, of course, it's ridiculous. I can hardly afford to keep myself. What have I got to offer a wife? And someone like you, brought up in a place like this, wearing clothes like this . . .' His hand swept round in a gesture which took in not merely her dress but the whole castle. 'But I have to say it once, just so that you know.'

'So you've said it.'

'Ginny darling, don't push me away. I don't want to wait. I want you now. Please, Ginny.' He pulled her into his arms, pressing kisses over her face and neck.

'I'm sorry,' she said, twisting away from him. 'I'm not ready for any commitment. I just want to be left alone.'

Flushed and panting, it took him a moment to compose himself. 'What's wrong?' he asked quietly.

'I should have thought you might have guessed. Why did you bring that woman here, Princess Fiori?'

'I didn't bring her. Why should I want her to turn up? I didn't invite her or even suggest – '

'You laid the trail that led her here. Fed her with information.'

'She's known your father from way back.' Mark's uneasiness showed in his eyes. 'Anything she wanted to know, he was the person to ask. What information could I possibly provide – ?'

'Oh, shut up!' exclaimed Ginny. 'Asking a question is a neat way of not quite having to tell a lie, isn't it?' She hesitated for a moment. 'Sitting in your new car, trying out your cassette player, I just happened to pick on the tape you must have hoped I'd never find out about. From the day in Italy when you wired me for sound.' She was making neither a confession nor an accusation; merely issuing a warning to prevent him from persisting in any attempt to deceive.

Her statement had the effect she expected. Mark stepped back, pale and apologetic.

'I'm sorry about that,' he said. 'I shouldn't . . . It's a horrid feeling, being in a situation where everybody else knows what's going on and you don't.'

'I know the feeling exactly.' She did not intend to tell him what she had overheard amongst the ruins that afternoon, but she paused in order that he could, if he chose, bring her up to date with his discoveries. He said nothing. 'You arrived here as Princess Fiori's spy. You went to Italy as Princess Fiori's spy. You're still Princess Fiori's spy. What do you expect me to feel, for heaven's sake?'

'Yes,' said Mark miserably. 'Yes, I can see that you're fed up with me. I really *am* sorry. I won't push it now, but everything I said earlier stands. I love you very much. Please remember that, later on.'

He let himself quietly out of the bedroom. By the time Ginny came down to breakfast the next morning, he had already left the castle.

20

Two days later Ginny received a phone call from Ness.

'Any chance that you could come to Oxford? I've got so much work to get through that I daren't take any more time away, but there's something I'd like to have a chat about.'

'What's wrong with now, over the telephone?' Ginny asked her.

'That's all very well for you, sitting comfortably. But I'm standing up at a payphone in a draughty corridor, liable to be overheard by every passer-by; and my phonecard will run out in the middle of the conversation. If you can't manage it, don't worry. But I would very much like to see you if poss.'

'Is anything wrong, Ness? Has anything happened?'

'Well, Mark has paid me a visit. I don't know whether you'd count that as a happening.'

'What did he want? What did he say?'

'I really meant it about the phonecard,' said Ness. 'My time is ticking away. Come if you can, and all questions will be answered at leisure.'

'Okay. I'll be with you on Thursday, nineish.' Disturbed, Ginny put down the receiver. Was Mark transferring his attentions to Ness and, if so, what did that signify? Should she warn her sister? That would mean revealing all her doubts and discoveries. Sooner or later, naturally, she intended to confide the truth, but only when she was certain what it was.

The journey was not as simple as it had been in the days when she could climb into her own car and speed down the motorways. Princess Fiori had left the castle soon after Mark, and with no visitors to be entertained any longer both Andrew and Hilary had disappeared; Andrew to Edinburgh and Hilary, driven by Gip, to England. But there was a good train service between Carlisle and Oxford, and the office which she shared with Dorothy was well supplied with timetables. She left the next day, spent the night at a hotel and presented herself at Christ Church soon after breakfast.

'Let's walk by the river,' said Ness, grinning with pleasure at her sister's arrival.

'Don't you have to go to lectures?'

'Don't have to. Don't want to. I stayed up till two this morning to get my profound thoughts on Aristotle on paper, so there's nothing I need do until I read the said thoughts aloud to my tutor at five o'clock. Are you wearing sensible shoes? Good.'

In the crowded street outside the college, buses and coaches were disgorging their cargoes of shoppers, tourists and language students, whilst motorists crawled round the one-way traffic system; but as Ginny and Ness crossed Folly Bridge and took the steps down to the towpath they found themselves abruptly moving from noise and pollution into silence and solitude.

'I love walking here,' Ness said. 'Especially early on Sunday mornings, when the mist is rising. I like to think of all the people who've come to study in Oxford for hundreds and hundreds of years. Too much has changed in the centre of the city, and there's too much traffic. But here it's almost the same as it was five hundred years ago. It's a marvellous feeling, being part of a tradition that's very old and still alive. I mean, just look.'

She put out a hand to draw her sister to a halt.

'Look at that; across the river, across the Meadows. That's Magdalen Tower, that's the back of Merton, and that's Christ Church, of course. Seething with intellectual life inside, and so peaceful outside. Stone walls, stone towers, trees and gardens and fields and water – and thousands of young men and women bursting to make the most of the greatest opportunity they may ever have in their lives. It's so exciting. Don't you think I'm lucky, spending four years in surroundings like this?'

'Yes,' said Ginny, surprising herself by the firmness with which she spoke. 'The last day or two, I've been thinking. You were right when you said that I ought to have gone to university. Of course, I may be too old now, but – '

'Not too old at all.' Ness's expression revealed her pleasure. 'A lot of girls arrive here while they're still too young, in my opinion. Ginny, I'm so glad you've come round to it. I was going to have another shot at persuading you. Will you try for Oxford?

'Heavens no. I wouldn't have a hope. Anyway, that's not exactly what I want. I might as well make use of whatever talents I've got. A degree in business studies would be the thing, with an international flavour since I've got the languages. Perhaps at a European university. I'll get some addresses from a library while I'm here and write off.'

'Good for you!' exclaimed Ness – who then added curiously, 'What made you change your mind?'

'I just realised that I needed to get away from home. I know that I'm useful, working for the Trust, but being employed by my father isn't something that any other potential employer will take seriously.' That was not the whole truth, but she was not yet ready to explain why she needed to escape from home; why she no longer felt at ease with her father. 'I need a proper qualification and then a spell of working for an outside organisation, don't I?'

'Yes,' Ness agreed enthusiastically. 'And it's more than just a question of jobs. The whole business of living, really. It may not always be a lot of fun being on one's own, but it's an important stage to go through. If you move straight from being Andrew's daughter to somebody's wife, you'll never have a chance to be yourself.'

Ginny's attention was caught by a single word in that little sermon. Ness had never previously called their father by his Christian name. But to comment on it would be a distraction.

'I can promise you,' she said instead, 'that I'm in no danger of suddenly becoming somebody's wife.'

'Really?'

'Really. To be honest, though, that's a factor in the decision. Stuck at home, I'm never going to meet anyone I might like to marry. I mean, there are all the sons of Mother's friends, but they're not exciting somehow.'

'I thought you found Mark Lacey exciting.'

'Yes, I did, and that's part of the problem. The only new acquaintance I've made in two years, and who is he? Someone who turns up completely out of the blue, someone I know nothing about – '

'You could say that that's the usual system, that people marry people they know nothing about.'

'But if you're working – either like you, as an undergraduate, or like Tory – you have time to do things together casually, find out what you have in common, before it all gets serious. I need a wider society to move in. You must know what I mean, Ness.'

'Of course I do. I've been trying to tell you that for years. All the same, Mark Lacey is more than just a statistic, the one new acquaintance: he's a chap. Rather an unhappy one at the moment. It's Mark that I wanted to talk to you about. Let's stop here for a moment.'

There was a wooden seat beside the towpath. As they sat down a flotilla of ducks sped like an arrow towards them, protesting loudly when they proved to be empty-handed. Ness, considering what to say, remained silent, and Ginny did not interrupt.

After a while, Ness sighed.

'I told you, didn't I, Mark came to see me?'

'What did he want?'

'First of all to weep on my shoulder. And then to ask me to use my influence with you.'

'About what?'

'He's in love with you. Says he is, anyway. This is all quotation, not my own opinion. He wants to marry you. Presumably he's made you aware of this.'

'Yes. But he doesn't really want to marry me – or anyone else – yet. It's just that he thinks I'm the sort of girl who won't, you know, without the promise of a wedding.'

'Is he so wrong?'

'I suppose he looked at Father and Mother, happily married for donkey's years, and then at me still living at home. Unadventurous. He was right at the time, but the time's past.'

'Meaning that you might, you know, even without that wedding in sight?'

Ginny didn't answer that question. She would have told Ness the truth if she knew it, but her mind was still in a muddle. A few months ago – much later in life than most girls – she had reached the moment when she was ready to fall in love, and at that moment Mark had arrived on the doorstep. Now she was ready to jump a second hurdle, but between two possible tracks lay a minefield. She could envisage the loss of her virginity as an act of trust in anticipation of marriage or, alternatively, as an experiment, a physical coupling to be experienced light-heartedly, without strings. But if it was a sign of maturity to embark on an affair which might continue for years and yet might end at a moment's notice, she was not yet mature.

Ness, who had smiled affectionately as she asked the question, did not wait long for an answer.

'Yes, well, as what you've just said suggests, he didn't feel that his proposal was exactly received with rapture. Hence his request that I should speak up for him. I'd better confess at once that my first reaction was to say to him what I've just said to you – about letting you have a few years to establish your independence. The real thing is, of course, that I personally consider it's dangerous to marry young. But we both agreed that the first of those points was none of my business and the second was my business only, and not yours.'

'And so?'

'What's worrying him, Ginny, is that *he* thinks that *you* think that he only wants to marry you for your money. He believes that you do like him, love him even, and that it's only since he started getting serious that you've started backing off.'

'He knows better than that. Are you expected to argue on behalf of his sincerity?'

'What I tried to point out was that you haven't in fact got money of the sort that can be married for. I mean, Andrew earns a quite enormous salary and obviously we live in the sort of style which must certainly make any outsider think that we must all be loaded. But I don't believe that Andrew and Hilary are the sort to toss the odd million across as a dowry. They'd never let you starve: but if he was really a fortune-hunter, then I'd say he was chasing the wrong quarry.'

'I think Mark may have bigger game in mind,' said Ginny quietly. 'He knows that Isabella Fiori is still alive.'

'Is that something which you believe as well?'

'Yes. But I haven't found out yet who she is. Mark's ahead of me. He knows.'

'If he knows, why do you think he doesn't tell?'

'Obvious, isn't it?'

Ness shook her head. 'One possibility may be obvious. Fortune-hunting, as you say. But you ought not to let that blind you to alternative scenarios. For example, that he might have found out the true identity of Isabella Fiori – and realised that she doesn't want anyone to know about it. That puts him rather on the spot, you see. Because, although I haven't known him long, it does seem to me that he's a considerate, honourable sort of chap, not wanting to muck up other people's lives. And he can see that if he comes to you and says, "I love you although I know for certain that you're not Isabella," you're going to throw the question straight back to him: "Then who is?"'

'Well, what's the answer? Who is Isabella?'

'I am,' said Ness.

21

Stunned by the force of the unambiguous statement, Ginny slowly turned her head and saw that Ness was crying.

'Sorry,' she said, dabbing her eyes. 'I get all emotional whenever I think of it. It's such a mess. But it's *my* mess. I don't want it to spill over on to you.'

'How long have you known?'

'Depends what you mean by knowing. First I wondered, and then I felt sure. Not with the kind of sureness I could prove – and I didn't *want* to prove it – so I pretended to myself that I was fantasising. But I did know really.'

'When, though?'

'Well,' said Ness. 'Do you remember that after our A-levels we were allowed a weekend at home? Mine was earlier than yours, because we were doing different subjects. So I was at Kilcraigie a few days before our eighteenth birthday. An envelope arrived addressed to the Misses V. Craig: obviously a birthday card. It disappeared, and I assumed that Mother – I mean Hilary – was collecting everything until the right date. But it was never produced again. I would have recognised it because of the Australian stamps.'

'Ah!' Ginny was beginning to guess what was coming.

'I was curious. And after all, it *was* addressed to us. So I poked around until I found it. It had been opened already. "To dear little Virginia and Victoria, who aren't so little any more, with congratulations on your coming-of-age from your first Nanny, Evelyn Saunders." Well, that was odd, wasn't it? I may have been a horrible baby, but not so terrible as to be cut out of a birthday card eighteen years later, surely.'

'So that started you wondering?'

'Right. I wrote to Evelyn Saunders. To thank her for the card, how nice it was to hear from her, that sort of tosh. Signed it with Tory's name but sent an envelope for a reply to Miss V. Craig here at Christ Church. And asked her to tell me what had happened to Vanessa. Didn't like to raise the subject with my parents, I said, since it would naturally upset them.'

'And did she tell you?'

'I didn't hear at once, naturally. I knew it would take a bit of time. Something happened before she answered. Do you remember that it was on our eighteenth birthday that we were allowed to explore the Fiori suite for the first time?'

'The great Bluebeard's secret of our childhood? Yes.'

'Well, there was a family portrait there. Prince Fiori's grandmother, I think. It looked just like me. Not much like you or Tory, but like me as I could have looked if I'd put my hair up and pulled my shoulders back and worn an elegant décolleté dress. I couldn't think why no one commented on the likeness. To be honest, I came to the wrong conclusion at first. Thought that Hilary must have had it off with Prince Fiori. I can remember delving into all sorts of medical books to find out whether one set of quads could actually consist of two sets of twins and if so, whether the two sets of twins could have different fathers.'

'But that theory wouldn't fit with the birthday card.'

'Right. And Mrs Saunders wrote back, eventually – a gooey letter about poor little Vanessa and how she'd almost been strangled in the womb by the umbilical cords of her two sisters and that was probably why Hilary had never liked to mention it in case I – that's Tory – and Virginia might feel personally responsible. There was never any chance that Vanessa could live long, she said, and while she was alive, at whatever age, she would always have had to be nursed as an incontinent baby who couldn't even turn herself over in bed. And it was decided that it wouldn't be fair to the two healthy children to have her needing so much attention at home. That was why there was only that one joyful-sad christening day between leaving the hospital and going into a nursing home.'

'So it began to seem a little unlikely to you that a brain-damaged Vanessa Craig could have won a place to Oxford on the strength of three A-grade A-levels?'

Ness nodded. 'In the Christmas vacation I looked in the family photograph albums and found that there weren't any snaps of us all together in Weybridge, except the christening one. The other thing I did was to buy such a fragile Christmas present for Nanny Mackay that I had to drive over with it.'

'No wonder she looked startled when Mark met her by my hospital bed and started asking questions.'

'She gave me a clear answer. Three little girls, right from her first day at Kilcraigie, but one of them – me – very small and a little backward for her age. A difficult birth, she'd been told. I was slower to walk and talk than the others. But I soon caught up.'

'Because you weren't suffering from brain damage but were actually two or three months younger than us.'

'Once you know, it all fits in. But at the time . . . I felt that I ought to be capable of working out what had happened. It was still impersonal at that stage. As though I was trying to solve a detective story which didn't have much to do with me. Testing different theories for size. The Isabella theory occurred to me quite early on, but the dates didn't fit. There were already three little girls at Kilcraigie before Isabella was kidnapped. I had to move into the realm of wild guesses – or shall we say, extreme hypotheses? And with one of them the whole jigsaw seemed to fall into place. Still no actual proof. But I was sure, all the same.'

'Ness,' said Ginny, 'why didn't you tell me? Once you knew, or guessed at least, why did you keep it a secret?'

Ness stretched out a hand to squeeze hers. 'Because I didn't want anything to change between you and me,' she said. 'I wasn't interested in inheriting a fortune if it meant that I wouldn't be your sister any more. Cut off in some way. Diverted into a different life. I thought that as long as I kept quiet, we could go on as we were.'

'But you must have realised – '

'What I didn't realise was that the coming-of-age time had changed since we were born. I thought that if Andrew had planned to tell me anything, my eighteenth birthday would have been the time. You were more in touch with the Tantivy Trust than I was. You'd have known that twenty-one was the operative date there, but I forgot. I did wonder if Andrew might be cheating on me.'

'That's what Mark thought too.'

'Well, I considered that and decided that I didn't want to challenge him. Because it was important to me that I should still have you; more important than money.' She withdrew her hand in order to dab again at her eyes and blow her nose violently. Tossing the tissue on to the water, she watched as the current carried it away. 'Litter lout!' she reproached herself, and then managed to smile. 'It's not something one says to a sister very often, is it, but I really do love you, Ginny. I don't know that I have a particularly faithful nature. I rather suspect that over the years boyfriends may come and go. But anyone needs just one person to be honest with, don't you agree? I couldn't bear to lose you.'

'You won't ever. Although concealing the truth is an odd prerequisite for hanging on to a confidante.' Ginny couldn't help grinning. 'But then what has made you change your mind about telling me? Was it knowing that Mark was on the trail?'

'Not exactly. Mark seems to be doing his best in an

awkward situation. When you think that he could set himself up for life with a single phone call to the *News of the World*! He didn't even tell *me* what it was he knew, in case he might prove to be shooting the gun. He did no more than drop the sort of hint which I could pick up if I understood it.'

'You still haven't said when you did find out for sure.'

Ness sighed at the memory. 'It was that day I came home to ask about buying a house in Oxford. Andrew had been meaning to make a formal announcement on what is supposed to be my twenty-first birthday, although actually, of course, it's only yours and Tory's. But it did begin to dawn on him when I turned up suddenly that he was letting me get into a false position and that perhaps he'd better give me warning.'

'Why should that have made you so angry with him?'

'How did you know? Well, yes, we had a flaming row. I suppose it could be heard all over Scotland.'

'Tory and I thought perhaps he'd objected to you living with David.'

'I never even got to the point of mentioning that. No, he told me that I was Isabella Fiori, and then he began to explain all the changes which would take place on my twenty-first birthday. He intended to issue a statement then to make the situation clear. I said I didn't want him to do that and he said he had to under the terms of my father's will and of the Tantivy Trust and that anyway I was the last of the Fioris and I had an obligation to my heritage just as Andrew himself had a responsibility to his dead friend and there couldn't be any argument because it was going to happen.'

'I can see – '

'Can you? Bloody cheek, I call it. It's all very well to talk about laws and auditors and people who've been dead for years, but it seemed to me that the most important person involved was me, and he didn't seem to be taking any notice of that. I mean, if he knew that this was how it was going to end, he's been doing everything wrong for years. Letting me love him as a real father, Hilary as a real mother, and then turning round suddenly to say, "Well, actually . . ." as though I couldn't be expected to care.' She was crying again.

'I suppose,' said Ginny, 'that the original plan would have been different. Presumably your father never had any intention of letting go of you while he was alive. He'd just have wanted to feel that you were in a safe home where he could visit you whenever he liked. But after he died, and then after the real Vanessa Craig died –'

'You know about that, do you?'

'I only found out about the death a couple of days ago. And I didn't know which of the three.'

'That must have made it easy for them to fib about me. They could use Vanessa's birth certificate and keep quiet about her death one. I suppose they got Uncle Tod to make sure that the legal side was all right. But they should have told me earlier. Not let me go on thinking . . . Oh well. Can I borrow a hankie? I've used my last tissue.'

'Course.'

'Since the row,' said Ness sighing, 'I've had a long letter. With a copy of some extraordinary document. Four pages of it: four alternative proposals that Andrew drew up twenty years ago. At the bottom of one of them it says, "Agreed. Tony Fiori." Just that, in a handwritten scribble. My whole future, an enormous fortune, all casually handed over to someone else. I mean, suppose Andrew had been a crook!'

'Presumably Prince Fiori felt sure that he wasn't,' said Ginny. 'And it can't really have been casual. There was all that background of the kidnapping and the divorce and other things that we probably don't know about.'

'No doubt. I can see that to anyone except the person most involved it must have seemed a neat and tidy solution, to give me a family life and save me from being kidnapped or spoiled.'

'Then can't you give them credit for acting in your best interests?'

'In theory I can. Applying the cold light of reason. But I find it hard to be reasonable for more than a moment or two at a time. It went on too long, that's the real thing. Either earlier or later I might have been able to cope. I can see that a small child couldn't be expected to keep a secret, but when I was fifteen or sixteen, I should have been told then.'

'Would it have made so much difference?'

'Given five years' notice I could have prepared myself for life as a rich bitch. Or else, if I'd had a few years as an independent adult, I'd have settled on a way of life that suited me and then I could have made the money fit into it. But this is absolutely the most hopeless time. I've always thought of these years at Oxford as being a kind of golden period – a breathing space before diving into the serious business of husbands and children and earning a living. I suppose that was a frivolous attitude. But it means that I haven't worked out yet what sort of person I want to be.'

'Isn't that true of most undergraduates?' suggested Ginny.

'Maybe. But most undergraduates have time to come to terms with the future gradually. I'm going to be pitchforked into a situation which I never wanted – and in a hideously public way, with everyone watching all my mistakes.'

'Did Father explain why he didn't tell you earlier?'

'He thought it would complicate family relationships. And that sooner or later I'd boast or lose my temper or in some way let the cat out of the bag; whereas he saw it as important to reveal the truth in a controlled way. So at the age of twenty I suddenly find that I'm not the person

I thought I was and need to develop a new persona, from scratch, and fast.'

'Is that really necessary?'

'Well, pretend it was you. From what Mark has told me, there must have been moments when you thought it might be. Didn't it frighten you a bit, thinking about it?'

'I don't think I considered it in that way. It was the idea of having all that money that took my breath away. But then, for the past couple of years I've been helping to spend it although it wasn't mine. If someone tries to spend a fortune all on herself, life may get complicated, but giving it away is easy. Buy a couple of Van Goghs, give them to the nation and you're a pauper again.'

'How much is involved?' asked Ness. 'Andrew didn't say.'

'I only know about the charitable part of it. That has an income of about three million a year. From a capital investment of roughly thirty million. But there's another hunk of capital which has been compounding the interest until Isabella's twenty-first birthday. I'd always assumed that after that it would be moved across into the charity, but Father would have known all the time that he was saving it for you. I've no idea how that part stands. You could find yourself with anything between fifty and a hundred million.'

'My God!'

'Look at it from Father's point of view,' said Ginny earnestly. 'He can't have expected to be left with sole responsibility for you. But once he was, he couldn't prevent you from being rich one day. All he could do was to put the day off. A moment ago you were claiming that it's dangerous to be a millionairess too young. Think what it would have been like having photographers buzzing around when you were at school. And young men queuing up to make your acquaintance at Oxford. As it is, you've got David. Loving you for yourself, not for your money, because he didn't know about it.'

'Well, that's another thing,' said Ness. 'I mean, the obvious first thing for me to do with a tiny fraction of this money is to fund David's research; and I shall. He gave up Texas for my sake. Now I can make sure that he doesn't lose by it and he can go on to get his doctorate – and in due course, no doubt, a Nobel prize – and we ought both to live happily ever after. He'll feel duty bound to stick close to me but that's what he wants to do anyway so it's not really a duty.'

'I don't see the problem. You love him, as well.'

'Yes, I have till now, but I might not always. I mean, how can you tell? You feel as if it's for ever, but when you look around you soon realise that for most people "ever" is quite a short time. It's tempting to say, "Right, I'll marry David because I know for certain that he fell in love with me without knowing how rich I am," but actually I don't want to get married yet – and when I do, it may not be to him. Making love's one thing, but when it comes to settling down and sharing my life I'll want to choose someone who uses the same vocabulary as me. I mean, if David tries to tell me what he's been doing all day, I can't understand any of the words; but it's the most important thing in the world to him.'

'Would that matter if you have your own interests?'

'It would be a bind. He'll never want to travel away from his lab. He won't even take a Sunday off if there's some culture or other just coming to the boil. He needs to marry another scientist, as clever as himself – or else someone who'll give him a cosy home and lots of casseroles which won't spoil when he's late for supper. But he hasn't realised that yet. He'll try to go too fast with me and then think that I'm turning him down just because I'm a stuck-up rich girl.'

'Oh, come off it, Ness. You must have talked it out

before. You can talk it out again. You and he aren't suddenly going to become different people.'

'Yes, we are,' said Ness. 'We have already, although he doesn't know it yet. I can't not fund him, but the moment I write the cheque for his first fifty thousand pounds then our present relationship is wrecked. He may be in love with Ness Craig, but he won't be able to cope with Isabella Fiori.' She gave a wry shrug of the shoulders. 'He may even decide that it would be simpler to go to Texas after all.'

'You're making the situation sound far too complicated.'

'I can't make it more complicated than it is. Little things keep bobbing into my mind when I ought to be working. For example, I've thought of myself for years as a non-practising Anglican. Now I find that I'm a lapsed Catholic, which sounds much worse: I can practically feel the fire of hell tickling my toes. And then there's the question of my mother.'

'Princess Fiori?'

'Yes. Does she know about me?'

'Not yet, because Mark hasn't told her. But she knows it's one of us. She's been to inspect me and now she's in London looking up Tory. Father was fierce about how you mustn't be distracted until term was over. Do you need to have any kind of relationship with her?'

'Yes, of course I do. Wouldn't you be curious? And besides, Andrew pitched a great spiel about how she rejected me as a baby. She must feel bloody guilty about that, and I'm the only person who can tell her that it's worked out all right. But first of all I have to convince myself. Be quite sure who I am. Not Vanessa Craig. Not the person I thought I was at all. Isabella Fiori, naked and new-born.'

'I can see that it must be frightening.'

'Terrifying. Have you any idea what it's going to be like when the papers get hold of this, Ginny? Actually, one of the few decisions that I've made is about Mark. He's been so decent about keeping quiet that he deserves a reward. On the day that Andrew issues his statement to the press I shall be out of the country and I shall stay out for the whole of the long vacation. Any newspaper which wants a photograph of this long-lost heiress will have to apply to Mark Lacey, who already has one set of the said heiress wearing jeans and a baggy sweater and who is about to be offered the chance of a second sitting with the best I can do in the way of glamour, wearing evening dress and anything which Andrew cares to produce out of the Aladdin's cave of Fiori jewels. If he plays his cards right, he ought to rake in a small fortune – and make a reputation as a photographer.'

'There's the portrait, too. He has copyright in that even after he's sold it.'

'Right. So he can get himself known as a portrait painter as well. It's just what he needs at this stage in his career, a fillip of publicity. And then, when he's earning a decent living, he'll be able to get on terms with you again instead of feeling inadequate.'

'He's stirred up a lot of trouble,' Ginny pointed out.

'Not intentionally. He was simply asked to find out about the Trust to start with; and then when it became a search for Isabella he must have thought that her mother had as much right as anyone to the facts. It was only when he fell in love with you that he began to realise the damage he could do.'

'And he did it.'

'You're not giving him credit for his damage-limitation efforts, Ginny. When he asked me to argue on his behalf that he loved you whether or not you had a penny to your name, he knew that my quickest way to do that was to tell you that I was Isabella, if I was aware of that, but he didn't drop any hint that it might be so. In my view Mark Lacey is tactful, intelligent, talented and sensitive. And loyal – it was just that his loyalty was to Princess Fiori at first. He's

337

also had a very sound classical education. I wouldn't at all say no to the idea of having him as a boyfriend-in-law.'

'Sounds to me as though you've found your replacement for David,' suggested Ginny wryly. 'Someone you can talk to.' It would be ironic, she thought, if Mark were to end up by marrying an heiress after all.

'Don't be an idiot. I'm not in the business of stealing my sister's boyfriends. And it's you he's in love with.'

Ginny sighed. 'I haven't trusted him,' she said. 'He came into my life as a spy. I was right to be suspicious of him, just as he was right to be suspicious of Father. But how can one have a decent relationship unless it's based on trust? Even if *I* can forget that I didn't trust him, how can he?'

'That's his business. You know what your trouble is, Ginny? It's only just occurred to me. You never lose your temper. I bet you went on being polite to Mark all the time you were seething with anger at being snooped on. Am I right?'

'I suppose so. I was chilly more than polite, but I didn't bawl him out.'

'A mistake. What you need is one hell of a row. A loud, blazing, no-holds-barred row. A thunderstorm to clear the air. Be so rude that you'll expect him never to speak to you again. If he's got any spirit, he'll fight back and you'll both walk away in fury. After that, you can start again from scratch. The new Virginia Craig, with all cards on the table. Requiring, no doubt, a certain amount of courage, but not half as much as *I* shall need to slough off Vanessa Craig and appear as Isabella Fiori. I'm far too sorry for myself to feel much sympathy for anyone else. A fresh start, that's what we both have to promise ourselves. And where better to make good resolutions than in Oxford, where metamorphosis is built into the system?' She stood up, ready at last to continue their walk. 'A new life for you and me as pseudo sisters,' she said. 'Starting with a brisk trot to Donnington Bridge and back.'

22

'Why don't you ever stay with me when you come to London?' demanded Tory.

Hilary laughed affectionately. 'Because I like to sit and sleep more than four inches above the floor. Your flat is immensely elegant, but I do find everything rather a long way down. Besides, what's the point of having privileged status at the Fiori Hotel and not making use of it?'

'True. And there's no doubt that you get a better breakfast here.' Tory, always an early riser, had accepted her mother's invitation for a seven o'clock meal but was working her way through the elaborate menu with an enthusiasm which suggested that she regarded it as lunch. 'And now you have to tell me, who is this Princess Fiori woman who keeps phoning up and wanting to meet me?'

'She's the ex-wife of your late godfather, as I'm sure you realised. An old acquaintance of Andrew's and mine who suddenly bobbed up again.'

'But why should she be interested in *me*?'

Hilary was silent. It was not in her nature to keep secrets. Although, many years ago, Andrew had asked for her approval before putting to Tony the plan which could only be operated with her help, and although it had been clear at the time that the arrangement proposed was in little Isabella's best interests, she had become increasingly unhappy about the need to continue the deception as the girls grew up. Her solution was to put the truth out of her mind and love Ness as though she were truly Ness, her own third baby. When Andrew at last came out with the truth, Ness – Isabella – had claimed the right to break the news to Tory and Ginny herself, at a time of her own choosing.

'Not a word!' she had demanded furiously. 'Not a word to either of them until I say so. You owe me that, at least.'

That prohibition had made it difficult recently for Hilary to be as straightforward with her two true daughters as she would have wished. Luckily Tory had another question to ask.

'And how does she come to be involved with Mark Lacey? Well, I know how they met, but that was in New England six years ago. It seems odd that they should both breeze into our lives at about the same time.'

'Tell me what you think of Mark. And have another croissant.'

'Thanks. I like him.'

'Just like him? Nothing more?'

'I find him attractive. We had quite a dizzy time for a couple of weeks. But then he met Ginny! And anyway, at heart he's a bit staid for me. Not at all the bohemian sort of artist. I suspect he'll grow up to be like his father one day: respectable and settled and Conservative.'

Hilary smiled. 'Conservative', in Tory's vocabulary, was a dirty word. 'So you think Ginny – '

'I worked out a theory about Mark,' said Tory earnestly. 'He was fascinated by the whole idea of triplets from the first moment I met him. I don't suppose he'd ever come across one before. And I suspect that he's fallen in love with a single Craig girl – all three of us blended together. He and I could have had a sizzling affair if we'd chosen. The chemistry was right; it was just that he wasn't quite frivolous enough. And he admires Ness enormously because she's intelligent and clear-minded and they like talking about the same things. He seriously wants to have her as a friend. But Ginny's the one he wants to marry – and quite right too, because I'm sure she'll choose to be respectable and settled as well.'

'What does being a triplet mean to you, Tory?'

'Same as when I was three. Same as when I was seven.'

Makes me feel bolshie. Not wanting to be one of a group. I like having the other two as sisters. When Ginny had her accident I was terrified in case she was going to die. And when Ness had her quarrel with you and Father, I was on her side even though I still don't know what it was all about.' She paused hopefully, but Hilary made no comment. 'But there's none of this "prick her and I bleed" feeling. I'm just their sister, and separate.' She showed no sign of curiosity at her mother's questioning. 'Oh, luscious!' she exclaimed instead, as a plate of sliced tropical fruits was brought to the table.

Hilary wished that she could warn Tory that one of her sisters was about to escape from what she saw as the bondage of being a triplet, but could think of no way which would not upset Ness. Instead she enquired how work was going, and they continued to discuss that subject until Tory announced that she must get to the office. 'And you never answered my question about this princess!' she exclaimed.

'She's just curious to meet you. And there's no reason for you to evade her. Dinner at the Connaught isn't something to be turned down lightly.' If all went well, within a few hours Hilary hoped to persuade Ness that there should be no more secrets within the family, and then she could apologise to Tory for keeping her in the dark.

It was time for Hilary herself to leave, for she had finished all her business in London the previous day. 'Oxford now,' she told Gip. It was time to make her peace with Ness, who had evaded any discussion of the Isabella situation since the day of the disclosure. The car drew up in front of Christ Church soon after nine. Ness, who liked to work late into the night, was not noted for rising early, and only after protracted knocking on the door of her set did Hilary recognise that its occupant was not sleeping but absent.

Secretly relieved by the postponement of what might

prove to be an uncomfortable interview, she left a message on the wipe-off board which was fixed to the door and went for a walk. Two hours passed before she attacked the door for a second time. No answer had been written to her suggestion of lunch, and there was still no sound from inside; but even as she listened she heard footsteps approaching up the staircase. Turning, ready to smile, she was taken aback to see not only Ness but Ginny, whom she had left three days earlier at Kilcraigie.

'Hilary!' It was Ness who stepped forward to be kissed as though nothing had changed between them; although the name she spoke showed that everything had changed. 'Have you been here long? I should have told you the system. Carol opposite keeps a copy of my key, and I keep hers, because we're always locking ourselves out. She would have let you in.'

'In my day,' said Hilary, accepting the neutral topic, 'we weren't *allowed* to lock our doors. It was assumed that the only reasons for needing privacy were drugs or a man.'

'In your day perhaps sneak thieves weren't quite so adventurous in getting right to the top of every staircase,' suggested Ness. She turned the key in the lock and gestured for the other two to go in. 'Coffee?' She switched on her electric kettle.

'Lovely. I wasn't expecting you to be here, Ginny.'

'Perhaps you'd like me to make myself scarce for a bit.' Ginny turned towards the door, but Ness put out a hand to stop her.

'No, you deserve your coffee after that walk. And we have no secrets.'

'Good,' said Hilary, comprehending at once the significance of that remark – but Ness allowed her no time to follow what had seemed to be a cue.

'What have you been doing while you waited?' she asked instead. 'Reliving your youth?'

It was an unexpected question; for Hilary, after all, had

paid several visits to Oxford during the past two and a half years without feeling herself to be more than the mother of an undergraduate. But it struck its mark.

'I didn't intend to,' she said, taking her mug over to the chair at the desk. 'I went to the Botanic Garden to see if it had any good ideas to offer for the gardens at home. But it's odd, isn't it, the power of places. I was remembering one May Day with Andrew. Sitting in a punt at six o'clock in the morning and listening to the choirboys who were singing at the top of Magdalen Tower. Not that we could hear them very well. And then having a picnic afterwards. But we were lazy and the river was crowded, so we didn't go far. Just moored by the bank of the Botanic Garden. I sat on that bank this morning and tried to look at myself from outside. Fifty-one years old. Sensibly dressed for sitting on a charitable committee. Starting to go grey, and needing to wear glasses but not quite prepared to admit that yet. And yet still feeling the same person as when I was twenty. Not remembering it, but *being* it. Magdalen Tower, I said to myself, has changed more than I have. It was black and crumbling then; wearing a smooth clean complexion now. I know it's all sentimental nonsense, but it took me over for a bit.'

'Were you engaged to Andrew by then, on that May Day?' asked Ginny.

Hilary took a moment to register this second use of a Christian name. It was easy to guess why Ness had stopped saying Mother and Father. Perhaps she had persuaded Ginny to make the change at the same time in order that her own choice of words might not seen too pointed a withdrawal from a family relationship. If so, that was a good omen for the future.

'No,' she said. 'I was in love with him, but nothing was settled. I was in a sort of limbo: no degree, no job, no fiancé or husband; not committed to any particular way of life. All the big choices still in front of me. A brief period of freedom. Freedom to make enormous mistakes, of course. I ought to have been terrified. But I was happy.'

'You must still be happy now, then,' said Ness, making herself comfortable on the floor. 'Otherwise you wouldn't be able to have that same-person feeling. It would be spoiled by regret at wrong decisions.'

'Did you ever, afterwards, wish you'd married someone different?' asked Ginny. She was still standing up, moving restlessly about the room. 'Did you ever fall in love with anyone else?'

'No. Never. Not even before I met Andrew. Terribly dull, I'm afraid, and amazingly old-fashioned. We lived through the Swinging Sixties almost without noticing them.'

'What about Prince Fiori? Wasn't he in love with you?'

Hilary turned her head to look curiously at Ginny, who had come to rest beside the window and was staring out across the quad as though she had no interest in the answer to her own question.

'I didn't meet him for the first time until after I was married,' she said carefully. 'We became very good friends later. But I never wanted anyone but your father.'

'I thought perhaps he might have wanted you, though. Written you love letters, that kind of thing.'

Hilary began to feel as though she were walking through a minefield. The purpose of this visit was to sweep away the memory of the deception which had so upset Ness and to re-establish a relationship based on truthfulness; but it seemed to be running out of control. Ginny had the air of already knowing the answer to her question.

'He only did that once,' she answered, concealing her reluctance to admit it beneath an air of openness. 'And even then I don't think I was ever intended to read it.' She paused, remembering the shock she had felt on first deciphering the bloodstained letter which Andrew had brought back from Peru. It had taken her a long time to come to terms with the suspicion that Tony had perhaps

344

for years been expressing in writing the desire that he had felt for his best friend's wife, and had been trapped into a failure to destroy the evidence only by death. Andrew, when she finally offered to let him read the letter, was far quicker than she to understand that it did not represent a betrayal, but instead proved the strength of the friendship which prevented Tony from giving any hint of his feelings during his lifetime. 'You have to remember that he and your father – '

'Yes,' said Ginny. 'My father. That's the word I wanted to explore. I asked Andrew straight out a little while ago whether he was really my father, and he said that of course he was. But it's quite possible, isn't it, that he doesn't know the truth?'

23

'What!' Hilary could hardly believe her ears. Was this really Ginny who was making such an accusation? Of the three girls, it was Tory who from childhood had been positive to the point of aggressiveness in demanding what she wanted. Ginny had been the most pliant of the three: easy to please, grateful for any suggestions as to what she should do, and always anxious to avoid a quarrel.

'You told us,' she said now, 'about how Andrew had mumps on your honeymoon. Sometimes that makes it impossible – '

'Difficult, not impossible,' Hilary interrupted. 'It lowers fertility, but doesn't kill it altogether.'

'All the same.' Ginny pressed on. 'Nothing happened in the ordinary way. It was only after you went to a fertility clinic. And not even then for the first few tries – is that right?'

'It's not something I want to talk about,' said Hilary.

'Oh, come on.' This new, assertive Ginny was not to be diverted, although she attempted with a smile to make the words sound less hostile. 'We're big girls now and we know the facts of life. I have to be grateful to you for persevering through what must have been an unpleasant process; otherwise I couldn't be here today.' She waited, her silence forcing her mother into a comment.

'It was very early days for that sort of treatment. Nowadays doctors can perform miracles in test-tubes, but at that time it was still a bit hit and miss.'

'Which makes me wonder whether perhaps your dear friend Prince Fiori might have decided to lend a hand. He knew the specialist who ran the clinic, didn't he? Perhaps

346

he made an enquiry and discovered that it was never going to work, the way you were trying. And because he was such a good friend, he would have looked around to see whether there was anything he could do to help.'

'You're going too far, Ginny! You've no right to talk like this.'

'But it's important to us. I suppose that to you it's all past history, but Ness and I need to know where we stand. I'm not suggesting that you and the prince had an affair. I mean, not if you say you didn't. But, just to be coldly clinical for a moment, you allowed yourself to be inseminated. Andrew assumed that he was the donor. But that might not actually have been the case. One has to wonder why the process should suddenly work when it never had before?'

'It fits!' Ness had been listening to the conversation with an absorbed expression which suggested that she had had no suspicion of what Ginny was going to say. 'That story we've been bored with so often, about little Tony Fiori wanting to come top of his class in maths. "Friendship shows itself in giving someone what he needs, not necessarily what he asks for." Andrew wanted children. He only needed to *believe* they were his own, whether or not that was the case.' She turned excitedly to Ginny. 'So what you're getting at, Ginny, is that we *are* still sisters after all. Half-sisters, at least.'

'Stop it, both of you!' said Hilary. She felt herself becoming agitated, and struggled to maintain control. 'You're letting your imagination run wild. Tony knew – it was one of the very first things I told him – that I was never going to keep secrets from Andrew. My definition of friendship, of love, was always different from his. I believe in sharing, in not ever holding anything back. I would simply not have been capable of deceiving Andrew for all these years on something so terribly important.'

'As you've just said, Prince Fiori would have known

347

that,' Ginny pointed out. 'And he was your friend as well as Andrew's. He could have applied the great maths coaching argument to you as well and given you what you needed, although you could never have asked for it. He would have realised that if Andrew was never to find out, he ought not to confess even to you.' She came across and put her arms round Hilary's shoulders. 'No one could ever accuse you of cheating, Mother. All I'm suggesting is that you don't actually *know*.'

It was reassuring to be 'Mother' again – although no doubt that was a slip of the tongue – but in the long silence which followed Hilary found herself struggling not to cry. For a second time within a few minutes Ginny had scored a bull's-eye. Twenty-one years ago a smiling Dr Sussman had told her that her latest pregnancy test had proved positive. She had made no attempt then to control her tears: tears of joy and relief. But even in that moment of euphoria she had wondered . . . Dr Sussman owed Tony an enormous debt of gratitude and might have been able to persuade himself that behaviour which strictly was unethical could be condoned when it was so clearly intended for the best. It was tempting to ask, but she had resisted the temptation both then and later.

That restraint had not prevented her from indulging in occasional fantasies – especially in the weeks after Tony's death, when she read and reread the bloodstained letter, learning for the first time how he had repressed fantasies of his own. But from the moment when Isabella was carried secretly from New York to Kilcraigie she had ceased to search for family resemblances between the three little girls and had discouraged the process in anyone else. Ginny was right to guess that she had not wanted to know the truth; and she did not wish even a suspicion of it to emerge now.

'You would hurt Andrew very much indeed if you suggested anything of the sort to him,' she said quietly to

348

Ginny. 'He's always loved you as your father. Why should you want to feel that he might not be that after all?'

It was Ness who answered. 'Because I want Ginny still to be my sister.' Crossing her legs, she stood up gracefully, like a gymnast.

'That doesn't give you the right to rob Andrew of a daughter.'

'It gives me a weapon with which to try. After all, he – '

'He's been a father to you Ness, ever since your natural father died. When you've had time to get over the shock, you'll be able to appreciate everything he's done for you. As for this other business, there's no way in which anyone can find out the answer.'

'Well actually,' Ness pointed out, 'there's DNA.'

'You'd have no co-operation on that from me. It would be very wrong for either of you to press the question. Ginny, Ness, you should be looking to the future now, not the past. With David, perhaps; with Mark.'

'Mark will have to wait,' said Ginny (and Ness, under her breath, murmured, 'And David.'). 'The future builds on the past, so we have to get that straight first. We're not ready for the happy-ever-after bit yet.'

'It isn't such a big thing, being sisters,' Hilary argued. 'What's really held you together, you two and not Tory, is that you're friends.'

'But that's not as strong as a family tie,' Ness objected. 'It's only a – a sort of feeling. I don't think you understand, either of you, you and Andrew, how tough it's going to be for me suddenly to become Isabella Fiori. I've got to have someone special. Someone I can trust to – well, just to stay the same towards me.'

The phrase tugged at Hilary's heart. Almost the same words had persuaded Andrew to give up his job and become Tony Fiori's trusty. She was ashamed of herself for not realising just how lonely Ness would feel in the new life which was to be thrust upon her.

'You could say that ties dissolve more easily than feelings,' she suggested. 'People break their marriage vows, quarrel with their families. But friends, real friends, do what's best for each other, are glad to see each other, throughout their lives.' She laughed at an unexpected memory which perhaps would not have re-entered her mind had it not been for the surprising morning of feeling twenty again on the banks of the Cherwell. 'Though as a matter of fact Tony and Andrew did tie themselves together – literally. In some kind of prep school ritual.'

'What was it?' asked Ginny.

'Have you got a piece of string?' While Ness searched for it, Hilary picked up a pencil.

'No luck. Would a shoelace do?'

'Yes.' Hilary knotted it round the pencil in a manner which left a loop above the knot and the two ends protruding below it. 'That's a highwayman's hitch, if I've got it right,' she said. 'Used to tether a horse. All the highwayman has to do is to lean down from the saddle and tug one end and he's free to gallop away. But then – ' She made two unsuccessful attempts to make it work – 'The man who was headmaster of Tantivy when your fathers were there, invented a variation. One more twist like this –' This time she was successful. 'You two hold one end each. Now, as long as each of you goes on pulling, the other one can't undo the knot. But if one of you lets go, the whole thing collapses. He called it the Tantivy Twist. It had no practical application whatsoever, as far as I know. But the boys used it to swear eternal friendship. Tony and Andrew, for example. You two could turn it into a tradition if you wanted to: Craigs and Fioris.'

They had come close to watch her make the knot, and now she put one end of the dirty white shoelace into Ness's hand and one into Ginny's.

'All you need now is a little mumbo-jumbo,' she said. 'Cross your hearts and hope to die, or whatever. I'll leave you to work that out for yourselves. Where's the nearest lavatory, Ness?'

'One floor down on the right. It says John on the door, to discourage the tourists.'

'I'll wait out in the quad afterwards. Come down when you're ready and I'll take you both out to lunch.'

It was only an excuse to leave the room. The ritual must be private if it was not to seem absurd. Well, of course, it *was* absurd. But it had worked once, for Andrew and Tony. And it had worked a second time when Hilary – an adult: a married woman – had been taught the knot and encouraged to repeat the ridiculous prep school promises. It was a very special kind of trust which could take deceit in its stride and convert it into a very special kind of love. Would Ness understand that one day, as her father had always understood it? It was Andrew who had formulated a definition of friendship, but it was Tony who perfected the art of making gifts which could not be refused – perfected it, perhaps, to the supreme point of leaving the recipient ignorant of the gift.

'Thank you, Tony,' said Hilary aloud as she waited patiently in the quad, surrounded by the bustle of under-graduates hurrying back from lectures and making their way to the hall for lunch. Smiling, she rose to her feet when the two young women appeared at the bottom of the staircase. Whether or not they were sisters was of no importance: but they were friends for life.